A TIME FOR PASSION

Jordan reached out and lightly untangled the ribbon from her hair. His finger brushed her shoulder and Elle inhaled at his touch. It was so gentle it made her skin tingle. He allowed his finger to brush over her collarbone and then cupped her chin in his palm. "You are the most mysterious woman I have ever known. Who *are* you, Elizabeth Mackenzie?"

"I . . . I told you. I come from the future. From nineteen—"

His finger on her lips stopped her words. "Please. Just for tonight. Don't . . ."

She almost kissed his finger, but stopped herself just in time. Instead she smiled, and her voice was deep and seductive. "Just for tonight," she repeated his words. "I can be anyone you want."

He groaned as he pulled her into his arms. Strong, secure arms that seemed to almost hunger for her. He leaned down, his mouth mere inches from hers. And then he did it. Right there in front of every one of those women who had been flirting with him all evening.

He kissed her.

BOOK YOUR PLACE ON OUR WEBSITE AND MAKE THE READING CONNECTION!

We've created a customized website just for our very special readers, where you can get the inside scoop on everything that's going on with Zebra, Pinnacle and Kensington books.

When you come online, you'll have the exciting opportunity to:

- View covers of upcoming books
- Read sample chapters
- Learn about our future publishing schedule (listed by publication month *and author*)
- Find out when your favorite authors will be visiting a city near you
- Search for and order backlist books from our online catalog
- Check out author bios and background information
- Send e-mail to your favorite authors
- Meet the Kensington staff online
- Join us in weekly chats with authors, readers and other guests
- Get writing guidelines
- AND MUCH MORE!

**Visit our website at
http://www.zebrabooks.com**

CONSTANCE O'DAY-FLANNERY

A Time for Love

Zebra Books
Kensington Publishing Corp.

http://www.zebrabooks.com

ZEBRA BOOKS are published by

Kensington Publishing Corp.
850 Third Avenue
New York, NY 10022

Zebra and the Z logo Reg. U.S. Pat. & TM Off.

First Printing: December, 1991
10 9 8 7 6 5 4

Printed in the United States of America

FOR T. S.—who taught me the true meaning of self-esteem and sacrifice. *Thank you for the laughter and the love.*

ACKNOWLEDGEMENTS

CARIN, ROBERTA AND WALTER—for their patience and understanding.

COLLEEN AND LINDA—for believing I could do it, in spite of everything.

ADELE—for the laughter and encouragement, and working with me through an impossible situation.

HY LIT—a legendary disk jockey in Philadelphia—for taking the time, and sharing with me a wealth of research. It was truly appreciated.

AND MY FAMILY AND FRIENDS ... Thanks for always being there, for believing in me when I forgot to believe in myself. Each one of you share in this one.

Chapter 1

She should have known that day would irreversibly change her life. There should have been some warning. But then, back in the beginning, she had been such an innocent . . .

The fear rose up inside her, like an invisible monster that clutched at her chest and possessed her imagination. Every instinct was telling her to get up and leave—to run. But then she was here, in this place, this position, out of need . . . a desperate, undeniable need.

"It's okay. Just relax." The voice was soft, soothing, and meant to weaken her resistance. "I can't get it in. Open wider . . . please?"

Elizabeth Mackenzie looked up into the brown eyes of the man above her and shook her head. "I—I'm sorry. You're so patient and I'm so . . . ." Her voice trailed off as she mentally searched for the proper word.

"Frightened?" The man supplied it.

She nodded. "I know it's silly. I'm supposed to be an adult and everything, but being here, in this place, terrifies me."

"Elizabeth . . ." He smiled at her. "Are you always called Elizabeth? Do you have a nickname?"

She started to shake her head, then stopped. "My . . . my family calls me Elle."

"Ellie?"

She shrugged. "Sounds the same, just spelled differently. My cousin couldn't pronounce Elizabeth, so El became Elle and stuck, unfortunately." Convinced that she was beginning to sound like a babbling idiot, she murmured, "I don't usually tell anyone . . ."

He grinned. "You don't know me very well and it must be hard for you to trust, but all I want to do right now, Elle, is take an x-ray of your tooth. I can promise you this won't hurt."

His expression was kind, like a parent, yet all she could envision at the moment was the large, dark man who had yelled at her to stop crying . . . the dentist who had slapped her twelve-year-old hands and then made her sit on them while he pulled a permanent molar from her mouth. It was because of that nightmare that she was fanatical about her teeth, for she had made a childhood vow never to endure a repeat performance.

"Look, you came in here because you were in pain. I can't properly treat you without knowing exactly what's causing your discomfort, can I?"

Trying to be reasonable, Elle shook her head. She knew an x-ray was painless. "I'm sorry. Of course, you can take it." And she slowly opened her mouth to show her trust.

Within thirty seconds it was over and Elle breathed a sigh of relief as she watched Dr. Eisenberg or Macdade walk out of the office to develop the x-ray. She felt foolish for acting like a child and even more so for having

10

forgotten the dentist's name. Now she was far too embarrassed to ask him to repeat it. She figured the easiest way was to wait until his assistant called out to him. Unfortunately, that hadn't happened yet.

Resting her head back against the chair, Elle closed her eyes rather than look at all the frightening equipment that surrounded her. It looked right out of Star Wars. Drilling. Probing. Hi-tech torture. As the throbbing in her cheekbone continued, she took a deep breath and told herself that she hadn't any other choice. She simply could not function with this kind of pain, let alone make a presentation to the head buyer of Mictronix Communications tomorrow morning.

Wichita, Kansas. She would probably laugh about this sometime, but not now. Maybe back in Pennsylvania. Nobody in the office had wanted to make this trip, but Elle had thought the personal presentation was necessary to close the deal. Five years ago Mictronix had been a small communications company. Today, it was a valuable account, and Elle wanted it to be hers. Three years ago when she'd accepted the position of Computer Sales Rep for Keystone, she hadn't realized that she would be the only woman in an office of twenty competitive men. And right now, back in Pennsylvania, there were ten of them that didn't think she had a chance at landing the account. It hadn't been easy, but she'd won the respect of most of the other reps. And she'd done that by working just as hard as any of them, by taking advantage of every opportunity; by working at night, preparing, while everyone else in the universe had a social life. And now this disaster . . .

The filling had been cracked for weeks, but she'd fooled herself into believing that if she was fastidious

11

about her dental hygiene, it would all go away. Last night when she'd finally reached her hotel, all she could think about was room service and a hot bath—in that order. Maybe she should have ordered something soft, like what older people with dental problems eat. Maybe then the filling would not have left the molar and mingled with her BLT. The shock of running the tip of her tongue around what seemed like a crater in her back molar was nothing compared to the pain that had started two hours later. She had spent a sleepless night, devouring Tylenol, pressing warm wash cloths to her cheekbone, and then switching to cold when nothing else worked. And nothing did. By dawn she was rolling from side to side in agony and, down deep, she knew the sharp ache that was paralyzing part of her face was not going to go away.

She'd finally called the front desk and they had read her a list of emergency dentists. The manager had recommended the offices of Drs. Eisenberg and Macdade. He had said his wife and son were very happy with their services. It was beyond her comprehension how a child could be happy with a dentist, but at the time it had sounded like a pretty solid recommendation. A Pediatric Dentist. That was just about right for a twenty-nine-year-old coward. When the cab had pulled up to the office she had initially thought the driver had made a mistake. It was in a renovated train station. The Victorian building with its gingerbread trim was now a dental office. It was charming inside, decorated in late-nineteenth-century country and far less frightening than a typical medical facility. Even the receptionist worked behind a glass ticket window that looked like the original. Miniature silent trains ran over tracks that bordered the ceiling. The multicolored cars weaved in and out of tunnels and disappeared into the recesses of the offices. As she waited to be called, she found herself staring at the ceiling, waiting for the train to re-enter the reception area. How she wished she could shrink to its size. And when it came into this examining room, she would hop on board and be swept away . . . away from here. Away from the pain, the—

"Elle? I'm afraid I don't have good news."

She opened her eyes and saw sympathy in the expression of the nameless dentist. Forgetting about her fantasy, she clutched the fake leather arms of the chair. "Doctor?"

He sat down next to her on a small movable stool. Holding up the x-ray for her to see, he said, "There's no other way to put this, except to say it—"

"I don't think I want you to," Elle interrupted. It already sounded ominous and she straightened in the chair as he prepared to speak.

"How old was that filling?" the doctor asked, switching to another tack.

She tried to remember, but her nerves were shot . . . along with her memory. "I don't know. I think I was fifteen, or sixteen." What was he trying to say to her?

The kindly man looked down to her chart. "And you're thirty now—"

"Twenty-nine," she insisted. "Until next week."

He nodded. "Elle, that restoration was at least fifteen years old. It should have been replaced years ago. As it is," and he shook his head sadly, "I'm afraid there isn't any way to save that tooth."

"*What?*" Her fingernails sank into the arms of the chair and her entire body tensed, as if shocked with an electrical current.

He came closer and patted her hand in sympathy. "I know this seems drastic to you, but there really isn't any other way. I wouldn't even suggest root canal. I believe the decay has gone too far. And even that wouldn't completely solve your problem, because the pain would continue until the entire root was removed. It would take more than one visit. Your own dentist could complete the procedure and then place a crown on it, but you risk infection, especially flying back to Pennsylvania. In many cases such as this the air pressure of the cabin magnifies the problem."

"You—you couldn't save it?" she whispered in a frightened voice.

He shook his head. "I wouldn't recommend trying. It isn't an easy procedure to begin with, and you'd be doing it for a tooth that, in my opinion, is beyond saving. You stand a very good chance of losing that tooth even if you decide on root canal."

She stared into his eyes. They were kind eyes, behind brown tortoise shell glasses. And his smile was warm and sympathetic. He was about her height, and not handsome in the conventional way. He would never make the cover of GQ, but he probably made some woman a great husband. He was a man to be trusted. As if on cue, the pain in her upper jaw increased and she said in a small voice, "I'm very, very frightened of dentists. I'm sorry, but I am. I want to say take it out and stop the pain, but I keep remembering this incident from my past."

She told him her horror story and drew strength from the angry expression on his face. When she was finished, she watched as he shook his head, as if deploring such actions, and leaned closer to her.

"Listen, Elle, I'm sorry you ever had to go through

something like that. I completely understand how you feel, but I want you to know that most dentists today would never act so unprofessionally. You would be completely anesthetized. There are methods such as gas . . . you could even be put to sleep—though I don't think we would have to go that far for this procedure."

She immediately perked up. "Put to sleep? You mean I won't feel anything?"

He looked at her chart before answering. "Remember when we took your blood pressure?"

She nodded.

"It was slightly elevated. Now, considering your fear, that could account for the rise, but I'd rather just use sweet air—nitrous oxide. You won't need anything else, Elle. Trust me."

She wanted to. The throbbing in her cheek was becoming unbearable. She hadn't had any sleep and she was tired of fighting the pain and her fear. If she could just trust him . . .

"Okay. Take it out."

He smiled. "It's going to be all right, Elle. You'll see."

She was breathing through a rubber mask and floating, up above the chair and sweet Dr. Eisenberg or Macdade. It felt wonderful, a little sexual, as if she'd had three or four quick drinks and she didn't really care that the good doctor was telling her to open wide. She knew he held a syringe behind his back, knew the tip of it was going to puncture her gum, and she wanted to tell him not to hide it from her. But he was so nice, so sweet. He didn't want to frighten her. And she again thought how lucky his wife was. He was probably very attentive, very sensitive . . . Why was it that the men she found were more concerned about their own egos, and about as sensitive as a charging

15

water buffalo?

She was alone. It was her choice . . . well, almost. She just hadn't met anyone yet that she could trust with the rest of her life. Long ago she had made her peace with life. She wasn't foolish enough to believe that a woman could really have it all. Something always had to give, and Elle had promised herself that she wouldn't make the same mistakes as her mother. She was convinced that she could make it if she protected herself, for she didn't think she would be able to withstand any more heartache. She liked herself. Well, most of the time she liked herself. She didn't need a man to be complete. She supposed being alone was better than doing laundry for someone who drank beer on her living room couch while watching Monday Night Football. Okay, so that might be overstating it but she would just bet that even Carl Sagan indulged in an occasional Monday Night Male Bacchanalia. She didn't want to do anyone else's laundry, and she had little patience for the macho ego. But right now, at this moment, she could certainly use someone's arms around her. Someone to tell her that it was going to be okay . . . but she would handle it, just like she'd had to handle every other emergency. That's what happens when you're alone. You learn how to get through with the least amount of pain. She deeply inhaled the sweet air as images of water buffalo roaming her beautiful living room rose up in her mind. Beer-guzzling water buffalo . . . Her imagination grew fertile and she giggled.

"Enjoying yourself, Elle?" From very far off she heard the doctor's voice.

She nodded. "This is wonderful." Every word seemed distant and her lips tingled, as if just kissed.

She thought she heard the young dental assistant

16

laugh and Elle smiled. Wasn't everyone so nice here? Didn't everything seem better already?

"Do you think you could open very wide now?"

"Oh, yes," she answered in a deep obliging voice. She would have done anything they asked.

She felt the pinch of the needle. It hurt. She didn't care. If they had wanted to remove every tooth in her mouth she would have let them. She was soaring. As they waited for the Novocaine to take effect, Elle watched the tiny train appear at the ceiling and she wanted to smile, but her lips felt big and puffy—a nice kind of puffy, just awkward. She liked that train. She liked this office. Why were the lights flickering? Wasn't that odd? She was giddy and feeling wonderfully foolish.

"Am I drunk, or are the lights going off and on?"

"There's a storm outside. Breathe through your nose, Elle. Take nice deep breaths."

A storm. How pleasant . . . She had always loved the sound of rain on the roof. It was great for lovemaking . . . Oh, yeah. Right. As if she'd had a lot of practice. As if a man had touched her in almost a year. She hadn't even shaken hands with a male that wasn't friendly and businesslike. Maybe she put them off. Intimidated them. Maybe—

"Nice deep breaths. C'mon."

Inhaling, she did as she was told and listened as the doctor instructed his assistant to check on the auxiliary generator, in case they lost power. Who cared? Elle thought. Just as long as the gas lines continued to work. She closed her eyes and enjoyed the sense of freedom— freedom from worry, responsibilities, pain.

"Okay, Elle. Open again. This time stay open."

She felt the probing, the pressure, eventually heard a

crack, and then the dear doctor was telling her that he was taking two stitches, and that her own dentist could check to see that they dissolved. The unseen assistant lifted the mask away from her nose and she was told that it was all over.

She blinked several times in disbelief and actual disappointment as she clamped down on a large wad of gauze.

"You did very well, Elle. Now just sit here for a few minutes until the gas leaves your system—I don't believe this! Don't move."

She was confused. Only moments before she had been floating in a warm haze of contentment and now she was cast into a cold darkness. Everything stopped. The train halted upon its approach into the room, the lights flickered out, the music ceased.

"Waas amatter?" she mumbled into the darkness as she brought her fingers up to her mouth to check her swollen lips. She had the oddest sensation that she was dribbling.

From very far away she heard the dentist say that they had lost the electricity and Elle closed her eyes, trying to recapture that feeling of security that she'd had only minutes ago. No matter how hard she tried, it didn't work. She was confused. She felt dizzy and frightened, and she didn't like being in the dark. Shivering, Elle could hear the storm raging outside. It was like the roar of a train. It sounded just like a train outside.

For a moment, her heart skipped a beat before thundering on. Didn't they say tornadoes sounded like trains? And wasn't this Kansas?

Kansas! Tornadoes!

Her eyes opened in horror. Dear God! She was getting

18

out now! Pushing herself up from the chair, Elle's shoulder hit the movable tray and she shoved it away. She reached out in the darkness, like a blind person, to find her way, all the while attempting to call out in her mumbled, garbled fashion. "Hey, waas happanin out dere?" She realized her voice sounded like a cheap imitation of the Cosby dental skit, yet she sputtered on, fighting against the thickness of her lips to speak.

"Wilw someone anther me? Where is evwy one?"

As if in response, the sound of shattering glass broke through the eerie stillness and was almost immediately followed by a blast of wind whirling through the room, a wind so strong, so powerful, that it knocked Elle to her knees. A brief flash of brilliant light crackled around her causing her to hide her eyes against her arm and hold her breath against whatever force was in that room. Clutching the doorjamb, she hung on for dear life and it was only moments later that the wind subsided as quickly as it had come. Frightened, she slowly lifted her head. From far off she heard the sound of voices and Elle breathed a sigh of relief. She was alive. She was okay. Whatever had happened, she had survived. Finally, she released her breath.

God, how she hated dentists' offices!

Fighting a wave of dizziness, Elle very slowly rose to her feet. In the dim light she brushed back her hair and smoothed down her slacks. She had to get out of here. Without the numbing effect of the gas, this dental office was even worse than the others. Maybe they forgot about her. She was obviously finished. Perhaps she was supposed to just go out to the receptionist and pay?

More than a little confused, Elle used her hand to guide her along the wall and leave the examining room.

There was light, a dim light in the distance. Maybe she should move toward it. She had gone no more than two feet into the hallway when she stopped and stared at the incredible, unbelievable, sight before her.

People, dressed in old-fashioned clothes—women in floor-length dark dresses and bonnets, men in suits or cowboy outfits—were milling about a waiting room—only it wasn't the waiting room she had left earlier in the morning. The comfortable cushioned chairs were gone, replaced by hard wooden benches. The receptionist in her crisp white uniform was now an elderly man with a huge gray handlebar mustache.

Everyone, everything familiar was . . . *gone!*

Chapter 2

"I don't know, Traver. You think it's her?"

The old man wiped the side of his leather glove over his mouth to muffle his words. "Sheeet, boy, look at 'er! If that's the new missus, then the Cap'n is in for one hell of a surprise."

Kyle Reavis jammed his thumbs behind the thin cord that tied his chaps together and slumped his shoulders with indecision. She was wearing pants! Trousers! "Well, what'll we do?" he demanded of his older, hopefully wiser, companion. From the corner of his eye, he glanced back at the woman. She was the only one in the depot close to the right age. All the rest of the females were either too old or too young. But Traver was right. If this one was the Cap'n's, then all hell would break loose once they got back to the herd outside of town.

"I say you go over there, boy, and find out."

Kyle quickly straightened and shook his head. "Not me. You go."

Traver Diggs glared at the youngster. Almost nineteen, Kyle still hadn't learned to follow orders and that

21

annoyed the hell out of Traver—especially since he'd been assigned to teach the lad on this last drive to Wichita. After three months on the trail and almost another month in this cow town, it was past time to go home, back to the Triple Cross. "Go over and ask if she's Cap'n McCabe's new bride. That's clear enough."

"I will not ask such a question," Kyle mumbled back. "If'n it ain't her I'd look the fool. I don't know why the Cap'n had to go marry some stranger anyhow. Lucia was more'n happy—"

"Shut your mouth, Kyle Reavis," Traver admonished. "Don't you ever bring up Lucia in front of this woman!'"

Kyle rolled his eyes toward the wooden ceiling. "We don't even know if'n it is her, so don't yell at me, you old fool."

He'd let the boy get away with too much over the years. It was plain as day to Traver that he had been lax in his teaching. Ever since he and the Cap'n had come across the skinny little yearling wandering out on the prairie after his folks was killed . . . well, he had a soft spot for the youngster. He had treated Kyle almost like a son— considering his age, maybe a grandson. Anyway, he'd have to straighten the kid out real quick, 'cause Kyle Reavis was near a man. And it was time to act like one.

"You want to go back to the Cap'n and tell him we didn't get his woman?"

"Proxy bride." Kyle's mouth screwed up with distaste. "That's the way them immigrants get hitched. Ain't fittin' that the Cap'n advertise for a wife. Just ain't fittin'."

Traver raised a single bushy, gray eyebrow. "Cap'n ask your opinion, did he?"

"'Course he didn't."

"Then you stop flappin' about what's none of your business and come with me. And brush back that mess of hair from your eyes, boy. We're about to meet the new missus."

Traver glared at Kyle with a murderous expression that clearly stated he was to follow. Both men were nervous and clutched at worn wide-brimmed hats as they approached the strange woman who stood alone by the wall.

She was dressed in a man's suit of clothes. Imagine! Navy blue trousers and an odd suit jacket that had a pin on the breast pocket. The bar of multicolored ribbons resembled one Traver had once seen on the chest of a naval officer. How this woman had come to wear something that belonged to a military man was beyond him. It even had a strange, tiny, bronze animal hanging from it. Around her neck was a chain of silver which clipped to a large blue paper that lay on her upper chest. She wore a paper napkin as easily as other women wear pearl necklaces! The poor Cap'n! The only woman things about her were the frilly lace collar of her white blouse and the long brown hair that was streaked blond in places by the sun. Even though her lips looked larger on one side than the other, she did have a sort of pretty face, square-jawed, like she could be real stubborn if she put her mind to it. Her cheekbones were high, kind of like the Indians or them Russian farmers they had passed on the drive north. Her face was flushed a pretty pink, but as they got closer, Traver could see that she was even more nervous than him and Kyle. The woman's wide amber-colored eyes showed fear.

"You waitin' for Cap'n McCabe, ma'am?"

She blinked several times at the cowboys. The one that

spoke was old, his skin weathered like a shelled walnut. His nose and ears seemed too big for his face, as if they had kept growing while the rest of him had aged and shrunk. He wore a plaid shirt and leather leggings, just like the younger one—only the young one's had fringe at the bottom. The leggings, they were called chaps, she thought, were tied together right below a huge belt buckle and worn tan leather gloves were casually tucked behind the string at their groin. Both had wide-brimmed hats that they held at their side. The young one nervously tapped it against his leg as they both waited for her answer. They each looked like they had stepped off a movie set and, despite her fear, she recognized a tiny fascination. These people could see and hear her, and they expected an answer. She was to actively participate in this dream. Her observation was made in mere seconds, yet it seemed like minutes before she could get her mouth to work properly.

"Macdabe?" she tried to pronounce through her thick, numb lips. "Eisenberg and Macdade? The demmtipts?" She wiped her mouth and tried again. "Dentists?"

The cowboys first stared at her and then cast alarmed glances at each other. "We're here to take you to Cap'n McCabe, ma'am," the old one volunteered. "McCabe, right?"

Elle swallowed down and shifted the wad of gauze in her cheek. "Macdabe. Right." They would take her back to the dentist. Once again experiencing that odd sensation, she touched the corner of her puffy lips to check for dribble. She was embarrassed by their looks of bewilderment and tried to explain. "My mouff, you know?"

"Yes'm," the younger one said, before clearing his

throat and glancing at his companion. "Traver?"

The one named Traver stared at her long and hard before abruptly nodding. "We'd best take her. Let Cap'n McCabe decide what to do."

The old cowboy motioned with his hands for her to follow and Elle moved forward, convinced that she was still under the effects of the gas. What other reason could there be for all these strange people, in their strange clothing, giving her even stranger looks as she passed them by?

There isn't any other explanation, she reasoned as she walked between the two men out of the building and into the street. She was obviously hallucinating. Soon, she would wake up back in the dentist's chair and be told it was all over.

In the meantime, she decided it wouldn't hurt to follow these fascinating men. Elle was amazed by the power of her mind, her imagination. Never would she have believed that she possessed such highly developed faculties. Having never done drugs . . . well, once she'd tried pot in college and had found it only made her hungry, then extremely tired. She'd had the sense to realize it wasn't an experience that she ever wanted to repeat, so her life had remained drug free in an era when yuppies and pushers were doing big business. But this . . . what she was experiencing now . . . this was probably what everybody in the sixties was talking about when they described "tripping."

And it was certainly turning into one hell of a trip. . . .

It wasn't frightening, or painful. Instead, Elle was filled with a sense of awe, of wonder, as she viewed her surroundings. She was led out onto a dirt road and she paused to look back at the train depot. No longer was it the Victorian building with its lacy gingerbread. Now it was just a plain white frame structure, with the word *Wichita* in large block letters painted on the front. Across the street was another building with a sign that read, *Charles Marsh—Coal Dispenser/Business Manager for the Santa Fe Line.* On either side of the street were long lines of railroad cars, the boxcars filled with cattle. Men, some in dark suits, but most in cowboy outfits, appeared preoccupied as they went about their day as if nothing out of the ordinary were happening. There were horses and wagons and the distinct odor of animals. Lots of animals. It was simply incredible. Never before had her dreams been this vivid, nor her senses more acute.

"Can I help you up on the buckboard, ma'am?" the young cowboy asked in a polite voice.

She turned away from the depot and smiled. "Thanks," she said while holding out her hand. Elle settled onto the wooden seat next to the older of the two men and grinned. Who'd believe it? She had to be dreaming, imagining this old town while a dentist yanked out her tooth! Talk about the miracle of modern dentistry. Vaguely, as her tongue again touched the wad of gauze in her cheek, she wondered why the gauze was in her mouth in the first place. . . . Something was weird, but she shook off the notion and decided to stop questioning and just go with the flow. Whatever was happening to her now had to be easier than being awake, and watching a stranger pull out a tooth that she had grown very used to in the last two decades. Yes. Sweet air, the dentist had called it, was sweet indeed and she didn't want any part of reality just yet.

"No other baggage?" the man named Traver asked, interrupting her thoughts. How clever. Her subconscious had even named these two men.

She smiled and shook her head.

Traver nodded. "Your trunk, it came three days ago and we brung it already. The Cap'n said we was to apologize if you were on this last train. 'Cause of the storm and everything, he had to stay out with the herd. Near stampeded into the Arkansas River." Traver flicked the reins over the horse's back. "Them Herefords, they hate lightning. Spook real easy. Even more'n the Longhorns."

Elle didn't know what she was supposed to say, so she merely nodded. Why was he telling her this?

"He waited three days for you to come. In town, here at the hotel. And got mighty worried when your trunk come off that train without you. We all figured something was mixed up. If it weren't for this emergency, well, he sure enough would've met you hisself."

She wasn't listening to the younger cowboy. Grabbing hold of the edge of the seat, Elle hung on as the buckboard started moving up the wide main street of the town. The buildings were mostly of wood, very few of brick, and almost all two stories. There were businesses and saloons, and on the corner was a huge place called The New York Store—a dry goods and clothing emporium. Elle grinned. What a great imagination she had! One place advertised in huge letters: Guns, Pistols, Ammunition, Hardware and Tinware. The people on the wooden sidewalk in front of the establishment stopped and stared as she drove by. Some of the men wore large white aprons and the women were dressed in dark gray or brown dresses with little or no other color. They looked at her as if she were the odd one, the person out of place. She could only smile, or try to smile, since her mouth was

27

still numb. She raised her hand to wave, but hesitated for fear of overdoing it. Instead, she'd just let the experience continue until they woke her up.

Beginning to enjoy herself, Elle watched the men and women on the street, real characters taken right out of every Western movie or television series she had ever seen. As they weaved in and around other wagons or men on horseback, she listened to the sounds of the wagon wheels squishing in the muddy ruts on the streets. She heard the flicks of leather against hides, the ring of metal spurs and the murmuring of low voices all blending together into a delightful and noisy reverberation of humanity. As they left what was the center of town, Elle even recognized what must have been a brothel. Up on the second floor two women sat on windowsills, looking bored, and Elle glanced up and smiled. Their faces showed their shock and they stared at her with what could only be described as intense interest.

Suddenly, without any warning whatsoever, a man came flying out the wide door of the house and tumbled into the street right in front of their horse. Elle tried to scream, but the sound that came out of her mouth sounded more like a high, strangled gurgle.

"Damnation!" Traver muttered as he fought to bring the horse under control. The old man used considerable strength to stop the beast from crushing the body in the mud. Within seconds, the horse slowed and the wagon came to a stop off to one side of the dirt road.

Elle gulped in air and hung on to the seat for dear life as she listened to Kyle yell out from the back of the wagon. "What the samhill you doing, Jake Beard? We could've killed him! Maybe us, too!"

A huge red-haired man with a long beard of the same

unusual color stood in front of the brothel door. His hands were on his hips and Elle could see that he wore a gun strapped under his large belly.

"Bill Armstrong's been gettin' a mite too rough for the ladies. Only doin' my job, is all. What'cha got there, Kyle Reavis? I can't tell if it be man or woman."

Elle listened to the red-haired man's laughter and watched as the one named Bill Armstrong struggled to his feet. She could almost feel Traver stiffen next to her as he yelled back, "Watch your mouth, Jake, or you'll answer to Cap'n McCabe."

"Cap'n McCabe? This here's the one he's been waitin' for? *She's* the one?"

Elle watched the man named Bill Armstrong straighten out and brush the mud from his jacket sleeve. When he looked up at them, she couldn't suppress a shiver of distaste. He must have been in his forties, yet he could have been younger and just looked aged by the sun. His skin was a deep leathery brown; his hair a strange blond, almost white. He was dressed in all black, except for a red handkerchief that he checked to make sure was still there before stuffing it deeper into his chest pocket. His eyes were cold and angry; his jaw set in a fierce, grim line. Never in her sheltered life had anyone frightened her like this, and Elle felt foolish—for in a strange way, she was mesmerized by the malevolence in his expression. He seemed to dismiss her and drag his attention back to the red-haired man who had thrown him into the street. The same man who was still shouting things to Traver and Kyle. Things that sounded vaguely insulting to her, yet she couldn't figure out why. . . .

And then, the oddest thing happened. As casually as if he were taking out a pack of cigarettes, the white-haired

29

man pulled out a small pistol from his coat. Even from five yards away she could make out the carved ivory handle.

"Hey," Elle tried to interrupt as she pointed across the muddy street. "He hath a gum . . . a *gun!*"

Traver immediately yelled out to the horse and pulled the wagon away. It all took place so quickly that she would later question whether it ever happened, but for the moment Elle clutched at the rim of the wooden seat and clung to it as the wagon sped down the street, away from whatever was happening behind her. She involuntarily jerked around when she heard the loud explosion of gunfire, but Kyle grabbed hold of her shoulders to keep her from seeing beyond him.

"Nothing you should witness, ma'am. Just appears like Boot Hill got another citizen, is all."

The town passed in a blur as people came out of the stores and ran toward the brothel. Elle didn't look back. It didn't happen. It couldn't have. She did not just see two men shooting at each other. This was only taking place in her head, in her imagination. All she had to do was remember that and stay calm.

She stared at the rear end of the horse, watching its hind muscles undulate, the sheen of sweat appear on its brown hair as they left the town behind them. Even though she didn't know that much about drugs, Elle was fairly certain that this hallucination was now taking a turn for the worse.

"Waare are we gowing?" she mumbled as she saw a river directly in front of them.

"Goin' to catch up with the herd. Don't rightly know how much the Cap'n wrote to you." The young cowboy spoke up from in back of the wagon as they crossed over

30

a narrow wooden bridge. "He's real proud of them Herefords. Going to crossbreed 'em with the Longhorn. He even bought himself an Angus bull. Imagine that!"

Traver glared back over his shoulder. "Kyle Reavis, watch your mouth. This here's a lady."

Even though she saw both men glance at her gabardine slacks, she still smiled as they left the bridge behind them and rode out into the flat countryside. "Thaas okay," she said as best she could. She dabbed at the corner of her mouth with the blue paper still hanging from her neck. "I don't mind."

Traver harrumphed loudly before urging the horse on. "You still watch your mouth, Kyle. The Cap'n wouldn't like it."

Elle thought whoever this Cap'n was, he sounded like someone she wouldn't like. She wanted to ask the old cowboy when they would get back to the dentist's office, but decided against it. Every time she spoke she had the distinct impression that they were horrified by her voice. One would think she was the only one in the world who had trouble speaking after being shot up with Novocaine!

She had never been in such an isolated place. Mile after mile they rode in silence. Probably in reality it was only seconds, but to her it felt like almost an hour had gone by and still they kept to the deep rutted road that seemed to lead to nowhere. If it weren't for the occasional prairie dogs, which she thought were cute and Traver proclaimed as danged nuisances, Elle would have sworn they weren't even moving. She thought that if she were to stand in the center of the plains and twirl completely around, she would see the same sight, the same horizon before her. It was that flat. So when she actually saw the herd of cattle, the white shape that turned into a covered

31

wagon, Elle sat up straight in the seat and became interested.

"What's dat . . . that?" she mumbled, starting to feel a tingling in her lips.

"That's the Cap'n, and the herd we're goin' to take back with us to the Triple Cross. Nothin' like the seven hundred we drove up here, but these sixty are special. Plan to crossbreed 'em, the Cap'n does . . ." Kyle's voice held a note of pride and Elle wondered just who this paragon of virtue was to have inspired such respect. Glancing at Traver's angry expression, Kyle added, "But I already told you about that."

Within minutes, the wagons grew larger and the cattle became real living things as they moved about. She could see men on horses riding at the edge of the herd, swinging their hats to bring a stray cow back to the others. Traver drove past the cattle to the covered wagon that stood before a campfire. There were perhaps ten cowboys standing by it, drinking coffee and staring at them as they approached. One of them, taller than the others, moved forward as if to greet them. His steps were long and graceful, filled with purpose and authority.

As if on command, the sun came out from behind the fat clouds and Elle shielded her eyes against the sudden glare. Squinting, she stared back. The lone cowboy wore a brown coat that reached beyond his calves. It looked like a raincoat of sorts, with an attached shawl of leather over his shoulders. Even from this distance, she could see that the leather was worn, even ripped in spots. When he walked toward them the long coat fell to his sides and she was able to make out his jeans and shirt. He wore an olive green scarf, a bandana, at his neck and it lay on his chest, as though he had just pulled it down from his face.

Unconsciously, Elle swallowed as they came closer. She couldn't see his eyes because of the wide hat, but she could distinguish the lower half of his features, the mustache and beard, the dark brown hair that touched his collar. And for some strange reason, Elizabeth Mackenzie held her breath as Traver stopped the buckboard and the cowboy swept his worn leather hat from his head.

He was, she reluctantly admitted, the most gorgeous man she had ever seen. God, but her imagination was fertile! For only with the help of sweet air could she have conjured up this hunk. And that's what he was—a hunk. A rugged, hunky cowboy. A combination of Tom Selleck, Mel Gibson and Gary Cooper all mixed together. And to think she never even liked cowboys! Not even in the movies. They simply weren't her type. She liked three-piece suits, expertly tailored, not tight jeans and beards and light blue eyes that looked at her with . . . with *anticipation?* As if he were expecting her?

This man, this wonderful image from her drugged mind, came up to the side of the buckboard and smiled.

"You're here . . ." he said, as though not quite believing it himself. "I'm sorry about this. About the way you were met at the station. It isn't how I had wanted us to finally meet."

His voice was low, a little embarrassed, and he brushed back his hair in a nervous gesture. "I'm glad you're here."

She smiled as best she could. "Tanks . . . thank you." Wiping the side of her mouth she strained to speak correctly. "Do you know where Doctor Macdade is?"

The smile on his face quickly disappeared. As if remembering himself, he reached out his hand to her.

33

"Doctor? Here, let me help you down. Would you like coffee? Anything I can get you? You must be tired after your trip."

She nodded and stood up. What a great voice he had. "You're not kidding. This has beewn unbewievable!" Damn it! Why did she have to sound like Daffy Duck now? In front of *him*. She was about to explain about her mouth when she noticed the low murmurs of the other cowboys who stood by the campfire. Looking up, Elle saw their shocked expressions and she glanced to the tall cowboy in front of her. His eyes narrowed as they took in her legs and his mouth was set in a grim line. Why did her clothes seem to evoke such negative reactions from everyone? This was truly a crazy dream. One would think these men had never seen a woman in slacks before.

His hands were strong as he lifted her down from the wagon, and Elle again marveled at the hallucination. It would be just her luck for the real Doctor Macdade to wake her now, now that she was getting to the interesting part. The cowboy set her away from him and she had the impression that she had somehow just disappointed him. She didn't know how, or why, but she could tell by his eyes that something wasn't right.

He cleared his throat, aware of the interested men behind him. "We've . . . ah, I have been waiting. I was . . . was worried," he added, clearly embarrassed. "Was there a problem with the connections? Is that why your train was delayed?"

God, he was great looking! Never again would she be frightened of the dentist. If a little gas could create this man, she knew she would be back for more. "My twain? It was dewayed? Delayed?" She smiled apologetically. "I'm afwaid I don't know what your tawking about.

Talking about." As if it weren't bad enough that she spoke like a cartoon character, she actually, in front of all these staring men, began to dribble from trying to push the words through numb lips.

"Sheet, man . . . look at that!"

"My God, the Cap'n—he's gone and married a . . ."

"A blubbering idiot! That's what!"

"Aww, Geez. Look at her! She's *afoamin'.*"

"Shut up. Don't let him hear you."

But he had. And so had she.

Wiping the corner of her mouth with the paper napkin that still hung from her neck, Elle glanced up at him. The Captain. A tight knot began in her stomach and squeezed at her muscles. He was furious, and he was looking at her as if she were the cause. His left cheek was moving rapidly, probably from clenching his back teeth. And his eyes. Eyes that she had thought to be outstanding only a moment ago, narrowed and turned cold.

"We'll talk later. We've already been delayed three days and I have to make up the time. I'm sorry for the inconvenience, but there isn't any other way." He turned around to the men and added in a low threatening voice. "All right, ladies, if you're done with your gossiping, then let's get started. We've got a long trip ahead of us."

They were like jackrabbits that had been caught in a beam of light. Frozen in indecision and fear, no one moved until the tall cowboy roared, *"Now!"*

Elle jumped along with the others. The cowboys started scurrying about the camp while the man, the Captain, turned back to her.

"You'll ride with Cooky, Arlyn," he corrected. "Your trunk is in my wagon. I expect you'll want to change."

She looked down to her slacks. "What's wrong with what I'm wearing?"

He inhaled deeply. "I was hoping you were so attired because of losing your baggage. A lady would never—would never—" He shook his head with impatience. "Why am I discussing this? We're breaking camp immediately." He jammed his hat back onto his head and added, "We'll continue this discussion when we stop outside of Caldwell."

"Wait a minute," she called after him as he walked away from her. "Wait just one minute." She was happy to note that her speech was definitely more clear.

He turned, and she saw that the annoyance in his expression had turned to anger. "What is it?"

"Look, I think there's been a mistake. I want to wake up now." She tried smiling at him. "It's not your fault. I suppose you're nice enough, but I don't think I'm going to wike this . . . like this." She waved to the wagons and the cattle beyond. "I'm not the outdoorsy type. I hate camping. L.L. Bean . . . all that stuff. It's just not for me."

His mouth dropped open in surprise and she felt a twinge of pity for this figment of her imagination. It was too bad that it was over, but she'd had enough. It was getting too confusing. Surely the dentist had to be done by now. "Hey, it's okay. Just tell me what to do."

He leaned closer to her, so close that she noticed the crinkles at the corner of his eyes—blue eyes that narrowed even more so with anger. His nostrils actually flared and she observed a single gray hair in his beard. He was plainly furious, but she stood her ground instead of backing up. And when he opened his mouth to speak, she could detect the scent of coffee at his lips.

36

"I have already told you what to do, madam. Do not continue with this spectacle—"

"But I told you," she interrupted. "There's been a mistake."

He looked deeply into her eyes and she actually cringed from the fury building within his expression.

"I believe you are correct," he said in a low, almost menacing voice. "There *has* been a mistake. Mine. You, madam, grossly misrepresented yourself."

"What?" Highly offended, she straightened her shoulders. "How dare you? Why, you're not even real! You . . . you . . . *Captain!*"

His eyes locked with hers over a stormy war of words. "That's right, madam. A captain. Retired, Confederate Army. And I'm giving you an order right now. Get in that wagon with Cooky, or by God I'll leave you right here on the Kansas plains. That hair would make some Osage chief very happy."

She blinked several times. How odd that only minutes ago, she was plagued by an excess of saliva, actually dribbling onto the blue napkin at her neck. Grasping the paper in her fist, she pulled it off. Now, her mouth felt as dry as a desert. What did he say? *The Confederate Army?* How ludicrous. This was a hallucination. A delusion.

"Who *are* you?" she demanded of the illusion.

He looked at her as though she'd lost her mind. As if straining for patience, he enunciated each word, "Jordan Dillon McCabe. Please make up your mind. We're moving out."

He turned and walked away, leaving her in front of the wagons. She watched a cowboy put out the campfire and smelled the acrid odor of doused flames, as coffee was poured over it. Other men threw things into the back of

37

the wooden wagon while giving her sidelong glances.

Something was definitely wrong. Who did McCabe think he was?

Dear God . . . he was acting as if this were real.

Real?

Thinking the word, hearing it in her mind, frightened her even more than saying it aloud. For suddenly, without any explanation, instinct was telling her it was so.

This was not a dream!

It was happening . . . now!

Chapter 3

"Okay! Hold it!" Elle's voice was surprisingly strong,
considering her state of shock. "Wait just one minute,"
she called after the cowboy. He stopped, stood very still,
and then slowly turned back to her.

She walked the few yards to meet him, knowing he
would never come forward. It was a power play. She'd
gone through it herself in business a hundred times. But
she was good at it and knew just how to advance and when
to retreat. Aware of the attention they were receiving
from those around them, Elle also knew this man would
hate to lose face—it made good sense now to come to
him, to save him from any further embarrassment.

She stood in front of him, refusing to allow his
frightening appearance to alter her course. He wasn't real
anyway. Her ridiculous thoughts of moments ago were
not worth considering. Somehow, some way, she had to
stop this fantasy before it turned into a nightmare.

"Mr. McCabe? That is your name, isn't it?" She didn't
wait for an answer before continuing. "Look, I've had
enough. Something happened during the storm this

morning. Maybe I can't handle nitrous oxide, or something. Maybe there was a surge in the electricity before it was knocked out, and I got a double dose of laughing gas—only I'm not laughing anymore. Who knows why I'm here, or why you're here . . . although that's certainly a more interesting question. Probably has something to do with my love life. Or lack of one. Come to think of it, I hope I'm not spouting all this to Eisenberg or Macdade, or whoever he was, and that nurse of his." Placing her hand onto her hip, she shook her head. "They're probably hysterical right now, aren't they? Listening to me talking to you. A fantasy. My God, I must seem pathetic."

She took a deep breath and tried to return to her original thought. "Anyway, I don't know how this sort of thing is supposed to work, but I need to go back now. That's really what I wanted to say." She almost grinned. "And I'm saying it pretty well, now that I'm getting some feeling into my lips. Well, what do you say, Mr. Cap'n Cowboy? How do I get back?"

He continued to stare at her. And when he spoke, his voice was a whisper of angry disbelief. "What are you talking about? You want to *go back*? I believe we have already discussed that. It's the rest of your speech that I find—"

She nodded and tried to smile as she interrupted him. "Yes, well . . . this time I'd appreciate an answer, instead of an order. How do I get back to Wichita?"

His nose actually flared, and Elle couldn't stop staring at his expression. He looked so angry that she found her stomach muscles tightening in defense. Honestly, why couldn't she have conjured up a more accommodating figure for this dream? This guy, although gorgeous in a

40

rough kind of way, was becoming a real pain.

Slowly, as though it had a will of its own, his arm rose from his side and pointed to the left. "That way. You go back that way. The same way you just came."

She looked to the barren horizon. There was nothing here, absolutely nothing. "Will your men take me back? Traver and Kyle?" It was the least they could do.

"My men are preparing to go home. Something we're all impatient to do. We've wasted three days waiting for you, madam. I am not about to squander another hour and a half to take you back to Wichita. You'll have to wait until Caldwell to get a ride east."

"You mean you won't take me back? What am I to do out here?" Her voice was rising, along with a frightening hysteria. He'd actually leave her in this desolate place!

He bent his head, his face mere inches from her own. She swallowed down an excess of saliva and glared back at him.

"I've already given you your alternatives. You ride with Cooky—or, you walk."

Elle's chin rose up in defiance, while her eyes narrowed dangerously. She would have dearly loved to tell him exactly what he could do with his suggestions, but her sense of survival rose to the surface, taking the edge off an intense anger. Instead, she allowed the full measure of her distaste to be heard in her voice.

"Cowboy!"

For a modern, cultured, sophisticated Easterner, at the moment it was the worst thing she could think of to say.

His mouth dropped open and she smiled at his shocked expression. "I have endured enough, madam," he said finally and with great patience. "When we reach

41

Caldwell, we shall both see about rectifying this mistake."

Without another word he walked away, leaving her in the middle of a camp that was rapidly being dismantled. She sensed the stares of the men as they worked around her and she turned her head to face them. Quickly, they averted their eyes and continued their chores, tying barrels and shovels to the sides of wagons, checking the harness of the lead horses. There wasn't a doubt in her mind.

These men thought she was crazy.

Of course she hadn't done much to dispel that image. They had said she was foaming at the mouth. Maybe a little dribble could create a curiosity, but *"a foamin'?"* C'mon . . . she'd been numb. Her lips had felt like a Mick Jagger nightmare. And then there was McCabe's reaction to her words. Perhaps to someone, a cowboy, it might sound strange. She shrugged. A little strange. As she thought over her morning, her tongue played with the sodden gauze in the back of her mouth and she felt like gagging. Enough was enough.

As casually as she could, she brushed back her hair and allowed her hand to pass over the front of her face, while as delicately and as stealthily as possible, Elle spit out the gauze into the blue napkin that she clutched in her hand. Hoping no one would notice, she walked closer to the doused campfire and dropped the offending material. Just as she was about to kick some dried mud on top of it, a voice called out from behind her.

"Ma'am? You hurt, or somethin'?"

Elle jumped in surprise, but quickly recovered and turned to the young man at her side. "I . . . ahhh . . . I had a tooth removed this morning," she said promptly to

42

Kyle as he stared down at her attempt to cover the bloodied gauze. "It's . . . it's nothing. Really."

"You sure? Maybe you should—well, you know, tell the Cap'n. Or somethin'?" The boy was obviously embarrassed.

Elle actually laughed, or she hoped it sounded like a laugh. My God, her mouth hurt! "Don't you dare say anything to that man. He's a pompous jackass. And neurotic about time! He couldn't even spare a wagon, or anyone to take me back to Wichita. His precious wagon train might be delayed. Can you imagine?"

"Yes, ma'am. I can. He's the boss. And this here isn't a wagon train. It's more like a trail drive back home to Texas." He appeared uncomfortable talking to her and cleared his throat. "I'm to show you Cooky's wagon. All right?"

He looked like he expected her to argue with him and Elle softened at his fearful expression. She didn't have a problem with the young man. Smiling, she said, "Sure, show me Cooky's wagon. I might as well ride this dream out. I'm certainly not making any headway going against it."

She followed Kyle to the large covered wagon and waited as he introduced her to an old man who was throwing supplies into a huge box that was bolted to the back of it. It looked like a large dresser with massive drawers for storing food and cooking utensils. Vaguely, Elle wished she'd had a cup of coffee this morning back at the hotel. It didn't look like it was going to be an easy afternoon.

"Cooky? This here's Miz Cynthia. The Cap'n's new missus. She's ridin' with you."

Elle barely had time to acknowledge the old man's

grunt of displeasure when Kyle's words registered.

Now it all made sense! Of course, they thought she was someone else. She opened her mouth to speak, to correct the mistake. Surely now they would take her back to Wichita. But as she started to talk, a red haze of pain washed in front of her eyes, making her tear at the effort to control it.

It was obvious the Novocain had finally worn off. What perfect timing. Here she was, in the middle of nowhere. With no way to get back to civilization. To her way of thinking, she didn't have much of a choice. And as yet, no one had ever accused Elizabeth Mackenzie of being a fool.

She watched the man named Cooky tie down the canvas across the back of the wagon. He had long gray hair that didn't look like it had been washed in a month. His matching beard hung in long wisps that reminded her of the fake cobwebs people used at Halloween to decorate their doors. Even his hat was gray. Once, it might have been black, but over time it must have faded to blend in with the rest of him. He was a genuine character, mumbling his displeasure at her company. Without a recognizable word, he took his seat in the front and waited for her to join him.

Here it was . . . the decision. Should she stay and wait for the dream to end? Surely now that the Novocain was wearing off, the effects of the gas would dissipate. She gazed to the bleak horizon and hated to admit that it didn't look promising. Or . . . she could join Gabby Hayes here and stay with people, or illusions, until she woke up. Within moments, she concluded that anything was better than being alone in this fantasy . . . even old Gabby.

Climbing up next to the silent and somber-faced driver, Elle tried to compose her expression. "How do you do, Cooky?" she said as calmly and pleasantly as possible. "You can call me Elizabeth." Even though she was definitely in pain, she smiled down at Kyle. "No one ever calls me Cynthia."

It wasn't a lie.

It was so goddamned unfair that if he actually thought about it, he might stampede the herd himself. Guiding the Angus bull, Jordan realized he was barely able to manage his own emotions. How the hell could this have happened? How could this harridan, this . . . this *shrew* be the same woman whose sensitive letters had moved him so? The woman who had answered his letters had written with intelligence and sensitivity, perception and enthusiasm. The female driving Cooky to distraction with her stream of chatter hardly filled that description.

He had been deceived. And Jordan Dillon McCabe prided himself on his judgments. It wasn't often that he made a mistake, but this . . . surely this qualified for something larger than a mistake.

It was a disaster.

Granted, he hadn't met Cynthia in person, but they had written for almost a year. They had even exchanged photographs. It didn't matter to him that she looked nothing at all like the image she had sent him over six months ago. His own picture hadn't captured him either. With such formal clothing, somber expression and a brace to hold his head still, Jordan had been unsure, yet the photographer had said it was an appropriate gift for a lady. He had not been pleased to send it off to Atlanta, yet

45

was impatient for Cynthia's reply. He remembered actually being apprehensive waiting for *her* approval!

Following behind the chuck wagon, Jordan shook his head as he watched the woman hold the side of her face. At least she wasn't talking anymore. He hadn't expected a great beauty in Cynthia. He thought he knew what he was getting this time around. This time in his life, he wanted stability and intelligence—someone to build a home with. He gazed down to the lead animal. It was all supposed to be part of the plan. He'd worked on it for years . . .

With Scottish backing, Jordan had established one of the finest cattle spreads in Texas. Every four months, he sent exactly one-third of the profits to Scotland, with his thanks and gratitude. Without James Magonicle, there would be no Triple Cross. The Scotsman had invested in the dreams of a defeated soldier, and trusted him to make good. It was an immense source of pride that three years ago, the Triple Cross had shown its initial profit and now James would be visiting for the very first time in less than two months. Two months . . .

Peachtree Point was finally completed in the same antebellum style as his family home in Georgia. Not exactly a replica of the one that had been burned and gutted by an invading army in the fall of '64, but it was a sweet reminder of more innocent days. And it was an accomplishment to have re-created that splendor amid such wild land. Four huge white columns greeted any guest to his front door. Every brick of soft peach and white had been brought in by wagon and applied to the facade and the walkways that bordered the small orchards on either side of the house. Even though the peach trees had never yielded a single fruit, Jordan liked to look at the blossoms in the spring, remembering a time when he could gaze out a window of his family home to a sea of soft white . . . but that was another lifetime ago. He would never be that innocent or trusting ever again. Through war and defeat and sorrow and sheer hell, Jordan Dillon McCabe had been reborn into a survivor. He might be able to recapture the outward trappings of a lost life, but inside, where honesty was so often brutal, Jordan knew a vital part of himself had been lost.

He had thought perhaps Cynthia might have been the one to bring it back. She had written all the right responses in her letters, expressed the same dreams for a future.

She must have been play acting, saying and doing anything to get a husband. He had been so foolish. Lucia had laughed at him for marrying a woman he had never met . . . for advertising in the *Atlanta Journal* for a wife. But he'd had Cynthia investigated! How could he have been so deceived? He and Alexander Foy had grown up together. They had even formed the Kenesaw Mountain Volunteers at the tender age of nineteen. Never mind that their small group of mostly gentlemen cavalry soldiers had been absorbed into General Johnson's army. Alex Foy had been a trusted lifetime friend—a friend that had sworn to him of Cynthia's soft, gentle nature. Alex had written that Miss Cynthia Warden was a woman of virtue and gentility. Her people went back to the first settlers of the Georgia colony. Alex had recommended her, saying she would make a perfect wife—that she was everything the South, the old South, had once envisioned in a woman, and that Jordan was fortunate to have found her, even in such a bizarre fashion. Alex had not only met Cynthia, he'd also stood in as Jordan's proxy

47

for the wedding in her aunt's home last month.

Nothing made sense anymore. Nothing. His oldest friend had misled him, and the woman in Cooky's wagon had deceived him in the most despicable manner. Anger renewed itself and surged up inside of him as he glared ahead. How she must be laughing at his pathetic need for a wife.

For the widower Jordan McCabe, it was the second time he had made a drastic mistake in marriage. And this time he wouldn't wait for Fate to step in and solve his problem. He was going to rectify this one as soon as they reached Caldwell, for he couldn't imagine bringing this woman home to Peachtree Point. Picturing his mother-in-law's reaction almost brought a smile to his lips. The ever-proper Hester Hunt Morgan would take one look at those trousers and collapse in apoplexy.

So absorbed in his own thoughts, Jordan didn't even realize that Cooky had slowed the chuck wagon and was preparing to stop for the night until he almost rode right up to it. He looked to the sky and then brought his horse next to the driver.

"What are you doing?" he asked the old man. "There's at least two more hours of good daylight—"

He stopped speaking when he glanced at the woman next to Cooky. The vibrant, fearless woman of this afternoon was gone. Somehow, in the last four hours, a pale, shaking creature had taken her place. The pain in her eyes was clearly visible. She was holding her cheek, cradling it in the palms of her hands, and when she looked at him, really looked, his chest tightened with remorse as he watched the thin tears roll over her fingers.

She was obviously ill. And she was looking at him as if he had somehow caused it.

"What's wrong?" he asked Cooky.

The old man shrugged. "She's been like this for the past couple 'a hours. I didn't think she could take much more." He wrapped the leather reins around the brake and hopped off the wagon. "Ain't gonna hurt nothing if we settle in a few hours early tonight. All I know is I ain't drivin' another mile with a crying woman next to me—"

"I mean what's wrong with her? Is she hurt?"

Elle swallowed down a sob of pain and frustration. "Why don't you ask me? You *can* talk to me, you know. I am able to answer simple questions." Trying to glare at him, but finding it took too much of an effort, she sniffled and groaned aloud at the movement. How could she have ever thought he looked like Mel Gibson? He had the compassion and sensitivity of Attilla the Hun!

Taking a deep breath, the cowboy said, "Then tell me. What's wrong?"

Elle's lips trembled as she tried to speak over the racking pain that enveloped the entire side of her face. "I have to know . . . is this hell? Just tell me. Have I died and gone to hell?"

He could only stare at her. *My God, what had he gotten himself into? Not only was she a shrew, she was also deranged!*

Chapter 4

He found her pacing beside the wagon, holding her face and silently crying. When Kyle finally told him about her tooth, Jordan felt terrible. Why hadn't she told him herself? It would have saved so much. But then he remembered that arrogant, stubborn streak he had seen in her when she'd first arrived. That, too, was something he never detected from her letters. Cynthia Warden was a complete surprise. As he approached her, he was shocked to realize that she was now Cynthia McCabe. Legally. But not morally. And he was going to see that it remained that way.

She spun around to face him. "Did you get something?" she asked in an anguished whisper.

He felt a moment of real contrition for having put her through an afternoon of torture on the trail. "Here's a poultice Cooky made. Some cloves for the pain and tea to draw the blood." He held out his hand while wondering why he never thought she was truly attractive in her photograph. Even in her pain, as she flung her long brown hair back from her face and stared at his hand, she was . . . well, almost pretty.

"I beg your pardon?" Elle looked at the thing in his palm. He was offering a small ball wrapped in a yellowed cotton material. "What is that? I asked you for something for the pain." Sniffling, she wiped at her nose. She no longer cared what anyone thought. "Don't you have . . . drugs?"

"Drugs?"

God, talk about big and stupid! "Yes. Drugs. I'll even settle for an aspirin. Please, don't you have anything?"

He held out his hand. "Why don't you try it?"

"I have had a tooth extracted, Mr. McCabe, not my brain. Cloves and tea are not going to stop this kind of pain."

He stared at her, as if fighting for his patience, but she couldn't have cared less at the moment about his injured male ego. Not with pain like this! My God, she felt like her face was on fire. The blinding, stabbing ache went deep behind her upper jaw. It was an unleashed horror, attacking her nerve endings and producing a throbbing spasm that wound its way up behind her eye and temple and back down to the empty socket in her mouth. It was the worst pain she had ever endured and it was relentless. Dear God, she needed some relief, from somewhere.

She wasn't even surprised to see her shaking fingers reach out and take the poultice. She stared at it for a few seconds, almost missing his next words.

"I . . . ah . . . that is, I thought it might help if you soaked it first. I'm sorry I don't have anything less potent. I didn't expect—"

"What is it?" she interrupted, while gaping at the bottle he had pulled out from the pocket of his long coat.

"Whiskey."

52

"Whiskey?"

"I apologize. Under normal circumstances I would never have offered. A lady . . . a . . . a woman—"

Elle reached out and grabbed the bottle from his hand. "Give it to me," she nearly ordered. Desperate for relief, in any form, she held the cotton ball to the mouth of the bottle and tipped it over. She repeated the action until the poultice was soaking in the liquor. "I'm in agony," she offered as an apology for being so short with him. "I'll do anything . . . even this."

She opened her mouth and gingerly inserted the saturated ball. When she tried closing her jaw, she hissed in pain as her raw gum came in contact with the homemade remedy. Without further thought, she brought the bottle up to her mouth and tilted her head back.

"Cynthia!"

She ignored his shocked protest and took a deep swallow. Losing her breath as the alcohol burned its way to her empty stomach, Elle sputtered and bent over, gagging at the strong taste. She fought with her body, somehow managing to catch her breath and control her rebellious stomach at the same time. When she finally straightened, it was to come face to face with the self-righteous cowboy.

He held out his hand for the bottle, but she clung to it, hugging it to her stomach. "Let me keep it," she said. It was a statement; she wasn't asking. Hating herself for it, she wiped at her nose with the back of one hand while clutching the whiskey to her as if it were more precious than gold. What a pathetic sight she must make! "And I told Cooky and Kyle nobody calls me Cynthia." The whiskey must be starting to work, for she didn't even care

53

how furious he was becoming. "I prefer Elizabeth."

It was true. Only close family were permitted to use the childhood nickname. Everyone in business who tried to hang a Betty, Beth or, God forbid, Bess was met with a polite reminder that her name was Elizabeth . . . period. And she certainly wasn't a Cynthia. Not his Cynthia, at least. For a fleeting moment, Elle wondered where the woman was. If she was still waiting in Wichita, or if there really was such a woman at all. She shrugged her shoulders and tried smiling up at the cowboy.

"Call me Elizabeth. Everybody does."

She could see that stopped his angry thoughts, for his mouth merely opened and closed. No words came out. Elle walked closer to the wagon and leaned against it for support. Dear God, she was tired. If she could only stop the pain, the throbbing, then maybe she could sleep. Yes. That was it. If she could only fall asleep, then perhaps when she awoke it would be all over. She would be back in the dentist's chair, or in her hotel room . . . maybe even home in her own bed. Maybe this was all a nightmare.

That was it! She had to go to sleep.

But to get to sleep, she had to stop the pain. And the only thing she had was the whiskey. Shrugging her shoulders, she grabbed hold of the wagon wheel and slowly, gingerly, lowered herself to the ground.

"What are you doing?"

She gazed up at him. He didn't look so frightening. Come to think of it, he was starting to look like Mel Gibson again. Funny what a little whiskey can do. "I'm going to sit here until I fall asleep. And then you're going to be gone. All you guys are going to disappear back to prairie heaven, or wherever you come from." She waved to the men who were settling in the cows for the night.

She smelled the food Cooky was working over and her stomach muscles tightened in response. She hadn't had anything to eat in . . . since last night when that rotten BLT had started this bad dream. But she wasn't hungry. She had swallowed too much blood to even contemplate food. And then again, her jaw hurt too damned much to . . . to masticate. Elle brought the whiskey up to her lips. Great word . . . masticate. She couldn't be drunk. Not if she could think of it. What she needed was more whiskey. Feeling more in control of the situation, she tilted her head back and sipped. She shivered in distaste, yet wrapped her arms around the bottle and held it to her chest for protection. Already she felt different. There was a distant buzzing in her ears and her lips were beginning to tingle again. Now if she could just keep drinking until the rest of her was numb, she'd be set. To her tortured mind, it was perfect logic. Obliterate the senses, then pass out.

When she woke up, it would all be over.

She'd be Elizabeth Mackenzie again. Competent. In control. Ready to take on the world—

"Do you mean to tell me you intend to sit there and drink?"

"You've got it," she answered, angry that he had intruded on her positive thoughts.

"In front of everyone?"

She blinked several times before tilting her head up to see him. "Look, what is your problem? Is it because I'm a woman? You cowboys seem to have this distorted idea about a female's endurance. If you, or any of these men, were trying to wipe out this kind of pain, no one would give it a second thought. But because I'm a woman, I'm expected to clamp down on herbs and endure?" She took

55

a deep breath to steady her raw nerves. "No thanks. I'll take the liquor."

"Cynth—" He shook his head in frustration. *"Elizabeth,"* and he said her name with exaggerated patience, "you're going to make yourself sick. You should eat something. Cooky's heating up stew from last night. Maybe you could try it."

He was only a dream, a product of her imagination, and she really didn't have to answer him if she didn't want to . . . but something inside of her made her wave him off. "Now that would really make me sick. I can't eat." She leaned her head back against the wooden wheel and closed her eyes. "I just want to go to sleep. Everybody looks busy. Don't you have anything else to do besides keeping me awake?"

When he didn't answer after a few moments, she opened her eyes and looked up to where he had been standing.

For the first time all day, she breathed a sigh of relief. He'd already gone.

"Wake up, Elizabeth."

Still clutching the whiskey bottle to her chest, she stirred in her sleep. "Huh? Oh, okay . . ." Her eyes remained closed.

"Elizabeth. You cannot sleep on the ground. Please. At least let me put this blanket under you so you don't catch cold."

She opened her eyes and smiled and, for a moment, Jordan caught his breath at the sweet expression. It only lasted a fraction of time, but for an instant her guard was down, her face relaxed. And her amber eyes were peaceful, almost beautiful. Her skin was pure, soft and unblemished. He was sure when she was cleaned up, she would be quite lovely. Clearing his throat, Jordan tried again.

He reached out and touched her.

Wrapping his fingers around her arms, he pulled her up to him. She tried to help, but her efforts were weak and she clung to him as she stood.

"Hey, McCabe," she slurred in a sleepy voice, "what're you doing?" With great effort, she pushed the strands of long brown hair away from her face.

"I'm trying to get you to stand, so I can put a blanket down. Maybe you'd like to sleep in Cooky's wagon. There's not much room, but you'd be off the ground." He almost smiled at her efforts to awaken. She was blinking rapidly as she gazed up at him and he could feel how unsteady her legs were as she swayed in his arms.

His arms . . .

It was odd to hold a woman again. Especially this one. Actually he wasn't holding her, merely keeping her upright until she was able to stand by herself, but the fact remained that this was the first time that he had held the woman all others thought of as his wife. A wife. It was too bizarre to contemplate. Instead, he took her hand from his arm and placed it on the wagon for support. "Can you stand?" he asked.

She nodded and leaned against the cook's wagon. Her head bobbed drunkenly as she tried to overcome the effects of the whiskey. Once more he felt the urge to smile. He never would have believed the proper woman of those long months of correspondence would behave with such total abandon. Elizabeth, as she'd made it clear she preferred to be called, was turning out to be a complete surprise—in more ways than he expected.

"I have a quilt and a small straw mattress. It isn't much, but if you won't sleep in the wagon it'll keep you from getting a chill." He spread the old quilt over the mattress and smoothed down its edges. "There you are," he said, his voice sounding far brighter than his mood.

She sank to the quilt, her fist still clutching the bottle. "Did I sleep?" she asked as she squinted toward the campfire.

Sitting next to her, he offered the plate of stew. "For a short time. Look, I brought you some food. You've got to be hungry. Maybe you could dip the bread into the gravy."

She shook her head before slowly allowing it to fall back against the wagon wheel. Closing her eyes, she muttered, "You go ahead. I can't eat."

He watched her for a few moments, seeing how the return of pain made her expression tense, her body achingly taut. In all honesty, he didn't blame her for bringing the whiskey to her mouth and gulping it down.

"Are you all right?" he asked, observing her cough and sputter in the aftermath. When she didn't answer, he held his plate in one hand and whacked her on the back with the other. She seemed to catch her breath after that.

"Jesus!" Her face was red from the exertion. "How mad are you?"

"I was trying to help you," he said defensively.

"Right. I think my lungs are now located in my throat."

He stared at her.

"I suppose you're now waiting for me to thank you for rearranging my internal organs?"

58

He paused for only a moment before smiling. "You're welcome."

It was the smile. He never should have done that, Elle reasoned. If only he had remained the stiff, overbearing cowboy that made this nightmare so appalling. Instead, he had smiled at her. For the first time. And something inside of her melted at his wide friendly grin. She must be drunk to be so affected by a smile . . . from a cowboy, even a great-looking cowboy, and she ran her hand over her eyes as the next wave of pain washed over her face. What an imagination! It must be the whiskey. She wasn't used to drinking. Not like this. An occasional glass of wine after dinner maybe. Whiskey? Straight from a bottle? Hardly.

Knowing it was the only thing that was going to get her through the night, she reluctantly brought the bottle back up to her lips and took another sip. Her entire body shivered at the strong taste and she let her breath out in a prolonged gasp. "McCabe?" she asked in a hoarse voice.

He swallowed the food in his mouth. "What?"

"I think we're lost. Both of us. I should be in Wichita, or back East . . . and you? You should be where?"

He took off his hat and looked up to the stars. "If I could be anywhere right now?"

She nodded while staring at his profile. Mel Gibson with a day-old growth of beard . . .

"Back at Peachtree Point."

"Your home?" From the warm tone of voice she realized it could be no other.

"I wrote you about it. Don't you remember?"

Now would have been the perfect opportunity for her to tell him the truth—that his proxy bride was still missing. But she knew she wouldn't. Not yet. In truth she was afraid of his reaction. He might just leave her out here and she hated to admit that even his company was preferable to being abandoned. Swallowing down her guilt, Elle said in a low voice, "Why don't you tell me about it again."

She listened as he spoke of this place, Peachtree Point. It was obviously special to him. She could hear it in his voice. She might have consumed more alcohol today than she had in a year, yet she was still able to detect the difference in his words. The pride and honest affection for his home was genuine.

"Nina has been working very hard. Under Hester's tutelage she has organized all the servants—"

"Servants?"

He glanced down to her. "There are several women whose husbands work the ranch. All are Mexican, or part Indian." His eyes narrowed. "Does that bother you?"

She shrugged. "No, why should it? I was just surprised you have servants."

"We need them. There are sixteen rooms. Hester would never be able to manage alone."

As the ache in her upper jaw returned, Elle brought the whiskey back to her lips. Once she caught her breath, she asked, "Who's Hester?"

He was sopping up heavy gravy with a thick slice of bread when he said, "My mother-in-law. You remember. I wrote to you about her several times."

Cradling the side of her face in her palm, she could only stare at him. *His mother-in-law?* She must be drunk! Blinking several times, she muttered, "Your mother-in-law?"

"Charlotte's mother."

Elle slowly nodded her head, as if she understood,

when the entire thing sounded ludicrous to her. How could he have brought this Cynthia woman out from Georgia to marry him when he was already married? It made no sense, unless— "Are you a . . . a Mormon, or something?" she mumbled.

It was his turn to gape at her. He looked deeply into her eyes in the most uncomfortable stare. Elle felt he was searching her face for the truth and she had to look away from him to the campfire.

"Don't you remember, Elizabeth? I told you all about Charlotte, and how she died."

Her head snapped up. Their eyes met for an instant, and a frightening heat entered her body and settled in her chest. It only lasted a fraction of time, but it was enough that she was uncomfortable . . . and he knew it. *His wife died!* She looked back out to the campfire. Even though it was becoming more difficult to focus on anything in particular, Elle tried to concentrate on the scene in front of her. She strained her eyes, forcing them to take in Cooky as he handed out a second helping of stew to Kyle. The old man named Traver sat with several other cowboys on the ground, drinking coffee as they leaned back against their bedrolls.

The light from the campfire illuminated the area and Elle could see the cattle not far away. Even if she weren't able to see them, she could certainly smell them, and the horses that were tethered to a line of rope, starting at the front of the wagon and ending ten feet away with a notched stick in the ground. A city girl, through and through, she couldn't understand why the creatures didn't break away from the flimsy restraint.

Perhaps they're like me, she thought as she gazed out beyond them to the dark night. They have nowhere else

61

to go. At least here was some form of shelter and food and refuge from the unknown. She was no better than the beasts, with even less courage, for she could not find the words to tell this man sitting next to her that she was Elizabeth Mackenzie from Yardley, Pennsylvania . . . not his mail order bride.

Bride.

How many years had it been since she allowed herself to even think that word and what it implied? Certainly not since she had grown up and realized that term would probably never be applied to her. It wasn't as if she hadn't dreamed once . . . when she was young and naive and needing a fantasy to take her away from the struggle of growing up.

Once, when her father had come home from Conran's bar and had started yelling at her Mom, Elle had shut herself in her closet with the only flashlight in the house. Alone, away from all the shouting and crying, she had written down on a piece of paper the names of her future children.

Patrick and Shannon.

In that tiny dark closet, she had closed out the frightening adult problems and promised herself that when she was a bride she would marry a man that never got drunk and hit people. Her husband wouldn't lose job after job and always blame his bad luck on his wife and children. In her childish mind, she had pictured a tuxedoed groom with the breathtaking looks of a movie star, the wealth of an Arab sheik, and the patience and temperament of a saint. And he would love her. He wouldn't call her names like ugly and scarecrow and stupid. Not like her father and sometimes the boys in school did when they were mad at her. No. If she were ever a bride, then somebody, somewhere, was going to love her just the way she was.

Elle's eyes widened as she continued to stare into the flames of the campfire. My God . . . what a pathetically unhappy and unrealistic child she had been. She hadn't allowed herself to think about that time in her life, and couldn't understand why it had sprung to mind now. Especially when years ago Fate had decreed that she would remain alone. She had accepted that and built up her protection.

Really beginning to feel the effects of the whiskey, Elle leaned her head back against the wheel and looked at a deep purple sky that seemed to fold its arms over the edges of the earth. Hundreds of stars shimmered like jewels and she smiled at the unusual thought. For someone who normally thought of the night as dark and the stars as bright, it was near poetic. It must be the whiskey. Come to think of it, she felt almost numb. Tired, but nearly pain-free.

It was working. Surely she must be close to passing out. Vaguely, she remembered that had been her plan: to drink until oblivion and then wake up from this nightmare. Safe. Sound. In her own time.

She glanced to the man at her side. He sat erect, not slouching, nor leaning against the wheel for support. Despite the cowboy attire, there was something about him that suggested breeding and discipline. What had he said before? A Confederate soldier?

Impossible. She couldn't have heard correctly. Even her imagination couldn't have come up with that one. It was simply ridiculous. Her eyelids fluttered to stay open as she watched him finish eating. He was certainly good-looking in a rough sort of way. Not that she was ever really attracted to that type of man. As if just becoming aware of her scrutiny, McCabe surprised her by turning his head and catching her not too subtle inspection.

Dear God, his eyes were blue. Not just blue—a startling light blue that was more pronounced by his deep tan and his dark brown hair. There was a tiny scar above his eyebrow, a thin line that was more interesting than detracting. Too bad he would be gone when she woke up.

"Here's your coffee, Cap'n. Brought some for the Missus, too."

They both looked up to Cooky. The old man stood before them offering steaming mugs. McCabe murmured his thanks and reached up to take them. When he turned to her, Elle shook her head.

"I don't want to take the chance that it might sober me up."

He put her cup on the ground by his boot and then, finally, leaned back next to her. She watched as he brought the mug to his lips and sipped the strong coffee. It didn't even appear to bother him to swallow the scalding brew. For a moment his eyes closed, as though he were very tired, and then he spoke.

"We must talk, Elizabeth."

He said it simply, plainly, yet she felt like he had just issued a command—one she did not wish to obey. She could barely stay awake. "Now?" she asked weakly, purposefully touching the side of her face to remind him of her pain.

He took a deep breath and stared at her, as if studying her features. "Tomorrow, then. There are some things that we must discuss. We are both . . . how shall I say this?" He cleared his throat and looked out to the campfire. "I believe we are both a bit disappointed."

64

"I'm not especially disappointed. I mean, for a cowboy, you're . . . you know," she said in a sleepy voice. "Sexy. Great buns," she added while trying to stifle a yawn. God, it hurt to move her jaw! Imagine, telling a man she admired his rear end. Closing her eyes, she grinned. Good thing he was only a figment of her imagination. She would die of embarrassment if any of this were real.

Jordan nearly choked on his coffee. It took him a few moments to regain his composure. "Perhaps baffled is a better word. It's been a confusing day, to say the least, and I've been short-tempered and most disagreeable. I apologize for my behavior. Had I known that you'd had a tooth extracted on this trip then I would never have made you travel further. However, I believe we both need to discuss our plans before we reach Caldwell tomorrow."

He straightened his shoulders and continued. "I would like you to know that should you . . . should *we* decide that a mistake has been made then there will be time to take the proper action before we go into Indian territory—Elizabeth?" He turned his head and looked at the woman next to him.

She was asleep.

Frustrated by the strain of giving a speech that hadn't been heard, Jordan let out his breath and gingerly removed the nearly empty bottle from her fingers. She released it and further startled him by moaning in sleepy contentment. He studied her face in repose, the high cheekbones, the fringe of dark lashes that matched her hair. He found himself mesmerized when the tip of her tongue grazed over her dry lips, only to disappear the next moment. She twitched in her sleep, as if startled, then settled back to a fitful slumber. From the corner of his eye, he watched as her head slowly slumped down to her shoulder. Then, as if they had been married for years, she turned in to him and placed her head on *his* shoulder, all the while making tiny noises in the back of her throat, disturbing noises that could be taken for either pleasure or pain.

Of course it must be pain.

He didn't move. He sat completely still and listened as his breathing matched hers. He could feel his heart pounding beneath his shirt and he glanced up at the men who gathered about the fire. Each in turn cast him sidelong looks of curiosity and embarrassment as this woman, Elizabeth, by law his wife, wound her arms around his and pressed closer.

Ignoring the stares of the men, Jordan used his free arm to pour a measure of whiskey into his coffee cup. He had to concentrate to keep his hand from shaking. His elbow, the back of his arm, was trapped between her breasts! When he swallowed the mixture, he detected her heartbeat against his muscle. Sure and steady. Nothing at all like his.

He was sitting here beside this woman, a prisoner to her whiskey-induced embrace. Nothing made sense. She was drunk and she was legally his wife. But there was something about her . . . something that made him feel differently toward her. Perhaps it was admiration for the way she had stood up to him today. He could even understand her inebriated state. What he couldn't understand was how this person next to him was the same sweet compliant woman who had written to him over the last half year. Too many things simply didn't make sense. It was certainly a puzzle, one that he hoped to solve in the morning. And morning couldn't come soon enough.

She moved in her sleep and he found himself growing exceedingly uncomfortable as he brought the mug back up to his mouth. He gulped the whiskey-laced coffee and looked out beyond the campfire. How could this have happened? His only answer was the noise of the cattle, the whispers of the men and the crackling of the fire.

And what the hell did she mean by saying he had great buns? Surely she couldn't have meant . . . ?

Jordan Dillon McCabe knew with a certainty it was going to be one hell of a long night.

Chapter 5

"Coffee, Miz Elizabeth?"

One eyelid barely opened, a minute muscular response to the young voice. Immediately the pain registered, a sharp blinding light that penetrated her pupil and traveled with frightening speed to her brain. Groaning, Elle shut her eye against the rude glimpse of daylight and turned her head into the protection of her arm.

And then she smelled it.

The mildew of the blanket. The distinct odor of horses mingled with strong coffee. And worst of all . . . she smelled herself. Blood. Stale whiskey. And sweat. What the hell had happened to her?

Gathering all her strength, Elle raised her head and forced her eyes open. Squinting, she refused to believe what she was seeing. It couldn't be! She blinked rapidly, as if to clear her eyes, to wipe away the unbelievable scene. It simply could not be!

It was supposed to have been a dream!

"Cap'n said you was to get up now and eat. We'll be on our way in less'n fifteen minutes."

She stared at the young cowboy. Kyle. His name was Kyle. She remembered that. "What . . . what year is this?" she whispered, terrified of his answer before he spoke.

He appeared confused and more than a little embarrassed by her strange question. "1876, ma'am."

Her mouth hung open in shock. She could hear her own heartbeat in her ears, loud and swift, like a primitive drumbeat that kept increasing in volume. The louder it became the more she was filled with panic, until in a desperate effort to escape everything, she forced her aching body to move. She hit her head on a wagon wheel, yet ignored that added pain as she scrambled to her feet. It was essential that she get up, get away . . . *move!* And move she did, disregarding the shouting of her name as she stumbled and started running—away from the voices, the living reminders of a nightmare that refused to end.

She kept going, running as fast as she could through a field with nowhere to hide. She kept pushing herself into a sea of endless tall grass, forcing her legs to continue though her muscles were screaming at her to stop. She was gasping for breath, gulping in huge amounts of air to propel her forward, when a powerful force wrapped itself around her shoulders and drew her back.

"Elizabeth! Stop it!"

She could hear his breath by her ear as he pulled her against him. Desperate, she spun around and slapped at his chest.

"Get away from me! You don't exist! Go away . . ." She could feel the tears welling up in her eyes as she shoved him.

He grasped her arm and held her still. "Why are you

70

doing this?"

She looked up at him then. The Captain. He was breathing as heavily as she was and his expression was quickly changing from annoyance to concern. "What's wrong?" he demanded.

He was real! My God, he was real!

Accompanying that horrible thought was a wave of nausea so strong that she felt attacked by the contraction of her stomach muscles. Her eyes widened in dread and her hand shot up to cover her mouth as she reeled away from him and sank to the ground.

Digging her nails into the soft earth, Elle vaguely noticed grasshoppers flying through the air as she emptied her abused stomach into the tall grass. Her arms were shaking from supporting her as she hung her head in mortification. She was grateful that her hair fell around her like a tent, shielding her, yet through the strands she was able to see his hand. In it was an olive green scarf, the one he had worn around his neck. Reaching up to take it, she quickly realized this was the most humiliating experience of her life.

And the most frightening.

Because he was real. They were all real. . . .

"Can I help you?"

Wiping her mouth, she shook her head. She was afraid to speak, to move, yet she knew that she must. She tried to rise, and felt his hand on her arm as he assisted her. A hand—his. It felt just like any other man's, except his was covered in a worn leather glove. Like a cowboy. And in her entire life she had never known anyone like that. Dear God, was she losing her mind? The cowboy stood before her, quiet, patiently waiting for her to make the next move. What did he want from her? She couldn't

71

look at him, for to do so meant that she must confront what was taking place.

And she didn't know what was happening. Or how it had happened.

"You should have expected to be sick after last night," he finally said in a surprisingly gentle voice. Even though she wasn't looking at him, she could detect a note of humor in his tone.

Elle merely nodded. She had nothing to say. And what does one say to a ghost? For that's what he had to be. She remembered him talking about being a Confederate soldier. That had to be what . . . ? Eighteen sixty-something? How could it all seem so real? Trying to reason out the impossible made her head ache and the dull pain in her upper jaw returned, reminding her that at sometime yesterday she had left everything familiar and normal and had come to this. But what was this? The boy had to be wrong, or she had heard wrong. Forcing moisture back into her mouth, she pleaded, "Please . . . tell me. What year is it? Today. Right now . . . the year?"

For just a moment, his eyes narrowed as he stared at her. Then, he smiled sympathetically, as if her question sprang from nothing more than a hangover. "The year is 1876."

Elle could only stare at this apparition from the past. You're only dreaming, she told herself. This is only a dream, or a hallucination, or . . . or something. Dear God, it isn't real!

"We'd better get back now," he said.

She didn't move.

"Would you," he hesitated, as if searching for the proper words, "would you like some privacy first? I've set up an area . . . that is, we've hung a blanket on the line with the horses and you could change and . . ." His voice trailed off but his meaning was clear.

Fighting another bout of nausea, a drilling headache, and a jaw that felt like Mike Tyson had assaulted it, Elle simply nodded and followed him back to the camp. Stop fighting it, she told herself. It doesn't work. It doesn't make the nightmare go away. Just go along with it. Take it to its completion, and then it will cease, she reasoned. For this could not be happening. It simply could not be. Intelligence and logic told her so, and hadn't she always depended on those two factors to get her out of jams in the past? But intelligence and logic seemed pathetically inadequate in a world gone crazy.

If she thought her humiliation was complete in the field, then using a latrine, a mere hole in the ground, demonstrated that further degradations awaited her at every turn. Surrounded by curious horses, Elizabeth Mackenzie found out what *real* camping was like. She felt completely justified in having always hated the very idea of roughing it.

"Mind your own business," she nearly snarled to an inquisitive brown beast. Buttoning up her slacks, she kicked the dirt back into the hole and shuddered. It was not 1876! It wasn't! Somewhere right now, her hotel was waiting for her—a lovely room overlooking Wichita, with a beautiful bathroom . . . a real bathroom with hot water and soap and a toothbrush awaited her. And a toilet.

She looked back down.

A hole in the ground!

What she had to do was think about this, really think, and find a way back.

Back to her own time.

"Miz Elizabeth? Cap'n, he said you might want your trunk now and I was to show you where it was."

Turning away from the makeshift latrine, Elle pushed her hair back from her face and tried to smile. She might be totally humiliated, but there wasn't anyone here that had to know it. If she could handle men from the twentieth century, then these cowboys should be easy.

"Thank you, Kyle," she said. Even though she knew she looked terrible, that her navy gabardine suit was soiled, her hair hanging in knots and her face more dirty now than when she was a child, Elle raised her chin, as if she were walking into the Mictronix board room. Lifting the corner of the blanket, she stepped beyond it and faced the men.

They all stopped whatever they were doing and looked.

First she swallowed down her fear, and then smiled to Kyle. "I believe I would like to change." As regal as any queen, Elle held her chin high. She still wore the military pin with its bronzed elephant on the left side of her jacket. Her back was so straight, her attitude so commanding, that it might well have been a royal crest bestowed on her by the imperial crown.

The young cowboy nodded and led the way to the front of Cooky's wagon. He helped her up and then opened the canvas flap to reveal a large wooden trunk.

"Cap'n figured you must've lost the key, so's he opened it for you. I guess I'll leave you." He turned to go, and then stopped. "Cooky'll give you ten minutes or so and then we got to get goin', okay?"

She tried to smile. "Okay."

When she was alone, Elle closed the canvas and turned to the trunk. There was barely any room to move around in the wagon. Boxes were stacked everywhere. Carefully sidestepping a rather large one, she sat on another and reached out for the trunk. The lid opened quite easily. Even though Elle felt sick she was still able to marvel at the beautifully decorated interior. Padded green and rose chintz was edged in delicate lace. There were drawers with tiny glass knobs and neatly folded garments. It seemed a shame to touch anything, but she was desperate.

Reaching out a soiled hand, Elle pulled up a deep green two-piece dress with a tiny white collar. It was heavy and she would probably die in the heat this afternoon. She reasoned that she could always take off the top later in the day, but it was clean. And right now that was all that mattered. Within minutes she had placed her slacks to one side of the wagon. She rummaged through the trunk and found underwear, at least she thought it was underwear. Made of fine cotton lawn, the material felt soft next to her skin. She mentally apologized to the missing Cynthia for using her things as she pulled the green skirt over her head.

Suddenly she was assaulted by a wave of dizziness. It could have been the fact that she was hung over, or that she hadn't had anything nourishing to eat or drink in twenty-four hours, or even that she had lost blood. But inside, down deep, where explanations weren't quite so easy, something told her it wasn't any of that. It was something strange and uncertain. It happened when she put on the dress. It was as if she were taking over this woman's life . . . her place in this time.

Shaking off the ridiculous thought, Elle quickly buttoned the dress and bent down to open a drawer in the trunk. Just as she thought, inside was a brush and hand mirror, decorated hair pins, ribbons and a fine brown

75

hair net.

How did she know which drawer would contain such things?

Afraid of the answer, she reached out and picked up the brush and ran it through her hair. She ignored the pain as the sharp bristles pulled through the tight knots from the day before. Elle gathered her hair back and tied it with a thick white ribbon. She carefully replaced the brush and only then did she give in to the unexplainable need that made her fingers close over the silver handle of the mirror.

Slowly, already dreading what she would find, Elle brought the glass up to her face.

Her breath caught at the back of her throat. Her heart actually skipped a beat. She was staring at a familiar face, but it wasn't hers! It was her mother's image, as she looked when Elle last saw her. Sad. Weary. Defeated by life. In the glass was the perfect reflection of her *mother!*

It lasted only a few seconds, perhaps merely one or two, but in that minute span of time she was completely immobilized by the pain in the woman's face—the acceptance of a life that held no promises—the biding of time until it was over. My God, it was vivid! She forced her eyes closed, as if the simple action might wipe the insane image from her mind. Her mother! Confused, and more than a little frightened, Elle told herself that the very idea was crazy, impossible, yet she was hesitant to look again.

Compelled, yet fighting it, she slowly opened her eyes.

She released her breath in a sigh of relief. Thank God. Surely she must have imagined it all. The face staring back at her, though definitely grimy and smudged with dirt, was her own. Her own! Even in the insanity of her situation she had a brief surge of joy to find herself gazing upon her own face. *This cannot be happening,* she told herself for the hundredth time. Things like this do not happen to ordinary people.

As if to remind her of her mortality, a throbbing ache resumed in her upper jaw. She brought her fingers up to her cheek and gingerly touched it. The nerve endings under her skin felt raw and she tried to open her mouth to see her gum. Using her fingernail, she pulled back her lip.

There were two tiny black stitches.

She wasn't going crazy. That dentist *had* removed her back molar. She tried to think, to remember. He'd given her gas—nitrous-something or other. She'd felt like she was flying. Everything was great until . . . until . . .

Damn it, why couldn't she remember?

Something had caused this to happen.

"Miz Elizabeth? You ready?"

Startled, she dropped the mirror. "In a minute," she called out, though her stomach was already rebelling at the thought of moving. Slowly, Elle reached down and picked up the mirror. Turning it over to inspect the glass, she couldn't suppress a groan of frustration. Dear God, what else could happen?

"Seven years bad luck," she whispered in a defeated voice, while running a fingertip over a hairline crack in the upper corner. She was certain it hadn't been there before. "Seven years! I won't last," she murmured while replacing the mirror in the drawer and closing the trunk. "I can't believe I got through a day of this. It's like losing your mind, and knowing it . . ."

"You saying somethin', Miz Elizabeth?" Kyle asked from outside.

She closed her eyes and willed her stomach to remain

77

calm. "I'm coming," she said, though her body was telling her to find a bed and pull the covers up over her head. Forcing the inviting thought from her mind, Elle stood up and made her way out the front of the wagon.

She had done no more than open the canvas flap when she saw *him* behind Kyle. Damn it, if he wasn't just as good-looking as she had remembered. But she had thought that was only a dream. Even in the field she hadn't really looked at him, too humiliated by what had happened. Now, in the morning sunlight, he was most definitely alive . . . and male. He honest-to-God looked like Mel Gibson with now a two-day-old growth of beard. Only more cynical. And he was holding out a cup of coffee to her.

"I hope you like it black." He directed his words to her while looking at the young man. As if they had silently communicated in some strange cowboy language, she watched as Kyle left without saying another word.

Reaching out, she took the cup. "Black is fine," Elle murmured, sitting on the bench that served as a front seat to the wagon. She wrapped her hands around the tin cup for warmth. Even though she knew the day would grow hot, at the moment she was chilled.

In the back of her brain she knew it was because of what had happened in front of the trunk. About her mother. Maybe this had something to do with her mother. What if she wasn't all right? What if that bastard had hit her again? But she couldn't think about her parents, and why her mother refused to leave. Not now. Now she had to deal with this man who was staring at her as if she were from another planet. If it wouldn't have hurt her face, she might have laughed at the thought. Anything was possible, and nothing was as it should have been. Absolutely nothing.

She brought the cup to her mouth and sipped. The coffee hit her empty stomach like a twenty-pound sledgehammer and she moaned aloud.

"The men call it six-shooter coffee because you could float a pistol in it."

She tried to smile but was unsuccessful. "I believe it," she admitted. Nevertheless, she continued to take small sips of the powerful brew.

From the corner of her eye, she noticed that he appeared uncomfortable, as if he were waiting for something, or some opportunity. She couldn't tell from his face for half of it was obscured by the large hat that he wore. It had more to do with body language. He had changed his shirt, but he looked like he had slept in the rest of his clothes. And he stood very straight, almost formally, just like someone preparing to make an announcement.

Listening to him clear his throat, Elle realized that she was about to hear the reason for his behavior.

"I had planned to talk to you this morning, Elizabeth," he started off in a perfectly polite voice. "Since you're not feeling well, I believe I can postpone it until lunch. But then we must talk. Do you understand?"

She understood nothing, yet managed to nod her head—anything to make him go away, for when he lifted his chin she could see intense blue eyes, eyes that seemed to look beyond her features and recognize the impostor. Again she felt the need to tell him the truth—that she wasn't his precious Cynthia, yet something held her back. She needed to be stronger. Yes, that was it. She'd do it after lunch, when she was feeling better. And then they would be close to a town. He had said something

79

about a town. Caldwell. She remembered that. She would wait until they were near this place.

It made sense, for she had a feeling that she was going to need the protection of others when this man found out how she had deceived him.

As if enough hadn't happened to fill her with dread, now she would have this high noon verbal shoot-out with a cowboy. Seeing the sullen Cooky approach the wagon, she realized this day held very little promise.

She wouldn't look again. She told herself that if she did she had no one to blame but herself. They hadn't been on the trail for very long when she noticed that the countryside was littered with the remains of animals— skulls of cattle with horns over four feet in width, the bloated bodies of others, or half-eaten carcasses that fed dozens of birds. Each time her morbid curiosity made her glance toward the grotesque forms, her stomach would lurch up into her throat and she would clasp her hand over her mouth. But there was nothing else to do, save sit and look. It wasn't as if her traveling companion cared to chat. Cooky tended to grunt in reply to her attempts at conversation. And what she wouldn't give for a pair of sunglasses! She seemed tortured by the glare of the sun. It produced a monster headache that wouldn't quit. Okay, okay, she *was* hung over, but she was sick. She shouldn't be expected to make this pioneer trek into the wilderness. Mile after mile, they rode across the barren, empty land. There was little noise as the ground seemed to swallow up the trampling of the hooves behind her.

She and Cooky rode ahead of the others. Once, when

she had looked back, she saw that McCabe was far behind them, leading a huge lumbering black bull. In back of him was the herd of cattle she remembered Traver and Kyle telling her about—McCabe's precious Herefords, a sea of red bodies with broad white faces. Now that she thought about it, they were the reason he hadn't been in Wichita to meet his mail order bride. She started to grin. That's how she'd do it. She'd turn the tables on him and say if he'd cared enough he would have been there and this mistake would have never happened. When one thought about it, it was clearly his fault. She was high on drugs, or gas, or something, and couldn't be held responsible for her actions. He, on the other hand, appeared to care more about a herd of dumb animals than his new wife. Poor Cynthia, wherever she was, was better off. But then the guilt came rushing back. What happened to the woman? When she thought about all the lives that had been damaged by the situation, Elle's headache only increased.

She'd fix it. Somehow she'd find a way to turn everything around. Trying to ignore the intense pain in her head, the dull ache of her jaw, and the dry twisting of her stomach muscles, Elle turned to her traveling companion and widely grinned.

Filled with false goodwill, she said, "Do you mind if I just call you Arlyn? That is your name, isn't it?"

The old man grunted.

Again she smiled. She would not be defeated. "Well, *Arlyn*, where are you from?"

She ignored the long stream of spit that the man shot out to the ground.

"Around."

She nodded. It was a beginning. It was a word. "Around where? Here?"

"Texas."

Now she was getting somewhere. "Texas. I've never been there. Is it exciting?" Talk to me, she silently pleaded, for if left in silence she would think, and it was all too much to think about right now.

"Texas is Texas." A man of few words, Arlyn scratched the side of his face against his shoulder.

"How did you come to be a cook?" Please talk. "Do you like it?" She couldn't think of anything else to say to him. Most men loved to talk about their jobs, at least in her time—

"Cook's the most important member of the trail outfit. Just ask the Cap'n. He'll tell ya. Being cook means taking charge of the chuckwagon. All the food, stuff to cook it in and the extra supplies for the drive. Can't some ordinary man handle all that."

It was a veritable speech. She was impressed and hurried to answer for fear that he'd crawl back into his shell of silence. "I can imagine. I'm sorry I couldn't eat last night. My mouth was too sore to chew, but I did hear everyone saying how good it was."

Every cook loves a compliment and Arlyn was no exception. He grunted.

"Ahh . . ." Her mind searched for another topic of conversation. He wouldn't know business, nor care about her sales record, and she knew diddley about cattle drives. "How far away from Caldwell are we?" Somehow that town sounded like her only refuge right now.

Arlyn looked up to the sky and muttered, "'Bout half a day, maybe less." After once more spitting, he wiped his mouth on his sleeve and returned his attention to the well-traveled ruts in front of the horses. It was clear their conversation was over.

She didn't mind that he had the manners of a farm animal, that he looked like he hadn't come in contact with bath water in weeks. She even made a heroic attempt to ignore the fact that he smelled. Since she hadn't bathed since yesterday morning, she didn't feel particularly superior on that score. What galled her was being shut out, like she wasn't worth the effort it took to speak. She knew why she wasn't accepted—she had shamed their leader—McCabe. She was not the wife any of them had expected. She could just imagine their collective relief when they found out the truth.

Two hours later she couldn't have cared what any of them thought. She was in agony.

This time she was sure she was dying. No matter how hard she pressed her fist against the center of her forehead she couldn't stop the blinding pain. Her head felt too big for her neck to support and she was having trouble sitting upright. She felt the sun beating down on her like a hot wave and she wanted to strip off the heavy top to cool off. Every time the wagon hit a bump Elle thought she would scream, but even that would take too much effort. She told herself that she could make it until they stopped for lunch, that she wouldn't be any more trouble, but it was becoming more and more difficult to remain upright and silent.

And then they passed another carcass, this one dark and dry and leathery with a whitened rib cage bleached by the sun. The monstrous half-face of the animal seemed to look back at her with a cadaverous grin, as if it were laughing at her plight . . . and that's when Elizabeth Mackenzie's willpower broke. She simply could not go on.

83

"Please, Arlyn . . . stop the wagon. I'm going to be sick."

He merely grunted in response.

"I'm going to be sick," she repeated, hearing the rising hysteria in her voice. "Let me out."

The old man looked up to the sun. "We'll be stoppin' for lunch in about—"

"I don't care," she interrupted. "I have to get out. Stop the wagon! Now!"

He muttered something under his breath about being Prairie Loco and yanked back on the brake. She didn't even wait until the wagon had come to a complete halt. Stumbling down, she ran out into the field and collapsed into the tall, dry grass.

There was nothing left in her stomach. It felt so good to lie down, to close her eyes against the glaring heat of the sun. Her face was so hot that she must be sunburned. She simply could not get back on that wagon. This is where she had to stay. It was hushed and calm and still. If she remained here in the grass then she would at least die in peace.

"What are you doing?"

It was *his* voice. And it sounded annoyed. She didn't open her eyes. "I'm dying. Leave me alone." Her lips felt thick and heavy, and dry.

"Elizabeth, get up. Everyone's watching."

"Go away." She could sleep if he'd just leave her alone. But it hurt to think, to open her eyes, to move, even to talk. Surely she was dying. She would be like those grisly animals that had expired along the trail. Someday someone would gag over her remains.

"You are merely feeling the effects of last night's

whiskey, now let me help you up. Any minute now the herd is going to be coming. You could be trampled."

"Do not touch me." It hurt to speak. The herd. So that was the rumbling in the ground. She didn't care. At least she would be out of her misery. "I am not getting back in that wagon. Take your cows and go to . . . go to Texas. Just let me be. I can't go on." She felt an insect land on her cheek, but didn't care. "Please . . ." she barely whispered, "go away."

She groaned when he touched her, yet felt too weak to offer resistance.

"My God, Elizabeth, you're burning up!"

She tried to open her eyes to look at him. He was above her; his face was filled with concern. "Yeah? I am?" Finally it all made sense, why every bone in her body ached. She tried to help when he gathered her into his arms, but she could only grab hold of his shirt.

In her entire life no male had ever carried her. Not her father. Not a lover. No one. And now this stranger did so with ease. She was about to say something nice to him, to apologize for everything, when the most incredible and welcoming thing happened.

Darkness clouded her vision, like the closing of a tunnel, and she began to pass out. She could feel the black edge of it wrapping around her like a warm, comforting blanket. And for the first time since her arrival to this time, Elle stopped fighting and experienced peace.

"Cooky! Pull out that mattress. Make room for her in the wagon." He carried her back, feeling the heat of her body through the heavy fabric of her clothes. How could he have not seen that she was truly sick this morning?

Blaming himself, Jordan vowed not to neglect her again. With Elizabeth safely ensconced in the back of the chuckwagon, he rode up to Traver and told him the situation.

"I'm going to take her to that farm we passed on the way north. It's closer than Caldwell." He looked at the Herefords, the animals that he was building a dream on, and added, "I'll have to stay with her. You take the herd on. I'll catch up."

Traver scratched his chin. "Whatever you say, Cap'n. 'Cept that nester ain't gonna like you comin' on his land and askin' for favors. If I remember rightly, he had himself a Winchester and watched to make sure we didn't mess up none of his wheat crop on our way north. You're not steppin' into exactly friendly territory there."

Jordan breathed hard, impatient to be on his way. "You may be right," he admitted and reluctantly added, "Cut me out a weak one, Traver, one that would have trouble making it to Texas." He shook his head. "I didn't think I'd lose one this soon."

Traver touched the tip of his hat in respect. "Yes, sir. We'll wait up for you outside Caldwell then?"

Jordan glanced back to the chuckwagon. "No. You're trail boss now. We've lost too much time. Now that they're moving, I don't want them stopped for a day or two. You keep going and we'll find you. I'll send Cooky back as soon as we get to the farm."

"Good luck to you, sir. I'll watch over them as if they were my own."

"They *are* yours, Traver. You and every man on this drive has a percentage of the Triple Cross. You'll do fine." Jordan reached out and touched his friend's shoulder. Ten years earlier Traver Diggs had been his First Sergeant in a war that had destroyed the world as they had known it. Now, together, they were trying to build a new one. Before either man could comment, Jordan jerked the reins to the left and rode back to where Cooky waited for him.

"How's she doing?"

The old man glanced over his shoulder. "She was real quiet, but now she's mumblin' somethin'. Can't rightly make it out."

Delirium. The fever was rising. "Let's go," he ordered and rode next to the wagon as they left behind his dream, his future.

It took every ounce of willpower that he possessed not to look back.

Within an hour they came upon the small sod house, planted in the center of a wheat field. It looked dark, cold and uninviting, and as they came closer Jordan could see the farmer standing in front of the miserable place with his Winchester across his chest. He was clad in an old shirt that was streaked with sweat and dirt. His baggy pants were held up with huge suspenders. His hair was short, almost shorn, making his ears stick out. He was thin, near gaunt-looking, with cheekbones that stood out in relief. Deep circles framed his eyes. His beard was trimmed, yet hid the line of his mouth. Nowhere in the man's expression was there a hint of welcome.

"I have a sick woman. I need a place for her to recover."

"This ain't no goddamned hotelery," the man spat out.

"I got two young 'uns and my own woman. Ain't no room for yours."

"I'll pay."

The man's eyes narrowed. "How much?"

"How much you want?"

"Five dollars."

"Fine." He wasn't about to haggle. Elizabeth needed nursing.

"Where'd you get that cow?"

Now it was coming. "Wichita." Jordan could see the man's wife peeking out from behind the door. She was as pathetic and worn down as the man. "It's called a Hereford. I brought it to trade."

The gun lowered a fraction. "Trade what?"

"The woman needs nursing. She has a fever. Nothing contagious. I believe it's caused by the removal of a tooth. I can't nurse her on the trail. She needs a place to rest and someone to look after her."

"She your wife?"

He didn't hesitate. "Yes."

The farmer considered it for a moment then said, "Bring her then. Ain't had no beef in months. The young 'uns can sleep on the ground."

When Jordan turned to Cooky, the man added, "Five dollars a day it is, and you help me butcher the cow."

Looking up at his old friend, Jordan shouted out his agreement to the farmer, then said in a lower voice, "After we get Elizabeth in, Cooky, I want you to get back to the herd. When you reach Caldwell, buy a buckboard and send Kyle back with it. I want to get out of here as soon as possible."

"Yes, Cap'n," Cooky answered in a whisper. "He looks

crazy, don't he? Like he spent too long out here, or somethin'."

Jordan didn't glance back at the man who was shouting for his wife. "I don't have any choice. She's burning up." He cradled Elizabeth's shoulders against his chest. "Just don't waste any time in getting Kyle moving."

Between him and Cooky they managed to get Elizabeth out of the wagon. As he was carrying her up to the sod house, he heard the farmer's cold voice as the man addressed his wife.

"You tend that cattleman's woman, you hear me? And keep those bastards away from her. He says it ain't contagious but I ain't takin' any chances."

It was worse inside than he had expected. The children were lined up like frightened animals against a wall papered in old yellowed newspapers. It was dark and the ceiling still dripped in places from the rain two days ago. A bed of sorts was off to one dry corner and he called out to Cooky who waited at the door. "Bring me the mattress from the wagon and some clean linen from her trunk." Having no idea what she would need when she recovered, he added, "You'd better bring in the trunk and leave it."

Within minutes he was able to lay Elizabeth down and stand back. The woman and children gathered around the bed and stared.

"Is she a princess, Momma?" the small boy whispered. "Like in the stories you—"

He was hushed by an older sister. The mother, a small, weary-looking woman with severely pulled-back hair, nervously wrung her hands together. "This . . . this here's your wife, mister?" Her voice was hesitant, as if she didn't often speak with men.

89

Jordan turned to the ragged group and nodded. "Yes, she is. Can you help her?"

Before anyone could answer, he heard the short bellow of the cow as its throat was slit. He caught Cooky's angered expression and shook his head.

The farmer wasn't wasting any time and neither would he.

"Go on, Arlyn," he ordered in a clipped voice.

There was no need for further communication.

Chapter 6

She heard a rhythmic *ping*, like a badly wound alarm clock. It was steady and annoying, and it wasn't going away. She didn't want to pay attention to it, for to do so meant that she must also become aware of other things . . . like how her eyes felt heavy and scratchy, as if someone had thrown sand into them. Even without trying, she knew they would hurt too much to open. So she didn't. Yet her nose was sending messages to her sleepy brain, a signal for food, and her stomach contracted with hunger. Something primitive and wild stirred within her at the tantalizing aroma. Her once dry throat became moist as she actually salivated. Hungry, she knew she would have to open her eyes to discover the source of the teasing scents. Slowly, as if she hadn't done so in many days, Elle forced her lids apart.

And the nightmare continued.

No more than two feet away was a creature from hell. Huge and brown, it was covered in long hair. Its mouth was hidden behind immense whiskers, though its pointed nose seemed to hold her in disdain. But the most frightening was its two beady eyes, moist black caverns that appeared to swallow her up. A scream built up in the back of her throat, yet she was helpless to bring it forth. The muscles of her neck felt paralyzed and she was only able to issue a muffled squeal.

It was enough to send the thing scurrying.

"Noah! Get away from the lady."

Elle's eyes were most certainly opened now. A child, no more than five or six, stood at her side and grinned.

"Momma named him Noah 'cause every time it rains he comes in. He won't hurt you none though," the blond-haired boy whispered in amusement. He smiled at her shyly. "He's just a mouse—"

"Cory Woodson! You leave that lady be." A female voice lightly scolded the child and Elle looked up into the eyes of a pretty teenager. She and the boy must be related for they both had the same color hair, the same heavy sprinkling of freckles over their noses, and the same intensely curious expressions.

The girl smiled, showing dimples, and lifted her voice to call out, "Momma? She's awake."

Elle looked around her, certain she had gone from one nightmare into another. It appeared that she was in a room made out of dirt, with . . . with newspapers lining one wall, as if it were the most natural wallcovering, and old crates nailed up for shelves. There was canvas hanging over the area where she was lying and if she turned her head to look into the dimly lit room she could see black pots on the dirt floor to catch the occasional drip from the ceiling, the annoying sound that had intruded into her sleep. But into what had she awakened? What new kind of nightmare was this?

A small woman pushed past the children, quietly

92

telling them to go outside. When she stood next to the bed, she looked at Elle and said, "How are you feeling, Mrs. McCabe?"

Elle could only stare at her. *Mrs. McCabe?* Who was this person? Obviously, she was the children's mother. Her hair was brown though still holding a hint of the blond that must have been there years before. Parted in the middle it was pulled severely back into a tight knot. Her slight frame was covered in a long black dress. Brown stains smeared the front of an apron that she smoothed down with red, bony hands. But it was her face, a painfully thin mask of hardship, that tugged at Elle's heart.

It reminded her of her mother.

"Your fever's down?" the woman asked shyly while coming closer.

"Fever?" Elle's throat felt raw. "Who . . . who are you?"

The woman smiled and her face was transformed. There was a trace of the lovely girl she must have been. "Phoebe Woodson. Your husband brought you here."

"My husband?" Elle's brain refused to register that piece of information.

"He's out with Mr. Woodson, my . . . my husband." Phoebe appeared uncomfortable with the subject and quickly changed it. "I've made some soup with the beef you brought and my own put-up onions and potatoes and such. Maybe tomorrow we can have a real Sunday dinner?"

Elle nodded, thoroughly confused. Just as she was about to ask where this husband was, she heard a harsh voice coming from outside.

"Get your reedy ass over here, girl, and take this. Tell

your mother she can cook it up for me."

Elle looked up to the woman in front of her for an explanation, but Phoebe's worried expression only increased when they heard the child's hesitant answer.

"Please, Poppa, let me get a towel first."

"Now! I'm not gonna hold it forever."

Phoebe turned and grabbed a long dish towel off the back of one of the three chairs in the home and ran outside. Feeling the urgency in Phoebe's actions Elle held her breath as she waited for the next words. They shocked her, for they were familiar.

"Let her be, Woodson. Hand it here, if you must."

Jordan Dillon McCabe. She knew the sound of him and a mental picture filled her mind. Memories flooded back to her—of trail drives and tall, lean cowboys . . . and one in particular.

"Here, Joseph," Phoebe said in a conciliatory voice. "Why not let me take it?"

"Because I asked her. Ain't never gonna make some man a wife if she's treated like a child. Now get over here, girl, before I take a strap to you. Don't you shame me in front of strangers."

Something tightened inside Elle at the man's words. He was angry and domineering, depending on sheer strength and power to subdue. It was all too familiar and she hated him without even laying eyes on the man.

He sounded just like her father.

She pulled herself out of bed, holding on to the mattress for support. A wave of dizziness washed over her, but she fought it. Something deep inside was pushing her forward to the canvas-covered window. Her fingernails dug into the blackened earth wall as she steadied herself before pulling back the small curtain to look outside.

Nothing could have prepared her.

A man was holding out a bloodied object to the young girl, demanding that she take it. His arms were covered in slick red blood and bile rose in her throat when Elle was able to distinguish the thing that he shoved at the crying teenager. It looked like a . . . a tongue. Her brain scarcely registered the butchered carcass of the cow as her heart reached out to the frightened girl. Only minutes ago she had stood at the foot of the bed, smiling, silently asking for friendship. Now she was crying, cowering in front of the man. And Elle knew, just like with her father, that this bastard needed to feel superior and could only do it by bullying those who weren't able to defend themselves.

"Stop it!" The words burst from her throat in a strong, impassioned command. Everyone turned, as if frozen, and stared at her. And that's when she saw him.

"Elizabeth!"

For just a moment, before he had called out to her, she had seen contempt for the man in his expression. It pained him to be part of that scene. He, too, was wearing a long apron, the front covered in blood. They were butchering one of his precious cows. She knew, as if they had already communicated, that he was only there by circumstances beyond his control. Somehow she knew it had something to do with her and she was saddened to have put him in that position. Now, staring back at her, he only looked concerned.

"You tell your woman to mind her own business, McCabe. I don't have to take that kind of interference from a guest in my house."

Suddenly spurred into action, Jordan picked up a nearby bowl and held it out. "Put it in here and be done

95

with it, man. The child's too upset now. She'd probably drop it."

He could see that his words had their effect as the farmer weighed them and saw the possibility of his losing out on the delicacy. With a shrug, Woodson dropped the tongue into the wide bowl and went back to work on the carcass. Jordan handed the bowl to the small, trembling woman and then said to her husband, "Were my wife truly a guest in your house, sir, I would question your hospitality for creating such a scene. As we are paying, overpaying, for our lodging, I must applaud her interference."

Jordan turned back to the small opening in the sod and smiled. He was actually proud of her. Elizabeth, obviously still weak, shyly returned his greeting. Without another word, he left the angry farmer to his grisly task and walked to the windmill. Once there, he untied the heavy apron and wiped away the blood on his hands. He felt like grieving for the animal, but realized the stupidity of that emotion. It was only an animal. Better to think that it would nourish the overly thin woman and her children. Better not to think of the farmer at all, Jordan reasoned as he pumped water up from the ground. Holding his hands under the cool spray, he washed the blood from his palms and pushed Joseph Woodson from his mind. There was something far more important to concentrate on—Elizabeth.

As he scrubbed at his hands, Jordan silently admitted that he had been frightened at the possibility that she might not recover. Surely, it was only concern. He wasn't attached in any way. But there was something in the back of his brain that denied the possibility, and he refused to acknowledge it. Tomorrow, if she was up to it,

96

they would leave this place and decide their future. When she was well, they would have their talk.

He would either leave Caldwell with a wife, or return to the herd and the Triple Cross alone. Drying his hands on the front of his shirt, Jordan stared down at the dripping water. In truth, he wasn't sure how he wanted it to turn out.

"It's only tea, made from the bark of the willow. I used it to bring down your fever. Go ahead, it's good for you." Phoebe held out the cup to her.

Back in bed, Elle swallowed down her distaste. She didn't want to be rude, yet it hardly sounded appetizing. "Gee, I don't know, Phoebe. I don't have a fever any longer and to be honest it doesn't sound like something I'd exactly enjoy."

"Oh, go on with you," Cory teased and a dimple appeared on his freckled cheek. "It's not so bad. I had some when I was sick."

Thoroughly enchanted with the child, Elle grinned back at him. Despite his dismal surroundings he was full of life, of mischief. "Would you like some now? There's more than enough for the two of us."

He giggled with pleasure. "Oh, no you don't, Miz Elizabeth. That's for you. It'll make you better. Momma says so."

Elle grimaced, knowing the child was enjoying her reluctance. "You're sure it's good, Cory? You wouldn't tease me, just to make me swallow it, would you?"

He firmly shook his head, yet she could see him biting the side of his cheek to keep from laughing. He was absolutely adorable, a miniature Huck Finn. Because of

97

his short hair even his ears stuck out to complete the picture. He was all boy—and a vivid reminder that she would never have a son or a daughter to call her own. Shaking off the depressing thought, Elle smiled back at him. "I suppose I don't have any other choice, do I?"

Cory again shook his head. "Nope."

Elle sipped the tea, then grimaced at the bitter taste. The youngster laughed at her expression and fell onto the bottom of the bed in a fit of giggles.

"Cory, get up," his mother ordered gently.

"He's fine," Elle answered, wanting the child's company.

Hearing the laughter, Cory's sister walked over to the bed. Elle had noticed that the girl was subdued ever since the incident with her father. Wanting to ease her embarrassment, Elle had tried to smile at her each time the child glanced across the room. She knew her name from overhearing Phoebe calming her daughter and was only waiting for the right opportunity to draw the girl out. Although Cory was a reminder of the role that was denied her in the future, it was his sister, Julie, that Elle's heart reached out to—a child of poverty and abuse. How well she knew that child of her past . . .

Searching for a topic to include the girl, Elle smiled at her. "How old are you?" she asked in a polite voice. She didn't want to push, for she recognized that Julie was beginning to build a wall around her for protection. Elle had done it herself at about the same age.

"Fourteen," Julie answered without making eye contact.

"You seem so grown up for fourteen."

"Julie's a big help," Phoebe added. "Lonely for a girl out here, though."

Elle looked up to the woman. "It must be lonely for all of you."

"Sometimes we have play parties and dances—though not much dancing gets done. Word goes out and people come from all around. Wagons and buggies as far as the eye can see." Phoebe gazed down to her apron and used her nail to scratch at a stain. "Probably doesn't seem like much to someone from the city, but after months out here with nothing but the wind for company, it seems downright festive."

Elle smiled. "I'm sure it is."

"Mr. Handsen brings his fiddle," Cory chimed in. "Bobby Ray plays his mouth harp. Near everybody can call figures, 'cept me 'cause I'm too little. I like the games, like London Bridge, Drop the Handkerchief. Julie likes Spin the Bottle—"

His sister slapped his shoulder in embarrassment.

"Anyway," Phoebe continued, "we make do." She looked worn and beaten by life, just like Elle's mother. "Now, I'd better get back to my stove." She appeared uncomfortable. "Mr. Woodson will expect a fine dinner tonight. What with the beef, and everything . . ."

Elle nodded, hating to see the subservient attitude in the other woman. *But this isn't your time,* she told herself. *For whatever reason, you're stuck here with these people. It's not going to go away. There's a reason, Elle. You must think . . .*

"Don't you ever have to pee?"

"*Cory!*" Julie yelled at her brother.

"Cory Woodson, watch your tongue!" Phoebe looked at Elle and silently pleaded with her for understanding. "We don't have company very often. I'm afraid I'll have to work on his manners."

Elle couldn't help grinning as she looked at the scolded youngster. "Well, as a matter of fact, Cory has a point there. What are the . . . ah, the arrangements?"

Phoebe apologized. "I'm sorry. We have an outhouse and of course there's the . . ." and she lowered her voice, "the pot."

It didn't take long for Elle to make up her mind. The last time she had been forced with this decision it had been a hole in the ground. An outhouse sounded downright private. She took hold of the edge of the sheet and stated, "I think I'd like a bit of fresh air."

"Julie will help you," Phoebe quickly added. "I hope you don't mind that we opened your trunk. For your nightclothes, and everything. Once you broke the fever, your husband insisted that we change you as often as necessary."

Her husband? Jordan was that concerned? Of course he must have been to leave his herd and bring her here. Filled with a sudden warmth for the cowboy, Elle smiled at the woman. "Thank you for taking care of me, and of course I don't mind. Not at all."

Very slowly, she swung her legs over the side of the bed and Cory hurried to offer her a pair of high-top shoes. She looked for her own leather loafers with the shiny cordovan tassels, but they were nowhere to be seen. She felt like the stepsister in Cinderella as she tried to force her feet into the small old-fashioned shoes. Everyone was looking at her and she glanced up and shrugged. "My feet must have swelled with the fever," she offered weakly.

The woman and children agreed.

"Did you see any others?" Elle asked in a hopeful voice.

"Just the slippers you had on when you came."

"They're fine." Elle breathed a sigh of relief when she saw Phoebe open the trunk and pull out her worn but comfortable Aigner loafers.

They looked almost new. Someone had polished them to a fine sheen. Her expression must have conveyed the question for Phoebe said with a note of pride, "Julie used a small bit of saddle soap and brought the shine back to them."

Elle turned to the young girl. "Thank you."

Julie shrugged, as if to say it wasn't anything. But Elle knew better.

"You didn't happen to find a robe in that trunk, did you?"

Julie nodded and hurried to find it. She carefully handed over a soft white cotton robe, embroidered with a fine lemon stitching. As Elle put it on she could see how the young girl's eyes nearly caressed the lovely garment. At that moment, Elle made up her mind to leave it for Julie tomorrow. She hoped that Cynthia would understand the distribution of her things, and she then shrugged. What did she care? If she ever saw the woman she'd explain.

It took a moment to steady herself and then Elle smiled at the teenager. As her arm went around the young girl's shoulders, Elle could feel how thin she was. Life was so unfair. This poor child didn't stand much of a chance to live a life any different than her mother's. As they left the dirt house, Elle lifted her chin and breathed in the evening air.

"Ahh . . . that smells wonderful."

"The house gets musty after it rains."

"I didn't mean to imply anything—"

"That's all right," Julie interrupted as they slowly walked to the distant building. "It must look pretty bad to someone like you."

Not knowing what else to say, Elle murmured, "I'm sure it will get better in time."

"I saw you looking at the newspapers. They're better than plain dirt walls and Cory's learning his letters by spelling out the advertisements."

Elle nodded as they passed a pen built of light poles and brush. The wind was blowing up, and the two scrawny chickens inside the enclosure were greeting it as a welcome change. "You and your mother work very hard. I guess everybody does out here." She honestly didn't know if she could survive this, knowing there wasn't any way out. There was nothing but the field of wheat. No trees. No other houses. Nothing but the wind.

"They call us Sodbusters because we wear heavy plow shoes and our clothes are faded by the sun and wind. The people in town make fun of us because we build our houses out of sod and don't live like them. They look at us like we were the dirt beneath their feet."

Elle felt her shrug. "We don't go into Caldwell much anymore. Been near a year now."

Looking around the small farm, Elle said, "You can't have lived here very long."

"Three years. Poppa bought some Turkey Red wheat from the Mennonites and staked out this claim. Been here ever since."

Three years. That was a long time in a young girl's life. Wanting to cheer her up, Elle said brightly, "When we get back to the house, do you think you could help me straighten out that trunk? It seems I've packed far too much."

Julie's eyes brightened at the suggestion. "Of course. Won't be any trouble. After I help Momma with supper, I could help you."

Elle nodded. "I really feel much better. Why don't I help you and your mother and then we can attack that trunk?"

Julie's smile was bright with excitement, and it tore at Elle's heart. In that moment she made up her mind. Cynthia was going to lose more than a robe to this family.

He came in the door, filling it with his size. Phoebe glanced up and shyly bent her head back over her pots. Julie stared down at the shoes in her lap, as if she didn't trust men and couldn't look one in the eye. Elle raised her face and smiled at him. He didn't resemble Mel Gibson. He wasn't that pretty. But he was handsome, and he looked so male . . . standing there with his sleeves rolled up beyond his elbows, his shirt opened at the neck and his hat in his hand. Julie had told her how he had worked on the farm, mending the split rail of the chicken pens, straightening the tines on an old plow. He was probably trying to keep busy and stay away from Julie and Cory's father. But he was a man that believed in the work ethic and he had earned his place at the supper table. For some crazy, unexplainable reason, Elle felt very proud of him.

He was, quite simply, a man to be admired.

"Jordan." She said his name in a soft whisper, though loud enough for him to hear.

Nodding in respect to Phoebe, he entered her home. He walked over to the bed and smiled down at Elle. "You're better." It was a statement, yet she could detect a note of gladness.

"Thanks to you." She looked into his eyes and said sincerely, "Thank you. I know you didn't need this detour."

He shrugged, as if embarrassed. To change the subject, he indicated the trunk. "What are you doing?"

Elle laughed. "Trunk cleaning." She pointed to the shoes in Julie's lap. "They don't even fit. Julie tried them on and they're perfect. I think this blouse would look lovely on Phoebe, don't you?"

She held up a white blouse with a bib of heavy lace for him to see and Jordan, glancing at his shy hostess, noted, "Why I do believe the contrast would bring out the blue in Miss Phoebe's eyes."

Phoebe Woodson blushed a bright shade of crimson and hid her face as she peeked into another pot. But they all heard her giggle. It was a sound that probably didn't often grace this house.

"And," Elle added, "I cannot understand why we are carting all this to Texas, do you?"

Going along, Jordan shook his head. "It isn't as if we won't be going through another town if you'd want to replace something. I think you're right, Elizabeth. You should lighten the load. I was going to talk to you about that very thing."

She smiled at her conspirator as he pulled up a chair and sat opposite her and Julie. "I'm happy that you've recovered so quickly. We can be on our way tomorrow morning when Kyle arrives."

"Kyle?"

"I instructed Cooky to send him back with a buckboard from Caldwell. We'll catch up with the herd in a few days."

A few days. Alone with him. Why did her stomach tighten? Surely it was only hunger . . .

A rude, angry voice interrupted her thoughts. "I caught this little runt feeding corn to that rat of his." Woodson threw Cory into the center of the room. Scrambling away from his father, Cory ran behind his mother's skirts for protection. "I catch that Noah, I'll skin him and serve him up for breakfast. Make you eat the tail, too."

The man laughed at his own joke, though Jordan reached out his hand to restrain Elle from rising in the child's defense. Jordan seemed to silently talk to her, telling her that they shouldn't interfere in this family. She knew he was right, yet it galled her to sit and listen to the ugly chuckles of the man when only moments ago the house had been filled with the soft, feminine giggles of his wife. All he did was walk into the room and everyone became silent and depressed.

This, Elle decided, was surely a living hell.

"Supper ready, woman?"

Phoebe didn't answer. She moved like a servant as she placed the steaming black pot in front of him. It was some sort of signal to the rest of the family that they could join him in dinner, for Julie rose and pulled her chair back to the small table that she and Elle had set with unmatched, cracked plates. The children sat on up-ended packing crates and poor Cory's chin barely reached the edge of the table. Everyone ate in silence, attacking their food. Polite conversation was not welcome. They treated eating, even the rare meal of beef, as any other task—done without joy.

Elle glanced at Jordan more than once during dinner, yet kept her silence. As her own act of defiance, she grinned at Julie and winked at Cory when his carrot slipped off his fork. Her insubordination did not go unnoticed for at the end of the meal, Joseph Woodson broke the heavy silence by his simple observation.

"I would think a lady would come to my table properly dressed."

Jordan slammed down his fork. "That's uncalled for. My wife has been ill."

"She has fully recovered, if her appetite is any indication. She eats enough for a man."

Elle could feel the rage building up inside of her as she closed the front of her robe more tightly. In her fury, she no longer saw this crude farmer of the nineteenth century. She reacted as if he had been her father. Slowly, she stood up and very calmly replaced her fork on the wooden table. As if in slow motion she lifted her chin and stared back into his hateful eyes.

"Who the hell do you think you are—"

"Elizabeth! Let's go outside—"

She waved Jordan off. "Listen to me, you pathetic excuse for a man, maybe you can bully your family but don't you dare open your mouth to me. You have no power over me, and I'm not afraid of you. Jordan McCabe put the food on this table, *not you.*"

"Elizabeth, please!" Jordan had come up next to her and taken her arm.

"I'm not afraid of him," Elle stated, not yet breaking the man's odious stare. His eyes were bulging; his face fused with purple. But she wasn't through with him. "He gets off on bullying people because he's a failure as a man—"

"That's enough!" Jordan pulled her away from the table and Elle blinked, as if coming out of a spell. Julie

106

was crying and Cory was clinging to his mother.

"Get that woman out of my house," Woodson screamed, spitting food onto the planked table. "Get her off my land!"

Jordan pulled her to the door.

"Joseph," Phoebe pleaded, "They've brought the Hereford, and Mr. McCabe already paid you the five dollars—"

With lightning speed, the man backhanded her across the face. Julie shrieked in horror as her mother fell off her chair and onto the dirt floor. The young girl hurried to help her mother up, while Cory raced across the room and threw himself against his father.

"Stop it! Don't you hit her again!" His tiny fists pounded at his father's stomach in a feeble attempt to inflict pain. Woodson shoved the child off to one side to deal with the cowboy who was reaching for his shirt collar.

"Someone should take you outside and beat the living hell out of you," Jordan growled into his face. "I think you've had it coming for a long time." His breath came in short angry spurts. "Let's not subject this family to any more violence. Step outside, like a man."

He released Woodson's shirt as if it were contaminated and turned toward the door.

Elle would later remember it happening as if it were a movie. As soon as Jordan turned, Woodson picked up the knife he had used to carve the roast. She saw him raise it above his head, as if to gain momentum before plunging it into Jordan's back. She lurched forward toward Jordan, wanting to protect him, to warn him. Then Phoebe came up out of nowhere. She just appeared like an avenging, bloodied angel. She held the Winchester rifle in her hand

107

and screamed out her husband's name as she used the weapon like a bat to knock him off balance.

Woodson fell to one side, hitting his head on the corner of a crate that was nailed into the dirt wall. He stood for just a moment, a surprised look on his face, before his eyes rolled back in his head and his legs gave out. The children screamed again as he went down in a crumpled mass.

The adults all stood perfectly still for a few seconds, each gasping for breath, for a moment of sanity. And then Jordan moved. He walked past Cory and Julie who huddled together against the wall. Carefully, he stepped over their father and bent down to check. No one spoke as Jordan turned him over. The dirt room was filled with a silence, still and awful, as Jordan's fingers felt for a pulse.

Finally, after agonizing minutes, Jordan McCabe looked up to Phoebe and said, "I'm sorry."

The meaning was clear. Phoebe's eyes were wide with fear as she backed out of the room. Jordan rose and reached out to her for the gun. "It was an accident, Miss Phoebe. We all saw what happened. *Miss Phoebe!*"

The woman looked crazed, her eyes filled with panic, then she turned and ran past Elle out into the night, into the field where she had worked so hard alongside her husband.

Elle turned back to the children and forced her legs to move. She wouldn't think about the body in the corner. She couldn't! None of this can really be happening, she kept telling herself—none of it. As if sleep-walking, Elle lifted the edge of her robe and wrapped it around the two sobbing children. "Come with me," she whispered down to them. "Let's go out for a few minutes. Please . . ." She

108

had to get them away. She had to get herself away from that horrible sight across from her.

She was urging them up, begging them to come with her, when the gunshot broke through the night like the terrifying crack of a whip.

Jolted by the sound, Cory straightened in her arms. But it was Julie who threw back her head, screaming out the name in an anguished wail.

"Momma!"

Chapter 7

Elle and Jordan stared at each other in disbelief for only a second before he grabbed the oil lamp off the table and ran outside.

Barely able to stay upright, Elle closed her eyes and repeatedly whispered to herself, "This isn't happening. None of this can be happening . . ."

Cory moaned in her arms and she looked down into his small frightened face. "C'mon," she whispered, "let's wait outside, all right?" They had to get away from the nightmare. She kept swallowing down the panic that threatened to surface. What she wanted to do was run away. Anywhere. Back to sanity. If she could just get them out of here . . . gathering up Cory, she led Julie out of the sod house.

They stood for just a moment, watching the distant light in the field. Elle would have felt better if it were moving, if Jordan were calling out to her for help, but everything was so still. . . .

"Is there somewhere where we can go for a little while?" she calmly questioned Julie, fighting desperately for control.

The girl was in shock, yet somehow managed to point into the night.

"What is it?" Elle asked, feeling Cory's breath on her neck as he pressed his face against it. His tiny fingers clung to her shoulders as she carried him.

"'Fraidy Hole." Julie's voice was less than a whisper. It was only the wind that carried it.

A fitting name. Through the mental chaos taking place inside of her, Elle was able to remember the cyclone cellar that Julie had pointed out earlier when she'd used the outhouse. At the time Elle had thought it was no more than a mound of grass over a hole in the ground. Now it seemed like a blessed refuge from the horror that was taking place around them.

Julie reached down and exposed the entry. In the moonlight Elle was able to see the dark hole that lay beyond the rough wooden door. The space didn't look welcoming and she was about to suggest that they wait in front of it when the wind picked up, swirling the dry grass around their legs. She glanced down to Julie. The young girl was looking up to her for guidance.

"Maybe we can go in?" Elle wanted to settle the children before searching for Jordan.

"It's dark and cold." Julie sounded frightened.

"That's okay. We'll leave the door open and sit on the steps. All right?" She shifted the child in her arms. "Is that all right with you, Cory?" The boy only clung more tightly. He didn't answer.

Elle led the way. The steps were dug out of dirt. Everything on this farm came out of the earth. Trying not to think, she waited until Julie sat on the first step before lowering herself and Cory onto the second. The distinct scent of onions carried up to her. It was cold, or maybe they were all just in shock. Letting Cory cuddle into her chest, she reached out and placed her hand on Julie's shoulder as they stared out into the wheat field.

The light hadn't moved.

"You think Momma's dead?"

Elle wasn't prepared for the girl's question. She should have been, but she wasn't. "I don't know, sweetie. Maybe the gun just went off by accident. Maybe—"

"Then why doesn't Captain McCabe come back?" she interrupted in a dull voice. "Why doesn't he call out for help?"

Elle was wondering the same thing herself.

"Maybe we should go to him. I can see the light."

Sitting behind the girl, Elle shook her head, though Julie couldn't see her. "I don't think so. Look! He must be coming back." They watched in silence as the light moved out of the field. She didn't need to say anything to Julie. Both of them waited and watched, knowing only moments would pass before they had their answer. When they could see the light come closer to the house, Elle called out.

"Jordan! Over here!"

Dear God.

He was alone.

They made room for him in the cellar. He brought the lamp, illuminating the small shelter. It was no more than seven feet square. Lining its cold dirt walls were bins of potatoes, carrots and onions. She and Julie stood together, Julie's thin arm grabbing at Elle's waist.

Jordan brushed his hair back from his forehead and

113

slowly let out his breath. They could all hear the hiss of the oil lamp as they waited for him to speak.

Everyone knew.

No one wanted it said.

"Julie, honey, your Momma's had a terrible accident—"

"*Nooo* . . ." She turned into Elle's shoulder and cried. Trying to hold Cory and the girl, Elle looked over Julie's blond curls to Jordan.

He shook his head, indicating that Phoebe Woodson, that fragile, overworked woman, no longer existed. How could this have happened? How . . .

Then it hit her. It was as if someone had slapped her in the face. She had done this. It was all her fault for arguing with the man. If she hadn't, maybe Phoebe's husband would be alive, maybe Cory and Julie's mother wouldn't be out in a wheat field . . . dead.

With that revelation came a wave of dizziness so strong that she could barely stand. Her legs buckled and Jordan reached over to steady her as she sat down on a crate. Still hiding his face, Cory whimpered while listening to his sister's sobs.

"Will you be all right?" Jordan asked when the three of them were settled on the ground.

Elle couldn't speak. Her culpability rushed up and washed over her, almost choking her with guilt. She condemned herself for her impatience and lack of control. That anger had caused the death of two people, and irreversibly changed the lives of these children.

"I'll get blankets and a lamp. Maybe you should all stay out here for a little bit longer," Jordan suggested in a soft voice. "I'll bring back your Momma, Julie, and then—"

"I don't want to see her!" the girl nearly screamed, causing Elle to swallow down her own tears as she hugged the teenager closer.

"If she's dead, then just bury her!" Julie sobbed out. "Bury them both! I don't want to see them—I don't—"

"Shh . . ." Elle kissed the top of the young girl's head, letting her own tears finally come. "You don't have to. You don't have to do anything you don't want to. It's all right, isn't it, Jordan?" She could barely speak for the tightness in her throat and her own need to scream out at the injustice.

"Sure it is," Jordan quickly answered. He reached across and touched Julie's shoulder, rubbing his hand back and forth in a show of comfort. Leaning closer to her, he whispered into her ear. "Honey, I'm going to take care of everything for you. Don't you worry. Me and Miss Elizabeth aren't going to let anything else happen to either you or your brother. You stay here, Julie. I promise you, I'll take care of everything."

Grateful for his presence, Elle watched him leave through the haze of her tears. In her entire life, she had never met a man who so easily assumed the cloak of responsibility. She wanted to tell him, to open her mouth and speak, yet her guilt held her back. She was just waiting . . . waiting for him to point the finger of blame, and she wouldn't be able to deny it. How could she have thought so little of him, when everything he had done since they'd come to the farm had been done for others? Now he was faced with this last gruesome task . . .

She was grateful to him for the children who huddled against her for comfort. She was also indebted to him, for in truth she was a coward.

115

If any of this were real then she was as childish as Julie, for she didn't want to see the Woodsons. She was afraid because they were dead, because only a short time ago they had been eating and yelling and fighting. And now because of her they would never argue again. She wanted it all to go away. She wanted to wake up in Bucks County, Pennsylvania—away from this. She could have endured the trail drive back to Texas if that was how she was supposed to follow this nightmare. But this—why wasn't she waking up?

Was this now her reality?

"What's going to happen to us?" Julie mumbled through her tears.

Elle shook her head. "Don't think about it. Not now." Cory had quieted down. His breathing was steady, yet his hands did not release their grip on her shoulders. She pressed her own palms to his back, feeling his lungs expand with each tiny breath. Suddenly a wave of protectiveness, strong and powerful, washed over her. These two helpless human beings were now in her care and looking to her for guidance. All those years when she had told herself that she never cared whether she became a mother slid away. In that small dirt room under the ground, in a century that she should never have been in, Elle once more heard the voice of the doctor telling her that she could never have children. She had heard his regret, his long explanation of tests. She remembered feeling her own resolve settle in, closing off her heart to protect it.

And now that protection seemed selfish.

Now there were others more important.

Shutting her eyes, Elizabeth Mackenzie tightened her

116

hold on the children, vowing not to let any more harm come their way.

They were wrapped in blankets to protect them from the chill. She had no idea what time it was. She couldn't sleep. Her body was cramped from sitting against the dirt wall, yet she was afraid to move, to awaken the children. They had both fallen asleep hours ago. Poor Cory still twitched occasionally and Julie moaned, her head against Elle's breast. Yet they were asleep, and hopefully were graced with oblivion. Lightly caressing the hair at Julie's temple, Elle glanced up to Jordan.

"What will we do?" she whispered. "What will become of them?"

Laboring through the night to bury their parents, Jordan gazed down to the children. He had come back into the storm cellar ten minutes ago, exhausted, and now a look of deep sorrow seemed etched on his face. "We'll take them into Caldwell in the morning. Even if Kyle doesn't come, we'll use Woodson's wagon."

She blinked, afraid of his next words.

"First we have to talk to Julie. She would know about relatives. They have to have a family Bible with names." He shook his head before leaning it back against the dirt wall. "I don't know, Elizabeth . . ." His breath left his body in a weary, frustrated rush.

"You blame me, don't you?"

He straightened. His face and hands had been washed, yet the rest of him showed the hours of digging into the Kansas earth. "Why would I blame you?"

She swallowed down fresh tears, trying so hard not to

117

let them surface. "Because I fought with the man. I made you intervene. You . . . you told me not to . . . I couldn't help it. I wish to God I could take it all back—"

"Don't wake the children," he interrupted. "And, no, it wasn't your fault." Sitting on the dirt ground, with one leg outstretched and the other bent in front of him, Jordan rested his arm on his knee and rubbed his fingers over his eyes. "Joseph Woodson was a walking bomb. I don't know what his story was, or how he came to be out here, but I think he lost something of himself to this land. He didn't pick an easy life, and his poor wife paid the price." Staring out into the night, he shook his head. "Miss Phoebe wasn't herself when she ran into that field. Living out here in this loneliness—she was probably just holding on with a thread when we came along." Visibly weary, he once more leaned his head back and closed his eyes. "Stop blaming yourself, Elizabeth. It was bound to happen. If not tonight, then sometime when there wasn't anyone to protect the children."

His voice was thick with sleep, and she watched as his head nodded closer to his shoulder. "Don't try and figure out life," he muttered, as if an afterthought. "Just try and get through it."

Within minutes the tension left the muscles in his face. He relaxed in a deep sleep and she didn't have the heart to disturb any of them, especially the children who had finally found relief in the peace that comes with total exhaustion.

Everyone was at peace, even Joseph and Phoebe Woodson.

Everyone but Elle Mackenzie.

Her heart was troubled and she felt as if a heavy rock

118

had been placed upon her chest. Looking out into the night, she muttered, "Why am I here?" And then in a stronger voice, "I said, why am I here?"

Silence.

Her eyes narrowed with anger. "Look," she whispered tightly, "I haven't bothered you in over ten years. Now what do you want from me?"

Glancing down to the children in her arms and not wanting to awaken anyone, Elle continued the conversation in her head. *I don't even know if you exist anymore. You certainly never made your presence known before . . . when I really needed you, when I was all alone with no one to protect me. Like these kids. So you'd better be listening now, because I haven't made a pest of myself. And the way I'm feeling . . . you owe me.*

She took a deep breath, closed her eyes, and continued. *Okay. If I haven't lost my mind, or died, or something, well, then, I've walked out of the last decade of the twentieth century and into 1876. In which case, you must have a reason. Is it these children? Was I brought here for them? Because you're sorry for making me childless . . . and this is supposed to make up for it?*

Her breath left her body in a rush of anger. *Well, it doesn't! Do you hear me? I did everything right! I tried to be a good person, even when you saddled me with parents who hated each other and took it out on me. I begged you to help me then and you ignored me. Now, I'm telling you I need some sign, some reason for me being here.* She breathed heavily and gathered her courage, knowing she was arguing, plotting with God. But it didn't matter. Not anymore. What more could be done to her? She had to reason this out in her mind, make some sense of it.

119

Having been denied it during her childhood, structure was very important to Elle. And that's what she needed now—an order to things. She couldn't comprehend the reasoning behind the tragedy that had taken place on this farm tonight. Two people had died. Died! This wasn't a movie, or something out of a storybook. This was happening, and there had to be a reason.

Why did you allow that? If it's to rescue these children, then all right. I'll find a better home for them. I'll make a deal with you. If I promise to find the best place for the children, then do you promise to take me back to the twentieth century?

Silence.

Elle waited, not too patiently, and then she opened her eyes to look back out into the night. Nothing was happening. There was no shooting star, no howl of a coyote nor hoot of owl. There was nothing but the wind to break the silence of the night. Maybe that's how God works, she reasoned. Quietly. He'd certainly been quiet for most of her life. Well, there wasn't any flash of lightning, nor crash of thunder to indicate supreme displeasure. She waited a few moments . . . just to give him time. Finally, she felt it settled in her mind.

Okay, then. We have an agreement. I find the right home for these kids and you get me back to the twentieth century. Hey, I can even understand it now. Guess it's no different than any other business deal. We both give and take until we come to a common ground. You get what you want, and so do I. We're both happy.

She took a deep breath and slowly exhaled as she once more closed her eyes. A smile appeared at her lips. Too bad she couldn't tell anyone about this one. The guys in the office would drool. Striking a bargain with the supreme being didn't come along very often.

And winning . . . Hey, how much trouble could it be to find a home for these children? They were great kids!

Knowing she had a plan, and a reason for the insanity in her life, Elle Mackenzie joined the others by closing her eyes.

She'd finally found her peace.

Chapter 8

Caldwell, Kansas loomed on the horizon like a town that had magically appeared out of nowhere. They had been driving for more than an hour over the creek-veined prairie when suddenly the dark shapes of buildings emerged. Excited, Elle sat up straight and pointed out the sight to Cory.

"Look, that must be it!" she said in an eager voice. Dear God, a town! People! She couldn't wait. Surely somewhere in this place was a home for Julie and Cory, and a way out of her own nightmare.

Cory barely glanced up. His shoulders were slumped; his chin rested on his chest. He was in shock, along with his sister. Elle had tried to be strong for both of them when they had left the farm this morning. Just as they had been saying prayers over the new graves of Phoebe and Joseph Woodson, Kyle arrived with a wagon. Elle remembered being relieved to see the young cowboy, for they could finally leave that place of horror. She had helped Julie pack her and Cory's few belongings. There was a family Bible, yet no names were inscribed outside of Phoebe's. Jordan had gently questioned Julie about relatives and the child could only provide the name of her maternal grandmother. Unfortunately, the woman had died last year and Julie couldn't even remember the town where she had lived. Jordan had shrugged, whispering to Elle that they would surely have some information on the family in Caldwell.

Elle had looked at Julie and Cory, standing together, tightly holding hands. They had appeared so frightened and afraid of the unknown. These children struck a chord inside of Elle, for she could easily remember feeling the same way as a young girl. My God . . . how adults can make the innocent pay for their mistakes! And now these two guiltless children had been placed in her charge. Their safety and well-being were up to her. She felt a twinge of remorse for her pact with God, but didn't dwell on it.

She had to help these children. In one single day they had worked their way into her heart. When she had first awakened on the farm Cory Woodson had been the one to make her smile. Even out on the lonely Kansas plains, with no one to play with except his sister and a tiny mouse, Cory's zest for life hadn't been extinguished. No—it had taken something more horrible, more shocking to silence the boy. Not knowing what else to do, Elle had gathered Cory into her arms and held him close during the long ride into town. She tried not to mind that he held onto Noah, petting the mouse a few times before putting it back into his jacket pocket. How well she knew that everybody needed something to get through the night, and even if she did find the rodent thoroughly disgusting, she vowed to keep her opinions to herself. The poor child hadn't uttered a single word since last night and Elle mentally promised that somehow she would find him a home far better than the one he had left.

"They're going to make fun of us," Julie muttered as the two wagons slowly approached the town.

"No, they aren't," Elle answered softly. "Why would anyone make fun of you?" She glanced behind her to the wagon Jordan was driving. He and Kyle had deposited the children's belongings in it and tethered the Woodsons' horse to the back. They had set out feed for the chickens and opened the flimsy gate, for it was silently acknowledged that no one would be coming back to the farm. Perhaps not ever.

"When they find out what Momma did . . ."

Cory moaned. His first sound.

Holding the boy closer, Elle hurried to stop Julie. "What happened was an accident. No one is going to place any blame. It was tragic, but—"

"They'll all say Momma went crazy, that's what. I don't want to go. . . ." Julie started to sob and Cory's moans turned into pathetic whimpers, cries that tore at Elle's heart.

Gathering them both into her arms, she noticed how uncomfortable Kyle looked as he drove their wagon. She took a deep breath and lowered her head down between the two children's. "Look, guys," she whispered, "we have to report the accident. Jordan's going to take care of everything, but if you don't want to talk to anyone, I promise that you don't have to, okay?"

Julie sniffled and Cory wiped at his cheek with the back of his hand. Elle tried to smile. "Hey, you don't think I'm going to dump you somewhere, just to get rid of you, do you?" She didn't wait for an answer. "No way. We're going to find the best place, and we'll all know when it's right. Okay?"

All three looked at each other for a few seconds. Swallowing down tears, Julie glanced at her younger brother, made a decision, and nodded. "You—you're not just going to leave us?" She hiccupped and wiped at her nose, trying not to let Kyle see her embarrassment.

Elle shook her head and smiled at the teenager. "No, Julie. I told you. Not until we all know it's right."

Julie deeply inhaled, as if the act brought her sudden strength. While gazing out toward the approaching town, she raised her chin and Elle saw the young girl's shoulders tighten as a precaution. All the defenses were up and in position.

What kind of place was Caldwell to cause such a reaction in someone so young?

They had to have passed over ten bars while making their way up the main street to the sheriff's office. In addition to the smaller establishments, Elle took notice of such places as "The Lone Star," the "Alamo Gambling Hall," "Moreland House," a hotel that proclaimed itself *Home of the Cowboy*. Women that could only be prostitutes sat on wide windowsills and surveyed the busy roadway with bored expressions. Occasionally, a very proper-looking woman stopped walking on the sidewalk to stare at their odd procession through the main street. These women were in direct contrast to those sitting by the windows. Serviceable dark dresses that swept the wooden walk clothed their frames, while small, plain bonnets sat atop heads despite the heat of the morning.

Filled with an odd fascination, Elle was sorry when their small caravan stopped in front of the law office. She hadn't really paid attention when they had left Wichita.

126

Then she had been convinced that it was all a dream, a hallucination. Now she knew differently.

Dear God . . .

"I'm scared," Julie whispered as she clutched the worn plaid shawl more tightly around her shoulders.

"You'll do all right." Elle gave her arm a squeeze as Jordan came up to the wagon and reached for Cory. Holding the boy on his hip, he held out his hand to her.

It seemed the most natural thing in the world to take it.

Natural and dangerous.

It was only moments, mere seconds of skin touching skin, yet *something* happened—a magnetic current of recognition ran between them. It was gone so quickly that Elle, suddenly confused, was left to believe that she had only imagined it, and she didn't really have time to consider the significance for Julie was tugging at her arm.

"I'm scared, Miss Elizabeth. My Momma—"

"Honey, no one can hurt your Momma," Jordan broke in gently. "She's finally at peace."

Elle looked at Jordan, so strong, so sure in his words. He spoke with so much conviction that even she believed him. He smiled that slow, almost warm smile of his and motioned for them to precede him into the sheriff's office, and Elle did it. Just as if she hadn't ever questioned a man's control. Here, in this time, Jordan McCabe was the authority and she would keep her mouth closed and let him lead the way. She didn't even bother to think what an interesting reversal that would make.

The law office was small, no more than the size of a good walk-in closet. The jail part, two tiny cells separated by rusted iron bars, was off to one side. The five of them stood before the sheriff's desk—Jordan still holding Cory, Elle with an arm around Julie's shoulders, and

127

Kyle, embarrassed and casting sidelong glances at all of them.

"What kinda accident you talkin' about?" the tall man asked while shifting his considerable weight in his chair.

Jordan cleared his throat and looked at Elle and Julie for just a moment before continuing. "Something went wrong with the gun and it misfired. Never saw anything like it before. Both of them killed."

The red-haired man reached over to a broom and broke off a length of straw. Using the thin end, he proceeded to pick at his teeth. Elle suppressed a shudder as she watched the sheriff dig the reed into the graying cavity on his front tooth.

"You the Woodson girl?" he asked Julie.

She nodded and leaned closer to Elle.

"You see this? You seen your Momma and Daddy?"

Julie didn't answer for a moment, as if considering the lie. Deciding the sin was worth taking on, she again nodded her affirmation.

"I need you to talk, girl."

Elle felt Julie swallow and catch her breath before muttering, "Yes . . . just like Captain McCabe says. Something . . . something went wrong with the gun. That's all . . ."

Sheriff Nathan Fuller scratched at his belly, like a lazy dog on a hot afternoon. He seemed to be digesting the story that was presented to him. After a considerably painful silence, the man sucked at the now empty cavity, let out his breath in a noisy rush and stood up.

"You say you buried them?"

Jordan nodded.

"Anything alive left out there I should worry about?"

Shaking his head, Jordan said, "Just some chickens.

We brought the only horse with us."

The sheriff's interest was aroused. "A horse? What do you plan to do with it?"

"I'll sell it, of course. The children will need something to start their new life."

Reluctantly, the large man nodded. "And what about them?" he asked, as if Julie and Cory weren't even in the room.

Silent until then, Elle lifted her chin and spoke up. "I'm going to find a place for the children. Perhaps you might tell me where I can begin."

As if just noticing her, the sheriff eyed Elle with a new regard. "And you are?" He tried to smile, and attempted to suck in his ample belly, which only served as a pathetic reminder that he was well past his prime.

"Elizabeth . . ." Elle stumbled over a last name and Jordan stepped in to rescue her.

"Elizabeth McCabe. My wife." He said the name with authority, refusing to look at Elle.

The sheriff's attitude immediately changed. A wife was respected property. Almost as much as a horse. He cleared his throat. "Well, then, Miz McCabe, I'd have to steer you to the Messenger of God Church. Reckon the Reverend Cates and his missus would be of help there."

"Then we're free to go now?" Elle asked, anxious to get out of the small room and back into the fresh air.

The sheriff drew in a deep breath that filled his belly. He let it out slowly, staring at each one of them in turn. Elle could feel the others holding their breaths along with her. So much depended on whether this man wanted to challenge them.

Finally, he spoke.

"Well, then, as long as the girl here agrees with your

story, I'd say that's the end of it. Tragic, is what it is. Them sodbusters woulda' rotted out there if you people didn't come by. Lucky for these kids you did."

Elle glanced at Jordan and although he tried to hide it, she could read the relief in his expression. It was an accident. Everyone in Caldwell would believe that it was a terrible tragedy and the two children would be safe from ugly rumors.

She was right to trust Jordan. Trust—a totally new emotion where men were concerned and, as they left the sheriff's office, Elle looked at this rough cowboy in a completely new light. Maybe he wasn't as flawed as the other men that had entered her life. Perhaps this one would change her long-held belief that most men were threatened by a woman of equal intelligence and power.

Once more out on the street, Jordan pointed toward the opposite end of town. "I think the church is down that way. I have to stop at the telegraph office and see if Traver left any messages." He placed Cory on the ground and absently tousled his blond curls. "Why don't I meet you in, say, a half hour? That way I can stop at the land office and make sure the Woodsons' farm is properly registered to Julie and Cory now."

She smiled at him. A genuine smile. He was thinking of everything. It was hard to believe that less than twelve hours before they had all been in the midst of such horror. Now the sun was shining and Elle could feel herself grow warm—an embarrassing Barbie doll glow of admiration for this remarkable male. "That would be fine," she heard herself saying, as if everything that came out of his mouth was agreeable to her. And what a mouth! A now heavy beard sexily wrapped around his jaw and cheeks, making his blue eyes look even lighter by contrast. Suddenly robbed of reasoning, she began to picture his mouth on hers, his arms wrapped tightly around her waist, pulling her closer, deeper into the hard contours of his body.

She shook her head to wipe out the ridiculous thoughts, just as he tipped his hat and smiled before turning away. Elle took a deep breath as she watched him walk down the street. She imagined the straight muscled back under the familiar leather coat . . . his hips, his legs . . .

Dear God, she was becoming as simple-minded as any air-headed bimbo in spandex. She mentally shuddered at the comparison and tried to gather her senses while leading the children in the opposite direction. Yet, her traitorous mind told her to take just one more look, one more peek.

And she did—in an evasive, sly way.

Her heart reacted to the sight of him and it startled her. When had she changed her mind? Was it when he had first brought her to Woodson's farm instead of staying with his precious herd? The way he had tried to brighten Phoebe's dreary life with his gentle and innocent flirtation? Or was it the way he had taken charge and spared her and the children any more horror last night?

She didn't know when it had happened, but sometime in the last twenty-four hours Jordan Dillon McCabe had become an honest-to-God hero in her eyes.

The discovery was amazing.

"I won't go to any church orphanage. You promised."

Elle brought her attention back to the children. Julie was holding Cory's other hand and her pretty young face held a look of terror.

"I told you we would make this decision together. But

131

we have to do the right thing here. The sheriff said we should talk to this Reverend person. He can help us, Julie." Elle tried to smile at the teenager. "I don't know anyone in this town. Not even the state." *Not even this century,* she mentally added. "Face it, honey. We need some advice."

They walked toward the church with an uneasy silence, each filled with their own thoughts. Caldwell had its share of merchants, bankers and grocers, and even though their minds were occupied Elle and the children couldn't help but notice the fancy saddles in the window of one shop. The three stopped for just a moment to admire the workmanship before moving on. Another store displayed high shiny boots tipped in silver and ornate Spanish-looking belts that had to be too heavy to wear. Each establishment—from the barber to the brewer, the laundress to the lawyer—offered something for the cowboy. One store boasted that everything a person might want could be found behind its doors—from a five-hundred-dollar diamond to a pint of salt.

Even though they were delaying the outcome, all too soon Elle, Julie and Cory found themselves in front of a small building with a large black and white sign.

Messenger of God Church . . .

It looked very much like the other stores, except for the large cross someone had painted on the door.

Elle took a deep breath and squeezed Cory's tight fist. "Well. Here we are. It looks . . . proper." Privately, Elle thought the place appeared far too somber and forbidding, but then she wasn't exactly a church-going person so she couldn't judge.

She moved the children forward and knocked softly before opening the door.

The hair at the base of her skull tingled when the heavy wooden door creaked on its rusted hinges. They crossed over into a dark room, cold for a summer morning. She felt Julie shiver next to her and pulled Cory closer to her side.

"What're you doing here, girl?"

All three jumped at the sudden harsh question. Elle giggled nervously as she sighted the small man who had entered the room from a side door.

It had been some time since anyone had called her "girl," yet she let it pass when she realized the expression was common for this time. Instead of her usual sharp response, Elle forced a smile.

"How do you do?" she said as pleasantly as possible. "My name is Elizabeth . . . Elizabeth Mackenzie." She decided not to lie in this house of the Lord. "And this," she moved the children forward, "is Julie and Cory Woodson."

She waited for some greeting, some sign at least of manners if nothing else. The man stood before them and stared. Elle sensed a subtle hostility emanating from him and she instinctively squared her shoulders as she stared back.

He was small in stature, yet he made up for that by the strange gleam in his eyes. In a more friendly man it might have been perceived as intelligence. Now it was frightening, almost scary. He looked like someone she couldn't place, someone spooky . . . all that wild hair, as if he'd just awakened . . .

"I asked you a question. State your business."

His voice held the distinct note of impatience, yet she refused to give in to her need for a response. She had promised to find a place for the children and she wouldn't blow it because of her temper. "We're here to seek your advice," she said in an even voice. "You see, their parents were . . . were killed last night, and the children will need a good home. The sheriff said you would be able to help us—"

"He did, did he?"

"Well, yes, he did." Why was the man frowning? "These children need help."

"This isn't a charity. We can't take every stray—"

All Elle's good intentions were blown away with the man's last words. "They aren't *strays,*" she interrupted. "I thought this was a church."

"And it is, Miss Mackenzie. We just can't afford to shelter every single unfortunate that comes in." He walked down the center aisle that was flanked by rough wooden benches.

Elle couldn't fathom how anyone could find peace in such a place and she shivered as the Reverend Cates approached them. He stopped less than a foot away and looked more closely at the children. Elle could see that he barely took notice of Cory, but Julie seemed to hold a particular interest for him. Warning bells rang inside her brain and she pulled Julie beside her.

"Can't use no boy, but this one might help Mrs. Cates with her duties." The man didn't even bother to hide the leering smirk, or the zealous fire in his eyes. "Don't I know you, girl? Didn't your people have that place out past Blutt Creek?"

Nodding, Julie looked ready to cry.

"How old are you?"

"Fifteen," Elle answered. "Look, the children can't be separated. Isn't there someone else?" Even as she asked the question, Elle knew she wouldn't leave Julie and Cory

134

with this man, for it finally came to her why Reverend Cates reminded her of someone. He bore a strong chilling resemblance to her father.

Gathering her courage, Elle turned the children around behind her and faced the man alone. "Thanks, anyway, for your help," she said in a calm voice as she pushed Julie and Cory down the aisle. The hair on the back of her arms was standing straight up as she heard the man following them.

"Where you going?" he demanded. "I said I'll take the girl off your hands, didn't I?"

"Well, thank you, but I said they stay together and you've made it clear that you don't have a place for Cory. We'll find someplace else." *Dear God*, she prayed, *get us out of here!*

"Nobody else is going to take her in and give her the right training she needs to become a proper, God-fearing Christian woman. Are you prepared to take on that responsibility?"

Something snapped inside of Elle and she pushed the children out the front door before whirling back on the preacher. "You listen to me, you hypocrite. How dare you even insinuate that your interests have anything to do with religion. You're no different than any other man out there," and she indicated the street with her head. "You're all ruled by your crotch, so don't pretend that your charity springs from anywhere else. You want to make Julie into a proper, God-fearing Christian woman?" Elle pointed to her chest. "*I* made a promise to save her from assholes like you—"

"How dare you?" Cates demanded, his face bright red with indignation. "May God strike you for your insolence, your foul mouth . . ."

135

Elle laughed, secure in her position. "Hey, I got the Big Guy on my side in this. See, we've got a deal going. I don't leave the kids with cretins, like you, and he takes me back to my own time."

Reverend Jack Cates stared at the woman across from him. Four years ago he had given up running with the Randall gang and settled down in Caldwell when a shot of lightning knocked him off his horse. It was just like Saul in the Bible, he told Mona, and convinced her that God had sent him a message to preach The Word. Well, he hated the preaching and he hated the poverty, and he especially hated the nearly celibate life with only the questionable pleasures of his wife. So he'd strayed, more than a few times. Maybe some of the things he'd done hadn't been right for a man of the Lord.

And now God had sent him this demon woman.

"Demon!" he shouted as she walked out into the street.

She had three, very well-constructed answers to that accusation, but she sweetly smiled at the children and steered them back toward the center of town. "Let's find Jordan," she said in a surprisingly calm voice. In actuality, she was really looking forward to seeing him. He was, at least, a decent fair man. Quite a rarity in this time, she reasoned. Smiling, she knew he would understand her decision to take the children to the next town.

He was, after all, a lone gentleman among the rest of these dullards. When she told him of their visit to the church and her decision, he would certainly understand, perhaps even applaud, her integrity.

It surprised her to realize that his opinion was important, for it had been a very long time since any

136

man's opinion mattered.

He stood in the telegraph office and stared down at the message that had been forwarded from Wichita. It made no sense.

Jordan, please understand. stop *Have changed my mind.* stop *Turned back in Topeka.* stop *I can't live like that.* stop *I'm sorry.* stop *Lost luggage.* stop *Will explain everything when I get back to Georgia. Cynthia Marie Warden.*

Jordan looked up just in time to see Elizabeth approach the office with the children.

Elizabeth? Cynthia? What the hell was going on?

And suddenly, as he watched the woman lean down and say something to the children, it all became clear.

He pictured her in his mind—in pain, clinging to the whiskey bottle. She had pushed her hair back from her eyes and said, "I told Cooky and Kyle nobody calls me Cynthia. I prefer Elizabeth. Call me Elizabeth . . . everybody does."

Elizabeth.

He'd kill her.

Chapter 9

"Oh, Jordan, you wouldn't believe that Reverend person. He was horrible. Why, he—" She stopped speaking and stared at him. His eyes fairly blazed his anger and the muscle in his left cheek tensed as he ground his back teeth together. "What's wrong? Has something happened to Traver and the herd?" It was the only thing she could think of that would bring about such a reaction.

The words seemed to struggle just to move past his clenched teeth. "*Who the hell are you?*"

Elle's eyes opened in shock. "I beg your pardon?" Surely she couldn't have heard correctly. She must be still angry over her encounter with that crazed preacher. "Is something wrong?" she repeated.

Without further words, Jordan grabbed her arm and led her out of the telegraph office. When they were on the street, he pulled her into an alley beside the wooden building. Startled by his actions, Elle finally recovered and jerked her arm away from his hand. "What do you think you're doing?" she demanded, her earlier appraisal of him diminishing.

He thrust a piece of paper into her hands. Briefly glancing at the children who stood a few feet away, Elle looked down to the telegram. What in the world could he have—

Suddenly, as the words began to register, her heart started pounding against her rib cage and her mouth lost all moisture.

Damn it . . .

Cynthia. The woman's name annoyed Elle. She sounded so prim and proper and her telegram certainly didn't speak well of her. So she'd turned around and gone home . . .

Elle looked up and said the first thing that came to mind. "I'm sorry. It's probably for the best. She doesn't sound like she would have been happy out here anyway."

His jaw dropped in astonishment and he grabbed for the paper, as if she might have harmed it. "I asked you a question, madam. Who the hell are you? And what kind of game do you think you're playing?"

She squared her shoulders at the verbal attack. "Wait a minute. I told you who I was, but you didn't want to listen." She cleared her throat and lifted her chin. "I'm Elizabeth Mackenzie."

"Elizabeth *Mackenzie?*" He said her last name as if it were a curse.

"That's right. Now before you start yelling again, let me remind you that I never claimed to be this Cynthia person. You and your men just assumed—"

"*What?*" He stared at her as if he were seeing her for the first time. "You mean you let them assume you were Cynthia? Why? What did you hope to accomplish? Were you so desperate to marry someone that you deceived

140

everyone in order to gain a husband?'' The color in his face had gone from a bright red to an ashen gray, and now returned to crimson.

"Marry someone? Are you joking? The very last thing I want is to be married.'' She couldn't look at the children who were huddled together off to one side. How could she possibly explain to any of them? Pushing back the hair from her eyes, she swallowed down her frustration and started again. "Look, Jordan, I can imagine how you feel. I didn't mean to deceive you. If you will remember I had just had a tooth pulled and wasn't exactly making much sense myself. When Traver and Kyle came up to me I thought . . . I mean I really thought they had said they were taking me back to Dr. Macdade's office. Of course, now I know they were saying McCabe—''

Jordan shook his head. "Wait a minute . . . wait a minute. You went with my men because you thought they were taking you to a doctor's office?''

Elle nodded. "A dentist. The one who'd extracted my tooth.''

"And he's in Wichita . . . this dentist?''

"Well, yes. But not exactly the Wichita you know.''

Jordan balled his hand into a fist. "I don't know what you mean by that. The Wichita I know? The only thing I do know is that if you thought they were taking you back to a dentist, then why did you travel over one hour in the opposite direction?''

Even the children seemed interested in the question and she didn't have an answer. At least not one that any of them would understand. Jordan was looking at her as if he had trapped her and before she knew it, she blurted out, "Look, I'm from 1991 . . . okay? I thought I was hallucinating.''

141

No one spoke. Even the sun chose that moment to hide behind a fat cloud. It was an odd sensation . . . total silence.

Finally, Jordan whispered behind clenched teeth, "What did you say?"

She wanted to laugh at his expression, but she knew it was nerves, for there was nothing funny about this situation. "I said," she began in a careful low voice so the children couldn't hear, "I don't belong in this time. I'm from 1991." She smiled as if it might take away a little bit of the shock.

"You're insane. I should have known it when you came to camp with that paper necklace, wearing men's trousers and drooling and slobbering—"

"Hey! Hey!" Now she was equally angry. "Now just you wait a minute, Mr. Macho Cowboy. I was not drooling and slobbering—well, I was, but there was a reason for it. My entire mouth was numb from Novocaine. That paper necklace, as you so charmingly call it, was put there by the dentist. Everybody wears one, everybody in my time. And as far as the men's trousers . . . you should know they were mine. I have lots of them, and I wear them whenever I please. You see in my time, a time of considerable improvement I might add, women have progressed to where they wear whatever pleases *them,* not men."

He pointed his finger at her. "I was right! You're a suffragette!"

Somehow, from his tone of voice, that label was as condemning as a cheat or an outlaw. "Well, I'm not, but I'd like to know how to become one if it has anything to do with encouraging women's rights in this century. Honest to God, I can't believe women haven't banded together and risen up against the lot of you!" Feeling quite righteous, Elle nodded abruptly, as if to make her point.

There was no need. By the expression on his face, it was quite clear that Jordan had understood. "I'm not going to stand here in the middle of a street and argue with you about women—"

"Why not?" she questioned. "Because you know I'm right? And by the way, this is an alley, not a street."

She smiled.

He glared.

"I will give you enough money to get back to Wichita," he said in a clipped voice. "What I should do is turn you in to the sheriff—"

"Forget the sheriff," she blurted. "You've already told him I was your wife." Her smile widened. "Reversing that would take a lot of explaining and probably make him doubt everything else you've said. Who knows, he might even think you had something to do with what happened at the farm. And you can forget about Wichita," she added. "I have no reason to go back there, unless of course you can find the Wichita that I left in 1991. Then I'd be eternally grateful to leave you to this uncivilized reign of male macho schlock."

He was breathing heavily, clutching the telegram in his fist. "I take it that expression is an insult?"

"Oh, most definitely."

He stared at her and then quickly glanced to the children. "Exactly what do you intend to do? I assume you didn't find any help at the church."

She could tell he was trying to overcome his anger and she decided not to further antagonize him. After all, what she was about to propose wasn't exactly what he was

143

expecting. "I wouldn't leave a stray cat with the Reverend Cates, let alone children. Besides, he made it perfectly clear that he could only take in Julie," she whispered. "And I'll let you use your imagination as to what his intentions were. Anyway, I thought we would just go with you . . . until we reach the next town. You see, Jordan, I told the children that I wouldn't leave them until I found the right home. You can understand that, can't you?"

He shook his head in disbelief. "Let me get this straight. You deceived me in the most despicable manner. I have left my herd, my men, because of you. I became involved at the Woodsons', lied to an officer of the law—"

"You make it sound worse than it is," she stated, smoothing down the front of Cynthia's copper-colored skirt. "And, besides, it was your guys that took me away. Who knows, I might have gone back. They could have interfered with fate, or something."

"It must be something, because I haven't the faintest idea what you are talking about. You might have gone back where?"

"I told you. 1991. That's where I'm from—"

He looked ready to strangle her. "Don't say it!" he commanded in a strained voice. "Do not say that you are from the next century. It is more than likely, madam, that you have escaped from a madhouse. And now I have had the misfortune to cross your path." He shook his head, as if to brush away the confusing thoughts. "What do you intend to do with the children? They seem attached to you."

Glancing up the alley to Julie and Cory, Elle smiled before turning back to glare at the tall cowboy in front of her. How could she have ever thought he was a *hero?* She mentally shook herself. Dear God, she had actually thought he was different.

She squared her shoulders. "I thought I made that perfectly clear, Captain McCabe. We're going with you to the next town. But don't worry, it's only until I can find the right home for Cory and Julie."

Jordan looked back to the children and took a deep breath. "And then what?"

She could sense his impending compliance and quickly added, "Why then I'll go back to my own time, of course. It's sort of a deal I've got going."

The sarcasm was loud and clear. "I'm afraid to ask with whom."

"Then don't." She smiled. "You wouldn't believe me anyway."

"You're right. I don't think I'd believe anything that comes out of your mouth. You, madam, are an impostor, a charlatan and a liar. And a poor example for the children, I might add."

Her jaw tightened. "I don't think you have to add anything. My God, you're so uptight. I have only those kids' best interests at heart. All I'm asking is that you let us tag along until you catch up with the herd or come to the next town. We'll find a place. I'm sure of it."

He seemed to be considering her words and she couldn't tell by his expression what he was going to do. What she didn't expect was for him to march away. He brushed past her and walked toward the children. Without any pretense, he approached Julie and Cory and asked in a voice loud enough for her to hear, "Do you actually want to place yourselves in this woman's hands?"

Jordan stooped down and rested on his haunches in front of the boy. "Cory, would you want me to find a place for you here in Caldwell? I'm sure if I—"

Cory's face screwed up into a painful grimace and his small lips puckered and trembled. It was obvious he was trying very hard not to cry. Small tears betrayed him, escaping the corners of his eyes and running down his freckled cheeks. He brought a fist up to wipe away the moisture and stared at the man in front of him.

"No!" Julie cried out. "Don't make us do this! Miss Elle said we all have to agree. That means her, too. Right, Cory?"

The boy glanced up to his sister and nodded. Julie looked at Jordan and shook her head. "We stick together." She put her arm around her brother in a show of solidarity.

Elle could have kissed those kids for their allegiance as Jordan let out his breath in a frustrated rush before standing. His hands on his hips, he turned back to her. Even from such a short distance, she could easily see the strain in his face. He was fighting a mental battle. Her? Or the children? They came as a package deal, and it was obvious this agreement was not to his liking.

Finally, he spoke.

"Then I guess we have no choice but to put up with *Miss* Elizabeth Mackenzie. But only for one week. Does everyone understand? She's got one week to settle this, and then I'm going home to Texas . . . a goddamned bachelor." He tore off his hat and swiped at the dust on his thigh. "Shit!"

She stood next to the children and all three watched the angry strides of the tall cowboy as he walked away from them. Elle took a deep cleansing breath and whispered to the kids, "He'll be okay. He's just upset because his precious Cynthia dumped him."

Julie wrinkled her nose. "Dumped him?"

Elle couldn't help smiling as she watched Jordan disappear into a store. "That's right . . . dumped him. Hmmm? Isn't that interesting? I don't imagine that sits too well with Captain McCabe."

Julie was looking up at her, a shy expression on her face. "Miss Elle? Where did you say you came from? We couldn't really hear."

Elle glanced down at the children and grinned. "Far away, guys," she said simply.

Chapter 10

He simply couldn't believe that he'd been so thoroughly taken in by her. He felt like a fool. It wasn't the first time a woman had deceived him, yet this bit of trickery was especially galling. He had thought he was safe, for too many years and far too many memories had taken away his innocence. He had married once and Charlotte had taught him a thing or two about women in their short union—mostly, that they were not to be trusted. How could he have allowed himself to forget?

Crossing another stream, Jordan gazed up to the cottonwood trees that lined the moist bank. It had been a while since he'd thought about his first wife. Not that the image of her wasn't imprinted on his mind. He doubted he would ever be able to erase the memory of her death. They called it childbirth, but there had been no birth, no giving of life. Instead, it had all been taken away. He had tried to forgive Charlotte for not wanting the child, and he'd told himself a thousand times that she simply hadn't been thinking when she took the buggy out. Even though the doctor had told her to stay in bed, for some reason

Charlotte had ignored her mother's pleas and left the house. They had found her a half hour later. The rig had overturned and Charlotte was unconscious and in hard labor. She never regained consciousness in the torturous hours that followed, yet her body expelled the tiny lifeless form of his son. The unwanted child, forced to leave its protection four months before it had any chance of survival, continued to haunt him. And in those moments, when visions of the child overwhelmed him, he hated Charlotte. Perhaps it was merely guilt, that somehow he must have been found lacking for his wife not to want their baby. Even the rumors that followed about the child not being his couldn't dispel the haunting image of a son . . . a lost son.

But it was the marriage itself that had been such a bitter disappointment, and the scar Charlotte left on his soul ran deeper than the loss of a child. His dream, his vision of a future, had been ripped away. And, Christ, it was the only thing that had kept him going since the war. It was that need to restore, to rebuild, that had led him to place an advertisement in the Georgia newspaper. Hester, his mother-in-law, had fought him at every turn. Jordan understood her reluctance in admitting another female into the house, and he had gone out of his way to assure the woman that she would always have a place at Peachtree Point, but it did little good. Hester Hunt Morgan had spoiled and indulged her daughter, yet ruled the household with an iron glove. Everyone who worked in the place lived in fear of her displeasure.

It had all started after Charlotte's death, when he tried to drown his grief in whiskey. For over a month, he either shut himself in his room, or came home drunk after visiting The Double Aces Saloon. And in that time,

Hester took over the running of Peachtree Point. Nothing was ever said. No questions were ever asked. She just stepped in and took hold. Now he didn't know if she could ever let go. There was a time when he was glad for her efficiency, cold as it was. But now all he wanted was the warmth of a home, instead of a showplace.

And he'd thought Cynthia had understood and shared his visions of the future. She had seemed so . . . receptive to his ideas. Now he felt foolish. Cynthia Warden realized her mistake and turned back, without ever meeting him or giving him a chance.

Why didn't he just face it? He was not meant to have a meaningful or lasting relationship with a woman. The example of his parents' marriage was from a time past. A time before the war had ripped away everything normal and decent in his life.

The hot fiery image of Lucia Perez flashed across his brain and Jordan sat up a little straighter as he drove the wagon toward the small Oklahoma farm in the distance. Now Lucia he understood. Their union was purely physical—straight, undiluted sex with no promises or expectations. At this moment Lucia was the only honest woman he knew—completely unlike the woman in the wagon ahead of him.

Miss Elizabeth Mackenzie was about as honest as a snake oil salesman. And as hard to read . . . surely she had to have escaped from an asylum. *1991!* Why would she even tell such an outrageous story? Was she on the run from the law? Now he was stuck with her until they found a place for the Woodson children. Well, he had given her only one week. Five more days, and he was determined to stay as far away from her as possible.

He would never admit it. He wasn't even ready to

consciously accept it, but Jordan McCabe had felt connected to the strange dark-haired woman in the short time they had spent together. He told himself it was because she had deceived him into believing that she was his bride. That it was only because she was vulnerable and in pain that he had reached out to her. He only felt protective because she had been sick, and it certainly couldn't have been pride that he felt when she'd stood up for Phoebe and the children.

He shook his head to drive out the thoughts. He refused to think about her. He would give her the remainder of the week to find a suitable home and then she was out of his life.

Hester and Lucia were right. He didn't need a wife.

Wiping the sweat from his upper lip with the back of his glove, Jordan glanced up at the blazing sun. What he needed was a drink.

Julie pointed out the different trees as they passed— the black walnut, hackberry, sycamore and willow. Sunflowers blossomed like lofty golden sentinels guarding the more fragile asters, columbine and verbena. Elle admitted it was a pretty sight as they came closer to the small white framed house—almost like an Andrew Wyeth painting. Now if only the occupants turned out to be as gentle and agreeable as the setting. This was the fourth farm they had encountered in the last twenty-four hours. Elle had found fault with each of the others—two of the families were too poor to take on any children, one was only looking for someone to clean house for them and refused to consider Cory, and Elle just plain disliked the coarse wheat farmer who spat tobacco juice precariously close to her shoes. There wasn't any way she was entrusting the children to the care of such people.

152

Somewhere there had to be a place.

Maybe this one . . . this time.

"They must be rich," Julie murmured in a nervous voice. She reached out and clutched her brother's shoulder.

Elle was worried about Cory. He hadn't spoken since his parents' death. No matter how hard she or Julie tried, the boy refused to talk. When pressed for an answer, he would either nod or shake his head, but words had not passed his lips. It was frightening to watch the five-year-old emotionally shut down, his freckled face void of expression and response. He would sit for hours in the wagon and pet Noah, just staring out across the prairie. Elle wondered what thoughts occupied his young mind.

Desperate to bring about a reaction, she leaned down and whispered, "Do you hear the dogs barking? They've already noticed us. Maybe you could play with one. What do you think?"

The child looked out to the yard, but said nothing. Elle gave him a hug anyway and let out her breath. She could feel the tension in his young body and her stomach tightened with remorse. There was nothing else she could do. It wasn't as if she could entertain the thought of keeping the children. She had nowhere to call home herself.

Please God, let this be the place. Let them find a good home with people who will give them the love they deserve.

"Got me a daughter already, but I could probably use the boy in the field." The robust farmer scratched at his chest as if to dislodge annoying parasites.

Trying to overlook this unfortunate, but seemingly

153

common affliction, Elle tried to smile. "Well, Mr. Wynings, you see, Cory and Julie must stay together. We couldn't split up a family. You understand that, don't you?" She looked to the man's wife, who stood just behind him.

Sun and wind had robbed her of beauty, but Grace Wyning's face still retained an aura of past loveliness. And she was kind. Elle could sense that in her expression.

Smiling with embarrassment for her husband, Grace said, "Miss Mackenzie, our daughter, Amanda, is plenty of help in the house and I'm not sure we could take in another, but I would like to have me a son. The good Lord chose to take away my Neddie. Near broke my heart, it did. I'd like a son—wouldn't you, Poppa?" She touched her husband's arm.

Mr. Wynings glanced back at his wife. "Girl would only be a liability. One more mouth to feed—"

"But the boy, Poppa," Grace whispered, a note of pleading in her voice. "We could adopt him all proper and we'd finally have us a son. Just look at him." They both gazed down at Cory.

Elle could see the farmer weakening with his wife's appeal. She turned and looked up to Jordan. The cowboy was standing to one side, as if the entire encounter wasn't his business. Yet, she could tell by his expression that Jordan was listening to every word. It was as if he were letting her run the show and Elle knew that if she failed the blame would be hers alone.

She drew her attention back to the couple in front of her. Grace was kneeling down in front of Cory, speaking to him, trying to draw him out. Her husband stood just behind, waiting patiently for the child to answer. Elle glanced up to Julie and saw the teenager's lips tremble.

154

That familiar knot of apprehension began to tighten deep in her belly. That same feeling returned, just as it had at each of their other stops. Call it instinct, or a premonition, but something was forcing her to find fault with every single home they had passed, and if she didn't, she could easily invent a reason to take the children on to the next town or farm.

Like now . . .

"Should you take the children," she began in a deceptively calm voice, "then what provisions would you make for their education?"

"Their education?" Grace glanced up and her husband frowned.

"Don't rightly need more than his sums for figuring seed and grain, and Grace, here, will make sure they learn passable readin'. Same as our Amanda."

Grace smiled at her husband. Everyone had noticed that the man had said *they*.

The knot tightened, straining her abdominal wall. "I'm afraid that won't do."

Jordan moaned with frustration.

Ignoring him, Elle grinned at Julie before turning her attention back to the Wynings. "The children need a more formal education. Isn't there a school nearby, someplace where they can benefit from a more broad base of knowledge?" She knew that possibility was remote and the knot inside of her was easing considerably, especially since everyone was reacting as though she had just spoken in an ancient dialect.

Not knowing what else to do, she merely shrugged. "I'm sorry, it's just that I can't see Julie and Cory being denied those necessities." It was obvious that this farm would be a dead end for the kids. Didn't Julie tell her

155

about Cory learning his letters from reading advertisements that papered the sod house walls? Well, she'd made a promise and somehow she intended to keep it. Julie and Cory were special. There was a reason she had been sent to them. Somehow they were important, and they needed more than *learnin' sums* and *passable readin'*. There had to be a town where they could receive schooling on a regular basis. She wanted to turn and ask Jordan what was the next place on their itinerary, but she didn't. His scowling expression stopped her cold.

Amid Grace's disappointment, Jordan stepped forward and grabbed Elle's upper arm. Leading her beyond the small group, he ignored her muttered protests until they were a good fifteen feet away.

"What are you doing?" he demanded. He released her arm as if it were something distasteful. Despite the heavy leather gloves, he wiped his palm on his thigh. "Just what the hell are you pulling?"

She actually glared at him, yet her expression couldn't dissolve his anger and frustration. *Just what the hell was the woman up to now?* "Let's hear it."

He could see her shoulders tighten in defense. Her chin lift in defiance. He wanted to thrash her for her manipulations, for exploiting these children for her own reasons. He was sure those reasons had to be perverted, selfish and bizarre—and crazy. Because she certainly was.

"How dare you?" She seemed to force the words beyond her lips. Her mouth appeared like a white slash of anger across her reddening face. "I'm trying to do what's best for the kids."

"You are not," he accused. "You're doing what's right for you. You're using those children as a cover—so I'll

156

keep hauling you all over the state until you find whatever the hell you're looking for."

He was glad to see that she was finally speechless. It was a moment to savor . . . and press on. "The Wynings are good people. They'll provide for the children and maybe even come to love them in time."

Unfortunately, the woman found her voice and rudely interrupted in her usual cheeky fashion.

"Don't you see? *That's* the problem." She seemed to struggle for the right words. "Maybe in time they'll come to love them. God, Jordan, nobody, especially kids, should have to wait like that to be loved."

He couldn't say anything. He had no answer. Something about her impassioned speech ripped at his gut, his very foundation. She was so worried about those kids. It was incredible for a woman who had impersonated his bride, deceived his men and made a complete fool out of him . . . yet she sounded so straightforward, almost as though she were speaking from personal experience. Somewhere, in the depths of her amber brown eyes, he recognized a shared pain.

Of course that was ridiculous. Miss Elizabeth Mackenzie was an accomplished actress and a professional liar. He wanted to shake his head to clear out her image. "Are you going to let them stay?" he asked, needing to fill the uncomfortable silence as they stared at each other.

She didn't even blink, and he almost admired her determination when she slowly shook her head.

"No. I have five more days. You promised."

He was breathing heavily and he wasn't sure whether it was entirely from anger. It took a moment to gain control. He felt her determination and knew no amount

157

of talking was going to get her to change her mind. She was the most stubborn woman he'd ever had the misfortune to meet up with, and he expelled his breath in a rush of pent-up frustration. "All right, then. Five days. But by God, woman, you mark my words. You will find a suitable home for those children, or I'll do it for you."

He strode back to the wagon and instructed Kyle to harness the lead horse. He couldn't wait to be on his way. Anything to put distance between him and that woman. But as he said goodbye to the Wynings and offered his apologies, Jordan couldn't quite shake off Elizabeth's words.

Nobody should have to wait like that to be loved.

He was afraid those words would come to haunt him.

The small circle of light illuminated those who sat around the campfire, bathing them in a soft yellow glow. The scent of burning elm mixed pleasantly with the tantalizing aroma of sizzling prairie chicken. Mouths watered in anticipation since it had been over two days since any of them had eaten meat. This afternoon Jordan had ridden on ahead and had returned with the delicacy. After Elle had nearly gagged at the thought of preparing the creature, Kyle and Julie had willingly taken over. And now the time had finally come to enjoy the unexpected luxury. She could hardly wait. . . .

"Miz Elle," Kyle interrupted her thoughts as he handed her the tin plate. "Sure smells good."

She accepted with thanks and politely waited until everyone else had been served. She used her hands to pick up the hot meat and was shocked that it almost came second nature to her now. But then a lot of things in her

158

life had changed. She hadn't had a bath in three days and her body was beginning to smell. Well, not just beginning. There wasn't any doubt in her mind—it did. Good God, she remembered sitting next to Cooky and barely being able to take a deep breath. Now someone would think the same thing about her. She hadn't worn makeup in days. Things like deodorant, toothpaste and soap seemed like distant memories. Dear God, how she had changed, she thought as she licked the grease from her fingers.

The chicken, well, sort of chicken, was delicious and she told Julie.

"My Momma showed me how when I was just little. She said you can never tell when you might be caught out on the prairie alone, and we should learn to fend for ourselves. Guess nobody ever taught you is all."

Elle nodded, ignoring Jordan's sudden interest. "No, I guess not," she said, remembering microwave ovens and quick, prepackaged dinners for one. "Give me a little time, though. I'm a quick learner."

"So's Cory," Kyle pointed out. "He helped, too, didn't you, Cory?"

Everyone looked to the small boy who was seated Indian-style in front of the campfire. Nodding, he continued to stare into the flame. But he didn't answer. When was he going to start talking again? It was beginning to worry everyone. All made an effort to draw the child out, even Jordan, but to no avail. Cory Woodson seemed to be going deeper and deeper into himself. Perhaps, thought Elle, he was trying to find a safe place, a spot in his subconscious where no one could hurt him again.

She didn't blame him, but she knew it couldn't go on

159

much longer. He might never come back.

They continued to eat in silence, as was their custom. The first night on the trail, Elle had tried to start up a lively conversation, but found that everyone else merely wanted to concentrate on eating. It took her two more days to realize why. Food, dinnertime, was a means of surviving—not a pleasant, lingering repast with friends. This was entirely different.

She no longer tried to inject witty dialogue into a discussion of how long it might be before they hooked up with the herd. Now she just listened, and ate, and watched.

Her mind yearned for the banality of television. As she became mesmerized by the fire, Elle absently chewed the meat while wondering what was happening on "thirty-something." Was Melissa ever going to find the right man? Would Hope ever stop whining and letting everyone know just how perfect she was? Such important, heady questions—but now she might never know the answers. Last week she would have laughed at the thought of even caring about fictitious characters on a TV show. Now, realizing that she might never watch TV again made her downright maudlin. Everything had been taken away from her—her home, her job, friends—even her way of kicking back and forgetting about her problems. She didn't even have a decent book to pass the time.

Wait a minute, wait a minute . . .

Was it only her imagination, or was young, healthy, eighteen-year-old Kyle Reavis looking at fourteen-year-old Julie Woodson like a lovesick calf? And could it be that the very pretty blush on Julie's cheeks was brought on by something more than her proximity to the campfire?

Was it only her imagination, or had the two of them been spending more and more time together in the last few days? Elle recalled how Julie had volunteered to ride the Woodsons' horse for exercise, rather than remain in the wagon. Elle remembered being jealous of the diversion. Nothing in the world could have prepared her for days on a hard wooden bench, her posterior muscles screaming in protest of every rut and furrow that slashed across the prairie. Yet every time she thought of complaining, her gaze settled on Mr. Perfect Cowboy and she swallowed her grievance.

If he could do it, then so could she.

She forgot about Julie and Kyle and concentrated on Jordan Dillon McCabe. The man was every cliche about a male and the West rolled into one. He was strong, silent and rugged. He was sullen, withdrawn and ornery. She reluctantly admitted that he was also dependable, responsible and drop-dead gorgeous. The latter rankled her the most. Why couldn't he look like Cookie, or Traver? But he didn't.

As if some strange, magnetic pull existed between them, McCabe lifted his face and caught her staring. She tried to look away, yet for a few seconds she was captured by his gaze. He studied her across the campfire and she couldn't break the spell. Eerie shadows from the fire danced around them, making it all seem unreal.

His face looked like it was sculpted from hard granite. His eyes were hooded, lazy, as he continued to stare at her. It was almost as if he were thinking aloud his questions and she could hear them. *Who are you? Why have you come into my life?* She had already told him the truth . . . and he'd thought she was crazy. As Jordan

161

wiped the edge of his mouth on his sleeve, Kyle turned his attention away from Julie and back to his boss.

"So you think by tomorrow or the next day, Cap'n?"

"What?" Jordan looked confused as he glanced at the boy.

"Traver and the boys. Do you think we'll hook up with them before the Red River Station?"

She watched Jordan shrug, trying to recapture his composure. "They must be making good time," he said. "I expected to catch up with them before we left Henessey—"

Elle listened as the two males talked, and names and memories mingled together as she thought of the places they had passed on this incredible trip. Enid. Dover. Bullfoot Springs. The Arkansas River. The Cimarron River. North Canadian River. Amber and Tuttle, where they had stopped at the Silver Creek Trading Post. There Elle had seen real Indians. Not the tall proud savage portrayed so often in books and movies, but a more quiet, humble version. She didn't think she would ever be able to erase that difference in her mind. It was one thing to read about the conquest of the West. It was quite another to actually witness that it had been obtained at the expense of an entire race.

"When we get to Rush Springs tomorrow, Miz Elle, you and Miz Julie can wash up and all before we hit Alexander. Nice little town, huh, Cap'n?" Now that the eating part was over, Kyle was ready to make conversation.

All Elle heard were the words, *wash up*. "What do you mean?" she asked Kyle. "How can we wash up? Is there a hotel?"

Kyle looked at Jordan and both men smiled. Kyle

162

shook his head. "No, ma'am. There's springs. You know—bubbling water that comes up from the ground."

"Outside?" Julie asked, a note of astonishment in her voice.

Kyle nodded. "Sure. Right out in front of God and everybody. Better'n any bath I ever had in any hotel. Don't you think, Cap'n?"

Everyone's attention turned to Jordan. He smiled at the young man. "You're right there, Kyle. There is definitely something to be said for being one with nature at Rush Springs. After the last few days, I can hardly wait for tomorrow."

He glanced at Elle and she felt her face become flushed. Traitorous threads of anticipation snaked their way down her body and settled uncomfortably in her thighs. She shifted her hips and tried to change positions, but everything she did only heightened the unwelcome sensations. She peeked at Jordan and was mortified that he was studying her. It truly was as if he could read her mind. She had the uncanny suspicion he knew exactly what she was thinking . . . and feeling.

It was humiliating.

It was also exciting.

That admission worried her.

Chapter 11

"C'mon, Cory, you have to get in. We all are."

The small boy stared at the damp ground in front of him. He didn't refuse. He simply didn't respond. Not to anyone.

Jordan tried again. "Listen, son. It's really very nice. Your sister and Miss Elizabeth are only on the other side of this tree. They're in the water already."

The child made no move.

Sighing, Jordan reached out and tentatively pushed a tiny yellowed button through its hole. The small blue collar opened and, receiving no protest, Jordan proceeded to unbutton the rest of Cory's shirt.

When he pulled the material away and helped Cory to remove his arms, Jordan caught his breath at the sight of the small, white chest. There was nothing remarkable about it. A little thin for a five-year-old, with the clear outline of a rib cage. But there was also innocence. There was no hair yet to hint at puberty, nor definition of muscle. There was, in fact, nothing to indicate the difference of sexes.

And at that moment, as he helped young Cory Woodson remove his shoes and trousers, Jordan felt the stab of his own loss. His son would have been about Cory's age. A little younger perhaps, but still the same fragile innocence . . . before life stripped it all away.

And then he looked into Cory's face and saw that this child had been denied even that. His world had been shattered, the same as any seasoned veteran's. And it was too much for his young mind to comprehend. As Cory stood nude in front of him, he saw the child shiver even though the wind was warm. Something broke inside the man then, something undefinable . . . a wash of tenderness, perhaps, for a kindred soul.

Aware that Cory stood waiting, Jordan hurried to shed his own clothes. Kyle was already in the water and Jordan didn't even hesitate before picking up the young boy and holding him close to his chest. There was a certain feeling when the child's skin made contact with his own. He wasn't quite sure what it was. He only knew it felt right, like something that had been denied him.

Holding Cory in his arms Jordan entered the warm springs and sat down, placing the child next to him. Cory sat on a dirt ledge, the warm bubbling water reaching his shoulders. It was soothing and relaxing and it even tickled, yet the child merely sat and stared.

A warning chill ran up Jordan's back. Something was very wrong with this child. And he hadn't the slightest notion of how to fix it.

He lifted his chin and looked beyond the willow tree that separated the males from the females. Long graceful branches fanned out and down to the water, creating a natural curtain. Almost. If he strained his eyes he could make out the faint outline of a shapely back and long, dark, wet hair that lay flat against it.

Maybe she would know what to do with the child.

He shrugged. He might as well ask. What the hell did he have to lose at this point?

It was sheer heaven. She couldn't even bear to talk to Julie. All she wanted was to relax and let the warm bubbles caress her skin. She felt blessed by nature that it would provide this luxury when she had thought she might never be clean again. A feeling of well-being permeated her system just as the soothing water entered her pores. Maybe everything was going to work out in the end. Maybe she would find the perfect place for the children and then be taken back to her own time. She realized as she lay back against the flat rock that she hadn't been exactly open to any of the prospective parents that they had thus encountered. But all that would change. Kyle had said that this town of Alexander that they would hit this afternoon was progressive. Surely there they would be able to find—

"Ahh, excuse me, but I was wondering if I could talk to you for a few minutes?"

She let out a little squeal and crossed her arms over her chest, cupping each breast in her palms. "What the hell do you think you're doing?" she demanded of him as Julie moved away and hid herself behind a heavy, swaying, willow branch.

"Look, I know this isn't the best time, but well . . . you're here and I couldn't see what harm it would do—"

"Oh really?" she interrupted, as she sank down until the water reached her chin. "Well, I would think that if you had something to say, Mr. McCabe, then you had

167

ample opportunity in the last week." She flipped her hair back from her face and glared at him. "You've done a pretty good job of pretending I don't even exist."

"Yes, I know," he said in an apologetic voice. "And I'm sorry. But now I want to talk to you about Cory." His voice lowered and he glanced back toward the other side of the tree. Running his hand over his face, he pushed the wet hair back off his forehead. "Something's wrong with the child."

Her mouth opened. "And you just noticed this?"

He made sure that he stayed on his side of the tree, but she could still see him shake his head. "Well, no. I mean the boy's been quiet, but this is . . . it's strange."

"He's in shock," she said. "Remember what he's been through." Her hair floated about her like a dark water lily and yet she could do nothing about it without first letting go of her breasts. And she wasn't about to do that. "Maybe there's a doctor in Alexander that can help him. A psychiatrist?"

"Who?" Jordan cupped his hands and brought water up over his head.

Elle found that her speech was being affected as she watched the sun reflect off the rivulets of water running down over his cheeks and chin and chest and arms. Biceps and triceps . . . Dear God, his stomach looked like a washboard. . . . "Ahh, psychiatrist. Sigmund Freud?" When the hell did modern psychiatry come into use?

"I don't know what that is. But I'm sure Alexander has a doctor. The town has really grown over the last few years with all the cattle drives that's come up from Texas. But do you really think a doctor can help Cory? I mean, it doesn't seem like it's anything physical. Do they have medicines for this?"

Even though he would move in and out of shadows to avoid looking at her, she could tell by his expression and the sound of his voice that he really cared. Something had happened in the time since they had entered these springs. Captain McCabe had changed and taken an interest in the children, at least in Cory.

Maybe her mission wasn't going to be so hard after all. Now, at least, it appeared that she had an ally. Who would have thought Mr. Jordan Dillon McCabe, strong, silent, self-righteous, would be so affected by a small child?

She had to bite the inside of her cheek to stop the smile. Why, she almost felt a spark of warmth ignite inside of her. Perhaps he wasn't so bad after all?

She no longer felt guilty wearing Cynthia's clothes. She chose a white cotton blouse with heavy lace at the collar to go with the brown gabardine skirt. What did it matter anymore? No one made any mention that these things belonged to another woman and, in truth, Elle was beginning to feel like the trunk and its contents were as much hers as Miss Cynthia Warden's. Anyway, Cynthia had chosen to turn around and go back to the safety of Georgia. She probably didn't ever expect to recover the trunk, and Elle needed clothes—even if they were meant for a woman taller than five-foot-four inches. Tucking the shirt in, she rolled the waistband of the skirt to shorten it and took a deep breath. There was only so much she could do to look presentable. She had already braided her hair and tied the thick end with a tiny white satin bow. After all, Jordan had said they were going into a real town, with real stores and everything. For a fleeting moment she thought of the plush interiors of Macy's and Wanamakers' and yearned for her soft, worn Ralph Lauren jeans, her prized Donna Karan cardigan. Who was taking care of her *things* now? Her apartment? Her car? Her job? Had she lost it? What about her mother? What was Margaret Mackenzie thinking? Was she grieving over the loss of her daughter?

Elle shook her head. Her mother probably took the news in stride—the same way she accepted every other rotten thing that had happened to her. And thinking of her mother, Elle absent-mindedly picked up the silver mirror to check her appearance.

It happened again. The shock of seeing her mother's worried face in the cracked glass took Elle's breath away. She wanted to drop the mirror, but something in her mother's expression made her fingers tighten on the ornate handle.

Margaret Mackenzie's eyes looked . . . tormented, as if her life were over and she just hadn't accepted it yet.

Dear God, why was this happening?

Frightened, Elle closed her eyes to shut out the image, wondering for the thousandth time why her mother just didn't leave her father and make a new life. How many times had she begged, had offered to help her Mom out of the nightmare?

Go away. Please, she mentally commanded. *I can't do anything about it now.* Now she had to concentrate on her mission, her real mission for being thrown back in time.

The children.

When she returned, she'd try again to talk to her mother—to get her to leave that impossible situation. But she couldn't do anything about it now, except worry. Taking a deep breath, she opened her eyes and was

170

relieved to see her own reflection.

Her face was sunburned; her freckles stood out in relief. But it was her own image that stared back at her and even though she didn't wear a speck of makeup, Elle was overjoyed. Whatever weird occurrence took place when she looked in the mirror . . . it was over.

Running a fingertip over her cheekbone, she couldn't help but wonder why Margaret Mackenzie was haunting her through a mirror when she was alive and well in 1991.

She *was* well.

Wasn't she?

Elle caught her breath for a moment, wondering if her father had started to beat her mom again. Her jaw tightened with past memories of her mother begging her to hide while the fighting took place, of screams of pain and terror, of police banging on the front door and dark closets that held the only comfort for a small child.

Elle shook her head to drive out the memories as Julie walked up to her and asked a question. She barely listened to the teenager. Instead, she stared off across the bubbling springs and mentally reached out . . .

Mom, be careful. Hold on. I'm coming back. I promise. And this time I vow to stop it.

In the midst of tall bluestem grass and the shorter blue grama and buffalo, the town of Alexander, Oklahoma rose up on the prairie like a heaven of civilization. It seemed to welcome all visitors and announce itself as being a place where a grand celebration was in full swing. A huge red, white and blue bunting was hung from Glenmartin's Emporium on the east side of the street to Nordhoff's Barber Shop on the west.

Founder's Day Race and Picnic

Even Elle was elated as they drove up the wide center street. There was an air of excitement in the town. Men checked on last-minute preparations; children ran wild while mothers merely smiled as they added their own contributions to tables already laden with food. Everyone was friendly and Elle had a good feeling about this town. The sun was shining and she looked up to a fat white cloud that kaleidoscoped the brilliant rays. When she was a young child walking home from school, she remembered stopping on the sidewalk and watching almost the same picture. At the time she had thought those rays were God's heavenly graces coming down to earth. Like at the end of a rainbow, she was certain something good would be found. Now she wasn't quite sure. She wasn't exactly ready to rid herself of the childish image of God's kindness to mankind. After everything that had happened to her in the last week, she was reluctant to rule out anything, especially something Divine. But maybe, just maybe, this was a good sign. Perhaps Alexander was going to be the magical place.

And then she could go home.

Already her heart felt lighter.

"Gonna enter the race, Cap'n?"

Jordan shrugged while glancing around the center of town. God, it was good to be with people again. What luck that they should come on this day. Surely this celebration would spark an interest in Cory. Reaching for the child, Jordan said, "What do you think, Cory? Should I do it?"

Cory merely blinked.

"Well, I'm gonna do it," Kyle announced to everyone. "Said the first prize was a twenty-dollar gold piece."

172

"Really?" Julie asked her young friend. "Do you think you could win?" A pretty blush heightened the color in her cheeks and she glanced down to the dirt road.

"Why sure," Kyle declared, pushing back the rim of his brown hat. He was filled with young male bravado. "And if I couldn't, then the Cap'n would save the day. Mark my words, the Triple Cross'll capture that gold piece."

Jordan laughed. "Wait a minute, Kyle. I like your confidence, but remember that our horses haven't had a good run in over a week. Be pretty hard to compete against the rest of the field." He tousled Cory's blond curls and smiled at the females. "I'd imagine the others have been practicing for weeks just for today."

"Ahh, c'mon, Cap'n," Kyle appealed. "You know we can do it. Let's register."

Julie appeared excited and Elle grinned as Jordan looked at her.

"What do you think?" he asked.

Elle was so shocked he had asked her opinion that she could only shrug.

"Well, then, let's go," Jordan said, while placing a hand on Cory's shoulder. "We'll give it a good try, won't we, son? 'Bout time those nags got some exercise."

Elle's mouth opened with surprise as she watched Jordan lead them in the direction of the registration table. The big, tough cowboy looked . . . almost young and happy while paying the dollar fee for both Kyle and himself.

He turned around and surveyed the town of Alexander, like a young kid let loose in a candy store. "Race doesn't start for another two hours yet. Let's see what else we can discover until then. Hey, Cory, a greased pig contest . . .

Look over there," he pointed in the direction of a square tank of water and a large barrel-chested man sitting on a small slab of wood. In huge red letters above him someone had crudely painted the words, *Dunk The Marshal*. It appeared, from the line of youngsters waiting their turn, that this was a very popular game.

Taking Cory's hand, Jordan led him toward the crowd of children and adults, each hooting and hollering and waiting for the chance to see the large man fall into the water. Elle followed, clearly fascinated by the turn of events. Whatever had happened at Rush Springs had changed Jordan. He had plainly taken Cory under his wing.

It was odd.

And, in a weird way, it was wonderful.

As she stood in back of them, she shook her head. He was certainly keeping her confused. One moment he was attentive and sweet. Of course that was before he had known that she wasn't Cynthia. Then he had become withdrawn and resentful. And now . . . now he was . . . nice.

Her smile grew wider as she watched him bend down to talk to Cory. She was positive Cory didn't respond, but Jordan acted as if he did. He walked up to a short man who held a small basket of balls and paid him a coin.

After joining Julie and Kyle at the front of the crowd, Elle found that her hands were tightly clasped together in front of her. Jordan was going to try and dunk the marshal. She shouldn't have cared whether he succeeded in this childish game, yet some shred of loyalty sprang forth inside of her and she silently cheered him on. Standing next to Cory, she reached for his small hand and squeezed it tightly as the first ball glanced off the

174

metal lever.

"Hey, stranger, what're you trying to do? Came pretty close to gettin' in trouble with the law there."

There was a murmur of laughter and Jordan called back, "Sorry, Marshal, just passing through. Pretty hot day, though, huh?"

The lawman played along. "Sayin' I'm gettin' hot under the collar there, mister? Think you're the man to cool me off?"

Laughing, Jordan shook his head. "Not me. I'm just helping out here. This is only my contribution to the Founder's Day Fund."

The marshal grinned. "Okay, then let's see what you've got. That first ball was nothin' more than a lucky break."

Jordan looked at Cory and winked. Elle glanced down and was glad to see Cory paying attention. That glassy look was gone from his eyes. His attention was, in fact, completely centered on Jordan. It was painfully obvious that this small child was starting to fixate on the cowboy. A short pang of sympathy tugged at her heart and she squeezed the child's hand before lifting her head.

He was looking at her. Over the heads of the women in straw bonnets and the men in cowboy hats, Jordan was looking directly at her.

It was only for a second, yet a quick stab of excitement ran up her thighs and settled in her belly. It was stupid, childish, yet when he brought back his arm and the marshal went falling into the water tank, Elle threw her arms up in the air and jumped as high as any actor in a Toyota commercial.

She wanted to run up and throw her arms around him, but others were already slapping him on the back. Amid

175

the laughter and congratulations, Jordan made his way to the tank and offered his hand to the lawman. When the marshal was again seated on his perch, dripping with water, Jordan then turned and looked over the crowd to her.

He smiled.

A real, genuine, totally male smile.

And that's when Elle Mackenzie knew she was in trouble.

Chapter 12

"All right, gentlemen, you all know the rules. Three revolutions 'round the town, back up Main Street. No shoving, kicking, whipping—and, for the womenfolk, no undue foul language." Amid the nervous laughter was also a distinct charge of excitement.

The race was about to begin.

Elle stood off to one side of the street with Julie and Cory. Her gaze never left Jordan and Kyle. The two men from the Triple Cross sat atop tall horses. Jordan's was black with white stockings. Kyle's was spotted brown and white. Both men looked determined, just like all the others in the field. Farmers and merchants controlled their mounts alongside cowboys and old wranglers. Everyone was eager for the race to begin, confident that the shiny twenty-dollar gold piece would soon warm their palm.

Elle looked down the dirt street. Women and old men lined the wooden sidewalk clear to the end of town. People were waving at the riders, calling out encouragement. Everyone was smiling and the excitement was contagious. No matter that Alexander was a small, struggling community on the edge of the Oklahoma border. Right now it could have been Churchill Downs. It was obvious this race was more than an afternoon's contest. It was the Event of the Year.

An old cowboy walked in front of them, juggling two small apples, a green ball and a yellow sphere of yarn. He talked to the children as he passed, reminding them of the sack races, the egg contest and the square dance that night.

A dance.

She felt a mixture of dread and anticipation. Would they go? And what would they all do if they did? Julie and Kyle might dance, but—she couldn't even finish the thought. Turning her head, Elle was startled to find that Jordan was staring at her. While others seemed to struggle to control their horses, he did so with ease. She wanted to tell him good luck, yet neither of them said a word. There was a strange communication taking place and she almost felt the distance between them disappear. It was eerie, and totally unsettling, just like at the dunking cage. She sensed he knew her thoughts, for a small grin played at the corner of his mouth, and she found her own lips answering in a smile.

Then he nodded.

Just like he *knew* that she was thinking about the dance.

But why did he nod? What the hell did that mean?

The smile left her lips as the stout mayor lifted his gun to signal the start of the race. She held her breath as she tried to clear her head. Dear God, why is all this happening now? Why now, when there is absolutely nothing that can come of it?

The gunshot shattered her thoughts, and as the race began, Elle's attention was centered on the riders, just like everyone else in Alexander.

Jordan and Kyle bolted forward and stayed at the front of the field. Perhaps six horses remained at the lead while the others kept close on their heels. Elle was shocked at the speed, for all the while they were on the prairie, she had never seen the horses do more than trot. Now, in a flash of color and movement, they were leaving the main street and circling the town. She could hear the thunder of their hooves and found that she, like everyone else, was leaning out and looking toward the right—waiting for the field to appear as it re-entered the main street.

When it did, she was struck by the magnitude of force that flashed in front of her. She was keenly aware of animal muscles shining with sweat, the blur of flaring nostrils and wild eyes, the thunderous roar of hooves crashing against the ground and the dirt—the flying dirt that was kicked up as they passed.

It was primitive and basic entertainment. There was no artificial machinery, only two of nature's creatures joining together in competition. Man and beast. It was wonderful.

Especially since Jordan was a good five feet ahead of Kyle and the rest of the pack.

She hugged Cory to her stomach when Julie yelled, "He's going to win! Captain McCabe is going to win!"

Elle couldn't contain a smile and her heart swelled with pride, as if Jordan really belonged to her. "He is, isn't he?" she giggled, like a young girl Julie's age. She tightened her hold on Cory. "What do you think, Cory? Do you think he can do it?"

Before she could say anything more, the crowd started

yelling as the field of horses came back into view. She could see Jordan's blue shirt as he bent low over his horse's neck. He was still leading. He looked young and happy, almost carefree, as the wind pushed the hair back off his face. He looked like he knew he was going to win, that nothing could stop him—

It happened as if in slow motion. In one moment, the scene was set. Jordan ahead of the others, sure of victory. In the next, the yellow ball of yarn that the old cowboy had been juggling fell into the street and a small girl of no more than three or four ran out after it—right into the path of the oncoming horses.

Elle's scream joined scores of others as Julie turned her head into Elle's chest to hide her face. Elle clutched Cory's shoulder as the terrible nightmare continued . . . the powerful force of hooves pounding the earth and bearing down on the child in the tiny white pinafore.

Elle was sure the child was doomed, for no one could possibly outrun the horses and save her. She wanted to turn her face away, to hide like Julie, yet if she had done so she would have missed a man's finest moment.

As if he had planned it all along, Jordan changed direction, left the front of the pack and, reaching down like a rodeo trick rider, swooped the little girl up in his arms. All the others roared by on their way to the finish line. He slowly stopped, as though the race had meant nothing more than exercise for the horse, and deposited the child into the arms of a sobbing woman. Jordan didn't dismount; he merely walked the animal to cool him down while the winner of the race came back to discuss what had happened.

Half the people were applauding the young cowboy from a local ranch and the other half were crowding around Jordan. It was clear to the populace of Alexander that there were two winners that day, and both men were being treated as heroes.

Elle was shaking as she stared across the street to Jordan. Everyone had crowded around him and he looked uncomfortable with their attention. She could see he was trying to move through them but they were blocking his way.

"I always thought of horse racing as sweating hides and young men's prides. But you must be pretty proud of that husband of yours."

She turned at the sound of the voice. An older woman in a heavy black dress and a matching ruffled bonnet smiled at her.

Not knowing how else to respond, Elle nodded.

"Takes some kind of man to do that. These your children?" The woman's face was open and friendly as she looked at Julie and Cory.

Elle glanced up at Jordan. He was still surrounded by grateful people, trying to make his way through them. Realizing she would have to do this alone, she turned to the older woman and said, "This is Cory and Julie Woodson. They . . . ah, they lost their parents. I . . . Jordan and I," she corrected, "are hoping to find them a good home."

The woman was immediately sympathetic. "Oh, I'm so sorry. Indians?" She reached out and patted Julie's shoulder.

Elle shook her head. "No. Nothing like that. It was an accident. In Kansas . . ." Her voice trailed off.

The woman nodded. "This is a harsh life and it's so hard to figure God's ways in these matters." She lowered her voice and leaned closer to Elle. "You are fortunate,

181

though, that you've come to Alexander. These tragedies have happened far too often in the past years—what with the Chickasaw so upset with the cattle drives and everything—well, we've had to establish an orphanage."

"An orphanage?" She and Julie said the word together.

"I believe it's the first in the territory."

"An orphanage?" Elle repeated in an incredulous voice. "Here? In Alexander?"

"Why, yes. Miss Avoula Turner founded the Turner Guardianship. I do believe there are seven or eight children there right now."

"An . . . an orphanage," Julie whispered, and Elle could detect the note of horror in her voice.

She didn't have time to respond, for the crowd of people that surrounded Jordan moved with him as he made his way toward her and the children. As she waited, she tightened her hold on Cory's shoulder to make sure he wasn't swept away in the sea of townspeople that preceded Jordan.

It was plain ridiculous.

He had handed his horse over to Kyle and now tried to maneuver himself through the multitude of outstretched palms that either shook his or slapped him on the back. He couldn't help grinning, but it was more with bewilderment than any other emotion. He hadn't done anything differently than anyone else. And he certainly wasn't this hero that these people were making him out to be; he'd just been in the lead and better able to get to the child. He had tried to explain that, but no one seemed inclined to listen. And so he'd smiled and nodded and attempted to push his way to Elizabeth and the children.

It was the oddest thing. When he had safely deposited

the little girl into her mother's arms, the first thing he'd thought about wasn't the race, or his loss. It was Elizabeth. And Julie. And especially Cory. Were they safe? It had taken him a few moments to locate them and then he'd been surrounded and barely able to make it across the street.

For some strange reason he needed to touch them. To connect with her and the children. It was as if they were . . . he was about to think "family," but that was absurd. They were nearly strangers, which made his reaction all the more foolish. But as he reached the wooden sidewalk, his gaze locked with Elizabeth's and something really frightening happened.

It started in his belly and curled its way down his legs and back up to his groin. She was so goddamned beautiful it almost hurt that she wasn't really his. And as he came closer, he knew it wasn't just because of the way she looked. Elizabeth Mackenzie was the most remarkable woman he had ever known.

He also acknowledged with a sinking feeling that he wasn't ready to give her up.

Not just yet . . .

"Are you all right?" she asked, licking at her lips as if they were dry.

Nodding, he bent down and picked up Cory. It barely mattered that the child didn't speak. It was almost as if they silently communicated. How else would Jordan know that Cory's small hand clutching at his shirt collar only meant that the boy had been frightened, and was now happy that it was all over and everyone was safe?

Jordan closed his eyes for a moment and slowly expelled his breath. Smiling, he felt the tension leave his body. "I'm fine," he finally answered. "Although everyone is certainly making far too much out of losing a race."

Her smile increased. "Oh, I don't think so."

"You're too modest, Mr. McCabe," the stout woman at Elizabeth's side added. "Miss Amy Furgusson will grow up knowing she owes her life to you."

He was embarrassed and didn't know what to say. Thankfully, the mayor had at last made his way up onto the sidewalk and joined the group.

After taking deep breaths to recapture his wind, the man said in a voice loud enough for all to hear, "The town council has conferred and we declare two winners today. Jake Jacovic from Bent Fork and Mr. Jordan McCabe. Abner Coulten from the bank has generously put up the additional prize money."

Cheers went up all around them and Cory buried his face against Jordan's neck, as if to hide from the enthusiastic applause. Holding the boy tighter, Jordan raised his hand to ask for quiet. He tried not to sound as bewildered as he felt. "Thank you for the offer, but I can't accept. Alexander had one champion in the Founder's Day race, and the victory should go to him alone."

Denials came from all around.

"No. You can't refuse. You were ahead."

"Everyone knows you were the sure winner."

"You saved a girl's life, young man. You must accept this honor."

"How else can we repay you?"

Jordan tried to interject an answer. "You don't have to do anything—"

Someone interrupted him. He couldn't see who, nor would it have made any difference. It was as if these people were determined to make him out to be more than he was. He looked at Elizabeth and shook his head in amazement.

"All right, then listen," the loud male voice interposed. "You and your wife and children will be my guests at the hotel for as long as you stay in Alexander."

"And new clothes from my store. Bet the missus would love a pretty new dress for the dance tonight."

"Nonsense. Mrs. McCabe will be outfitted by *my* shop."

Another voice joined the others. "And when you leave, I'll equip you with fresh supplies." The offers came from all around them.

"Well, you can't say Alexander doesn't know how to show its appreciation," the mayor said, then laughed at Jordan's dazed expression. "Come," he added, steering Jordan, Elle and the children through the crowd, "you and your family will join mine for the picnic and we can discuss the finer points of horsemanship. You wouldn't know to look at me now, but in my day I was considered quite an equestrian."

Giving up, Jordan merely smiled. He was only half listening. It had just dawned on him that neither he nor Elizabeth had corrected the man when he'd called her *wife.* For just a moment, Jordan had wished it were so, then the idea was so ludicrous that he shook it from his head. He never reasoned that by his silence he was pretending Elizabeth Mackenzie somehow belonged to him.

How could he even consider it? He and Elizabeth? It was an idea that scared the hell out of him.

*   *   *

The room was large for a hotel in a small town. There were two double beds separated by a marble-topped washstand. The hotel owner had apologized for putting them all together but added that this was the very last available room in town. He had gone on to explain that farmers and ranchers came from over seventy-five miles for this weekend's festivities. Elle kept nodding, dreading the moment that they would be left alone. What in the world would they say to each other?

"Well, I guess I'll see you all tonight at the dance. Be sure to save me a reel, Mrs. McCabe."

Elle could feel the heat of a blush creep up from her throat. She tried to smile, knowing she must look laughable. Dear God, she was a computer sales rep, respected in her field, and here she was blushing like a shy teenager. It had nothing to do with dancing with the man. It had everything to do with being called Mrs. McCabe.

The man nodded to Jordan and then left.

Jordan turned around to her and shrugged.

"I'm sorry. I didn't know what else to do. I should have said something, corrected them earlier—about us being married."

She didn't say anything. She couldn't.

He cleared his throat. "Well, ah . . . you and Julie can have that bed," he said, while pointing to the one closest to the window. "And, Kyle, Cory and me will take this one. Don't worry, I'll try and work out some privacy for you ladies. Right, boys?"

He looked to Kyle and Cory for help. Kyle nodded while nervously wiping the toe of his boot on the back leg of his jeans. Cory just stared.

"Okay." Jordan tried again as he pointed to a neat

stack of boxes. "All the bows and things you girls picked out have obviously been delivered. Why don't we get dressed first and then let you two have the room. We'll wait for you downstairs."

Elle quickly nodded. Grabbing Julie's arm, she headed for the door. "Sounds great," she muttered, before pushing the young girl into the narrow hallway.

When the door was closed behind her, she stopped and let out her tightly held breath. How in the world was she expected to spend the night in the same room with that man? Sleeping out under the stars was one thing. All of a sudden the confinement of that bedroom seemed stifling.

Maybe she would just dance all night.

God, she hoped the hotel owner had been serious and could dance.

For that matter, she hoped *she* could. It was a safe bet no one tonight was going to do anything even vaguely familiar.

Come to think of it, how the hell did one dance a "reel"?

Elle's loud groan made Julie look at her with concern.

"Are you all right, Miss Elle?" the young girl asked.

"Great," Elle answered. "Everyone thinks we're married. We all have to spend the night together. What else can happen?"

"Oh, Miss Elle, if that's what's bothering you we can always string a blanket between the beds. I'm just so nervous about tonight. I mean . . . a dance . . ."

Elle wasn't listening. A blanket between the beds— right out of "It Happened One Night."

Hmm . . .

Okay, if Gable and Colbert could get through it, then maybe she and McCabe stood a chance.

Maybe.

It was absurd.

No one could possibly wear all this gear and still be able to dance. She could barely manage walking. She'd already knocked over a vase of wildflowers just by turning around too quickly when Julie had asked a question. There was no doubt about it. Tonight was going to be a disaster.

Julie wore a blue-and-white candy-stripe muslin dress. It had a wide skirt, square neckline and full sleeves. With Julie's blond hair pulled back with a white satin ribbon, she reminded Elle of Disney's Cinderella. And as young as she was, she managed the hooped skirt quite well.

Elle, on the other hand, was a calamity waiting to happen. Try as she might, she simply couldn't get used to the ridiculous bustle on the back of her white gauze dress. That bustle was an instrument of torture that could only have been designed by a man—a man who hated women. When she had first seen the thing in the dress shop, she'd merely laughed, never dreaming it would be so awkward, and besides, she had loved the silky texture of the dress, the rich grass-green satin trim, the tiny purple and green flowers that decorated the hem. It was nothing at all like her own tailored, designer clothes. This was soft and feminine and totally unlike her. And yet, she had wanted it from the moment she'd seen it hanging in Miss Chatwin's shop.

She just didn't realize all the accessories that would accompany such a fragile costume. First there was the underwear. Now *that* should have told her something. She had ranted and raved to Julie, complaining that no woman could be expected to wear it all, especially since it was summer and they were almost in Texas, and what about the heat? And why do women allow men to dictate what is proper or not? Julie had just shaken her head as she tried to help Elle with the layers and layers of undergarments. First there was the chemise, then the open-leg drawers of white cotton with tucks, frills and lace that Miss Chatwin had practically cooed over calling broderie anglaise . . . whatever that meant. Then, as if that were not enough for a hot summer evening, why, there was a waist petticoat, a whalebone corset that she refused to tighten and finally, the true affront to the female form—the bustle. Or, as Miss Chatwin preferred to call it, the *tournure*. A polite name for torture.

This contraption consisted of numerous cane hoops and pads that increased in size from the waist to the hem. Looking at herself in the small hotel room mirror, Elle had cried out that she appeared deformed and Julie hadn't understood her reference to the Hunchback of Notre Dame's hump slipping to her behind.

It truly was absurd. Women were wearing padding and steel and bone hoops to bring attention to their derrieres by making them appear larger and more rounded. Back in 1991, women were sweating in gyms and courting asphyxiation in aerobics to trim those same fannies. It made no sense. Men never truly had a definition of the perfect male and were free to be themselves. Women, on the other hand, were constantly being told by others what was currently appealing to the opposite sex. And it always changed. In her own time she could remember her girlfriends laughing about ads to increase one's bust size, because lush curves and fullness were in. Next followed a period when women were told they should look like

189

adolescent boys, with no breasts or hips. Then, just when women reached the point of nearly killing themselves to look like Twiggy, the stupid ground rules changed again: it became vogue to resemble a man, to bulk up and build muscles that would make Arnold Schwarzenegger drool.

What's wrong with us, anyway? she wondered. Why do we continually, throughout the centuries, allow others to define us, and deform us, all in the name of fashion? How long will it take before we are comfortable with our bodies, however God created us?

She breathed a long, drawn-out sigh, knowing that her inner turmoil was caused more by her own frustration than anything else.

"I think you look beautiful, Miss Elle. If only you wouldn't scowl so. My momma used to say your face could stay like that." Julie smiled shyly.

Elle grinned. "I think all mothers use that line. I know mine did." She looked at herself in the mirror and again pushed down on the contraption at her rear. The white silk shot back into place when she removed her hand. "It's just this bustle. It looks so ridiculous."

"Oh, no," Julie quickly added. "Not at all. Didn't you see the fashion books in Miss Chatwin's? She said it was the latest rage. Though I don't think she understood when you laughed."

"Well, I'm not laughing now."

"Oh, please. Truly, you look lovely."

Elle critically examined her reflection. If it wasn't for the bustle, she might have been pleased. She had French-braided the top of her hair and Julie had wound a thin white satin ribbon through it, letting the long ends trail down to her shoulders. She didn't wear any makeup, yet found that her cheeks were flushed from the heat of her

190

bath and the warmth of the evening. Her eyes looked bright despite the lack of eyeliner and mascara.

She had to admit it. She didn't look one bit glamorous. She looked . . . healthy.

"Don't you think we should be going now?" Julie interrupted, nervously smoothing down the skirt of her gown.

Forgetting her own misgivings, Elle smiled. "Are you excited?"

Julie breathed deeply. "Oh, Miss Elle, I'm more scared than anything else. Just look at me, at this dress. I never had anything this fine before. I only went to play parties and square dances at someone's house out on the prairie. And I never actually danced. Not really. Except with somebody else's daddy. Not mine, not ever." Elle could see her chewing at the inside of her lip. "I mostly watched the young ones while everybody else was going four-hands-round and do-si-doing. And I've never been to anything in a town before, let alone a real dance. What if I make a fool out of myself?" She looked ready to cry.

Immediately Elle felt selfish. Here she had been thinking only about herself when this child was filled with teenage insecurity. She put an arm around Julie's slender shoulders.

"Okay, now listen to me. You don't have to worry about making a fool of yourself. For one thing, you're not wearing this damn bustle." Seeing the girl smile, she continued, "Julie, you look beautiful. I was skinny and gawky at your age, yet you seem to have bypassed all that and blossomed into a young woman . . . a lovely young woman. Just remember who you are today. Not who you were. And remember everything you've gone through to get here. You're strong. You're a survivor. Someday all of this isn't going to be anything more than a memory. Let's make it a good one, all right?"

She squeezed her shoulder and planted a small kiss on Julie's temple. "I promise you. There isn't going to be anyone at that dance tonight that's better than you, even if they do live in a town. But you have to believe it, too."

Julie didn't look up right away. When she did, her eyes were filled with tears. "What about tomorrow? About the orphanage? Are you going to leave us?"

A tight knot formed in Elle's stomach. Here was the question, the very subject, that she had been dreading and putting off. How like a child to confront it when the adult hides. Now who was the more grown-up?

She inhaled deeply to steady her voice. "I honestly don't know, Julie. We haven't even seen the place yet. But you know neither Jordan, nor I, would ever place you or Cory anywhere unless it was perfect. I promised you that in the beginning and I won't go back on it." She hugged the girl to her chest. "Try not to think of it tonight, okay? If it isn't acceptable, we'll just keep right on going until we find a place that is."

Julie sniffled. "I don't want to leave you."

Elle's heart nearly broke and she tightened her hold on the child. "I know," she breathed against the blond curls. "I know . . ."

"Oh, I'm so sorry! Please, excuse me!"

If she repeated those words just one more time tonight, Elle swore she was going to scream. Grinding her teeth, she bent down to pick up the three pieces of chicken that had fallen to the ground—or, more precisely, that the damn bustle had knocked to the ground. Holding them in her hand, she wasn't quite sure what to do with the dirt-encrusted food.

"Here, let me."

She looked up at Jordan and sighed before handing over the ruined chicken. "I'm sorry; I'm so awkward." She almost choked on her words. Dear God, she was all elbows and knees, as clumsy as an adolescent. First the flowers in the hotel room. Then when they had met in the small lobby, and she had seen that Jordan had shaved off his beard, she was so startled that she'd actually backed up into a small bowl of goldfish and knocked it over. Never would she forget the sight of those tiny, hopping fish and Jordan, Cory and Kyle joining all the others as they scrambled to catch the quick flash of fins and bright orange scales. Just to complete the picture of simpleton, once they had arrived at the outdoor party, her rear end had collided with more objects than a bumper car at Coney Island. It was humiliating. She had even tried to sit down, feeling that if she stayed put she couldn't harm anyone. But that, too, had proved to be a fiasco. She had nearly crippled herself by sitting down incorrectly when a steel rod from the damned bustle had practically sliced her tailbone in two. She never wanted to remember her howl of pain, or how she had shot out of the chair and into Jordan's arms.

She was right in thinking this night was turning into a disaster, she thought miserably while watching Jordan hand over the chicken to a woman behind the table. The young lady almost gushed as she took the mess from his hands.

That was another thing.

Was there a woman in this town that did not intend to flirt with Jordan McCabe? Good God, you would think

193

they hadn't seen an attractive man in years. It didn't help that he had enhanced his image by becoming a hero this afternoon. Oh, he'd tried to play it down. She would give him that. But, really . . .

Just how many women did he intend to encourage? Okay, so she couldn't actually see him encouraging them, but come on . . . women just didn't act like this without invitation. He was just sly. Or maybe they were desperate, or bored, or—damn it. Why did he have to look so handsome in his suit? A real suit! Well, it was almost a suit. The dark gray jacket over new denim jeans looked better on him than a Bill Blass. The crisp white shirt only highlighted his tanned face and blue eyes. And that thing he wore at his neck? She had the irrational urge to pull that chunk of turquoise down those leather strings and unbutton his shirt.

It was crazy. Totally unreal.

It was also wonderful.

She hadn't felt this attracted to a man in a very long time.

"Oh, Mr. McCabe, I just had to tell you how much I admired your riding this afternoon." A pretty young woman batted her eyelashes while flirting with him. They came out of nowhere. All day long, these women in all shapes and sizes have been trying to engage Jordan in conversation. "It was such a heroic thing to do. My heart"—and she touched her chest, just in case Jordan had forgotten where that vital organ was located—"nearly stopped when young Amy ran out into that street."

Elle ground her back teeth together. Didn't everyone think they were married? What was this? Sadie Hawkins Day, or something? Unless Jordan had told them differently, they were a couple, a married couple.

"Thank you," he said to the woman. "Truly, it was nothing."

As the woman argued prettily, Elle mentally mimicked his words *truly, it was nothing*. She felt like a teenager and wanted to say it aloud, but thought better of it. She was supposed to be an adult. Looking out to the dancers, she tapped her foot in time to the music. Julie and Kyle were standing together off to one side of the musicians. To anyone else they merely looked like they were enjoying each other's company. Elle knew better. Julie was falling in love with the young cowboy, and by all appearances, that feeling was amply returned. She could see it in the teenagers' expressions. For a brief moment, she wondered if she should do something about it. After all, Julie was only fourteen and Kyle merely two years older. Then she thought better of it. Let Julie have this night. The girl deserved it, and more. Who knew what tomorrow would bring for any of them . . . especially Julie and Cory.

"Are you sure you don't want to dance?" he asked again as another reel was announced.

She shook her head, while watching Julie and Kyle take their place along with the other dancers. Julie had no need to worry about her dancing ability, Elle thought. She hadn't sat out once. No sooner had they arrived when Kyle whisked Julie off to the dancing area. Elle smiled. She was glad it had turned out so well for Julie. Now, if only the same could be said for her brother.

Elle glanced over to the area set aside for the younger children. Cory was sitting on a bale of hay, appearing content to pet Noah and look over the festivities. He didn't talk to those around him and—

"Is something wrong? You aren't upset about any-

195

thing, are you?"

Elle blinked, as if she hadn't noticed all the attention women were showering on Jordan. "Oh, is your friend gone?" she asked while looking around her.

"Yes, she's gone. And I wouldn't exactly call her my friend."

Elle smiled brilliantly. "This is such a friendly town, isn't it?" She couldn't keep the sarcasm out of her voice.

Jordan scowled. "Are you sure you don't want to dance?" he asked for the third time. "You seem . . . I don't know, out of sorts."

"Out of sorts? I guess you could say that. I'm so clumsy tonight I think I'm safer just standing here. Thank you for asking, though." She gazed into the faces of several women who were eying Jordan. "But don't let me stop you from enjoying yourself," she said casually, as if the thought of him dancing with another didn't create a sick feeling in her middle.

"No, that's all right," he murmured, bringing the glass of beer up to his mouth. A light frothing of foam stayed on his mustache and he wiped it away with the back of his hand. "I just thought you might want to."

Now that the beard was gone, his chin looked lighter than the rest of his face. She wanted, God, for just a moment, she wanted to run her finger over the slight cleft in his chin, to feel the texture of his skin . . .

"With all the excitement back at the hotel, I don't think I ever told you how pretty you look." He smiled at her and Elle felt her stomach muscles tighten in response.

Chills ran up and down the backs of her arms, making her shiver even though the night was warm. No one had ever called her pretty. She had been called lovely, striking, even beautiful by a slightly drunk stockbroker. But never pretty. Pretty was something that had been denied to her as a teenager. When it appeared that everyone else had steady boyfriends and dates to proms, Elle remembered the pain of lonely, solitary weekends. But now . . . someone was looking at her and making her feel like she was eighteen again.

And pretty.

God, please don't let this happen to me. Not now . . . I can't afford to be hurt again. Someone always gets hurt in these things and it can't be me. She had to think of the children, of finding them a home. And then she would be taken back to her own time. If there was a man in her future, he certainly wasn't an ex-Confederate soldier making his way back home to Texas with a herd of cattle. He wouldn't have eyes the color of the evening sky, nor hair, thick and slicked back, just waiting for a woman to run her fingers through . . .

"And now," she vaguely heard a loud voice announce as if from far away, "I believe we would all be honored to have Mr. Jordan McCabe and his lovely wife lead us off in our first waltz of the evening. Besides, once he does, a few of us bachelors can then claim a dance." There was a round of applause as people seemed to converge around them.

Startled, Elle looked up into Jordan's face and saw his embarrassed smile. "I swear I didn't know anything about this."

His arm slid around her waist and she almost jumped at the touch. She had a moment of near panic, certain that he was too tall for her, sure it would be a clumsy, ungraceful match.

But she was wrong. Oh, God, was she wrong . . .

197

They fit together perfectly. Tall and short. Hard muscles and soft femininity. Somehow, it felt natural and right, almost as if she belonged there.

I will not be hurt she silently repeated, nearly mesmerized by the fluid, swaying motion, the graceful melody, the feel of his arm around her, steady and firm, yet gentle. *Protect yourself, Elle.* The warning echoed in her brain.

She wanted to ignore it. How long had it been since she was with a man? How long since she was able to enjoy the touch of a man's hand as it held her waist? The texture of hard muscles under her fingers? The clean scent of a man . . . what was that? Vanilla? She deeply inhaled as Jordan spun her in time to the romantic music. And it was romantic, despite the fact that the waltz was being played by four men with guitars and fiddles. To her ears the fiddles sounded like Stradivarius violins. Soon others joined them, but she hardly noticed. She kept staring at Jordan, not quite sure what was happening.

Be careful, Elle, the voice inside her repeated. Enjoy him, but you must protect yourself. The survivor in her rose to the surface and she thought, *If anything happens between us, it will have to be him that gets hurt.* She wouldn't allow anything else. And, yet, she didn't want him disillusioned either. She didn't know what she wanted . . . except at that moment she wanted to stay in his arms.

"You dance very well," he complimented her, swinging her in a wide circle.

"So do you," she heard herself answering. With great resolve Elle concentrated on him. She turned off her conscience, tired of its nagging, for she was really enjoying herself. She actually liked waltzing. It was an old-fashioned dance, full of grace and romance. Unlike modern slow dancing, in the waltz one was forced to look at their partner's face. And the face told so much about a person. Like Jordan . . .

He was staring at her, his blue eyes almost flashing with good humor. Tiny wrinkles fanned out from their edges, making him appear happy and carefree. It was a new side to Jordan McCabe. An admittedly attractive side.

"All those lessons my mother insisted I take." He shook his head good-naturedly. "Somehow, I never thought I'd be using them on the Oklahoma frontier."

She knew exactly what he meant. "Is your mother in Texas?" she asked, glad that he was in such a good mood.

"My mother died during the war," he said quietly.

"Oh . . ." Elle wrinkled her brow. The war? The Civil War? "I'm sorry." She wished she had never asked and was at a loss as to how to resume their carefree discussion.

"Did I tell you that Traver and the herd came through Alexander three days ago?" He, too, appeared to be searching for an alternative topic.

"Hey, that's great," she said brightly, a little too brightly. She stumbled and Jordan righted her.

"You okay?"

She nodded and smiled at the hotel owner who was steering an elderly woman in circles. Somehow she didn't think he forgot about their dance. "I'm not usually this clumsy," she said to Jordan as they danced past the man. "It's this damn bustle."

He grinned, making the cleft in his chin deeper. "I think it's delightful."

She grunted. "Delightful? You only think so because

you don't have to wear it. It's ridiculous, and damned uncomfortable—"

"You have a charming way of speaking."

She ignored his remark. "At least I'm honest. I don't go around pretending that this contraption isn't a male invention of torture."

He threw back his head and laughed. Right out loud. And then swung her even more into the swaying, graceful movement of the waltz.

She felt dizzy and it wasn't just from the dancing. It was that male/female thing happening between them. She'd gone through it enough in the past to recognize it now. The attraction was real, and it wasn't just one-sided.

I won't be the one . . ., she told herself. *I can't . . .*

He held her more tightly and she almost groaned. Dear God, had it really been more than nine months since a man's arms were around her? Almost a year of being alone. She was so tired of being lonely. It didn't matter what Jordan was offering; she probably wouldn't be here too much longer anyway.

What would it hurt? Did she always have to do the right thing? Always think of the consequences? Why couldn't she just enjoy the moment and let whatever was going to happen, happen?

The dance ended all too soon for her and she was pleased to notice that Jordan also looked disappointed.

"Thank you, Elizabeth. I enjoyed that." Looking into her eyes, he smiled. When they had walked back to the tables, he handed her a glass of cider and then did the most astonishing thing.

He reached out and lightly untangled the ribbon from her hair. His finger brushed her shoulder and Elle inhaled at his touch. It was so gentle it made her skin tingle. He allowed his finger to brush over her collarbone and then cupped her chin in his palm. "You're the most mysterious woman I have ever known. Who *are* you, Elizabeth Mackenzie?"

Her breathing was actually labored. She was so nervous that her voice cracked, yet there was nothing she could do about it. "I . . . I told you. I come from the future. From nineteen—"

His finger on her lips stopped her words. "Please. Just for tonight. Don't . . ."

She almost kissed his finger, but stopped herself just in time. Instead, she raised her chin so his finger slipped down. She smiled, deep and seductive. "Just for tonight," she repeated his words, "I can be anyone you want."

She knew her gaze was as provocative as her words, yet she couldn't stop. And, in truth, she didn't want to, for when she spoke again it was in an urgent whisper. "Who would you like me to be, Jordan?"

He groaned as he pulled her into his arms. Strong, secure arms, that seemed to almost hunger for her. He leaned down, his mouth mere inches away from hers. She could smell the beer and the vanilla and the cigar he'd had earlier. He was all male as he breathed the words right back into her mouth.

"Just be you, Elizabeth. That's more than enough."

And then he did it. Right there in front of the mayor and the hotel owner and Cory and Julie and Kyle and every one of those women who had been flirting with him all evening.

He kissed her.

*   *   *

201

She would never sleep. She'd been listening to Jordan and Kyle on the other side of the blanket wall that separated the beds. It just wouldn't happen. Julie, filled with homecooking and dreams of Kyle Reavis, was sound asleep next to her. But sleep eluded Elle like a nighttime fugitive.

She could still feel his kiss, the hunger of his mouth as it tasted her—first tentatively, gently, then with a longing that took her breath away. She knew, should she ever try to explain, that it would sound stupid, but her legs had grown weak. They had felt like they were made out of pudding and she had clung to his arms for more than support. She must have looked like a wanton. But it had been so long. And no one, not ever, had kissed her like that. There were no games. Just male and female. And a wanting, a craving, that shattered her composure. She didn't know how she would ever be able to look at him in the same way again.

Thank God for the blanket that hung between them.

Everyone had said good night over a half hour ago and was settled in bed. It had been a full day, filled with excitement, and no one appreciated that more than Elle. She strained to hear him breathe. Could he possibly have fallen asleep that quickly? Wasn't he over on the other side of that wool thinking about her? About their kiss? The applause of the townsfolk that had followed? Wasn't he picturing in his mind the way they had danced again, and again? How they had both been breathless with the exertion and yet eager to do it again so they could once more touch and be in each other's arms?

Can the male so easily turn off his mind while the female plays it over and over, like an old record, reliving each moment?

Well, by the sounds emanating from the opposite side of the room, it was evident that all three males were asleep. Elle brought her fingers up to her lips and lightly touched them. That kiss . . . it had done something inside of her that was frightening. It had brought up possibilities, dreams, fantasies about a future—

Don't do it, Elle. You can't be the one to get hurt. It can't be you this time. Protect yourself, your heart . . .

When she finally fell asleep, she was repeating those thoughts, like a mantra. It was her only salvation.

Morning came with a cool breeze that made her shiver and curl into the covers for warmth, but it was no use. Her brain had triggered the chilling gooseflesh and Elle groaned before stretching. Upon opening her eyes, she realized that she had to go to the bathroom and that thought brought forth a moan. If there was one thing she truly detested about this misadventure it was the lack of modern facilities. Well, she had two choices. She could either use the chamberpot under the bed, or throw on a robe and tiptoe out of the building to the outhouse.

There really wasn't much of a choice.

Shivering, she wrapped Cynthia's robe around her and slipped her feet into her shoes. She did tiptoe in order not to wake anyone up and was doing well until she passed the men's bed. She was almost to the door. She didn't have to look. And it would have saved her so much if she hadn't. But she was female, and curiosity was, unfortunately, part of the feminine gene pool.

There he was. Asleep. With a muscled arm around Cory's waist, cradling the child against him. She saw Cory's little hand clutching Jordan's thumb, as if for

203

reassurance that the adult was still there. She saw his shining blond curls mixed with the dark masculine hair on Jordan's chest, and something broke inside of her. Something hard and protective shattered at the sight of the grown man and the child—together, as if they belonged to each other.

Her body started to shake and she knew it wasn't from the morning chill. And then she knew . . . it was as if she heard it break away inside of her and a sudden heat permeated her body, making her warm and frightened at the same time. She wanted him, this man who could be both commanding and tender, stern yet funny, responsible, and yet sexy.

It was happening . . . the thing that she had feared. As she hugged herself, the tears streamed down her cheeks and fell onto her chest.

Finally she could no longer deny it. She heard it in her brain, felt it in her heart.

Oh, God . . . it's me. It's me. I'm the one who's going to be hurt.

Chapter 13

Was it possible? Did she love him? *Love* him? A cowboy from the nineteenth century? C'mon, Elle, she chided herself. Why, you're what is known in this time as a spinster. Unmarried. Unloved. Very soon to be on the down side of thirty.

She mentally shook herself back to reality. Blinking, Elle looked at the scene before her. Was it possible, she wondered, that tomorrow was her birthday? Was she really going to turn thirty in 1876? How could it be that this momentous occasion would take place in this insanity? But then . . . maybe it wouldn't count. Maybe she could remain twenty-nine. That was appealing. To be forever young. Well, almost young—

"I think it looks . . . very nice. Don't you?"

Jordan's voice startled her. They were standing in front of a large white Victorian home with an honest-to-God picket fence around it. Swings of long hemp rope and smooth, wooden seats hung from a stately oak tree. They actually swayed in the warm summer breeze, as if happy children had just jumped off. Talk about idyllic! The next thing she expected to see was little munchkins popping up from underneath the clusters of morning glories and verbena and pointing them in the direction of the yellow brick road.

"Hmm . . ." Elle reserved comment as she stood before Miss Avoula Turner's Guardianship. She gazed up to the scarlet gingerbread trim and sighed. In spite of the cheerful and inviting picture, she was disheartened. She didn't care that the birds were singing in the morning sunlight; it had to be too good to be true. As she and Jordan led the children up the brick walkway, Elle experienced another feeling of dread. She was counting, truly counting, on finding some fault with the woman, or at least the place—some reasonable excuse to whisk Cory and Julie away with her to the next town.

Squeezing Julie's hand, Elle glanced at Jordan as he knocked on the large wooden door. He, too, seemed distracted and nervous. Was he as suspicious as she of this perfect setup? Somewhere, lurking behind this promising exterior, might be a character right out of Dickens—a stern taskmaster who would beat and berate and extinguish the light inside each child. It had to be.

But it wasn't . . .

Avoula Turner was the picture of a perfect grandmother, so much so that Elle figured even Barbara Bush would come in a poor second. Tall, round, and apple-cheeked, Miss Turner opened the front door and immediately knelt down in front of Cory. Elle could see that her eyes sparkled with friendliness and her smile was filled with warmth.

"Ahh . . . now, I've been expecting you," she said to the child. She slowly looked up to the rest of them and grinned. "I'm afraid everyone in Alexander has had something to say about you, Mr. McCabe. I don't suppose a hero gets too much privacy."

Visibly embarrassed, Jordan removed his hat. "It's a pleasure to meet you, ma'am. Though I'm no hero," he added. "I keep telling everyone I didn't—"

Rising, Miss Turner held up her hand to interrupt. "I commend your modesty, but I wouldn't be surprised if by next year's Founders' Day you'd become a legend. I shouldn't have to tell you, Mr. McCabe, how quickly a tale like this will spread."

She looked at Elle and grinned. "It's one of the endearing qualities of the West . . . everything is exaggerated. No one just stops a wagon, you understand? The runaway team was spooked by a cougar the size of a bear, who first was spooked by the Indians that drove it out of the hills. In the end the hero in the tale had to fight both man and beast to save the day. Never mind that there aren't any cougars in this part of Oklahoma. The Indians have calmed down considerably and I haven't seen any appreciable hills since I left Ohio."

As if just realizing how she had been chattering, Miss Turner brought a lace-edged handkerchief to her mouth and pressed it against her lips. She clutched it tightly in her blue-veined hand and shook her head. "Oh, my! I do go on sometimes. Please, forgive me. It's my addiction, if you will, to Penny Dreadfuls. I've just finished the new Fess Tyson. *Passion's Price.* I think it's his best yet. Or should I say her? Rumor has it that he's really a she."

She looked at Elle, as if Elle should have recognized the name of the author. Feeling somehow illiterate, Elle nodded stupidly as the woman continued speaking.

"Forgive me for getting carried away, talking about my books, but that isn't why you're all visiting me this morning, is it?" she added quietly. Her smile included Julie and Cory.

Somehow, maybe through town gossip, Miss Turner knew why they had shown up on her doorstep. Everyone knew. Even the children. But no one wanted to say it. It was a tense moment as Elle looked at Jordan, for it was clear neither of them wanted to speak. Finally, Jordan shook his head.

"No, it isn't, Miss Turner. Unfortunately, our reason for being here is a bit more serious." He glanced at Cory and hesitated for just a moment. "The children need a home." His voice sounded rough and Elle quickly took over.

"Miss Turner. This is Cory and Julie Woodson. Their parents have . . ." her voice trailed off, hoping she wasn't going to have to fill in the details right away.

Tucking the handkerchief into her waistband, Miss Turner nodded sympathetically. She held out her hand to Julie and smiled. "I'm glad to meet you," she said in a friendly voice and then lightly touched Cory's cheek. "And this young man, too. I saw you both at the dance last night. What was that creature I saw making itself at home in your jacket pocket? A mouse?"

She waited for Cory to answer and in the silence that followed glanced up at Elle.

"Noah," Elle said. She smiled. "It's Cory's pet. He's really no problem," she added, as if she could bear to part with Cory, or Julie, or Noah for that matter. What the hell were they doing here, anyway? Did she really think she could walk away from them and leave them here? This place had to be too good to be true. What were the odds, that out in the middle of nowhere, they would find the ideal solution to their problem? An orphanage? In a

208

border town between Oklahoma and Texas?

"Please, come in," Miss Turner invited and waved them into her house.

Elle told herself that she was only going along with this to be polite. Sure Miss Turner appeared perfect, and Elle wasn't ready to voice her misgivings aloud, but she couldn't believe the time had come to make a decision about leaving the children. It was too soon, too—

"Wow . . ." Julie's exclamation interrupted her thoughts and for the first time Elle really paid attention to her surroundings.

The five of them were standing in the foyer looking into the most unusual room Elle had ever seen. It really was like going back in time . . .

The hardwood floors shone in the morning sunlight that came in through the long paned windows. Everything smelled of fresh air and beeswax. Sitting on marble-topped tables were glass domes with pink wax roses, albums, stuffed birds and figurines. Peacock feathers were anchored behind a wall picture of an elderly gentleman who looked down on the sitting room with a benign smile. A paisley scarf with pale green tassels and fringe was draped over a piano, and numerous daguerreotypes and tin prints of children were scattered about. Lightweight rice rugs for summer lay under the velvet-cut damask furniture. The high ceiling was plastered with a center medallion of ornately pressed tin. It was too busy for Elle's taste, but she knew it was quite a showplace for this period of time.

"How lovely." She couldn't help expressing her admiration.

"It's beautiful," Julie breathed in awe.

Miss Turner stopped and looked over the room, as if

she hadn't seen it in a long time. "Thank you. I brought almost everything with me from Ohio. It wasn't easy, as I'm sure you know, Mr. McCabe." She looked at the portrait on the far wall and smiled. "Several times, my Arthur was ready to leave me and my treasures on the plains. But he persevered, God bless his soul. I'm only sorry he didn't live long enough to see this house filled with children."

She took a deep breath, as though to wipe out the sad memory and motioned to the back of the house. "And speaking of children—there are a few in the kitchen that I'm sure would love to meet Cory and Julie. Perhaps you and your wife would join me for some coffee, Mr. McCabe?"

Jordan quickly glanced at Elle and then nodded to Miss Turner. "Thank you, ma'am." Elle noticed that Jordan didn't correct the woman. He was allowing her to think they were married.

Miss Turner led them down a narrow hallway and into a bright, sunny kitchen, and it was then that Elle first knew she was defeated.

Eight children ranging in age from around three to Julie's age were working in the kitchen. They appeared to be cleaning up after breakfast—washing and drying dishes, sweeping the planked floor. When they noticed the visitors, they all stopped what they were doing and stared, obviously very curious. Five young girls were dressed alike in dark blue jumpers and crisp, white pinafores. Their hair was parted in the middle and braided into long plaits that hung below their shoulders. The boys, the smallest younger than Cory, wore white shirts and dark trousers. The older ones had suspenders, as if that marked them as mature. To Elle, they looked like uniformed students in a private school.

Just as she was thinking they were probably too scared to move, that Miss Turner had them terrorized, a chubby, red-haired boy announced, "I don't care, Miss Turner, I'm not giving up my bed again."

The other children looked shocked and then laughed nervously as Avoula Turner brushed past her visitors and came into the kitchen. She went up to the child and tousled his hair in a show of affection. "Nobody even asked you, Peter Burnham, so I'd be minding that smart tongue of yours, if I were you."

She grinned at the others. "This is Mr. and Mrs. Jordan McCabe and their friends . . . and our new friends, Cory and Julie Woodson."

The children eyed each other, the girls definitely more open in their inspection than the boys. Since Cory barely glanced at any of them, it was Julie who asked the first question.

"Do . . ." she swallowed a few times before she could continue. "Do they all live here?" she asked shyly.

Miss Turner nodded. "They share rooms. The boys have their own and so do the girls. Although it could get to be too crowded and the older girls might have to start a new room soon. That's something we'll have to talk about."

Nodding, Julie clasped her hands in front of her and looked down to the floor.

"Would you like to know anything, Cory?"

There was a moment of awkward silence as Miss Turner glanced questioningly from the boy, who stared straight ahead, then to Elle. Elle shook her head, indicating the child didn't speak. Smiling sadly and with understanding, Miss Turner took a deep breath and

211

smoothly announced, "Well, while you children finish your chores, I promised Mr. and Mrs. McCabe a cup of coffee. Do you think Julie and Cory would like to help us make the ice cream later?"

She turned to Elle and Jordan. "Every Saturday we reward ourselves. Sometimes our arms get so tired from churning, but we take turns and it's always worth it."

"I haven't had ice cream since before the war," Jordan said wistfully, to no one in particular.

"Then that settles it," Miss Turner proclaimed. "All of you must spend the day with us. We'll all get to know each other a little better and Mr. McCabe will have a long-deserved treat." She turned to the children. "Won't that be nice?" she asked. "Look at all the extra arms. We might be savoring the ice cream before dinner."

She had never experienced anything like it before.

It was hard to describe. The texture, creaminess and taste were definitely different from Good Humor. Even the mighty Häagen-Dazs would kill for Miss Avoula Turner's secret ice cream recipe. Maybe it was the absence of stabilizers and preservatives. And then again it could be those hours of hand churning that made the anticipation even sweeter and more rich than any modern delicacy.

Elle closed her eyes for just a moment to appreciate the taste. It was wonderful . . . just like everything about Miss Turner and her Guardianship, and that thought made Elle open her eyes and look beyond the porch to the scene being played out in front of her.

Julie and Lillian, the oldest of the girls at the orphanage, were sitting on the swings and talking, while slowly eating their ice cream. Peter and Joshua and Martin had almost inhaled their serving and were now kneeling in the dirt, playing marbles, while Cory sat off to the side, watching. Milly, the youngest, was curling up on Miss Turner's lap for a nap; her head already nodding toward the woman's ample chest. The other girls sat with their dolls under the oak tree in an age-old feminine ritual. It was peaceful and easy . . . the kind of life she would have loved herself.

It was also time to admit it.

She would never find a better place for Julie and Cory.

Although he was seated next to her on the porch, Elle avoided looking at Jordan. She knew he was waiting for her to make the decision. Yet how could she do it? How could she leave the children?

"What about education?" Elle asked in a last-ditch effort to find some excuse. "I know you teach school here in Alexander, but what if one of them is really talented? How would they further their education?"

"Are you talking about going on to a university?" Miss Turner asked in a whisper as she gently stroked the sleeping child's hair.

Elle nodded.

"Well, I'm not a wealthy woman, you understand, but I do have a few connections back in Ohio. Joshua is a talented artist." The old woman looked out to her children and sighed deeply. "Of course there's not a large calling for an artist out here. But if Joshua could earn a scholarship, then I would do anything in my power to help him . . . or any of them. Every once in a while, we receive a donation from a benefactor that's heard of us from one source or another. And we make do in between times."

213

Jordan cleared his throat. "If we did leave Cory and Julie, I would like to provide for them on a yearly basis as long as I'm able."

Miss Turner smiled. "I would be most grateful, sir, for any help."

"We're the ones that would be grateful, Miss Turner," he answered. "You're doing a fine thing here."

There was a prolonged moment of silence until Jordan added jokingly, "And you make better ice cream than Aunt Celia. I didn't think it was possible."

Miss Turner laughed softly. "Where are you from, Mr. McCabe? Originally?"

"Georgia, ma'am."

"I could detect something of the southern gentleman in you, sir, beyond the Texas rancher. I would imagine leading a cattle drive clear through three states is far different than the life you left behind in Georgia."

Jordan looked out beyond the children to the horizon. "There was nothing left for me, ma'am, to miss. I've made a new home in Texas and it suits me fine."

Miss Turner nodded. "I'm sure it does, Mr. McCabe. Now, if you'd assist me in rising, I think I should put Milly down for her nap."

Jordan immediately stood up and helped the woman to her feet. She refused his offer to carry the child and told them she would return in a few minutes. Elle waited until Miss Turner had gone back into the house before speaking.

"What were you doing?" she demanded.

He sat down in his chair and stared at her. "What? What's wrong?"

"*I'm* the one that's supposed to make the decision—"

"I know," he shot back. "But you're interrogating her,

Elizabeth. Maybe you forget that she would be doing us a favor by taking Julie and Cory. This place is great. The children would receive everything you've been worried about, and more. You act like we'd be doing her a favor if we left them."

Elle felt a burning behind her eyes and she dug her fingernails into her palm to stop the tears from coming. "We *would* be doing her a favor," she said in a thick voice. "They're terrific kids."

Jordan looked out to the boys and their game of marbles. "I know," he admitted.

"Well, I don't know if I can do it," Elle muttered. "She would see them grow up—all those things that parents do. All those things I'll never do . . ."

He turned to her and she bit her bottom lip to keep it from trembling.

"Elizabeth. We have to make a decision. Look, I know it's supposed to be up to you, but I think I deserve a say in this too."

Elle couldn't speak. She was so afraid of what he was going to say, and she knew she wouldn't have any arguments, any rebuttal, for the answer was clear. She was just frightened because it meant everything was going to change.

And she wasn't sure any more of what she wanted.

"All right," she finally said. "What is it you have to say?"

He took a deep breath and said it. "I think they should stay. Look," he hurried to explain, "neither one of us can offer them a stable environment and children need stability. Miss Turner can do that. You have to admit, you're never going to find a better place for them. Once we leave here, we're into Texas and there's not another

215

town that even comes close to this for more than a hundred miles. And certainly not one with an orphanage. The thing is, Elizabeth, you have to do this for Cory and Julie. And not for you."

There it was. The truth. Plain and simple and painful.

She looked down to the empty fluted bowl in her hands. A fat tear slid down her cheek and she nodded. "You're right," she whispered and stopped speaking when her voice cracked with emotion.

He reached out and squeezed her hand. "I know it's not going to be easy, but I can't think of one reason for them not to stay. Can you?"

I love them, she wanted to scream. The same as I love you. But she couldn't say that. Instead, she shook her head. She had made her pact with God. She'd done her job and found the right home for the children. Her task was nearly complete. And then she would be taken from this time, from the children. And from Jordan.

Why didn't that make her happy? Wasn't that what she wanted?

She certainly didn't want this cowboy and his herd of animals. She wanted that faceless man of her dreams in a three-piece suit and BMW, and a house in the suburbs. Isn't that what every woman wanted? Isn't it?

Somehow, none of that mattered to Elle any longer. She'd already made her peace with life and her past mistakes. Marriage was out. Children were out. All she'd had was her career, and her success.

Now, in this time, if she left Cory and Julie, she would have nothing.

"Elizabeth?" He said her name softly, gently.

She looked at him then. How could she have ever thought he looked like Mel Gibson? His face was more weathered, more mature. Whatever his life had been like up until now, it hadn't been easy. He had the look of a survivor and at times she had caught a haunted expression on his face, almost as if he carried his own ghosts along with him. But he was a good man. That much she did know. He didn't have to cart her and kids across two states until they found this place. But he'd done it without too much complaining. And she knew it would cost him something to leave Cory. As much as he wanted the world to see the toughened cowboy, Jordan Dillon McCabe had allowed that small child into his heart. It wasn't going to be easy for either of them.

What would she do once the children were gone? There would be no reason to stay with him. If she wasn't taken back to her own time, she would be all alone.

The thought terrified her.

He repeated her name. "Elizabeth?"

She swallowed down the lump in her throat and nodded. "All right," she finally said. "Let's tell them and be done with it."

Even though her heart was broken, she knew she didn't have any other choice.

Okay, I'm doing it. Now you'd better give me the right words to say to them. You'd better make this right, or so help me I'll . . . She stopped and sniffled. What could you say to threaten God? *Well, you'd just better do it. That's all.*

"Oh, Miss Elle, don't go!" Julie threw her arms around Elizabeth, and Jordan watched as they hugged each other. He didn't know who looked more distraught—the woman or the child.

In truth, he was probably just as upset as both. He'd

foolishly allowed himself to become attached to them—this woman who had deceived him and shamed him in front of his men and countered just about every order he gave. And the children—Julie, standing on the brink of womanhood, sweet, shy, and obviously thinking herself in love with young Kyle. She would probably recover . . . but Cory? A tight knot formed in his chest when he looked at the boy.

How in the world could he leave Cory?

Kneeling down in front of him, Jordan placed his hand on the small shoulder. "You understand, don't you?" he asked the child. Not expecting an answer, Jordan continued, "If there was any other way, we wouldn't do this. But this is a fine place. You can see that. There's boys here for you to play with and Miss Turner will see that you go to school with them, so it won't be all that scary for you. You'll make friends and pretty soon you'll forget all about us—"

"Well, I'll never forget," Julie protested. "Nobody can make us stay."

Elizabeth hugged the girl more tightly to her chest. "Stop it, Julie. We're all upset." She placed a soft kiss on her cheek and brushed back a wisp of blond hair. "But listen . . . remember how you were frightened of coming into town back in Kansas? Remember when you thought you weren't good enough? Well, now you know you are. You'll live here in town and make friends—"

"But we have you and the Captain, and . . . and Kyle. Why can't we just go on the way we were?" she demanded between sobs.

Elizabeth pulled back from her so she could see the girl's face. "Look at me, Julie. I don't know where I'm going to be tomorrow, let alone next week, or the week after that. You and Cory need a home. I can't give that to you. I don't have one myself." She looked around to the empty yard. "Have you ever seen anything better than this? I would have loved to grow up in a place like this. You'll be protected here. It's hard now, I know. It's hard for all of us, but I promise you, you'll do fine. And we'll write. Won't we, Jordan?"

He nodded; his throat was too raw to speak.

"You see," she continued, though he could hear her voice breaking, "we'll keep in touch and if the situation ever changes, one of us will be here. Okay?"

Julie couldn't answer. She hugged her thin waist and stared out beyond the yard. Elizabeth reached down and picked up Cory. She wrapped her arms around the child and held him to her chest.

"What do I say to you?" she whispered into his hair.

When he saw the tears streaming down her cheeks, Jordan had to turn away. He couldn't look at her heartbreak, for it mirrored his own. He tried not to hear her as she poured out her love for the child, wanting Cory to remember them, to be a good boy, and how she knew he would grow into a fine man.

It was too painful to watch and yet he knew the time had come. For everyone's sake, they must leave.

He hugged Julie, like an older brother, or even a father. God, he hadn't expected it to be this hard. "I'll send Kyle with your things, so you can say goodbye. All right? Miss Turner knows how to reach me if anything goes wrong, but I know it won't. You'll be okay, Julie. When you stop hurting, when you get used to things here, you'll admit it was the only thing to do."

He placed a kiss on her damp forehead and waited for Elizabeth to hand over Cory.

He could do it. He told himself, he'd been through worse in battle. This was simple. There were no open wounds or gore, or hopelessness. This was only pain of the heart. Surely, this had to be easier . . . yet when the child's body was next to his, he almost lost it. He felt his arms tighten around the small rib cage and had to stop himself from hurting the child in his embrace. There were no words he could say. And, anyway, he and Cory hadn't needed words. Somehow they had known what the other was thinking. Cory would know now that he would miss him. That he . . . that he cared about him . . . loved him.

Cory would know. He would feel it, just as Jordan could feel the child's tiny hands tightening at his neck.

"*Jordan?*"

Elizabeth's voice was uncertain as she called out his name. When she whispered, "Look at him . . . Jordan, look!" he pulled away from Cory and stared at the child.

Huge, fat tears rolled down his freckled cheeks. His tiny chin was quivering with uncertainty and his eyes . . . his eyes held a mixture of recognition and despair.

"Jordan, this is the first reaction he's had since Kansas. Look, he's crying . . ." Elizabeth had to wipe away her own tears to speak.

"Because we're leaving," Jordan finished, and glanced up to the porch where Miss Turner waited.

It only took a moment for such a monumental decision. He turned to Elizabeth and said, "I can't do it. I know this is the perfect place, but is it the right one? What would happen if we leave him now?"

Elizabeth was nodding a little wildly. "I know. I know," she chanted. He could see she was biting her

220

bottom lip to keep from grinning. "He could completely close himself off, become a zombie."

"A what?"

She shook her head. "It doesn't matter," she cried happily and hugged Julie. As all four embraced, Elizabeth shouted over their heads, "I'm sorry, Miss Turner, but we're about to follow the yellow brick road . . ."

Everyone looked at her for an explanation, but she only threw back her head and laughed. Jordan caught his breath as he stared at her. Her face was flushed with emotion, her amber eyes sparkled with happiness. She was beautiful, but she was so much more than that. It went beyond the physical. He was drawn to something else inside of her. She possessed a gift for life, for living, that he had thought no one any longer retained after the war. It was as if she had never experienced that horror. Life for her was so simple, so easy. Elizabeth Mackenzie was the most extraordinary woman he had ever known.

And it was then, watching her giggle with the children, that Jordan first felt he might be falling in love.

Chapter 14

Texas. The name conjured up images of every cowboy movie she had ever seen. But this, this particular morning, was different. In sharp contrast to the plains with its blistering heat, ungratified thirst, the hunger and physical exhaustion; the crude wooden crosses that marked the resting place of those who never completed their journey . . . there was another side to this wild and beautiful land. And on the morning of her thirtieth birthday, Elizabeth Mackenzie held her breath in awe as she watched the sun rise over the horizon.

The prairie was covered with lush grass and dotted with larkspur, asters, goldenrod and geraniums. She knew they would soon pass out of this exquisite valley into the more arid part of the state, yet for the moment, she considered this her gift from God. Her own personal, living and breathing, birthday card. She grinned as she watched a mockingbird fly overhead and perch on the branch of a flowering bush.

It was almost paradise.

Quietly, Elle realized she had rarely appreciated

nature before. She had, in truth, taken it for granted. She'd been too busy trying to "make it"—whatever the current standing of making it was. And she'd missed this. For thirty years she had never really stopped, and looked.

The quiet brilliance demanded a response.

Okay, thanks for today, she silently prayed and glanced to Jordan and the sleeping children. *And thanks for them, too. I don't know. Miss Turner's just wasn't the right place. If it was, you wouldn't have let Jordan change his mind, would you?* She didn't expect an answer, or even the bird to move as a sign, so she just continued, *So . . . I guess you aren't about to take me back to my own time just yet, huh? Not until I fulfill my part of the bargain. If that's so, then why am I always thinking about my mother? If you're not taking me back, then why do I feel like she's in trouble? That she needs me?*

Elle deeply inhaled the sweet morning air and closed her eyes. Again, the picture of her mother's face haunted her. She didn't even need the mirror any longer. Now she would see Margaret Mackenzie's tortured image at will. The graying hair. The lined face. The sad eyes of a defeated woman. Had they ever held hope and promise? It was scary and frustrating, for there was nothing she could do to help the one woman she loved.

She shook her head to drive out the frightening thoughts. Today, thirty years ago, in another century, Margie Curran Mackenzie gave birth to her and now she was certain her mother was in trouble. Elle was positive it had something to do with her father. He'd abused her mother for as long as she could remember. Elle was fourteen the first time she reported her father to the police, but he always came back. And her mother took

4 BESTSELLING HISTORICAL ROMANCES BY YOUR FAVORITE AUTHORS CAN BE YOURS, FREE!

Kensington Choice brings you historical romances by your favorite bestselling authors including Janelle Taylor, Shannon Drake, Bertrice Small, Jo Goodman, and Georgina Gentry, just to name a few! Each book is filled with passion, adventure and the excitement of bygone times!

To introduce you to this great club which is part of Zebra Home Subscription Service, we'd like to send you your first 4 bestselling historical romances, absolutely free!   And once you get these 4 free books to savor at home, we'll rush you the next 4 brand-new books at the lowest prices available, as soon as they are published.

The way the club works is that after your initial FREE shipment, you will get our 4 newest bestselling historical romances delivered to your

doorstep each month at the preferred subscriber's rate of only $4.20 per book, a savings of up to $8.16 per month (since these titles sell in bookstores for $4.99-$6.99)! All books are sent on a 10-day free examination basis and there is no minimum number of books to buy. (And no charge for shipping.) Plus as a regular subscriber, you'll receive our FREE monthly newsletter, *Zebra/Pinnacle Romance News*, which features author profiles, subscriber benefits, book previews and more!

We have 4 FREE BOOKS for you as your introduction to KENSINGTON CHOICE! To get your FREE BOOKS, worth up to $24.96, mail the card below.

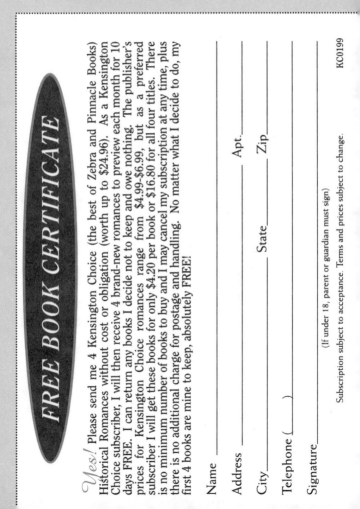

FREE BOOK CERTIFICATE

Yes! Please send me 4 Kensington Choice (the best of Zebra and Pinnacle Books) Historical Romances without cost or obligation (worth up to $24.96). As a Kensington Choice subscriber, I will then receive 4 brand-new romances to preview each month for 10 days FREE. I can return any books I decide not to keep and owe nothing. The publisher's prices for Kensington Choice romances range from $4.99-$6.99, but as a preferred subscriber I will get these books for only $4.20 per book or $16.80 for all four titles. There is no minimum number of books to buy and I may cancel my subscription at any time, plus there is no additional charge for postage and handling. No matter what I decide to do, my first 4 books are mine to keep, absolutely FREE!

Name _____

Address _____ Apt._____

City_____ State_____ Zip_____

Telephone ( ) _____

Signature _____

(If under 18, parent or guardian must sign)

Subscription subject to acceptance. Terms and prices subject to change.

KC0199

him back. It made no sense. What hold did John Mackenzie have over her mother?

"You're awake?"

Shaken out of her daydreams, Elle looked to Jordan and smiled. "Couldn't sleep." She gazed out to the valley and again inhaled. "It's beautiful, isn't it?"

Jordan sat up and ran a hand over his face. He yawned and scratched the new growth of beard on his chin before looking around him. "Sure is a lot prettier than at dusk."

She nodded in quiet agreement. For just a moment they sat in silence. It was glorious, though hushed, as if the world itself had not yet awakened. In those moments, Elle truly felt at peace. It was okay to turn thirty out in the wilderness, for no superficial party with friends could possibly compare with the grandeur that was displayed before her.

She didn't care that her hair was tangled, or that there was sleep in the corners of her eyes. Somehow, it didn't matter that Jordan wasn't seeing her at her best. The moment was special, for she felt like she was discovering a hidden part of herself and shedding the obsolete, those portions that were no longer needed.

She almost felt sorry for the old Elle, the one that had strived so hard for success. Perhaps it was her fear of being poor, like her father. It didn't matter anymore—and that knowledge brought relief, a freedom. For she knew that no matter what happened in her future, she had learned something here in the past.

She looked at Jordan.

She had learned about values.

*   *   *

225

"I'll tell you a secret," Elle said to Julie as they drove out of the valley. It was crazy how well she had learned to handle the horse and wagon. She didn't even mind wearing the huge leather gloves anymore.

"What?" Julie asked eagerly. "Who's it about?" She shielded her face from the sun with her bonnet and grinned. Clearly, the girl loved the idea of gossip.

Flicking the reins over the horse's rump, Elle laughed. "It's about me."

"You?"

She nodded. "Today's my birthday. I'm thirty years old."

"*No . . .*" Julie's voice showed her disbelief.

It made Elle feel even better. "Really, it's true. And I don't care who knows it. A few weeks ago I wouldn't have admitted that to anyone. Now, I'm proud of it."

She took a deep breath. "I'm thirty years old, and I'm here." She looked around the countryside. "Wherever here is."

Julie impulsively reached over and hugged her. "Why, you're with us, Miss Elle. Just where you should be."

As impossible as it seemed, Elle's grin widened. God, it was going to be a great day.

By mid-afternoon, her arms were aching from guiding the horse. She attempted to keep up her cheerful mood, even though she was tired. But it wasn't easy. In Alexander, Jordan had bought her a hat. He and Julie had pointed out the wide straw bonnets, but she had firmly shaken her head. She had remembered the intense heat and had picked up an expansive ten-gallon cowboy hat, one that John Wayne would have been proud to wear. It shaded her face, even her shoulders, but her arms were still exposed to the punishing rays of the sun. She was exhausted; her mind nearly brain-dead from the endless routine. No one was even bothering to talk anymore. So when she saw the silhouette of a man and horse on the horizon, she sat up and paid attention. She was about to call out to Jordan when he rode up. He reached out and slowed the wagon as the figure took shape.

It was a man, in middle age.

He looked pretty bad, as if he'd been out on the trail for a long time. The closer he came, the more Elle thought of the word *straight*. He looked straight. A tall, thin, powerful-looking man with a definite set to his jaw. The only thing that threw the whole image out of balance was the wad of chewing tobacco that bulged in his left cheek and made a little white spot on his tanned skin. His hat was low over his eyes, yet Elle could sense that he took in their every movement.

Finally Jordan pulled back on the reins and Elle stopped the wagon as the man rode up in front of Jordan.

He touched the tip of his hat in respect to her and said in a gravelly, dry voice, "Howdy, folks. Can you spare any water?"

Elle didn't wait to ask Jordan. She turned to Julie and nodded.

"Where are you heading?" Jordan asked.

Elle noted that the question sounded more like interrogation than politeness.

"North," the man answered evasively, as he accepted the canteen from Julie's outstretched hand. "How about you?"

"South," Jordan countered.

227

Elle thought the whole thing was silly. Why were they so suspicious of each other? "We're going to meet up with Jordan's herd of cattle. Have you seen them?" Elle asked in a friendly voice, glad to see a new face.

The man spit a stream of ghastly brown tobacco juice to the ground, before bringing the canteen to his mouth. Swallowing the water, he shook his head and smiled. "Why, no, ma'am, I haven't. A herd of cattle this time of year?" He shot Jordan a curious look. "Headin' south?"

Elle couldn't help shuddering and she didn't dare look at Julie for fear of her reaction to the man's manners. But then again, Cooky had done the same thing so this spitting must be a fairly common, though disgusting, practice. Thank God, Jordan didn't—

It was then she noticed that for some strange reason Jordan was glaring at her. In the awkward silence that followed, he slowly turned his attention back to the man. "She's mistaken," he said in a cold voice. "We're merely going home. Though I do expect to meet up with friends in Decatur." He hesitated for only a moment before extending his gloved hand. "Jordan McCabe."

The man nodded, looking like he had expected the name. He took Jordan's hand in his and said, "Harley Longham."

The two shook hands quickly, coldly, as if neither really wanted to do it.

Elle couldn't understand why Jordan lied about the herd, or why he was upset with her for talking about it, so she remained silent . . . like the rest of them. Presently, the man handed back the canteen and tipped his hat to her.

"Thank you, ma'am. I'd best be going. Good luck to

you folks."

Jordan nodded, and Elle noticed for the first time that his hand was casually resting on his gun. And so was Kyle's. What the heck were they doing? She was relieved to see Mr. Longham nod to them and quietly ride away.

"Well, that was real friendly," she muttered when the man had put enough distance between them.

Staring after Longham, Jordan said, "Don't you ever mention the herd again. Not to anyone."

"What?" Her mouth dropped open in surprise. "What's the secret? They aren't invisible, you know. People have seen them. I just wanted to know if he had, and how far away they were. I thought you might like to know, too."

"It's not your fault," Jordan admitted. "I should have said something to you earlier." Taking off his hat, he wiped his forehead on his sleeve. "I'm sorry if I growled at you, Elizabeth—it's just that you don't know how things are out here yet. You keep your business to yourself."

She could tell he was sincere in his apology and she decided that today was too special to argue. Instead, she smiled. "It's okay. I didn't know. Now, I do."

He looked into her eyes and held her gaze for a few exciting seconds before saying, "By the way, happy birthday."

Surprised, Elle was about to ask how he knew when he added, "Julie told me. We'll have to see what we can do to celebrate tonight."

He didn't give her a chance to respond. Grinning at her with what she would have sworn was flat-out flirtation, he rode away. She could only stare after him. Even when

Julie elbowed her and indicated that she should follow the men, Elle simply stared at Jordan's back. *What did he mean by that?* She mindlessly flicked the reins over the horse's rump and drove the wagon after him. Her arms didn't hurt any longer. She wasn't even tired. Instead, her brain was filled with possibilities. In her time a man hinting like that on a woman's birthday about *celebrating* might mean one thing. In this time, he could merely intend to show her how rattlesnakes dance. It was hard to tell.

It also meant she would spend the rest of the afternoon indulging in some great fantasies.

Rattlesnakes dancing? By God, she really was getting into this whole western thing.

"So anyway . . . like I was saying, there wasn't any more bizarre adventurer than one Sir George Grant. An upper-crust Englishman. He responded to the call of the West by advertising in the papers for a team of young bloods, preferably remittance men, to join him and found an English colony on a tract of land he'd bought from the Union Pacific."

"Where was this again?" Elle asked.

Jordan smiled across the campfire. "Kansas."

"Get out . . ." She couldn't help laughing. "An English colony in Kansas?"

He nodded, thoroughly enjoying himself, and Elle was sure this was the most relaxed she had ever seen him. They had just finished eating and were sitting around the campfire, talking, when Jordan had decided to contribute to the conversation. Julie and Kyle were sitting next to each other, as was their custom. Elle made a mental note to talk to Jordan about the teenagers and their obvious infatuation with each other.

Young love.

She tried not to be condescending.

They were cute to watch . . . all the shy glances, the casual brushing against each other . . . dear God, she almost described herself and Jordan tonight as everyone prepared the meal. The warm glances, the unintentional, lingering touching while passing the coffeepot. But she'd been thinking about Julie and Kyle. Right? What was happening between her and Jordan had to be her imagination.

As Jordan continued to speak, she had to concentrate, for the picture he presented, leaning up against the wagon, with Cory sitting close to his side, made Elle grow warm. And it had little to do with the campfire that burned between them.

"So when Sir Grant assembled his team and collected their hunting pinks, some horses, some sheep and some Aberdeen Angus cattle, he sailed away for America. In St. Louis he buys himself a steamboat and is real put out to learn that there's plenty of wind, but no rivers worth anything in Kansas. So now he has a steamboat and no place to take it."

Julie and Kyle laughed, and even Cory smiled. A little.

"All right, now this part is a little hard to swallow, but I swear it's true. These Englishmen, you see, have a strange and confused picture of the West. They probably figured on endless nights of poker and faro, a few buffalo hunts and fox hunts, a possible brush with wild Indians and maybe some wild women—"

He glanced at Elle and said, "I'm sorry. I forgot."

She shrugged. "Go on."

Jordan sipped his coffee and grinned. "Okay. Now hear this. These fellows, stuck with a steamboat and a dream, dragged the thing two hundred miles across the prairie and found a creek."

"What?" Kyle shook his head.

"C'mon," Elle challenged. "They dragged a steamboat two hundred miles?"

"I swear. It's true."

"But they only found a creek?" Julie objected.

Jordan laughed at their combined disbelief. "Ahh . . . they dammed it up and made a little lake. They could navigate for eight to ten miles up and down."

Now Elle laughed. "I don't believe it!"

"It's true. They had great fun, for a while. They shot jackrabbits and coyote and barged up and down the lake and tended their cattle. Stayed for about four or five years."

"Why did they leave?" Julie asked, and Elle looked at her as if the girl had lost it, for she sounded as if she really believed Jordan.

"The summer heat and the bitter winters got to them. Then there was a long drought. And, if you'll pardon me, the story goes that the few women they actually encountered were not up to legendary standards. One of the young bloods pronounced the whole thing a *deuced bore,* and they took off for home."

"That's it? That's the big finish?" Elle felt duped. Surely such a long story should have a point.

Jordan didn't disappoint them. "Well, in the end, Sir George Grant had the satisfaction of seeing his village named Victoria, after Her Gracious Majesty. And he introduced to the United States the Aberdeen Angus breed of cattle. Just like my bull."

As everyone showed their appreciation with the story, he looked exceedingly pleased with himself.

Elle muttered, "Well, if you ask me, I think there's more than a little bull in that story."

Jordan appeared shocked. "Elizabeth. I swear to you. That's exactly the way I heard it."

Nodding, she grinned. "Okay," she conceded. "It was a good story."

Jordan smiled at her. It was one of those smiles that extended to the eyes, where the eyes almost shine with merriment. Elle realized it had been an awfully long time since a man had looked at her with genuine affection. And this man . . . well, for this man it was special.

"All right," Jordan drew everyone's attention. "We all agreed that everyone has to contribute to this celebration. Kyle did his rope tricks and played the mouth organ. Julie baked us a fine pan cake and Cory helped. I, myself, regaled you with a thrilling, and informative I might add, narration. Now, Miss Mackenzie, it's your turn."

They all turned to her with expectation.

"Entertain us, madam."

She felt a blush of embarrassment creep up from her throat. "But I'm the birthday person. You should be entertaining me," she protested.

"Ahh . . . but we have," Jordan countered. "We agreed. *Everyone* has to take part. Now it's your turn."

"That's right, Miss Elle. It's your turn," Kyle added.

"C'mon, Miss Elle, you can do something," Julie prodded good-naturedly.

233

Elle sat Indian-style across the campfire from them. She felt their eyes on her and her brain picked that moment to turn to mush. She couldn't think of a thing to do. She wasn't talented in any of the creative arts. She could show them how to close a deal, put the pressure on a prospective client, but somehow she didn't think that was what they had in mind. Donald Trump might be amused, but not these people.

And then it came to her. The one thing they would appreciate. Now, if she could only remember all the words . . .

In her best Willie Nelson impersonation, she threw her head back like a coyote, took a deep breath, and howled to the sky, *"Momma, don't let your babies grow up to be cowboys . . ."* She couldn't look at them, for if she did she would never be able to continue. And once she started, she realized she didn't care anyway. She was having a good time. Enjoying every moment, she sang the first verse straight through, which was all she remembered anyway.

If she lived to be a hundred, she would never forget the astonishment on their faces. Bursting out laughing, Elle knew she had just blown her city-girl image forever. She also knew she had never felt this close to anyone. Tonight, they were her family. Kyle, Julie and Cory . . . and Jordan. She loved each one.

Regaining her breath, she smiled at them with affection and pride.

She was right. This had turned into a great day.

There were just two of them left awake. Kyle and Julie

234

and Cory were sound asleep in their bedrolls under the wagon. Elle and Jordan sat side by side against the wheel, watching the last of the embers die out in the campfire. It was quiet, except for the noises of the animals and Elle was feeling hypnotized from staring into the flames. They had begun the day like this, just the two of them, and it seemed fitting that it end the same way.

"Thank you, Jordan," she whispered. "It was the best birthday I ever had."

"The best?" he asked in a hushed voice. "Surely, you've had better. This was only—"

"Only the best," she interrupted sleepily. "I mean it. Everyone was great. I felt . . . well, I felt like you were all my family. I appreciate that."

"Do you miss them? Your family? You've never talked about them."

She smiled. "I don't, do I?" Shrugging, she added, "I guess that's because there isn't that much to say."

"C'mon, everybody has a few things to say about families. What was your father like?"

He was smiling, she thought. He thinks he's asking a simple question. How could she tell this man the truth? What would he think? He's a man of integrity, responsibility. How could he possibly understand John Mackenzie? And then the words came out, blurted from some deep well of emotion. "My father is an alcoholic."

Jordan looked confused. "An—an al-co-hol-ic? I don't understand."

She again smiled. "I didn't think you would." She said it more simply. "He's a drunk."

"I'm sorry. We don't have to talk about this—"

"I don't care," she quickly interrupted. "I thought I

235

would. I even tried to hide from it myself. He is a drunk. He abuses my mother, and he hates me because I wouldn't allow him to make excuses." She shook her head. "I'm sorry. I don't know why I'm telling you this."

"Because I asked," he said in a low voice. "Because I'm interested."

She could feel the lack of pressure. He wasn't prying. He was concerned. Like a friend . . . or more.

She looked at him then, really looked into his eyes. It was as if he were talking to her with them. She could almost hear him telling her to trust him, that whatever he heard would never be used against her in the future. That tonight, whatever happened between them, her mind and her heart were safe.

"My parents . . . my parents are Margaret and John Mackenzie," she began in a whisper, "and I'm from Bucks County, Pennsylvania."

"A true Yankee," he said, smiling with encouragement.

She decided not to inform him that the Civil War had been over for a hundred and twenty-six years. "I guess that's what you'd call me—a Yankee." She closed her eyes for a moment and shook her head. "But I guess I've always thought of myself as a rebel." When she glanced up at him, she had to swallow down the acrid taste of tears. "I've sort of made a mess of my life," she admitted.

He grinned. "Who hasn't? At one time or another."

For the next half hour she told him all about her parents, about growing up in fear. She thought it would have been difficult, explaining her father and his destructive personality to someone from another century, but Jordan was a good listener. Only occasionally would he gently interrupt with a question. In the end, she

236

found herself crying silently next to him, and it seemed the most natural thing in the world to wind up in his arms.

In truth, it was where she wanted to be.

"I have something for you. For your birthday," he said gently.

She raised her face and looked at him as he reached into the pocket of his shirt. Smiling, he brought out a gold chain and when he held out his hand, she could see a small gold locket was attached. A tiny flower had been etched into the front of it, so small, so dainty, that on first glance it might only have been part of the decoration. It was exquisite in its simplicity.

"Jordan, I can't—" She didn't know what to say. "It's lovely, but . . ."

"I want you to have it."

She glanced at him, saw the truth in his words. "But when did you get it? You didn't even know it was my birthday in Alexander."

He shook his head. "This is something I had purchased a long time ago."

And then she knew. "It was for Cynthia, wasn't it?"

He didn't answer at first, and when he spoke, his voice was low and serious. "Why don't we just say that I bought this for the woman I was meeting in Wichita?" He smiled, and his gaze grew warm as it roamed over her features. "I just didn't know it would be you.

"Here, let me put it on." He lifted the chain over her head and pulled her braid out so the gold would lie around her neck.

Elle touched the heart that hung between her breasts. She opened the locket and saw a miniature picture of him

237

on one side.

"I forgot that was in there," he said with embarrassment. "I'll take it out."

Before he could reach for it, Elle snapped the gold case shut. "No," she said emphatically. "I want it there."

They stared at each other for a few timeless seconds, neither daring to speak. And then he pulled her back against him, where she had been but minutes before. Her cheek was against his cotton shirt. The material was soft with age and she unconsciously snuggled against it. She could feel the warmth of his skin beneath it and she closed her eyes to remember the moment. It had been so long since a man had held her in his arms, so long since she had allowed another to comfort her.

"Thank you, Jordan," she said simply and honestly. It was the best present she had ever received.

His hand came up to stroke her hair. Gently. Softly. Over and over—following the line of her head and down her neck. She was astonished by the tenderness in his touch.

"Elizabeth." He said her name as a soft whisper against her forehead, and she knew it would never sound the same again. His lips were warm against her skin, brushing and grazing over it, and she closed her eyes to memorize the moment. She felt so secure, so protected . . .

His hands moved down her cheek and cupped her chin, bringing her face up to his.

"You are the most astonishing woman I've ever known, Miss Mackenzie."

She smiled at the irony of his words. "You have no idea how true that is, Mr. McCabe. I doubt if you'll ever meet another like me." Her mouth was so close to his that

238

she could feel his breath on her face and, by strange coincidence, she found herself breathing heavily, as if she'd just run up a flight of stairs.

"I don't mean that as conceit," she said, gasping for air. "It's just odd . . . everything about this. How all of you came into my life, just when I needed something to hold on to again, something to believe in again." She was so confused; she could barely think when he was looking at her like that.

"And what do you believe in now, Elizabeth?"

Dear God, his gaze was so warm she felt an adolescent flush rise from her throat to cover her cheeks. A weird tingling started in her thighs and quickly traveled to her belly, making her almost giddy with anticipation. What in the world did he have in mind? Why was his hand beginning to move down her back? How did he know she was a sucker for a back rub? It had been years since anyone outside of a spa had touched her like that, yet this man was doing it instinctively, as if it were the most natural thing in the world. Sighing, she closed her eyes and enjoyed the sensation. His fingers were so light, so gentle, that she found herself moving into his touch, waiting for the next place where his hand would caress.

She felt mesmerized by the soft feathering of his fingers over her skin. Like a drugged person, Elle fought to open her eyes. She lifted her face to his. "Jordan . . ." She said his name softly, yet even to her ears it sounded like a plea, an appeal for him to continue his stroking.

He was gazing into her face, as if memorizing it, and Elle had a moment to wish that he could see her as she was in her time. Impeccably groomed. Hair by Rudolpho at Toppers. Makeup by Lancôme. Clothes by Anne Klein or Ralph Lauren. And then it hit her. She wasn't that self-centered person any longer. That wasn't her. Jordan was looking at someone totally different, and he appeared to actually like what he was seeing. Beneath the hair and the makeup and the clothes was Elle Mackenzie. That's all. Just Elle.

Elizabeth.

Her hair was falling out of the braid that hung down her back. She couldn't remember the last time she had used makeup. The clothes she wore were useful, but didn't carry a designer's name and her scent was more natural and musky than she might have liked. In spite of all that, what she saw in Jordan's eyes was *appreciation*. Could it be that someone liked her for herself? That she didn't have to be, or fit, someone else's image? Someone could like her even if she weren't successful, or beautiful? It was too much to comprehend.

Touching the locket at her breast, she realized it was also the second best birthday present she had ever received.

Filled with emotion, Elle did something without thinking of the consequences. For the first time, she put aside all her defenses, all that heavy armor she had built around herself for protection. She felt . . . free.

Grinning, Elizabeth Mackenzie leaned those few inches toward Jordan and kissed him soundly on the mouth. She could feel the surprise in his body. It only lasted a moment and then his mouth became demanding. She gladly gave. Giving was easy now. He wanted her and there wasn't any reason to hold back. Her lips parted and she allowed his tongue entrance, permitting him to explore. She didn't know why she thought a cowboy from

240

the last century would kiss differently, but she made an important discovery. Kissing was the same in any time. Well, almost. This was better than any kiss she could remember. It was thrilling and provocative, breathtaking in its intensity. She could barely think, only react. And when he pulled his mouth away, she actually groaned in disappointment. And she didn't care.

Reluctantly, she opened her eyes to find him staring at her with astonishment.

"Lizzie . . . you're amazing," he breathed, staring at her as if she were from another planet, instead of another time.

She tried to recapture her breath. "Nobody calls me Lizzie," she muttered, licking her bottom lip. Didn't he also just say she was amazing? Her? Amazing? But this Lizzie thing . . . she had to straighten him out on this. "No one has ever called me Lizzie." She smiled to soften her words because he was a great kisser and she certainly didn't want to mess this up.

"I didn't think anyone ever did. And that's why I'm going to."

They were staring at each other. It wasn't a conflict; it was more of a challenge. *Lizzie?* It sounded like the name of a spinster aunt, but from his lips it also took on the significance of an endearment. It almost sounded cute. And even though she had never been termed cute, even though she would have cringed at the tag, she suddenly found it wasn't as offensive as she had once thought. Lizzie.

He didn't give her time to think as he pulled her back into his embrace and again captured her mouth.

This time when their lips met it was with eagerness, as

if they couldn't get enough of each other. She touched his face, running her fingertips over the hard planes of his cheekbones, the scratchiness of the beard on his chin. The nerve endings in her fingers sent waves of excitement racing up her hands, through her arms and shoulders and brain, and her brain was telling her to forget the reasons why this meeting and mating were impossible—just enjoy it, embrace it. Relish it.

"The children," she whispered against his mouth.

"They're sleeping," he countered, drawing her mouth back to his. He kissed her softly, gently, soothing her doubts. "It's all right."

His gaze met hers and held. As his hand moved over her face, tracing the outline of her eyebrows, her cheekbones, her lips, Elle thought back to the morning at the hotel in Alexander when she had seen him sleeping with Cory, when she knew that in this relationship she would be the one to get hurt. This was not a man to take lightly. If she gave herself, she knew she would also be giving her heart. Could she do it? It would take courage, for in the end she would always be alone. But just this once? Could she embrace happiness just this once, for as long as it lasted?

His hand had traced the slope of her shoulder and was moving downward—slowly, now hesitantly, as if waiting for a sign from her.

And then she knew what she wanted. Risking her heart, she took his hand and moved it so he could feel the loud beating behind her breast. Still staring at each other, they breathed almost as one.

"Lizzie—I . . ."

"*Well, now. Ain't this the touching scene?*"

242

They froze at the sudden question and turned quickly in the direction of the voice.

Stepping into the light of the campfire, Harley Longham walked toward them and Elle was again reminded of how straight he looked. He still had a wad of chewing tobacco in his cheek.

He also had a gun, and it was pointed right at them.

Chapter 15

Elle sat frozen in fear as the man growled, "Get those kids out here. Wake 'em up!"

He appeared nervous, and she could only stare at the wild look in his eyes. Without breaking the man's intense gaze, Jordan nudged her and said, "Wake the children, Elizabeth."

She glanced at Jordan, but he wasn't taking his eyes off Longham. "Do it, Elizabeth," Jordan ordered. Shaking, she turned back to the buckboard and leaned underneath it.

"Kyle. Julie. Cory. Wake up." She shook the young man and it was then she noticed his gun, nestled in its holster by his head. While the children stirred, making confused noises, Elle pulled Kyle's gun out and dragged it through the dirt as she withdrew from under the wagon. She didn't know what she would do with it. Her hands were shaking so badly that she could only hide it behind her as she gathered Cory into her arms and sat back with Jordan.

When Julie and Kyle were standing next to the wagon,

Harley ordered, "Everybody up. Let's go."

Terrified that the man would see the gun, Elle stumbled and Jordan had to help her and Cory rise. She was grateful for the long skirt, for Longham didn't appear to have noticed the revolver behind her.

"Hated to interrupt that tender scene, McCabe, but you've got somethin' I want." Longham spit a stream of tobacco juice into the campfire and everyone could hear it sizzle.

"And what's that?" Jordan asked in a surprisingly calm voice.

Longham grinned, showing gaps between his yellowed teeth. "The horses will do for a start," he chuckled, before becoming deadly serious. "But what I'm really after is the payoff you got for bringing that herd of cattle up to Wichita last month. I was in Wellington when you went through on your way north. Four hundred head is the way I heard."

"You heard wrong," Kyle muttered.

Longham swung in the direction of Julie and Kyle. "Was I talkin' to you, boy?"

He turned back to Jordan. "Now, you go get that money, McCabe, and there won't be any trouble." He pointed the gun at Elle. "Wouldn't want to hurt the little lady here, seeing as how you was spoonin' with her just a few minutes ago."

No one moved. Finally, Jordan said, "Look, Longham, I wouldn't keep that kind of money with me. Half of it was deposited in the bank at Wichita, and the other half is with my men."

"You're lyin'." Harley looked angry.

Jordan shook his head. "Why would I take a chance like that? I gave it to my trail boss."

Desperate, Longham yelled, "You, girl, you search that buckboard. I want everything out. Dump it all out until we find that money."

Julie was frightened, but did as she was told. They all watched as the young girl methodically emptied all the trunks. Elle held Cory on her hip until he was too heavy, and then she let him stand next to her. She could feel the fear in his young body and she pulled him close to her waist. Her mind was frantically searching for a way to reach the gun at her feet, or at least to let Jordan know that it was there.

When all the trunks were emptied, Harley ventured closer for a look. He was breathing heavily, anger clear in his expression. "Where'd you hide it, McCabe?" he demanded.

Jordan again shook his head. "I told you the first time you asked. I don't have it with me. You made a mistake, Longham. Why don't you just ride off and we'll all forget about this."

Harley laughed, and the sound sent chills up Elle's back.

"You think I trailed you fifteen miles for nothin'? Think again, my friend." He pointed the long pistol at Jordan as he came closer. When he was in front of them, Harley glanced to Elle and smiled. "That pretty necklace would sure get me one hell of a night in San Antonio. I heard them Mex bitches love anything gold."

Elle's hand came up to clutch the necklace and she could feel her heart thudding behind it. Harley laughed evilly and made a point of licking his lips as he said, "Maybe you and me can pick up where you left off when I'm through with McCabe. What do you think of that, little lady? How long since you been with a real man?"

247

"Leave her alone," Jordan ordered, anger clear in his voice. "That's not what you came for."

Harley looked back. Never once diverting his attention from Jordan, he said, defiantly, "Yeah, that's right. But I'm not about to walk away with nothing. Maybe I'll let you watch. Show you how it's done, McCabe. How'd you like that, Missy? Ever did it with an audience?"

"Get away from her, Longham."

Elle could feel the coiled rage in Jordan. Even though his voice was low and controlled, even though he didn't move a muscle, Jordan McCabe was a man about to explode.

"Empty your pockets, McCabe. Let's see what you've got in there."

Jordan didn't do anything for a moment; he merely stared at the man. Drawing in a deep breath, he finally dug into the pockets of his jeans. Elle watched as he brought out a folded stack of bills. It didn't look like much to Elle, certainly not enough to satisfy Longham.

Jordan held out the money and Harley moved toward it. To Elle's surprise, just as the gunman was about to take the money, Jordan flung it at him, startling the man for a moment.

It was all Jordan needed.

Amid flying bills, he tackled Longham, both of them landing in the dirt with a loud thud. The gun dropped to the ground, useless to the robber. Elle watched in horror as the two men wrestled, rolling over and over, each trying to gain the upper hand. When they parted, they rose like angry bears—crouching, arms outstretched, weighing the other in their minds. And then they came together again. Harley swung his fist. Jordan easily side-stepped it. Jordan brought his arm back and put the

248

strength of his body into it when he brought it forward. It connected with Longham's stomach. The thin man doubled over, but backed away too quickly for Jordan to follow with another punch.

From far off, Elle heard Julie scream as Longham charged Jordan, bringing him to the ground. He was a man possessed, a man fearing for his life. Tobacco juice spilled from his mouth as he gasped for breath. He clawed and scratched and ripped Jordan's shirt as he tried to overturn him. Frustrated by Jordan's strength, Longham butted Jordan in the face, causing Jordan to jerk backward and giving the thief time to draw back his fist. After it connected, Elle gasped as she saw blood pouring from Jordan's nose.

She had to do something! This could not go on . . .

Elle seemed rooted to the ground. She heard Cory whimper and saw Kyle move toward Longham's gun by the fire, just as Jordan's arm was reaching out for it. Even though she was sure her heart would soon burst through her chest, even though she was dizzy with fear, she knew she had to move, to push down the paralyzing fear. Shoving Cory toward Julie, she knelt down and picked up Kyle's gun. She was surprised by how heavy it was.

"Kyle!" She called out to the boy.

He spun around and she tossed it to him, just as Jordan overturned Longham. His face was now being pummeled with heavy, unceasing blows as Jordan began to dominate the battle. The horrible sound of the punches cut through the night, as did the man's short grunts of anguish.

"Jordan!" Kyle called out to his boss, yet Jordan seemed determined to punish Longham by crashing his face with his fist . . . again and again.

Kyle walked up to the two men and pointed his gun to the one on the ground. His hand shook and he had to use his other to steady his aim. In a scared voice, he announced, "I got him covered, Cap'n! You can back off now!"

The boy's words seemed to puncture the cloud of rage that had enveloped Jordan. His arm froze in mid-air as he stared at the young man who had ridden by his side for years. For just a moment, he looked confused. And then he pulled himself off of Longham quickly, breathing heavily, and wiping the blood from his nose onto the back of his hand.

"Good job, Kyle," Jordan muttered, spitting blood onto the ground.

Elle watched as Longham started to crawl away.

"Jordan!" she called out. "He's—he's—"

"Stay where you are, Longham," Jordan ordered, pulling the gun out of Kyle's hand.

Harley Longham stumbled a few times and then rose to his feet. He started running, slowly at first, and then faster, determined to put as much distance as possible between himself and those around the campfire.

"I said *stop*," Jordan yelled. "Or I'll shoot."

The man kept running.

She would never forget the moment. It all happened so quickly.

In a flash of movement, Jordan reached out and fired. Harley lurched forward, stumbling, trying to regain his footing, but failing. And then he went down.

He never rose again.

Elle sank to her knees in horror, her hand clutching the gold chain at her neck. Shocked, she watched as Jordan and Kyle walked over to the body. She could see

Jordan kneel down and then rise. In the stillness of the night, she heard him mutter to Kyle, "Get a shovel and bury the bastard."

Cory and Julie were crying and Elle could do no more than pat Julie's shoulder as she stood up and walked toward Jordan. He looked frightening. It wasn't just the fight that had put the strange look into his eyes. It was something more. Something so foreign, so forbidding, that Elle could barely speak. But then she must. For the question would haunt her forever if she didn't.

"Why?" Her voice pleaded with him for an answer, something that would make sense of it all. "Why did you kill him? He was running away."

He glared at her, the muscle in his cheek working furiously. "I will say this one time, Elizabeth," he announced in a clipped voice. "And then don't ever question me again. Longham wasn't just running away. Do you actually think he wouldn't have come back, trailed us for days until he got revenge? And if he couldn't do it alone, a man like him knows others that would help. He was going to steal our horses. Rob us. Rape you, if he could. And then probably kill us all. You tell me what choice I had, for I wish to God there'd been another."

Without another word he walked away from her to the buckboard and pulled out a shovel to help Kyle. He didn't look at her as he passed.

But Elle looked at him, and in his eyes she saw something even more frightening than before. He had the same haunted look as Cory.

As he pounded the hard earth with his foot around the

body of Harley Longham, Jordan touched Kyle's shoulder. "Go on back," he muttered. "I'll finish up here."

Tired, Kyle merely nodded and headed back to the camp not fifty yards away. Jordan stood at the grave. The lamp on the ground burned low; its light would soon fade. In the stillness of the night, with only the sounds of nature around him, Jordan McCabe watched the ghosts of his past rush up to greet him. Their faces were varied: men in their middle years, tired and weary from war; old men, who should have been living out their remaining years in peace; and, most tragically, the young ones, who would never have the opportunity. Years ago he had realized they were all the same. They weren't his enemies. They were all brave men, disillusioned by causes, wondering what the hell they were fighting for anymore.

But he had known. Each of them was just fighting to stay alive for one more day, hoping with every sunrise that it wasn't their last. That was what it came down to in the end. Survival. They did whatever was necessary to hang on, whatever it took. And it always took the form of death.

Looking down to the grave at his feet, Jordan felt the bile rise in his throat. He hadn't killed a man since the war; he'd seen too much and done too much to let it continue. There was nothing honorable in death, no matter what the novelists wrote. It was ugly and final.

And now he had taken part in it again. It didn't matter that the logical part of his brain was telling him that he'd done the right thing, the only thing, to ensure the safety of Elizabeth and the others. He knew. For years he had tried to bury the ghosts, those men he had killed in battle, and he'd been successful. But now, with Harley Longham forever still beneath his feet, he had to acknowledge the others.

They were still there. They would remain with him for the rest of his life.

He had seen the revulsion in Elizabeth's eyes, but it was nothing compared to his own awareness. That part of him, that piece of himself that he had thought safely buried—the person that could destroy another. It had risen to the surface with a terrifying swiftness. He knew now it had always been there, waiting.

And he also knew that it would never go away.

"You won," he whispered down to the grave with bitterness. For in his heart he realized that Harley Longham had succeeded in stealing something from him—

His peace of mind.

Chapter 16

Nothing was the same. Jordan was cold and withdrawn and his attitude infected the rest of them. Cory was the only one that he allowed close to him, and even then the child knew when to keep his distance. Jordan McCabe was like a stranger. He barked orders, and was impatient when they weren't carried out fast enough. He barely spoke to Elle, and when he did, his voice was clipped and impersonal. But it was his eyes that frightened her the most. They were hard, almost cruel, and they looked right through her.

Elle wasn't sure what had caused him to change— whether it had been the actual killing or her unthinking remarks. Later, after she had gotten over the shock, she'd realized that Jordan was right. He really didn't have much of a choice. She had tried to talk to him, to apologize, but he had only stared at her. It was as if he hadn't heard . . . or hadn't cared.

He was like a man driven by unseen demons, pushing all of them further each day, riding well past dusk. Only when it was impossible to see any longer would they stop for the night. And then he let everyone know he resented the interruption. It was as if a strained truce existed among them. Everyone knew to stay clear of him. Conversation ceased—unless it was Julie and Kyle whispering off to the side, or Elle and the children murmuring to each other.

Jordan didn't want to be a part of them any longer, and Elle had the feeling that he couldn't wait to get rid of them. They had always been, after all, a responsibility he had taken on reluctantly. Just because she had felt they were almost a family, that didn't make it so. They were strangers he had taken pity on, nothing more. No matter how much she wanted it to be different, she was powerless.

In her own way, she grieved for the loss. For just a night, a sweet, magical night, she had opened her heart and Jordan McCabe had crept in and taken hold. But now her own defenses were again in position. She couldn't afford the luxury of loving . . . not now.

Now she had to concentrate on herself and the children—and the children came first. She'd been sidetracked by her heart, that's all. She simply had to remember the reason why she was here. It wasn't for Jordan, nor even herself. It was Julie and Cory. Kyle had said there was only one more town they would pass through before Jordan turned off the trail and headed for home. Decatur. It sounded like a typical Texas cowtown. Now if only she could find—she stopped herself. She would *have* to find the proper home. This was her last chance.

Clutching the gold heart that hung heavily between her breasts, Elle felt her stomach tighten with apprehension as Kyle yelled out in a young, happy voice.

"It's them, Cap'n! Look—Traver and Cooky!" Letting out a wild, Indian hail of excitement, Kyle kicked his heels into the brown sorrel's sides and took off in the direction of the herd.

Well, here it is, Elle thought while trying to stay calm. We're back at the beginning. She looked at Jordan and was surprised by his lack of expression. Not even seeing his precious herd again seemed to make a difference. Maybe he, too, was thinking that this is how the adventure began for them. But now neither of them was the same any longer. So much had happened, and they had both changed.

She was stronger.

He was more distant.

The question was . . . how was it going to end?

"Miss Elle?"

Turning in the direction of Julie's voice, she could see apprehension in the child's expression. It was mirrored on her brother's face.

"Hey, it's okay," she said with a false brightness. "Those men work for Jordan. You'll like them." She called out to the man on horseback not ten feet away. "Won't they, Jordan?"

He turned his head, as if just remembering she was there. "What did you say?"

She ignored his rudeness; the act was becoming more difficult to pull off. "I said the children will like Traver and Cooky, and the others. Don't you think?" She was smiling.

As usual, he appeared impatient. "Why wouldn't they?" he asked shortly. He looked out to the covered wagon, the men on horseback, the large bodies of the cattle as they grazed on the tall, dry grass. "If you would,

257

for once, stop trying to solve everyone else's problem, and just do your job and drive the wagon, they just might find out for themselves."

He kicked his horse, spurring it into a gallop as he raced across the flat land. Elle watched his image grow smaller as he closed the distance between himself and his herd. She followed his image and her eyes narrowed with anger.

Enough was enough. She had just about had it with Jordan Dillon McCabe's attitude. Why couldn't he see how scared the kids were? What would it have taken for him to have been a little reassuring? Maybe she'd been a bit too understanding in the last few days. Perhaps her acceptance of his ill humor only encouraged it.

Flicking the reins over the horse's rump, Elle vowed that if she never saw the back end of a horse again it would be too soon. She also vowed that, at the first possible opportunity, she was going to let Mr. McCabe know just how closely he resembled that part of the animal's anatomy.

She was no longer smiling. She was, in good olde western lingo, pissed off.

"Miss Elizabeth. Glad to see you lookin' so much better." Smiling, Traver Diggs helped Elle down from the buckboard. Without questioning, he assisted Julie and then Cory.

She returned his smile. "Thanks, Traver, it's good to see you too. Is everyone all right?"

The weathered cowboy nodded. "Right as can be." He looked to the children.

Elle again felt annoyance that Jordan had deserted

them, leaving the explanations to her. She took off the wide cowboy hat and wiped her forehead. Later. She'd talk to him later. Right now she wanted to support the children, for Cory's eyes were wide with apprehension as he stared around him.

"Traver, this is Julie and Cory Woodson. They're traveling with us," she added, not wanting to explain more at the time.

Traver tipped the brim of his hat to Julie and glanced down to Cory. "Ever seen an Angus bull before, son?"

Cory quickly looked up to the older man and shook his head.

Traver grinned. "Well, then, come along. You've got yourself a treat. Think about now Lothario might welcome a new face." He put his wide hand on Cory's shoulder and led him away.

Elle laughed. "Lothario?" she called after them.

Traver turned and shrugged. "We got tired of callin' it *bull*. Cooky said it was a real classy name for a . . ." he seemed to struggle for a proper word. "For a bull," he added lamely.

Elle nodded and watched as the man and boy walked toward the animal that was kept at a distance from the cows. She sighed with resignation and turned to the chuckwagon. There he was, as cranky and ornery-looking as when she'd first met him.

Plopping the hat back on her head, she said to Julie, "Come on. I'll introduce you to Arlyn Sinclair, better known as Cooky." She grinned wryly. "It's quite an experience." Poor Arlyn. Now he'd have to put up with two females. He was probably cussin' already.

To her surprise Arlyn greeted her almost warmly. "Had us real worried there, Missy. Never saw nobody more miserable with gettin' a tooth yanked."

Elle ran her tongue over the healed socket. She had almost forgotten that experience. It seemed like ages ago. Thank God for dissolving stitches, for she didn't even want to think of how she would have had to deal with *that*. Hadn't it been Cooky who'd told her that in the West blacksmiths doubled as dentists? Talk about hoof and mouth—. Forget it, she told herself. She had other things to think about.

"I'm fine now," she quickly stated and glanced at the young teenager at her side. "Thanks to some very good nursing." Elle smiled at Julie. "You also have some tough competition here, Arlyn. Julie is an excellent cook. She might even teach you a thing or two. Bless her heart, she's tried with me. Not too successfully, I might add."

Cooky looked at Julie with more interest. "You can cook outside a kitchen?"

Julie nodded.

"You done the cookin' for the Cap'n?"

Again, Julie shook her head in answer to the question. "Kyle helped . . . and so did Miss Elle."

Now it was Arlyn's turn to shake his head in disbelief. "Kyle ain't no help at all and, beggin' your pardon, Miss Elizabeth, but you're even less." He stared at the girl in front of him. "If you managed to satisfy the Cap'n, then it looks like I got me a real hired hand. Been tellin' 'em I needed one for months now." He ignored Elle and led Julie closer to his wagon. "I'll even talk to the Cap'n about pay. Won't be much, seein' as how we're so close to home, but if you work out . . . yup, we'll see about back pay, too."

Elle watched them in wonder. What had happened to everyone? Cooky seemed . . . nice? In fact, as she looked

260

around her, she saw other cowboys smile and nod in greeting. Was she no longer the outcast? What had changed their minds? Surely Jordan hadn't said anything to them. It was curious, but she decided not to question it. Things were going to be tough enough.

She didn't realize at the time how prophetic that statement was as Jordan walked up to her. Slapping his gloves against his thigh with impatience, he said in a rough voice, "We're going into Decatur soon. Traver said there's a couple in town. They own the mercantile store, and they're childless. Be ready in thirty minutes, and bring the children."

Her mouth hung open as he abruptly turned away. She swallowed her shock, then called out after him, "Wait a minute!"

He stopped, yet didn't face her.

She crossed the few yards and circled to face him.

"What do you think you're doing?" she demanded, feeling a hot flush of anger creep up her throat.

He took a deep breath with exaggerated patience, as if he were forced to converse with someone of lesser intelligence. "I am trying to find a home for Julie and Cory. That *is* what we said we would do."

"I'm supposed to do it. Not you," she countered. Her eyes narrowed with anger. "You can't wait to get rid of us, can you?"

"I'm not going to argue with you in front of the men. Why can't you please do as you were asked?"

She lowered her voice, yet her tone bristled with indignation. "Look, what do you want from me? I said I was sorry. If you're mad at me then take it out on me, not the children."

He looked right through her. "I'm not mad at you, or

the children. Nor do I intend to discuss this further."

He started to walk away from her, but she quickly grabbed his arm. "Jordan. Don't do this. Don't dump the children, just to get rid of a problem. They'll feel deserted—"

"I've made my decision, Elizabeth," he interrupted, then added, "And you might want to give some thought as to your own plans. If you wish to go back east, I'll provide your fare. You've certainly earned it."

The pain would have been less if he had slapped her face. Stunned, Elle could only stare at him as he said, "Now we have twenty minutes. Please have the children ready."

She watched in amazement as he walked away from her. Jordan McCabe had turned into a cold, unfeeling man . . . and she thought herself ten times a fool for ever thinking differently.

Next to Decatur, Alexander seemed almost cosmopolitan by comparison. Decatur, Texas was a small cowtown with three bars, a hotel above one; a blacksmith, an undertaker, a small white building with a cross on top; a title office and the mercantile store. That was it. As Elle drove the wagon down the main street, she shuddered. This *couldn't* be the entire town! Jordan couldn't condemn the children to spend their youth in such a place. She glared at the man riding horseback in front of her, riding straight up to a store constructed of rough wooden planks. In front was a crudely lettered sign that read: *Cummings Mercantile est. 1873.*

Once he'd tied his horse to a post out front, Jordan stepped to the wagon and helped Cory and Julie down.

When he offered his hand to Elle, her eyes blazed her anger, and her refusal. Hopping to the ground, she straightened her short jacket and took a deep breath. "You can't be serious," she muttered to him.

Ignoring her, he placed his hand behind Cory and led him up to the front door. A bell clanged when they entered. Immediately she smelled the strong aroma of coffee beans, saw dust and gunpowder. She blinked several times and, as Elle's eyes acclimated to the darker interior, she was able to see a woman coming from behind a glass-front counter on which brightly woven Indian blankets were stacked.

Elle guessed the woman to be in her early forties. She wore a brown dress with white lace at the collar. Her hair matched her costume—brown, with threads of gray at the temples. She had a kind face. Her cheeks were ruddy, the complexion of someone in good health. Elle wanted to dislike her, but couldn't ignore the expectant, though nervous look in the woman's eyes. Clearly excited, she stopped in front of them, her hands clasped together at her waist.

She smiled. "Hello. I . . . I'm so happy to meet all of you." Turning to the back of the store she called out in a loud voice, "John . . . they're here!" She looked back at them and her smile widened nervously. "I'm Ardelle Cummings."

Jordan took off his hat and inclined his head in respect. "How do you do, Mrs. Cummings? I'm Jordan McCabe. This is Elizabeth Mackenzie and Julie and Cory Woodson." He smiled tightly. "I believe Traver Diggs talked to you about the children?"

Ardelle nodded as her husband came up to greet them. "Why, yes, he did," she said quickly, then added, "this

263

is my husband, John. We've been in Decatur since 'seventy-three. We live right behind the store. I can show you, if you like. We're members of the First Baptist Church of Christ, and—"

"Ardelle," her husband interrupted. "Calm down. Let me meet them first."

The woman looked embarrassed, and took a step back behind her husband. Elle noticed that Ardelle Cummings had either a great amount of respect for her husband, or an alarming degree of fear. Deciding it was too soon to tell, Elle watched as the older, heavy-set man shook hands with Jordan and turned to her.

It was quite natural for her to also extend her hand in greeting, though John Cummings looked taken back by her action. "How do you do, Mr. Cummings?" she asked in her best businesslike voice.

"Fine," the shopkeeper muttered, clearly upset by what he must have perceived as her manly attitude.

Elle grinned, just to throw him further off base. Instinct told her that she liked the woman, but the man was harder to read.

"Well, so these are the children," he stated, and Elle had the impression that he was looking them over as if he were attending a horse auction.

"That's Julie," Jordan said, nodding to the young girl who stood with her arms crossed over her breasts. "And this is Cory."

Cory half hid behind Jordan, and Jordan moved so Cummings could better see the boy.

"Perhaps they would like some taffy?" Ardelle offered in an eager voice.

Elle said nothing, waiting for the children's reaction. Julie shook her head defensively, clearly old enough to realize that her future was being decided for her. Cory merely stared at the rough-planked wooden floor.

"That would be very nice," Jordan answered for them, obviously annoyed by the lack of response.

Ardelle nodded and hurried to the back of the store for the candy, and Elle watched the woman's husband. He rubbed the whiskers on his chin, as if forming a question.

Finally, he cleared his throat and asked it.

"What happened to their parents? Your man never said."

Jordan didn't even blink when he answered, "They were killed in an accident."

John Cummings nodded, as though it were an everyday occurrence. "No relatives?"

Shaking his head, Jordan said, "None that we know of. They need a home, Mr. Cummings. They're good kids."

Ardelle rushed back and offered the sweets to the children. "Here we are," she said happily. In her hands were long sticks of taffy. Julie politely took one, but Cory moved further behind Jordan.

"The boy looks skittish," Cummings pronounced.

"He's just shy, John," his wife meekly offered.

Quiet until now, Elle cleared her throat. "The children have been through a great deal, Mr. Cummings. They would need patience and understanding. Besides a home, can you give them that?"

Cummings's eyes narrowed as he looked at Elle. "You sound like you're interviewing *me*. I've got the right to ask questions, madam. It's a big responsibility you're asking me to take on."

Elle nodded. "I agree. And part of that responsibility would be education. Can you also provide that?"

Cummings looked flustered. "If you mean do we got a

school yet, then the answer is no. Ardelle can teach them all they need to know." He looked at Julie. "Know your numbers yet?"

Julie appeared angry and Elle couldn't blame her, yet she nodded in answer to the question.

Cummings was pleased. "There you go . . . she can even help out in the store."

Elle looked pointedly at the tall man who stood across from her. "Jordan, could I talk to you for a moment?"

He appeared to be irritated by her suggestion, but walked with her to a pile of burlap sacks that had the word *Seed* stamped on the front.

"Yes. What is it?" he asked in a terse voice.

Elle took a deep breath to calm herself. "You heard him," she whispered. "He's only looking for unpaid labor. We can't leave the children, Jordan—"

"Now you listen to me. You will not pull that same act. Not here. Time's run out. It's now or never."

She could see the muscle at his cheek working furiously, as he ground his back teeth together.

"Then let it be never," Elle stated impulsively. "*You* could take them, Jordan. Cory already loves you—"

"That's it," Jordan interrupted and walked back to the group. In a firm voice, he said, "Mr. and Mrs. Cummings, I've decided that the children should spend the night with you. Give all of you a chance to get to know each other, without myself or Miss Mackenzie here. We'll come back tomorrow afternoon and you can tell us of your decision."

Elle was furious, yet he didn't offer her the opportunity for rebuttal as he whisked her out the front door. It wasn't until they were on the street that she realized he never even gave her the chance to say goodbye to the children.

Glaring at him, she drew off her hat and slapped his chest. "You are the biggest ass I have ever come across. How could you do that?" she demanded.

He chose to ignore her attack. Instead, he grabbed hold of her arm and led her up the street. When she insisted that he tell her where they were going, he snapped, "I am depositing you in the hotel. You can get a bath and cool off there. If you have any more questions, and if your level of maturity has risen, I'll be glad to answer them tonight. Right now, I have business to take care of."

Before they entered the saloon, he stopped and said in a low, threatening voice, "And don't get any ideas of going back to the Cummings place. Do you hear me? Stop being selfish, Elizabeth. Think of the children, not yourself."

She stared at him, wondering how it was possible to hate someone so quickly. "Are you saying I am not allowed to even say goodbye to them?"

"What I am saying, madam, is that if everything goes well you will have that opportunity tomorrow. But if they see you now, they won't give that couple a chance in hell. I'm ordering you to stay away from them until tomorrow afternoon. Is that clear?"

She could feel her face flaming with anger, feel her chest heaving with indignation. "Well, well, well . . . the macho cowboy rises to the surface once more," she taunted. Her chin came up defensively. "Do you think just because you're a man that I will meekly obey you? That I'm like that woman, Ardelle, who's scared to even stand in front of her husband? May I remind you that you are not my husband? And there is no law, anywhere, that says I have to listen to you and your damn orders? If I want to see those children, you can't stop me."

He leaned down, so that his face was level with hers, and said in a fierce growl, "You will not see those children, and you will give the Cummings a chance, because if you don't I swear to God I'll tie you to a chair and leave you there until morning."

She challenged him, eye to eye, chin to chin, and her mouth slowly opened. "Try it, and I'll have you arrested for assault."

Ten seconds could have passed, and to Elle it seemed like ten hours as they faced off against each other. Just when she was sure he would back down, Jordan took a deep breath and shocked her by sweeping her up over his shoulder. Too astonished to fight back, she found herself carried, fireman-style, through the saloon doors. When she heard the hoots and hollering of the men inside, she struggled to break free. But Jordan had a death grip on her, and his arms and back took the punches she delivered as though they were mere annoyances. He even managed to wrap her skirt around her legs and immobilize them against him.

"Put me down!"

"I want a room for the night," he announced, a statement that brought even more howls of appreciation.

"Put me down, you jackass," she demanded, more embarrassed than she had ever been in her life. She pounded his back for emphasis and tried kicking his groin.

Her skirt absorbed most of the kick and he merely grunted at her attempt to abuse his back.

"With bath?" a man's voice asked. Elle could hear the laughter in the voice.

She could also hear Jordan inhale, as if smelling the

surrounding air. "Definitely with bath," he announced to the renewed laughter of the males around him.

"I'll kill you," Elle muttered, absolutely mortified by the scene taking place and tried to elbow his head. It only caused his hat to fall off and the simpletons around her to snigger when she missed. "Help! Somebody help me."

"A real hellcat, you got there," some idiot observed.

"You don't know the half of it," Jordan answered, scooping up a room key and shifting her on his shoulder.

Elle grunted as his bone pressed in against her stomach. She would never forgive him for this. Not ever.

"Fourth door on the right," the first voice said. "I'll send up a girl with a bath after you get her calmed down some. She looks more pissed than a rattler at high noon."

Elle lifted her face and screamed, "I am! Isn't someone going to help me?"

Her already flushed face took on an even brighter hue when a loud male voice replied, "I'll help you, honey. When your man gets tired, give me a call."

She would not cry. She refused to give them the satisfaction. She didn't gather her defenses so much for herself, but for every female that had been subjected to the arrogant male supremacy of the nineteenth century. Raising her head as Jordan climbed the first step, she looked out to the group of drunken, leering faces and cried, "Go to hell, you ignorant cretins."

It didn't matter that her statement only caused more whistles, howls and catcalls. She felt vindicated.

Jordan opened the door and walked to the bed. Without ceremony, he flipped her over and deposited her on top of it. For just a moment, she couldn't get her breath and she grabbed her solar-plexus in pain as Jordan went back and closed the door.

"You son of a bitch," she gasped out as she tried to sit up.

"You brought that on yourself," he answered, and it further annoyed Elle that he didn't sound out of breath. What the hell was the man made of? Steel?

But this was no Superman, just Jordan McCabe, an unsophisticated backwoods cattle rancher, and she vowed that he would learn he had met his match in a woman.

"Get out," she ordered, needing more time to formulate a plan.

"I'll wait until your bath is brought up," he said, locking the door and sitting in a wicker rocker by the window.

His gaze never left hers as she brought her legs over the side of the bed. She was frustrated by the fact that when he had dumped her onto the mattress, her skirt had flown up to her chest, revealing her legs and everything else underneath. But his face was a picture of composure as he annoyingly rocked.

"And then what?" she challenged, while pushing her hair back off her face so she could see him better. "Do you intend to tie me up? Keep me a prisoner in here until morning?"

"That depends on you," he said calmly.

"I hate you," she answered, and meant every word. She resented that she felt powerless and had resorted to a childish reply. But at that moment she did hate him, and vowed that before the night was over she would extract her revenge.

A smile crept over her features as a soft knock came to the door. An idea was quickly forming.

When Jordan rose to answer it, he said, "I'll leave you

to your bath, and I'll send up your trunk. Don't try to escape. There isn't a man in this town that would help and you'll only make it worse for yourself."

He waited until the young, frightened Mexican girl had left the buckets of steaming water on the floor and hastily retreated back beyond the door. Just before leaving himself, Jordan said, "I'll look in on you at dinnertime, and then maybe we can discuss this more civilly."

She didn't answer him. She could only stare as he closed the door and locked it from the outside.

She sat on the bed, looking down at the multicolored rag rug under her feet. He had done this to her, after everything they had been through together. He had totally humiliated her in front of everyone. It was only turnabout fair-play that Mister Jordan—I'm so superior —McCabe experience the same.

She knew just how to do it.

For just a moment, the night of her birthday, he had shown her his vulnerable point. She had spent too many years in business, looking for just that, not to recognize it now.

Her smile increased as she rose and picked up a heavy pail of hot water. Pouring it into the high-backed copper tub, Elle started humming, *Momma, don't let your babies grow up to be Cowboys.* . . . It was quickly becoming her favorite song. Good ole Willy . . . how true his words.

For tonight, Jordan Dillon McCabe was going to be one sorry, miserable cowboy.

It wasn't just a wish. It was a damned vow.

Chapter 17

She sat in the rocker, waiting.

Everything was in readiness. The small wooden table was set for two with the best the saloon could offer. The bourbon stood, unopened, between two glasses. A slight breeze ruffled the thin white curtains, taking some of the heat from the room. She'd wanted everything to be right and had set the scene accordingly.

Nervous, Elle rose and hurried to the mirror for the fifth time. She checked her reflection with a businesslike detachment. There wasn't any vanity involved.

This wasn't a seduction.

It was a mission.

Even though she was hot and nervous, she pinched her cheeks to add color and highlight her eyes. What she wouldn't have given for her little black-and-white bag of makeup. She would really have been able to show him . . . but then she thought back to this afternoon when they had caught up with the herd. At the time she had wondered what had caused the change in the men who worked for Jordan. It wasn't until he had dumped her in this room that she had looked into a mirror for the first time in over a week. What she had seen had nearly struck her dumb.

She had barely recognized the tired, haggard face that had stared back at her. She looked . . . horrible. Only hours ago she had stood before this very mirror and cried over the transformation. She remembered bringing her hand up to her sunburned cheeks and touching the freckles that had disappeared with childhood, but now resurfaced with a vengeance. Her hair, fallen out of its bun on her trip upstairs, had been matted. *Matted.* Like an abandoned animal. There were circles under her eyes, and her lips were nearly white from dryness. Even her hands looked like a stranger's. Her skin was cracked; her nails were broken and split. It had seemed, at the time, an impossible task to transform from a hag into a seductress in one evening. But then her gaze had fallen on Cynthia's trunk. Sitting on top was her hat, the one that had dropped into the street when Jordan had grabbed her. She had picked it up and put it on. The woman who stared back startled her.

She looked just like all the other women she had seen on the trail. She looked like a pioneer. Sturdy. Weathered. Durable. And that was what had brought about her acceptance by the men. They didn't see her as the stuttering, confused Easterner. They saw a woman who had proved her worth by enduring, and that accomplishment demanded their respect. In spite of her plan to humiliate their boss, Elle took satisfaction in having earned the men's admiration. The past three weeks hadn't been easy, but she had also proved something to herself. She was a survivor . . . and she could even survive this damage to her appearance. She had hot water, clean clothes and Cynthia's trunk.

It only took three hours of scrubbing, creaming and brushing to bring about the change. She had even found a small vial of flowery perfume hidden under heavy woolen stockings, and took it as a good sign.

Elle inhaled the scent that still lingered on her body. Everything was set.

It was as if a stage director acknowledged her words and pointed to the door, for at that moment she heard the key being inserted into the lock. Racing back to the rocker, she barely managed to spread the white dress around her ankles when Jordan walked into the room.

A tight knot had formed in his belly as he opened the door. He half expected to find a pail of bathwater thrown into his face. Elizabeth was not a woman to take lightly, and she'd been fighting mad when he'd left.

But what he found made him stop for a moment in surprise. She was seated in front of the window, gently rocking. Catching the evening breeze. It was a portrait of serenity . . . and, he reluctantly admitted, one of unexpected beauty. Her hair hung around her shoulders in soft waves that caught the light from the nearby lamp. She wore the white dress from Alexander. It made her look delicate and feminine. As she turned toward him, his breath caught in his throat when she smiled.

"Hello, Jordan."

Her voice was low and peaceful, almost welcoming. Instinct told him to be careful. This was definitely *not* the woman he had left three hours ago. Besides looking as if she had spent a life of leisure, her attitude was totally unfamiliar.

Closing the door behind him, he remembered to lock it and pocket the key before coming further into the room.

"Elizabeth." He said her name calmly, though every hunch he had was telling him she was up to something. No one could make this kind of a transformation in three hours. This woman had been ready to kill him, now she looked ready to—to what? Was it only the memory of her kiss that made him think she also had other things on her mind? Shaking off the notion, Jordan walked up to the table set for dinner.

"They told me downstairs that you had ordered food. There are two places," he noted, lifting the edge of the white napkin to peek at the fried chicken underneath.

"You said you were coming back," she began as she rose from the rocker. He noticed she wore no shoes. "I assumed you wanted to continue our discussion over dinner." She stopped in front of him and he found himself inhaling the flowery scent of her. "Was I wrong?"

He was almost mesmerized by the seductive look in her eyes and quickly shook his head. "That's fine," he said and pulled out a chair for her. He wanted to put distance between them, even if it was only a table.

She was maddeningly slow as she swept herself into her chair, and he felt his blood thicken when she murmured a polite "thank you" and smiled up at him. It was that smile that unnerved him. Gone was any trace of anger. In its place was a warmth that he could only regard with suspicion.

Jordan sat down opposite her. As he placed the napkin on his thigh, his eyebrow rose in question while he watched her open the bottle of bourbon.

"A drink?" she asked sweetly, and innocently, as if she did that sort of thing every day.

Cautious, he nodded and watched as she poured a good

measure into his glass. It further surprised him to see her fill her own with the same amount.

Raising hers into the air, she smiled and said, "A truce, then?"

Now he knew she was up to something, but decided to allow her to play out her game. Lifting his glass to hers, he said, "A truce," though he knew no such thing could possibly exist. Elizabeth was no ordinary woman, and he acknowledged that even an ordinary woman might have a reason to be angry over being hauled through a saloon and locked into a room. Still, it would be amusing to lock wits with her, and he had to admit his curiosity played a major role in his acquiescence. If nothing else, Elizabeth Mackenzie was never boring.

As he sipped his bourbon, he watched as she did the same while trying to mask her distaste. He couldn't help smirking. "If you don't like it, why drink it?"

She swallowed and attempted to smile. "I'm just used to mixing it with ginger ale, that's all."

"Ginger ale?"

She nodded. "I remember the first time I had to order a drink in public. I had no idea what to ask for, and then a well-dressed man next to me said to the bartender— bourbon and ginger, with a twist of lemon. I liked the way it sounded, so I did the same." She laughed and shook her head. "I was surprised that I also liked the way it tasted. I've been ordering them ever since."

He leaned closer to the table. "Do you do that often? Walk into saloons and order drinks?"

She laughed again, this time low and seductive, and he was annoyed that a quick response coiled in his groin and slowly spread down his legs. He'd obviously been without a woman for too long.

277

"Oh, Jordan . . ." She leaned back in her chair and grinned. "You're such an innocent."

"I beg your pardon?" His knife and fork were poised in midair. That was one word a woman had never before applied to him.

She brought the glass back up to her mouth and emptied it. He watched, astonished, as she nearly slammed it back onto the table and gasped for breath.

"It's really got a kick, doesn't it?" she asked in a hoarse voice. Her eyes were actually watering and yet she was still trying to show that she could handle the liquor.

"Maybe you should eat something," he suggested, as she picked up the bottle and refilled her glass. Ten minutes of this and she would be drunk.

"Go ahead and eat," she offered magnanimously with a wave of her hand.

"I was talking about you."

She looked surprised. "Oh." With extreme care she lifted the napkin away and picked up her knife and fork.

He noticed that she used the utensils with a daintiness that would have made his mother smile with approval. Somewhere, Elizabeth had learned proper manners. And that just didn't fit with a woman who would feel comfortable walking into a bar and ordering hard liquor.

"You never answered my question," he said after cutting into his own chicken.

She smiled . . . again. "And which question was that?"

"Do you often walk into drinking establishments and order bourbon? And why am I an innocent for asking?"

"That's two questions."

He merely looked at her. Waiting.

She shrugged.

She wiped the corner of her mouth with her napkin and replaced it in her lap. "Okay. No, I don't often walk into drinking establishments, as you call them. And I said you were an innocent because you're judging me by standards from this time, when women were considered little more than chattel."

"Chattel?"

"You know—peasants, workers, possessions—"

"I understand the meaning of the word," he interrupted. "What I don't understand is how you can make that statement. Have I ever treated you like that?"

Her lips moved into what was now an annoying smile. "Perhaps I'm referring to when you threw me over your shoulder and carried me through a room filled with hooting males. Or, possibly I'm hinting at the actions of the man who dumped me on that bed and locked me in this room. I believe I'm still locked in. Is that correct?"

"Elizabeth, you were . . ." His voice trailed into silence.

"Yes?"

She had touched a nerve, and yet he couldn't deny that her words carried a ring of truth behind them. "You were unreasonable," he finally answered. "You wouldn't listen to reason. You left me with no choice."

She laughed. She actually laughed.

"You see, Jordan. *That's* why you're an innocent. You think of women as flighty creatures with an inferior intellect. Let me tell you something. I happen to be the top salesperson for a multi-million-dollar corporation, and would you like to know how I achieved that?" She didn't wait for a reply, and he, quite honestly, had no idea what she was talking about.

"I got there," she continued, "by using my brain. By

outwitting men . . . just like you. Men who harbored the preconceived notion that the male is born superior."

"You *are* a suffragette!" he announced triumphantly while picking up his glass. Without thought he threw back his head and gulped the fiery liquid. "I knew it," he muttered, irritated that his voice sounded husky and rough from the alcohol that continued to burn his throat.

"I'm a feminist," she said sweetly. "You see, in my time—"

He held up his hand. "We are not back to this, are we?"

She raised her eyebrows in question.

"Please tell me you are not about to state that you are from the future again. Surely now, after everything you've been through in the last few weeks, you can see how ludicrous that statement is."

She shook her head as if in sorrow for his lack of intelligence. Everything she did, every action, every statement, proved an annoyance.

"I fail to see how your denial renders that statement false."

"Alcohol does this to you," he stated, pointing his finger at the bottle. "Every time I've seen you drink, you start talking like this. About coming from the future. Some people see pink elephants. You think you've traveled back in time."

Ignoring his outburst, she continued, "As I was saying. In my time, the year nineteen hundred and ninety-one, men are just now beginning to understand. You—all males, really—can't be held to blame. It's evolutionary."

"What?" Now he was bewildered, though he hated to admit it.

"You're all confused. You don't know where you

belong anymore. And it's worse for the men in my time."

He didn't even bother to correct her. It was obvious she was on a roll and no amount of reasoning was going to stop her. Forgetting his food, he refilled his glass and settled back in his chair to hear her out.

"It's worse?" he asked, ready to be entertained.

She nodded and sipped her bourbon. "Since prehistoric times, homo sapiens have—"

"Wait! wait . . . *home sap*—?"

"Homo sapiens," she corrected. "Man. Early man." She appeared frustrated and said in a schoolmarmish tone, "Cavemen? First human beings descended from the apes?"

His mouth hung open. "You believe that men descended from apes?"

She laughed. "Not just men, though I've known more than a few that have acted like it. Everyone. Males and females. It's been proven that our ancestors are apes."

He sat up straighter, clearly offended. "My ancestors are originally from Scotland and Ireland. We have a family tree that dates back to 1612."

She nodded. "Yes, well, humankind has a family tree that dates back about four million years. With skeletal remains that indicate I'm right, but I'm getting off the subject. We were discussing the evolution of men's psyche, not their bodies."

She again sipped her drink, her food completely forgotten. "Where was I?" she asked herself. "Oh, yes. Since caveman times, human culture has developed into three stages. In earliest societies we had the hunter, a man who was valued for his ability to bring in wild animals for food. This man was seen as important. And the bigger he was, the stronger he proved himself, the more his worth. Then we had the farmer who controlled his food source, and the bigger and stronger he was the larger the field he could monopolize. The larger the field, the more wealthy and respected he became. If he couldn't do it himself, he dominated others to cultivate his land for him. And then comes the warrior, and the importance of his size and his skill to handle heavy, weighty weapons is obvious. He's needed to protect the land and those who inhabited it."

Enjoying her recitation in spite of himself, he said the first word that came into his head. "Fascinating." And he wasn't sure if he was referring to the story, or her.

She grinned. "But then comes the Industrial Revolution."

"The what?"

"Industrial Revolution. When people learned to run machinery with energy from coal and other fuel. Don't you see, Jordan, that's when everything started to change."

"I don't understand the point you're trying to make."

She took a deep breath and looked out to the bedroom, as if thinking of an explanation. "In my time size and strength mean something entirely different. A woman doesn't need a man to provide meat for her table. She can do it herself. A hundred-pound female can sit behind the steering wheel of a huge machine and harvest an entire field in less than one day. A five-foot Vietnamese woman can pick up an M16 rifle and bring down a two-hundred-and-fifty-pound man with one shot. We've learned to master the machinery."

He could feel her looking at him with almost pity as she continued. "Everything is so different. Where I come from, sometimes the bigger a man is, the stronger he is, the more he's perceived as being less intelligent. In my time, size and physical strength isn't valued. Intelligence is. For someone in my time to be successful, they need to possess intelligence, diplomacy, and the ability to nurture either an idea, or a nation." She leaned closer to the table, her face intense, almost triumphant. "And, Jordan, women possess those qualities in abundance. We are finally equal, only men haven't realized it yet."

He sat back, studying her. She had angered him, confused him, fascinated him, and now demanded his respect. In spite of himself he found that he did. "Elizabeth. I didn't understand half of what you said, but I have to admire your ability to weave a tale."

She looked sad. "It isn't just a tale. It's the future. It's what's going to happen, Jordan."

"Then I'm glad I won't be alive to see it. You can't disrupt the laws of nature without disaster. If what you say is true then why would a woman even need a man? And if she doesn't, then that spells the end of humanity, doesn't it? Males and females, together, that's humanity."

"A woman needs a man to conceive a child, to continue the race. A woman needs a man to be her partner, to share her life, if she chooses. But she doesn't need one to survive."

"And why haven't you chosen anyone to share your life, Elizabeth?" His voice was low, almost a whisper.

She wasn't prepared for it. "I don't know what you mean," she said evasively and picked up her drink.

"I think you do," he countered. "You're pretty enough to have attracted suitors. When you want, you can be pleasant, even charming. And yet, here you are. Thirty years old. Unmarried. Why?"

She nearly spit out her drink in surprise. "I'm not exactly over the hill," she contested, while patting her chin with her napkin. "My God, you make me sound like my life is over."

It was his turn to smile. "No. I'm just curious to know why you've chosen to remain unmarried."

"I still have time . . ." Her voice trailed off. "Why am I even explaining myself to you? The better question is why you chose to marry someone you haven't even met. I could say the same of you, Jordan. You're reasonably handsome. When you make an effort you can be pleasant, even charming. And yet, here you are, sitting across from a woman that you thought was your mail order bride. Why? Why marry a stranger?"

His eyes narrowed with anger and Elle sat back in her chair, sipping her drink, pleased that she had turned the tables on him. For the moment she forgot about his seduction. Now she was just curious.

"You do that very well, you know. Evade answers." He took a deep breath and added, "If you must know, I decided it was time to marry and wanted someone that shared a common background."

"And so you sent away for her, like ordering a pedigreed puppy?"

"Cynthia Warden comes from an excellent family. From her letters I was able to tell that she possessed grace and kindness and intelligence. Those are qualities that I desired in a wife."

"But she didn't have the guts to make it to Kansas," Elle blurted out before she could stop herself. Why did hearing Jordan extol the woman's virtues anger her? Why should she even care what he thought? Refusing to explore the reasoning behind her outburst, Elle murmured, "I'm sorry. I shouldn't have said that."

He nodded. "No, you shouldn't. I'm sure she thought she was doing the only thing she could. Whatever her reasons."

"That's very charitable of you."

He shrugged and finished off his second drink before refilling his glass.

Forgetting the knife and fork, Elle picked the chicken up in her hands and tore off a chunk of white meat. As she chewed, she studied his face, a face that had been scrubbed clean. He had shaved. His hair was cut. His black shirt and pants were new. He looked . . . almost modern, like a man from her time. But it was that face that fascinated her. She was surprised to see he wasn't angry. He appeared thoughtful, as if considering her words. She was not, however, prepared for his next question.

"Why haven't you married, Elizabeth?"

She found it hard to swallow the chicken. Dear God, the man just wouldn't quit. "I suppose I haven't found anyone I wanted to share the rest of my life with, that's all."

He nodded. "But you aren't getting any younger, you know? Soon you'll be past childbearing age. Don't you want children? Or doesn't that fit into your suffragette beliefs?"

She merely stared at him, and then she said it. Perhaps it was the bourbon that loosened her tongue. She would never know, nor, at the moment, did she care. "I can't have children. I never will."

His mouth opened, as if to say something and then clamped shut. He gulped his drink and reconsidered. "How can you say that? How do you know? Unless . . ."

285

He left the meaning hanging in the air.

"No. I haven't consciously been trying to become pregnant. I don't go around attacking men in an effort to prove differently. It's me. I've had tests. Medical tests."

"What kind of medical tests can prove that? I think you're wrong, Elizabeth—"

"Look," she interrupted, "I had an . . . an operation, and it was botched, done incorrectly, and I was left . . . left sterile." She was so close to tears that she pushed the chair away from the table and ran to the window. Maybe it was the drink that made her feel so emotional, so vulnerable. She just knew she had to breathe in fresh air, clear her head and her lungs— anything to wipe out the memory.

Gulping in the night air, she tried to stop the tears. My God, after all these years it still hurt. How long was she supposed to pay? Did the guilt never end?

"What kind of operation?" He had come up behind her. He was standing so close that his voice was at her left ear. She couldn't turn around. She didn't want to face him.

"Please, don't pry," she said in between deep breaths. She must control herself. She could never tell him the truth. Another woman might understand, but not him. He would never understand the shock of an unwanted pregnancy, the stark terror of being alone with the most horrendous decision pressing down on you night and day.

"When I came home from the war, I learned the truth about my sister's death," he whispered in a voice filled with pain.

She listened as he continued to speak.

"Sheilah was on the brink of womanhood when I left.

286

God, I was so protective of her. My parents gave a huge party when I went off to war and I can even remember not letting the Walken boys fill in her dance card until I had talked to them first. She was my sister and I wanted only the best for her. I wanted . . ." His voice stopped and Elle held her breath as she stared out the window and waited for him to continue.

"When I came home to Atlanta, when it was all over and everything I knew and valued was dead or destroyed, it was then my uncle told me the truth. Sheilah was . . . was raped by a Union soldier after my father died." His voice was strained, as though it were the first time he had ever said those words aloud. "Rather than telling my mother, when she discovered she was pregnant, she went to a . . . a woman. My beautiful sister, so young, so innocent, who never hurt anyone in her short life, bled to death in the back room of a shanty."

Elle spun around and saw tears in the corners of his eyes and her own tears fell over her eyelids and down her cheeks.

"Jordan . . . I . . ." She didn't know if she could force words past the raw tightness in her throat.

He brought his hands up to wipe away her tears. Holding her face he said in a rough, emotional voice, "Don't you see, Lizzie, you're alive. Alive. That's *all* that matters."

Her chin quivered as he brought her face toward him. When he lowered his mouth to hers she welcomed him with a fierce longing that took away her breath. At her response, his kiss deepened and she gloried in the feel of his hands as they traced her jaw line and slid down her neck to the top of her dress. With a frantic need of his own, he tore at the buttons until her dress parted and revealed that she wore nothing underneath. He pushed the material down her shoulders and stood back, staring at her.

"My God, you're beautiful."

She was breathing heavily, and still fighting tears, tears that were so close she had to swallow several times before she could mutter, "Don't say anything . . . please."

This time it was Elle who reached for him. She was driven by a need so strong, so intense, that her brain forgot all about her plans for revenge. Now she could only think about being held, wanted, loved . . . something so basic, so vital, that no human being can survive without it.

With total abandon, Elle led him to the bed. She sat down on the edge of the mattress and impatiently watched as Jordan unbuttoned his shirt. She prayed he wouldn't say anything to break the spell that surrounded them. It was an aura of raw excitement and sensuality, and she didn't want anything, not even his voice, to bring her back to reality. When he pulled the loose shirt away from his waist, Elle reached out and buried her fingers in the thick, dark hair on his chest. Breathing heavily, she stared into his eyes and was struck by the intense hunger she saw reflected there. He never pulled his gaze away from hers as he slid the thin leather belt through its silver buckle. That act, so simple and natural and totally male, marked the point of no return. Unable to watch anymore, Elle closed her eyes and slowly sank back onto the bed. Within seconds, she could feel his hot breath on her skin as he bent over her and she swiftly inhaled the clean scent of him. When his lips touched the inside of her knee, she cried out in pleasure. His mouth, his breath, both hot and wet, became a searing brand that traveled slowly, maddeningly, up over her stomach and ribcage until settling at the tender place between her breasts. She opened her eyes and stared at the ceiling above her, not really seeing the fading plaster. Nothing mattered any longer, she thought, as she wound her fingers through the silkiness of his hair. There was only the wanting, the hunger deep inside her. . . .

With a swiftness born of passion kept too long under control, Elle hugged him to her and turned over. The white dress draped open, revealing her, yet she kept it on as she bent over him. As he pushed it down her back, Elle stared into his eyes. She felt his heartbeat pounding against her breasts, reminding her of his words. *You're alive. That's all that matters.* His hands grabbed her shoulders and brought her closer, so that her unbound hair formed a dark tent around them.

And it was then she breathed the words into his mouth.

"I want you. I don't care anymore about anything else. Not tonight."

It was fast and frenzied. Quick, like summer lightning, and just as hot. For the first time in her life, Elle became the aggressor. She was free, free to be anyone she wanted. And she wanted him. There were no words. None were needed. They communicated in the most primordial way—with their bodies. The mere grazing of his skin over hers created a hot current of intimacy that quickly turned into an ancient dance, a dance that had been choreographed through the ages by instinct and longing.

She felt free of herself, of all the bindings and restrictions that had held her back in the past. Here, in this time, she was able to let go, to use and enjoy the sheer pleasure of two bodies moving as one. She gasped with astonishment at how perfect they were together, how her body seemed whole and complete when he was a part of it. There was no reasoning behind it. She only knew it was right. She was relentless, teasing him with her body, her mouth, her hands . . . until he was with her, at a point of near pleasurable pain that must be eased. He took her hands and tightly clasped them within his, staring into her face, holding her gaze, watching her, wanting her, letting her body move over him. It was as if he'd sensed she had to do this her way and was giving her the freedom. She knew it all without words. In her life she had never experienced such a moment, a timeless slice of joy that she could share with another.

Filled with the power of overwhelming sensations, Elle cried out as her blood became thick and hot and heavy, rushing to where they were joined together. She called out his name as wave after wave of exquisite pleasure washed over her, through her, and transferred to him. Knowing the enchantment would be swift, Elle forced her eyes open. She wanted to remember it all—the astonishment on his face, the passion in his eyes—when she brought him along with her. It was a moment to stir her soul, the end of a precious journey that they had completed together.

She collapsed against him, spent, satisfied, totally in awe, and he brought her to the mattress. She laid her head back against the pillows. Her eyes were closed. Her heart pounded against her ribcage. Her body still trembled. She couldn't think . . . not yet. It was too overwhelming.

He continued to hold her, stroking the hair back from her face. "My God, Lizzie, I—"

"Shh . . ." She was reluctant to hear his words, scared

he would break the spell and she wasn't willing to return to reality just yet. Instead of words, she captured his hand at her temple, kissed it gently, and wrapped his arm around her as she turned on her side away from him. She reveled in the heat of his body against her back. There was something so close, so intimate, about it and she knew whatever they would say to one another would have to wait. Snuggling into him, Elle closed her eyes and released her breath.

It was quiet, and peaceful, and beautiful in its own way.

She wanted it to last forever.

Chapter 18

She felt the kisses at the back of her neck, light and feathery, and a chill of pleasure raced through her arms. Drifting up from a deep sleep, she moaned and pressed into the warmth behind her. It was a wonderful dream, one that she was reluctant to surrender, and it wasn't until she sensed a masculine arm wrapping itself around her waist that she opened her eyes. It was dark, the middle of the night, and the oil in the lamp next to the table had burned out.

This was definitely not a dream. The scents and textures were too real, too vivid . . .

Suddenly, images came flooding into her brain and she clamped her eyes shut with embarrassment. Dear God . . . what had she done? It was the bourbon. The loneliness. No. The bourbon. That had to be it. Jordan. Her. Together. Not just together, but *together*. Man and woman together. Oh, please, somebody save me from this . . .

"Are you awake?" His voice was a whisper by her ear.

She shivered as his breath sent traitorous, delicious

waves of pleasure that traveled with lightning speed to her thighs.

She moaned again, a sort of noncommittal noise. What was he going to say? Fear clutched her heart as she waited.

"Am I allowed to speak now?" he asked, and she could detect a note of humor in his words.

Elle remembered almost forbidding him to talk during their lovemaking and afterwards. My God, she must have seemed like a wanton to him. He could never understand—

"Elizabeth, I have to—"

She turned over and pressed a finger against his lips. "Don't talk about it, Jordan. Please. I don't want to hear you say that you regret it, not even that it was the most wonderful experience of your life. It happened. We're both adults and—"

"Could I say something, please?" he interrupted.

She held her breath.

"I only wanted to ask if you would lift your head. My arm is asleep."

"Huh?" Even though it was dark, Elle could see his face reflected in the moonlight. His expression was half pained, half amused. "What? Your arm?" She raised her head and watched as he slid his arm away from her neck. She'd been sleeping on him!

Inhaling through clenched teeth, Jordan rubbed his shoulder to bring feeling back into his limb. There was no mistaking his pain.

"Oh, God, I'm sorry." Closing the front of her dress, she leaned on her elbow to see him better. "What can I do? Do you want me to rub it for you?"

"Please. Don't touch it!" he gasped, and almost laughed.

Elle found her own lips curling into a smile. And here she had thought he was about to tell her that last night had been magical. Or worse. It could have been a curt "thank you, ma'am. Do you remember where I left my pants?" Secretly, she knew she had been fearing the latter.

Relief that she wouldn't have to face the answer enveloped her and she relaxed. She even giggled. "Why didn't you wake me up sooner?"

He glanced at her. "I tried. You were sound asleep. Snoring to wake the dead, I might add."

Her back straightened. "I was not," she protested. "I do not snore."

He flexed his fingers. "Well, you did tonight."

He was definitely amused and Elle gritted her teeth. This was not exactly the impression she'd wanted to make. "It must have been the bourbon. I'm sorry."

"Don't be." Satisfied with the mobility of his fingers, Jordan reached over and pushed a long curl behind her ear. "Don't apologize tonight, Lizzie Mackenzie," he said softly. He did not let go of her hair. Instead he played with the end of it.

She wished she could see him better, for in the moonlight he looked . . . he looked tender, almost romantic. Like he wanted her. Again . . .

Surely it was just her imagination, yet an excitement spread through her body and she had to fight it off. "Don't call me Lizzie," she said. It was the first thing she could think of—and she certainly didn't want to think of the heat coming from his body, the masculine scent of

295

him, the way his finger was now tracing the curve of her chin.

"You don't like the name Lizzie?" His voice was soft, so soft she had to strain to hear it.

She shook her head. "Ahh, no. It, ahh . . ." She couldn't think straight when his finger was gliding over her skin to her throat. The heat coming from him was unbelievable. Maybe he had a fever. Maybe she had a fever. She suppressed a moan. "It reminds me of Lizzie Borden," she blurted out, desperate to say anything. "You know? Lizzie Borden took an ax and gave her mother forty whacks?"

He chuckled and she felt idiotic for quoting the childhood rhyme. "Well, it does," she said defensively.

"Do you know what it reminds me of?" he asked in that low voice.

She didn't say anything. In truth, she was afraid to speak.

He continued as though she had nodded. "It reminds me of Elizabeth when she's warm, when her guard is down. When she's happy . . . like a young girl." He leaned over and kissed the tip of her nose. "That's when you're at your best, Lizzie."

She felt like crying, or hugging him. She did neither. She stayed completely still as his lips kissed her cheeks, her eyes, her temples and finally her mouth. Unlike before, this time it was soft and, somehow, more intimate than when passion had been behind it.

"You are the most remarkable woman I have ever known," he whispered. "You're warm and witty, fiery and intelligent. You're stubborn and yet giving. You fight for equality as if you want to be a man and in the next half hour you're the most feminine woman I've ever known . . ."

He was making love to her with his words. And it was working. His finger continued its journey down her arm and over her hip. Slow and gentle and teasing. She was powerless to stop him, nor did she want to.

"Lie back," he gently ordered.

She stared into his eyes and was sure she saw something there beyond desire. She was afraid to put a name on it. It wasn't love. It couldn't be love. "Jordan, I . . ."

This time it was he who touched her lips. "Shh. Don't say anything. Just lie back."

She did as she was told. She could feel her heart beating faster, her blood racing through her veins with anticipation. He was letting her know that he would take over, he would direct, just as she had earlier. Now it was his turn.

As if reading her thoughts, Jordan slid his body over hers.

Face to face, heart to heart, they stared at each other until Jordan started to grin. Dear God, Elle thought, he looks so young, as if nothing in the world matters but this moment.

"Listen to me," he whispered against her lips. "Before? It was wonderful, but it was lust." He kissed the corner of her mouth and cradled her face between his hands. "This, Lizzie Mackenzie . . . this is making love."

There was something so peaceful about dawn—the way light slowly crept into the room, changing the colors from a soothing gray into the warm hues of another day. Each sunrise the world awakened with the same sounds . . . the song of birds, the barking of dogs. And yet this morning, Elle Mackenzie was certain no other day could possibly compare.

She sat in the chair by the bed, staring at the man who still slept soundly. She was still, quiet as the morning itself, hugging her knees to her chest, as a warm summer breeze blew in from the window behind her. She was also crying.

Tears ran down her cheeks and fell onto her arms. She didn't even bother to wipe them away as she continued to stare at Jordan. How could it be possible? she wondered. After all this time? And yet she knew with a certainty that her life was forever changed.

She was hopelessly in love.

Nothing in her life ever came easy. She'd always had to work for everything, but this? This took virtually no effort at all. It just *was*. There was no explaining it, nor had she ever been this positive of something before. It shouldn't be. There was every reason to deny it had happened. He was from another time, for God's sake. He wasn't an urban corporate executive. He was a cattle rancher. From Texas. They didn't share any common interests. He'd never heard of Motown, the Beatles, the Rolling Stones, or Elton John, although he'd probably hate rap music as much as she did. More than likely, he'd never been to the symphony or an art museum and she knew his preference would run toward thick, artery-clogging beef steaks rather than delicate French food. It was crazy. They were total opposites. He was capable of extreme violence. She was as passive as the proverbial dove. There was absolutely no reasoning behind it. Except that her heart was demanding she listen to the truth. She loved Jordan Dillon McCabe. And there was no denying it any longer.

But did he love her? Now *that* was the million-dollar question.

Again, her heart told her he did. He had to after last night. In the quiet of the morning, alone with her thoughts, Elle found honesty came easy. Last night had been . . . magical. This cattle rancher had shown her that making love could be tender, yet thrilling, overwhelming and at the same time soothing; passionate and also capable of stirring the soul. He had made her cry out at the pleasure and laugh at the humanness. It was a night of beauty and enchantment, and, she willingly admitted, one of love.

He simply *had* to love her. She couldn't have misread that. As she watched him stir, Elle knew she must tell him . . . when the timing was right.

She was crying. He could see it right away. He had awakened with a sense of ease, finally cast free of the ghosts of his past. With Elizabeth he had found something more important than himself. Last night he had concentrated on her enjoyment, showing her the pleasure that could be achieved between a man and a woman. And yet somewhere, in the middle of the night, he had been struck by the thought that no other woman had given him such a sense of power. He realized the truth that there is more pleasure in giving than in receiving, for whatever he gave was returned to him tenfold. He couldn't help but compare her to Charlotte. Perhaps it was unfair to remember his wife at such a time, but it was inevitable. Charlotte performed her wifely duties by submitting to him; she was never an active participant. He had tried. She had even tried. But he always felt she viewed the entire process as distasteful, although necessary to produce children.

Last night had been different. No one could ever accuse him of being a romantic, yet with Elizabeth he had felt a part of something larger than himself. It was as if they were partners. Perhaps it was only foolishness on his part, yet she had unlocked the anger that was strangling him, moving it out of his heart to make way for her. It made absolutely no sense. She was probably crazy, at the very least suffering from delusions. She was as different from him as night from day. He craved stability and respectability. Elizabeth claimed to be from the twentieth century and flaunted a colorful vocabulary and a suffragette mentality. But she also made him happy. He had laughed last night. He couldn't remember being that relaxed with a woman in a very long time. Perhaps before the war . . . and she stirred up the totally male instinct to protect her and make her happy. He wasn't sure what deeper feeling he held for this incredible woman. He only knew he didn't want her to leave. Not now.

But that was before he had seen her tears. There could be only one reason behind them. She regretted last night. A deep sadness invaded his soul as he sat up and forced a smile. Perhaps he did care for her more than he wanted to admit . . . for he was willing to let her go if that would bring her happiness. How ironic to have found this remarkable woman only now to lose her.

"Good morning." He cleared his throat and felt the beard on his chin.

She smiled shyly. "Good morning."

There was a moment of awkward silence and Elle wondered how two people that had shared such an incredible night of lovemaking could be so uncommunicative. Determined to speak, she squared her shoulders. "Are you hungry? There's all that chicken from last night."

He glanced at the table. "Maybe later. Why were you crying, Elizabeth? Are you ashamed?"

She was startled by his candor. Shaking her head, she said, "No. I'm not ashamed. I . . ." How could she say that she loved him? God, it would make her so vulnerable. What if he didn't feel the same?

He nodded his head, as if he understood her inability to speak. Taking a deep breath, he said, "Thank you for last night. It was . . . special. There's a stage leaving this afternoon for Oklahoma City. You can get a train there for back East if that's your wish."

She straightened as if slapped. "I beg your pardon?" she asked in a tight voice. "Back East?"

He looked confused. "That is where you said you were from, isn't it? I naturally thought you'd wish to return there."

Elle stood up and held the front of her dress firmly against her chest. "Oh, you did, did you?" She walked over to the bottom of the bed and picked up a ribbon. Throwing it into the opened trunk, she added, "How thoughtful of you to obtain that information. Have you made the arrangements already? Am I being paid off, is that it?"

"Elizabeth," he began, but she cut him cold.

"No. You listen to me, you egotistical male." She started throwing hairbrush and mirror into the trunk. "I have always been able to take care of myself. I did it very well before you and your men kidnapped me on this wild goose chase and I'll do it again. I don't need your money, or your advice. And don't you dare cheapen last night by offering me tickets and transportation. My God,

301

what an idiot I am! Someday, Jordan McCabe, somebody will teach you a lesson. I'm only sorry I won't be around to see it."

"Elizabeth, listen to me. I've handled this all wrong. I—"

She picked up his boot and flung it at him. Annoyed that he easily deflected it, her voice rose to a shrill pitch. "Pick up your things and get out. I don't want to hear anything else you have to say. Just get the hell out!"

Hurling the other boot into his lap, she whirled around to the window and wrapped her arms around her waist. She would not cry while he was in the room. She didn't care if she had to bite through her bottom lip to stop the tears. She wouldn't give him the satisfaction of seeing her unravel.

His voice came from behind her. "My room is down the hall. When you calm down, we'll talk. You've completely misunderstood my meaning—"

"Get out of here!" she shouted. Dear God, make him leave. It was only when she heard the sound of the door closing that she turned around.

The room was empty. And the door unlocked.

She was free.

Elle sank back onto the bed and stared at the door. Her heart was beating furiously against the wall of her chest. *Well, here it is . . . freedom. Now what do you want me to do? Why did you bring me here? Why did I have to go through all this, only to wind up alone again?* She looked up to the ceiling, her face distorted with anger. *What kind of God are you? Why did you bring him into my life, only to take him away? And what of the children? How am I supposed to leave them now? Now that I love them.*

Filling with righteous hostility, Elle brought the sheet

302

up to wipe away her tears. Her eyes closed as she inhaled the scent of him that still clung to the thin cotton. Jordan . . . the ache that filled her chest was unbearable. It was like a tight band of pain that clawed at her, reminding her of what a fool she had been.

Flinging the sheet aside, Elle abruptly rose. "I'm getting the hell out of here," she muttered and wiped at her nose with the back of her hand. "No man is going to do this to me again," she vowed, picking up the brush from the trunk and running it through her hair. She walked over to the mirror and stood before it. Staring at her reflection, she whispered, "You survived being thrown back in time, through fever, watching people die. You even survived the goddamned Chisholm Trail . . . you can certainly survive Jordan Dillon McCabe!"

Determined, Elle pulled the brush through the snarls in her hair. She was getting out. Out of this room. Out of Texas. Out of this whole lousy nightmare. And the sooner the better.

Chapter 19

"Why no, sir. There ain't no cause to be alarmed. Just a little fuss between a man and his woman, that's all."

The tall, lanky man ran his thumb over the ivory handle of his pistol. He stood in the middle of the saloon and frowned. "That isn't the way I heard it, Mr. Diggs. Traver Diggs, from the Triple Cross, isn't it?"

The trail boss nodded, and looked nervous. "I don't know what you heard, but—"

"What I heard, Mr. Diggs, is that Jordan McCabe forcibly dragged a woman upstairs and spent the night in her room. From all sources, this was not a woman who would ordinarily occupy quarters in this establishment. If that is the case, then there is cause for my concern. This woman's welfare and reputation has been put in jeopardy."

"You Reverend Slaughter?" Diggs asked.

The taller man nodded.

Traver's shoulders slumped in defeat. Christ! John Slaughter. How in Sam Hill was he supposed to explain this one? Everybody knew the man's reputation. John

Slaughter had come into the territory years ago and had staked out the Circle D ranch. Done real good, too, from all accounts. He was as wealthy as they come and as righteous as an old Baptist woman. He took upon himself the role of circuit preacher and kept the local citizenry in line by following the Good Book, and when that failed to work he didn't hesitate to use the carved ivory pistols in his gun belt. Traver himself knew of at least a dozen men who walked lame after trying to resist the man's authority. He was famous for his fire and brimstone sermons and his lightning-fast right hand. The Cap'n's timing couldn't have been worse. Decatur was Slaughter's home base.

Scratching his beard, Traver said in a placating voice, "Look, Reverend, I don't think you got anything to be concerned about here. The Cap'n and Miss Elizabeth are married."

The preacher's eyes narrowed with suspicion. "Married?"

Traver nodded quickly. "That's right. They were married by proxy over in Georgia. Atlanta."

"When?"

Traver thought for a moment and shrugged. "Can't rightly say the exact date. You'd have to ask them. Here comes Miss Elizabeth now."

Both men turned at the sound of a trunk hitting each wooden step as it was dragged downstairs. They stared at the back end of the woman who was muttering something under her breath.

"Damn stupid cowboys," Elle swore. "Damn stupid cowtown hotel. What I wouldn't give for five minutes in a Hilton." The trunk bounced down another step, jarring her arms and shoulders. "And a strong bell captain to carry this damn stupid trunk."

Finally reaching the last step, Elle sat down on top of the case. Her chest was heaving from the exertion.

"Mrs. McCabe?"

She spun around and leaned her head back to look into the face of the tall stranger. He reminded her of pictures she had seen of Ichabod Crane in a child's storybook. Tall. Thin. Long, graying beard, and the most piercing brown eyes she had ever seen.

"I beg your pardon?" Elle asked. "Were you speaking to me?"

"Mrs. McCabe?"

Elle laughed. "You've got to be kidding."

The man frowned. "I'm very serious. Are you, or are you not, married to Jordan McCabe?"

Elle's mouth hung open. "*Married* to him? Ha! I can't stand the sight of him, why the hell would I want to be married to him?"

The stranger turned to Traver. "I thought you said they were married."

Traver came closer and looked at Elle. "They were married by proxy. That's what the Cap'n told me. Miss Elizabeth?"

Elle shook her head. "Sorry, Traver. You and Kyle picked up the wrong woman in Kansas. Sweet little Cynthia turned back before Wichita." She grinned evilly. "I guess the mighty McCabe didn't want to admit a mistake, so he let everyone continue to think what they wanted."

Traver looked shocked and Elle rose to pat his arm. "It's okay. It's been one hell of an adventure, but I'm through. I'm getting the kids and getting out. Please say goodbye to everyone for me—"

"Just one moment, madam," the taller man interrupted. "Am I to understand that you spent the night with a man to whom you are not married?"

Very slowly, Elle turned to face him. "Who *are* you? And what business is it of yours where I spent the night?"

"My name is John Slaughter. Reverend John Slaughter."

Elle's jaw tightened at the man's self-righteous tone. "Well, Reverend . . . it appears that you are the only one in this place that might have voiced an objection. Everyone else seemed to have enjoyed the spectacle."

"You, Traver, go up and bring McCabe down here. I'm going to get to the bottom of this right now."

Having no intention of ever seeing Jordan again, Elle waved her hand. "Well, I'll be off then, fellows. Hope everything works out."

She grabbed hold of the leather handle on the trunk and began pulling it toward the front door of the saloon.

"Hold on there," Slaughter called out to her as Traver raced up the steps, two at a time.

Elle straightened. Clearly annoyed, she asked, "Are you the sheriff, or something? I'm not lodging a complaint. I just want to leave."

"I act on a higher authority than man's law. You and McCabe have broken God's commandment and flaunted it in the faces of the good people of Decatur. I intend to rectify that."

Elle could only stare at him. This was just what she needed. A born-again do-gooder meddling in her life. It took a full thirty seconds for her to regain the use of her voice.

"Look, Reverend, if you feel the need to preach a

sermon on the ten commandments then address it to Jordan McCabe. I'm out of here."

Again, she attempted to pull the trunk when his hand reached out and grabbed hold of her arm.

"You're not going anywhere, madam. Now sit down until I get to the bottom of this."

Elle continued to stare at him. Then she looked at his fingers, long, bony, gnarled with age . . . and wrapped around her upper arm. Feeling threatened, she pulled her arm free. "Don't you ever, *ever*, put your hand on me again. All my life I've listened to other people telling me what to do—what was right, or wrong. I've always played by the rules, but enough is enough. I'm going to do what I want to do, and what I want is to leave." It was only anger that held back the tears, as a group of men gathered around her. The expression on their faces was an irritating mixture of curiosity and amusement. "And none of you can stop me," she added defiantly.

Just then the group separated as Jordan walked through them. He glanced at Slaughter, as if he weren't important and turned to her. "Where are you going, Elizabeth?"

Damn it? Why wasn't anything going right? She and the children were supposed to be long gone before he even realized they were missing. Now what? She took a deep breath to collect herself. "I am trying to leave this place. Not that I don't appreciate the charming ambiance, or the gracious hospitality that has been extended to me," and she glared at the men around her, "but I do have to bid you all farewell. It's been bizarre, to say the least."

"Sheet! Will you listen to them fancy words?" a leering cowboy announced. "Sure is a feisty little thing, ain't she?"

Elle and Jordan turned to the man and said in unison, "Shut up!"

Slaughter stepped forward. "Watch your mouth, Jake." The admonished cowboy frowned and stared at the wooden floor. Satisfied, Slaughter continued. "Now, you know who I am, McCabe?"

Jordan turned his attention to the tall rancher and nodded once. "I've heard of you, Slaughter. You've made quite a name for yourself by meddling into other people's business."

The reverend's eyes narrowed. "It isn't my reputation that I am concerned about now. It's this woman's. Your actions yesterday have compromised her and sent the wrong message to the rest of the community."

"Look," Elle interrupted, "do you honestly think I care what anyone in Decatur thinks? I just want to forget I've ever heard of the place. So why don't I just leave and everyone can—"

"I will ask you to keep quiet, madam, just one more time. You may not be concerned about Decatur but I have worked hard to eliminate vice from this town. Too many have ridden up the Trail and passed through, only to leave destruction behind them. I want the message to spread that we won't tolerate strangers turning Decatur into a den of depravity and corruption."

Elle rolled her eyes upward. "Give me a break," she muttered, and crossed her arms over her chest.

Slaughter ignored her remark. Instead, he turned his attention to Jordan. "Are you, or are you not, married to this woman?"

Jordan stared at the man. The muscle in his jaw was bulging as he clenched his back teeth. Everyone waited for his answer, including Elle.

"I am not."

Traver, standing next to his boss, groaned loudly.

Slaughter seemed actually pleased by Jordan's answer.
A fanatical gleam came into his eyes and he stood taller,
as if about to make an important decision. "Then you
are publicly admitting that you committed the sin of
fornication with this woman last night."

"Oh, Jesus . . ." Elle swore. "Jordan, don't answer
that. He has no right to pry into anyone's life."

Slaughter spun around to her. "Silence! How dare you
take the Lord's name in vain? Have you no shame,
woman?"

Elle scowled right back at him. "Don't scream at
someone to be silent and then ask them questions,
because you sound obtuse. And, besides, the answers are
none of your business." She looked at Jordan. "We were
two consenting adults. He can't treat us like misbehaving
children."

Before Jordan could respond, Slaughter spoke up.
"*Consenting?* You allowed this behavior?"

Elle refused to answer. She merely glared at the man.

Taking her silence as admission, the reverend pulled a
worn black book from the inside pocket of his coat. "Then
you shall be treated like misbehaving children and taught
a lesson. One that will stay with you the rest of your
lives." He lifted his head and spoke to the men that
surrounded them. "Gentlemen, prepare for a wedding."

After a moment of stunned silence, the crowd of men
started cheering and whooping and hollering. After a
confused moment, Elle realized that it was as if a festival
had been announced and the entire town was invited to
participate. These were grown men talking in excited

311

voices about where the wedding should be held, whose wife would bring the ham and potato salad. And didn't Mary Alice make the best corn relish in the territory? What about bread pudding, or should they try to get Miss Louisa to whip up a cake? Did they have time?

Elle would have laughed at the preposterous idea of matrimony, except that she was fascinated by the sight of cowboys preparing a wedding. Dear God, they must live a dull life and any excuse for a party was welcomed.

"Excuse me . . . *Excuse me!*" Jordan shouted above the noise. Everyone stopped talking and all attention turned to the prospective groom. Jordan stood tall and fairly composed, considering the turn of events. "There will not be a wedding," he pronounced. "I will not marry."

Suddenly, and without any other reason than pride, Elle lifted her chin in anger. "And why not?" she demanded before another could ask the question. Who the hell did he think he was to humiliate her like this? It was one thing to be rejected in the privacy of the room upstairs, to be able to mask the pain in anger. Now, here, in front of all these men, was unbearable.

"Yes, why not?" Slaughter wanted to know.

Ignoring the preacher, Jordan looked directly at her. "I'm already married. To Cynthia Warden."

"By proxy," Traver filled in. "See, I told you, Reverend, he was married. To somebody . . ." he added lamely, while casting Elle an apologetic look.

She was staring at Jordan. How could he consider himself married to that woman? He'd never even met her. Last night really was nothing more than a roll in the hay to him . . . or on a lumpy mattress, to be more accurate. How could she have been such a fool to think otherwise? In his mind, he was married. So what did that

312

say about her? About his opinion of her? Maybe Slaughter was right. They were breaking commandments right and left. And this was the big one. The big A.

"He may have been married by proxy, Mr. Diggs, but it was to the wrong person." The preacher/gunslinger turned to Jordan. "Have you had physical contact with this woman? This Cynthia Warden?"

Jordan tore his gaze away from Elle and shook his head. "No. She was coming out west but turned back before Kansas."

Slaughter looked relieved. "Then there's no problem. I'll dissolve the marriage. It wasn't a marriage to begin with, and it was never consummated."

For the first time Jordan appeared nervous. "You can't do that. You don't have the authority."

Elle was getting more furious with every word that came out of his mouth. How dare he sound so panicked? What was she? A leper? Truly angry, Elle pointed her finger at him. "I'll have you know, Jordan McCabe, that plenty of men would be honored at the opportunity of marrying me."

"That's right," a middle-aged cowboy standing to her left agreed. Elle smiled into his heavily bearded face and didn't even cringe when he grinned back at her and showed several missing teeth. "If you don't want her, I'll take her."

"Me, too," another piped up.

"And me."

"Hey, Reverend, can you dissolve my marriage too? Betsy's gettin' mighty tiresome lately. I'm thinkin' I'd like a young, feisty one."

Slaughter held up his hands for silence. He ignored the remarks of the men and addressed Jordan's statements.

"I do have the authority, Mr. McCabe. Last month Governor Richard Coke appointed me Wise County circuit judge, and I hereby do declare the marriage of Jordan McCabe and Cynthia Warden null and void." He slammed the black book in his hands for emphasis, and the audience surrounding them cheered.

Elle was smiling. "No kidding?" she said in awe. Got to give Slaughter credit, she thought. Once he gets a notion into his head, he acts on it. Maybe it wasn't such a bad idea now that she thought about it. She could keep the kids and take them to Jordan's home. Hell, she didn't have any money, or any place to go. She'd been running away from him because he had humiliated her. Now the tables were miraculously turned and Elle had to admit it felt good. Justice . . . she liked the sound of that word.

"Just a minute," Jordan interrupted everyone's good mood. "You still can't force two people to marry. I am not—"

His words were cut short by the instantaneous appearance of a pistol aimed at his temple. The handles were of etched ivory. "You have done this woman wrong, McCabe, and you now have to pay for your weakness."

"You play, you pay," a lone voice muttered.

"That's right," another agreed.

Elle could have done without the gun, but she had to admit she liked the way the whole thing was turning out. Was it only less than an hour ago that she had said someday someone was going to teach him a lesson? And she had wished she'd be there to see it? She shook her head in amazement. Maybe God was listening to her after all.

Revenge, she realized, could be exceedingly sweet.

Smiling to the surrounding men, she batted her

eyelashes in her best Scarlett O'Hara imitation. "Gentle-men, could one of you strong men carry my trunk back upstairs? I have to prepare myself for my wedding."

As six cowboys fought for the privilege, Jordan called out to her. "*Elizabeth!* Have you gone mad?"

She turned and gazed at him with a serene expression masking the near hysteria bubbling up inside of her. He was handsome, sexually satisfying, wealthy and he had a home. It was the last accomplishment that made up her mind.

"Why no, Jordan, I haven't gone mad," she said in an almost victorious voice. "To quote a cliche: I don't get mad. I get even."

He stared at her and she would always remember the sight of him, dressed in the black outfit, his hair still damp, a slight stubble on his cheeks, a stunned expression on his face. She almost smiled again. Instead, she turned to a young cowboy who was standing on the step next to her. "Would you please go over to Cummings Mercantile and bring back the two children who are there? I'm going to need attendants."

She watched the man run out of the saloon and it was then the idea came to her. "Oh, Reverend," she called out. "Since you're also a judge, do you think after we're married you could legalize an adoption, actually two adoptions?"

Slaughter kept his pistol aimed at Jordan. Shrugging, the man said, "Why not? Might as well take care of everything at once."

Elle grinned broadly. "My thoughts exactly."

Before she turned to go back to her room, she stole a glance at Jordan.

He was furious.

Chapter 20

The town was alive with activity.

Women dusted off their party dresses and heated curling irons to bring festive ringlets to their hair. Quickly combining their efforts, they put together a haphazard meal that lay covered, ready to consume, on a long table. Men submerged in wooden tubs for the first time all week and brought out their Sunday best. They applied pomade to slick back their hair and doused themselves with vanilla extract in case a member of the opposite sex consented to dancing after the ceremony. Everyone in Decatur was in the mood for fun . . . everyone but the man standing under the wide oak tree in front of the saloon.

He was not alone. Three others had been assigned to watch the prospective groom, three men who kept their guns pointed at the tall, scowling rancher in case he tried to bolt. They had given up attempting to converse with the man who regarded them with disdain. Instead, they talked among themselves, knowing Jordan McCabe would overhear their words.

317

"There's worse things than marriage," Buck Nord-strom stated.

Henry Atz snorted. "Yeah, like prison. Spent a year and half over in Montgomryville on the chain gang. Come to think of it, Buck, I done both. Married and prison. Ain't that much different, I suppose, 'cept the food's better in prison."

Amos Grafton chuckled. "How many times you been married, Buck?"

"Three. First one was the only one that was worth a sheep's rump. Never did divorce number two before I hitched up with Mavis. Maybe I should get Reverend Slaughter to null and void it, like he did for McCabe here." Henry sniggered. "Only how am I supposed to do that without Mavis findin' out? Hell, that woman would have my balls in a wringer." He scratched his crotch. "And I'm mighty fond of 'em, boys. That I am . . ."

Jordan didn't even look at the cackling middle-aged men. His gaze was fixed on the swinging doors of the saloon. Any minute *she* would come walking through them. He could see the crowd of people growing as they began to gather for the ceremony, yet he refused to look at any of them. What was the point? It wasn't as if anyone would lift a finger to help him. Hell, they were having too much fun. But it was all at his expense. Even his own men were attending this fiasco. And that's exactly what it was. A disaster.

No matter that he told himself it was his own fault for being foolish enough to trust a female. He should have known better. Elizabeth Mackenzie was not a woman to take lightly. In the deep recesses of his mind, he could almost admire her resilience. Almost. She certainly knew how to strike back. When she had seen the way, she'd

318

grabbed hold and took it. How perfectly it had all worked out for her. She gains a husband, respectability and children all in one fell swoop. Her future was secured.

Or so she thought. He had no choice. Not right now. He'd go through with this sham of a wedding, let her think she had won this round. But the fight had only begun. Besides, none of this could possibly be legal. If he had to employ the best lawyers this side of the Mississippi, he'd find a way out. And then she'd learn the true meaning of revenge. In the meantime, he wasn't about to make it easier on her. A part of him was almost eager for the wedding to be over, so he could leave this place and teach her what happens when you play God with another's life. And he fully intended it to be a lesson she would never forget.

Jordan's eyes narrowed as Kyle walked out of the saloon. The cowhand looked like a choirboy with his pressed shirt and his hair still wet from his bath. Jordan fought traitorous feelings as Kyle brought his harmonica up to his lips and started playing some gay tune. How could Kyle Reavis, whom he had treated like a younger brother, take part in this— Jordan's thoughts were cut short as Cory held half of the door open for his sister. Julie wore the striped dress from Alexander and she carried a small bouquet of wildflowers. She looked flushed and nervous with all the attention she was receiving and she slowly walked in his direction as the crowd parted to make an aisle. So it was about to begin, Jordan thought grimly. He barely noticed that Slaughter had appeared beside him.

He was staring straight ahead at the door Cory held open. Any second now she would emerge and he wanted—

319

Jordan's mouth hung open as he watched her leave the wooden building. For just a moment he realized how lovely she looked. The same flowers Julie carried were weaved into her upswept hair. She wore a long green skirt that hugged her hips and a blouse the color of morning cream with heavy lace at her throat. As she came closer he could see the gold heart and immediately his own hardened. Especially when he noticed the man escorting her up to him.

Traver Diggs, his friend, looked guilty as hell.

Jordan could barely contain his anger. How had she managed to wrangle Traver into this? Traver, who had served with him during the war? He would have sworn his trail boss's loyalty. Hadn't he saved the man's life at Gettysburg? Christ, what other humiliation was this woman about to subject him to?

He received only a small measure of satisfaction in seeing how nervous she was. Avoiding his eyes, she kept her gaze to the ground in front of her. All around her people were smiling and the women were murmuring their approval as she passed. Every female in town must be feeling vindicated by this wedding, Jordan thought cynically. Although the admission did little to brighten his mood, he decided right then and there that fighting the situation would be futile. Besides, everyone here expected it. What would throw Elizabeth off balance was if he were to appear to accept his fate. And he dearly wanted her off balance.

Satisfied that at least he had a plan, Jordan forced a smile to appear at his lips. As she approached him, he nodded to Traver and held out his arm to her.

He almost laughed out loud at her shocked expression. Her eyes were wide, her face so pale that her freckles were more pronounced. And the flowers in her hands shook. *Oh, Elizabeth*, he thought, *the fun is just beginning . . .*

She tried to stop the shaking, but her body seemed to have a mind of its own. It was all so unreal, from the moment Julie and Cory entered her room. She had looked at them and realized she was about to take on the responsibility of parenthood. But what other choice did she have? When Slaughter had brought up the possibility of marriage it had seemed the perfect solution for all of them. All but Jordan. Okay, so she was smarting from his rejection, but a tiny truthful part of her admitted that she loved him. She had never loved another man and the realization just wouldn't go away. Maybe in time she would have gotten over him, forgotten the joy she had found last night, but today she had to acknowledge the love within her heart. She might not even stay in this time, but while she was here she would be with him and the children would be safe. Feeling more and more like Scarlett O'Hara, Elle told herself for the tenth time *I won't think about it now.* Just get through the ceremony. Never mind that there are three men pointing pistols at Jordan to make sure he goes through with it. And don't try and figure out that ridiculous seductive smile on his face. Forget that your mother isn't here to witness this marriage. Hell, you never thought there would ever *be* a marriage in your future. So get on with it . . .

Linking her arm through Jordan's, Elle tried to concentrate on the preacher's words.

"Do you, Elizabeth Ann Mackenzie, take this man to be your lawfully wedded husband—"

"I do," Elle quickly answered.

"I'm not finished yet," Slaughter countered, scowling

321

at her impatience. "Do you take this man to be your lawfully wedded husband in sickness and health, through riches and poor times, until death do you part?"

She nodded. "I do." There. It was over.

"And do you promise to love, honor and obey him in all things?"

Wait a minute. Where did this come from? Elle tilted her head to the side. Jordan still wore the stupid smile. "I think I might have a little problem with the obey part. Couldn't we just eliminate that from the vow? I'm sure I could love and honor him without—"

"Madam, I am not amused," the Reverend Slaughter interrupted. "The correct and only acceptable answer is, I do!"

Elle swallowed. It wasn't like this was a forever binding vow. Even God would understand that she couldn't promise forever if she didn't know where she would spend it. She filled the tense silence with a strong, "Okay, I do."

The preacher nodded with satisfaction and turned to the man next to her. "And do you, Jordan Dillon McCabe, take this woman to be your lawfully wedded wife, to love her in sickness and in health, through riches and poor times, until death do you part?"

There was no hesitation. "I do."

A happy murmuring spread through the crowd until Slaughter silenced them with a threatening glare. "And do you promise to love, honor and cherish her—"

"Now hold on a minute," Elle ordered. "What happened to the obey bit? How come I have to promise and he doesn't?"

Jordan looked pleased. "She's a suffragette," he said as if that explained everything.

"Oh, Lordy!" Henry Atz called out. "I wouldn't tangle with one of them she-men. How's a man supposed to marry a woman that wants to be a man? Somebody tell me that. Can't be done!"

His wife, who outweighed him by fifty pounds, elbowed him in the stomach. "Shut up, Henry. Let them get on with it."

Reverend Slaughter ignored the outburst and looked at Elle. His long fingers clutched the book in his hand. "That's the way it's written here in the Bible. Are you questioning God's words?"

Elle lifted her chin. "God didn't write that. Men did. In my time couples write their own vows and the word obey has been completely eliminated."

Jordan turned to her. With a far too superior look on his face, he said, "Really, Elizabeth, I don't think this is a good time to invoke your fantasy about the future. Everyone here wants to get on to the food and the partying that will follow this momentous occasion. Do you want to keep them waiting with stories that will most certainly have them questioning your sanity?"

She looked around her. Everyone was staring at her, even Julie. She hated to admit that Jordan was right. If she announced who she was, where she came from, this thing would never end. And now she knew that she just wanted it over.

"Go ahead," she said with resignation. What good would it do? No one would believe her.

Collecting himself, Slaughter shot her an impatient look before turning his attention back to Jordan. "As I was saying, Do you promise to love, honor and cherish her?" His expression clearly stated that the task wasn't going to be an easy one.

323

Feeling the crowd's new sympathy toward him, Jordan said in a martyred voice, "I do."

Now that the vows were finally done, Slaughter quickly added, "By the power vested in me by the Lord and the state of Texas, I do hereby pronounce you husband and wife."

Elle barely had time to digest the announcement when Jordan grabbed hold of her shoulders and turned her to him. Without warning, he lowered his lips to hers and kissed her soundly, thrusting his tongue into her mouth and holding her when she struggled to break free. She was thoroughly shaken when he released her just as abruptly and faced the crowd with a triumphant expression.

Angry, Elle had to stop herself from punching that self-satisfied smirk off his face. Instead, she forced herself to collect her thoughts. "Excuse me, Reverend," she said in a determined voice. "What about arranging the adoptions now?"

Slaughter looked down to the children who stood before him. "Oh, yes." He cleared his throat and said in a loud, official voice, "I also hereby declare . . ." and he opened his Bible to look at the paper he'd inserted inside, ". . . Cory and Julie Woodson to be legally adopted by this couple. From this day forward they shall carry the name of McCabe and be known as the son and daughter of Elizabeth and Jordan, and shall be entitled to an equal share in any inheritance that may be acquired by any natural children that may result from this union."

Elle and Julie hugged with happiness and looked down to Cory. The young boy was staring up at Jordan, waiting . . .

He could feel the child's eyes upon him and reluctantly

lowered his gaze to meet Cory's. Something broke inside of Jordan as he read the boy's expression. There was expectation, a little confusion, and something else, something that looked a hell of a lot like love . . . like the kind of love he'd felt once, a very long time ago, for his own father.

Reaching down, he gathered the child up into his arms and hugged him. If nothing else, he would admit his happiness about this. Jordan inhaled the clean scent of soap that clung to the child's skin. "What do you think about that, Cory? You're going to come home with me."

Cory smiled and tilted his head to look at Elizabeth and Julie. "And Julie, too," Jordan added. "Peachtree Point will be your new home."

Elle's mind was screaming, *and me, too! It'll be my new home, too!* But Jordan didn't say it. He didn't even look at her. Beginning to feel left out, Elle was startled when a heavyset woman came up to her and pumped her hand up and down. "Congratulations, Mrs. McCabe. Ain't you the lucky one? A husband and a ready-made family in one day!"

Mrs. McCabe? Those words hit her in the face like a rush of cold water. She really was married to him. Mrs. McCabe . . . but was she lucky? It could be the prelude to disaster. Judging by the expression on his face when he'd heard those words, it didn't appear promising.

"C'mon, now," Buck Nordstrom urged, pushing her and Jordan together. "You two got to lead off the dancing."

Julie grabbed Cory from Jordan as Buck led them toward a flat, grassy clearing. Eager to get on with it, three men stood off to the side, their fiddles ready at their chins. Elle saw no way out. The very last thing she wanted to do was dance with Jordan. It had been bad enough to stand next to him, but now . . . dear God, to have his arms around her might just prove her undoing.

The fiddlers began tuning their instruments as Buck settled them in the center of the dance area. "First dance is for the bride and groom, then everybody joins in," he said, as if giving instructions to children. He nodded to the musicians and stepped back to the waiting crowd.

Staring at the small white buttons on Jordan's shirt, Elle was startled to hear the first loud chords begin.

"They're waiting," Jordan announced grimly, sliding an arm around her waist and taking her right hand in his.

She looked up into his eyes. There was no warmth reflected in the cold light blue, only satisfaction. Or maybe, triumph. Elle had little time to figure it out as Jordan swung her in a wide arc in time to the music. She clung to him and was hard put to keep up. The song was fast, perhaps a polka, and she tried to remember the near skipping steps. Dozens of receptions flashed through her mind. It didn't matter whether they were held at the Four Seasons Hotel or a local fire hall. Every wedding had a polka and she had been cornered by more uncles, cousins or friends into dancing the old standard. It was a benchmark, a gauge of how well the party was proceeding. Usually it wasn't the first piece, though. In her mind, a polka wasn't something you tackled before a few drinks. After that, you didn't care what you looked like skipping and dipping to the maddeningly happy tune. Maybe that's what she needed—a few drinks. Immediately her brain rebelled. Isn't that how this whole thing started? If only she didn't drink that damned bourbon last night. Concentrating, Elle finally fell into step. It all seemed unreal. She was married and dancing a polka with her husband, just like all the other brides she had ever seen. Filled with a small sense of triumph, Elle realized that there was something reassuring in knowing her own wedding was no exception.

"You look pleased with yourself," Jordan observed, turning her even faster.

Elle was beginning to feel dizzy as the people surrounding them began to blur. Only moments before she had observed men and women clapping and tapping their feet. Even the Reverend Slaughter seemed festive. Now bodies and smiling faces became smudges of color and sound. "Slow down," she pleaded, forcing herself to study his belt buckle. She was going to be sick if he didn't stop.

"Oh, but this is just the start, Elizabeth. This is your wedding day, something you've obviously wanted a great deal. I fully intend that you enjoy every moment of it."

She immediately looked up at him. There was more than a hint of sarcasm in his words and his smile was almost frightening.

"And I do want you to remember it, Elizabeth. All of it."

Despite the heat of the Texas afternoon, a chill ran up her back. Her fingers dug into his shoulder as he spun her around again and again. What was he planning? Her mind filled with possibilities, all of them unpleasant.

It was plain, Jordan McCabe wanted more than retribution.

He wanted revenge.

"A toast to the bride and groom!"

Oh God, Elle thought, not another, as a loud cheer

went up. There couldn't be a man left in Decatur that hadn't showered them with a flowery little speech. Even Traver and Kyle and the men from the Triple Cross had added their good wishes. The trouble was she feared she might throw up if another claimed her for a dance or acted insulted if she didn't drink to their toast. If she never saw another glass of beer, it wouldn't be soon enough. Of course, Jordan made sure her glass was always full, and then insisted that she dance with the person who saluted them.

Amos Grafton cleared his throat and said a little drunkenly, "Here's to the McCabes, and to the best damned weddin' Decatur ever put on."

Everyone cheered. It was early evening and the hours of eating and drinking and dancing were taking effect.

Amos wiped his nose on the sleeve of his checkered shirt. "I just want to add that some of us here felt a little bad about not helpin' out Miz McCabe yesterday when she came through the saloon, but we're sure glad it all turned out so well. You might say we feel responsible for this union. And I just want to say we all wish you a long life and happiness."

The crowd around Elle broke out in fresh applause and shouts of agreement. Buck Nordstrom finished off his beer and slammed the glass mug onto a table. Wiping his large hands on the front of his shirt, he walked up to her.

"Play me a fast one, boys," he called out to the fiddlers and Elle groaned as his huge palm grasped her wrist.

"Thanks, Buck, but I don't think I can dance another—"

"Sure you can," Jordan broke in. "This is your wedding, Elizabeth," he said for the twentieth time that afternoon, as if she needed the reminder. "I'll tell you

328

what—after this dance we can call it a night and go up to your room if you're tired." His smile hinted at a deeper meaning to his words. And quite a few others caught the same meaning as hoots and howls followed his statement.

Elle actually gulped down the panic that was bubbling up in her throat. *Go up to your room?* The wedding night. She hadn't thought that far ahead. Pulling Buck to the center of the dance area, she heard Jordan's knowing laughter.

The sound of it grated on her nerves, yet she was forced to concentrate on other things, like keeping her balance as Buck dragged her in a wide circle while trying to find the beat. Buck Nordstrom might be a fine blacksmith, but he was no dancer.

And it was another polka. She winced as Buck's massive foot stepped on hers. "Sorry, Miz McCabe. These feet just got a mind of their own when they hear music like this." Elle smiled weakly and was immediately reminded of Steve Martin's skit on happy feet. Focusing her attention on Buck's happy feet, Elle made sure to keep out of their way.

"Me next," she heard Henry Atz shout as they skipped past. From the corner of her eye she saw the man scratch his crotch in nervous anticipation.

Near exhaustion, Elle swore no other bride ever hated her wedding as much.

Chapter 21

She sat on the edge of the chair and pulled the high-top shoe off her foot. Moaning at the pain, Elle's eyes actually started to water as she massaged her aching feet.

Jordan paused while unbuttoning his shirt and stared at her. She felt his gaze and involuntarily looked up. "My ah . . . my feet," she said stupidly. "I didn't know people could keep dancing like that."

He jerked his shirt out from the waistband of his pants. "That's probably the first party they've had in a year," he muttered, pulling the shirt off him.

Elle stared at his chest, the bare muscles, the silky black hair that trailed below his belt. She gulped and turned her attention to her other shoe. Oh, God. What was she going to do? She really hadn't thought that far ahead to this . . . a wedding night. After last night, it was almost absurd that she be this nervous, this apprehensive, with Jordan. But last night, they had been two human beings that needed each other and connected as man and woman. Tonight they were husband and wife. Correction. Reluctant husband and anxious wife. She

331

didn't know what he was planning. Maybe they would just go to sleep, and not deal with it. No. He was angry. Maybe she should try to talk to him, to explain why she went along with Slaughter's crazy idea. Okay. That sounded appropriate. They could talk.

"Jordan, I know you're upset, and you have every right to be," she quickly added, "but I want to let you know why I did it."

Unbuckling his pants, he spun around to her and she dropped her shoe to the floor.

"Why you did what, Elizabeth? Why you came into my life? Why you allowed me to think you were another woman? If I hadn't gotten that telegram you still might be passing yourself off as Cynthia." He sat on the edge of the bed and pulled his pants off. As if they had undressed in front of each other for years, he tossed the trousers onto the back of her chair. "You are a calculating and shrewd woman, and I underestimated you. You saw your opportunity and a way to get what you've been wanting all along . . . a free ride."

Her chin lifted, as if she'd been slapped. "I beg your pardon," she said slowly, deeply. "You actually think that's why I went along with Slaughter and this marriage?"

He stared right back at her. "I do."

Her entire body tensed with outrage and she had to dig her fingernails into her palm to keep from striking him. "I did this for the children," she said, even though a small part of her knew that wasn't the whole truth. "And I have always been able to take care of myself. Always. Why, when I—"

"Look," he interrupted, as he pulled down the covers and lay back in the bed, "I'm in no mood to hear your

332

stories tonight. You're a crazy woman, Elizabeth. I'm married to a crazy woman," he muttered as he settled himself against the pillows. "An irrational woman with preposterous tales about coming from the future." He shook his head, as if not believing his bad luck.

She tried standing up, but her feet hurt too much and so she merely leaned forward in her chair. "Just because you don't believe it doesn't mean it isn't true. Why would I make up something like that? Don't you think I know what it makes me sound like?"

He only shrugged.

"I don't have any proof," she said, hearing the desperation coming into her voice. "I wish to God I had my purse, or something that would make you believe me, but I don't have anything tangible. All I can say is that I am telling the truth."

He continued to stare at her; his expression was unreadable. Finally he said, "You expect me to believe that you're from the future? You honestly expect that?"

She quickly nodded. "From the year nineteen ninety-one. I know it must sound absurd, but one minute I was in a dentist's chair getting my tooth pulled and in the next his waiting room turned into Wichita's train depot. And that's when Traver and Kyle came up to me and assumed I was Cynthia."

He was shaking his head, so she hurried to continue. "You see, I'd been given this drug for the pain and it had made me feel drunk, more than drunk, and I thought they were all part of this hallucination I was having. Because even I didn't believe that something like this could happen."

"And that's why you went with them?" he asked doubtfully.

"Yes. It wasn't until the Novocaine, the painkiller, started to wear off that I realized something bizarre had happened. But by that time I was too frightened and in too much pain to deal with it. Rather than tell the truth, it had seemed safer to let everyone think I was this woman until I found out what was going on. I was wrong, Jordan," she said earnestly, wanting him to believe her. "I should have put a stop to it outside of Wichita, but everything seemed to snowball out of control. It all got too complicated after I got sick. And then there was Cory and Julie, and I didn't know what to do anymore. I guess the truth is I was just too scared to do anything." She waited for a moment to see if he would make a comment.

Needing to fill the silence, she said, "But that was the only time I deceived you, Jordan."

He didn't respond, just continued to stare at her. After a full minute, he took a deep breath and said, "Cory and Julie are spending the night in my room down the hall. I've left orders with Traver to wake them up by five o'clock. I want to get an early start for Peachtree Point, so unless you plan to spend the night in that chair, you'd better get undressed."

She had tried, honestly tried, to reach out to him. Filled with sadness, she rose and picked up the thin cotton nightgown that someone had placed on top of the trunk. She turned away from him, not out of false modesty, but because she couldn't bear to think that this man she loved mistrusted her so much that they couldn't even communicate true feelings. She could feel his eyes on her back as she slipped the gown over her head. How could she get in bed with him? What if he touched her? And what if he didn't?

She slipped beneath the covers without looking

334

directly at him. From the corner of her eye, she saw him reach over and turn down the wick on the lamp until the room was cast in darkness. She heard him settle himself against his pillow, letting out his breath in a long, tired sigh, and she waited.

And waited . . .

Surely he could hear her heart beating against her breast, she thought, and tried to relax. However, no amount of concentration could ease the nervous pounding, nor could it wipe away the vivid memory of last night and what had taken place in this very bed. How could only twenty-four hours have passed since he had held her and loved her with such tender passion that she had cried at its beauty? Thinking about it only made her want him now. What would happen if she reached out? Would he slap her hand away in revulsion, or would he pull her to him . . . because he must be thinking about last night too. Last night had been honest. Last night had been—

"Good night, Elizabeth."

She felt him shift onto his side, away from her.

Turning her head, she saw the silhouette of his body in the moonlight, the way his shoulder sloped down to his waist. Tears burned her eyes as she realized this was rejection, raw and painful.

What else did she really expect?

Her name was Mandy and she didn't care if her cousin Katie had only given her up because she'd got a bigger and prettier one. Mandy was the best baby doll in the world and she belonged to Elle. Elle loved the doll's soft blond ringlets that curled around her finger, her fat little arms and legs

335

with dimples on the knees. It didn't matter that one glassy eye stayed open when Mandy went to bed. She was just fine the way she was, and Elle hugged the doll to her chest in a possessive embrace. Inhaling the scent of rubber and talc that was so familiar, Elle squeezed the doll tighter. Mandy was her best friend and Elle had made a tiny playroom in the corner of her Mommy's closet. Private time. That's what Mommy called it. It was the only place to be alone, and Mommy said it was all right because she didn't use all the room in the walk-in closet. Elle looked up to the clothes that hung on either side of her. She could smell the sweet scent of her mother's dresses. It came from the little blue bottle with the shiny label, the one that Mommy had read to her. Evening in Paris. It sounded like the name of one of the movies her mother watched alone late at night.

She tried not to smell the other scent, the scent of cigarettes and stale whiskey that clung to her father's clothes. It was the same odor that was always around him. She wouldn't think about him at all, she thought as she carefully laid Mandy into the tiny bed she had created from an old dress box and worn-out towels. It wasn't as pretty as Katie's wooden bed where her dolls slept, but it was warm and—

"Please, John, not again. I can't take much more."

Without looking, Elle grabbed Mandy back up to her chest and clutched the doll in fear. They were going to fight again, and if her father found out she was in the closet he would beat her too. Elle shut her eyes and buried her face in Mandy's hair. I won't listen, she told herself as she put her hands over her ears, yet she couldn't help but hear her father's angry, loud voice.

"Where'd you hide it? I know you took it! Now, where the hell is it?"

Her mother sounded frightened and Elle started to cry,

even before the inevitability began. "*John, I do not have your bottle. I told you before if you want to drink yourself to death, do it. I don't care anymore.*"

Elle knew she should have never come into the bedroom at night. They always fought in the bedroom. He was going to hit her. Elle knew he would do it soon and she wanted to run away before her mother screamed. But she was trapped in the closet, trapped in her body—a body that was too small to stop him.

"*C'mon, Margie, of course you care. If I die what the hell will happen to you and that bastard you stuck me with, huh?*"

"*Stop it, she'll hear you!*"

"*What do I care if she does? Maybe it's time somebody told her the truth.*"

"*How many times do I have to tell you? She's yours. Why can't you believe that?*"

"*Because a man knows when a kid isn't his. Why do you think I drink so much? It's you, Margie. All this is your fault. You've driven me to drink. Now where is it, and I swear to God if you tell me you don't know again I'll beat the truth out of you!*"

"*John, please . . . I didn't touch—*"

The crack of his fist against her mother's skin made Elle recoil and wrap herself into a tight ball. She heard her mother scream, begging him to stop, but he wouldn't. Once she had come running into the bedroom and thrown herself around his legs to get him away from her mom. He'd just flung her against the dresser and went right back at it. Hitting and hitting . . . Yelling bad things . . . and there was nothing she could do, except pray it would all go away.

"*I hate him,*" Elle cried into Mandy's hair. "*I wish he would die and leave us alone. I hate him! I hate him!*"

She didn't know when the yelling stopped and the whimpering began. It was always like that, a familiar pattern. It meant he was gone. Wiping away her tears, Elle leaned forward and peeked out from the crack in the doorway. She couldn't see him anymore, just her mother curled up on the bed like a broken doll.

Elle pushed the door open and slowly crawled to her feet. Very slowly, she walked toward the bed.

"Mommy? Mommy . . ."

Her mother moaned as she tried to turn her face, but it wasn't a face at all. It looked like something bad on television that she shouldn't watch. Her mother's nose was pushed to one side and her face and mouth were covered with blood.

When Elle saw it she dropped Mandy to the floor and screamed . . . and screamed . . .

"Elizabeth! Wake up!"

Her heart was pounding. Her head was throbbing. Disoriented, she bolted up in bed and stared into the moonlit room. Tears were streaming down her cheeks and she tried to catch her breath.

"What's wrong? You were screaming. Elizabeth, are you all right?"

She turned her head. Jordan. She was in bed with Jordan. "It was a dream," she cried in relief and brought her hands up to her face. Overwhelmed with grief, her shoulders started shaking from the racking sobs that tore at her body. "Oh, God . . . Oh, God . . ."

"Elizabeth. It was a dream. That's all."

She lifted her face and moaned, "But it wasn't a dream! It happened—how could I have forgotten?"

"What are you talking about?" He sat up next to her.

"Now, calm down. You just said it was a dream."

She didn't care that he hated her for deceiving him. None of that mattered right now. She needed to say it aloud. To tell someone. "Don't you see? I blocked it out. I forgot. How could I forget?"

"Forget what? What are you talking about?"

She wiped her face on the back of her hand and looked at him. Even in the moonlight she could see the mixture of confusion and concern in his expression. She took a deep breath and said it. "My father. He—he used to hit my mother. Beat her. And I saw it," she cried, like the little child that hid in the closet. "I can't believe I wiped that out of my memory. She was—was beaten so badly that her nose was broken. Her lip was slit and . . . my God, why did she stay with him? Why didn't she leave? Was it because of me?" She was shaking with anger and grief.

"You don't have to say any more," he offered.

"No. Don't you see? I *have* to. For twenty years I buried that horror. Now it's here in my mind and I want to remember everything. He was gone. I didn't know what to do to help her. I didn't even know how to use the telephone—"

"The telephone?" he interrupted.

She impatiently shook her head. "I didn't know how to reach anyone for help, so I ran outside and went to the Freemans' house. Mrs. Freeman came back with me and called the police."

The tears stung her eyes and her throat almost closed with emotion. "They came and took her to the hospital. I think I stayed with Mrs. Freeman. I don't know why I didn't go to my grandparents. Maybe we lived too far away. I can't remember. But I do remember hearing the

Freemans talking about the police finding my father in a bar and threatening him with arrest. Mrs. Freeman was angry about that. She called him a drunken bastard . . ."

That word stopped her cold and a warning chill ran up her back. Her eyes widened in shock as she recalled her father's accusation. *Of course you care, Margie. If I die what the hell will happen to you and that bastard you stuck me with, huh?"*

Bastard. He *wasn't* her father?

"He said I wasn't his. My father . . . he called me a bastard," she said in a numb voice. Even though she was in shock, part of her was rejoicing at his denial. But then she heard her mother insisting he was wrong. What was the truth?

"Elizabeth, it was a dream. Okay, a memory," he quickly added when she shook her head. "But a childhood memory. You say you had forgotten it for twenty years. How reliable can it be? Don't agonize over something—"

"Listen to me. It happened. I blocked it out because it was too painful, but I remember it now. Vividly . . . I know now why I've always hated him. And why he's always hated me. He isn't my father. He can't be."

They sat in silence, each with their own thoughts, until Jordan finally said, "Were you beaten? Did he hit you?" His voice was hard with anger.

She closed her eyes. "Just once . . . and . . . and then I left home." Taking a deep breath, she wiped out the painful memory. "But before that, growing up, he never beat me, just her. I think he knew she would kill him if he touched me, that she couldn't fight for herself, but she would for me."

He breathed heavily, waiting for her to continue, but

340

she didn't. Eventually, he asked in a gentle voice, "Are you okay now?"

She nodded, unable to talk. Her mind was filled with questions and haunting memories.

"Then why don't we try and get some sleep?" he offered, lying back down. "We probably have to be up in a few hours."

She didn't say anything, merely slid down the bed. When her cheek was on the pillow, Elle brought her fist to her mouth to stifle fresh tears. Biting down on her knuckle, she realized why this memory had been triggered.

It was her wedding night. And now she was married, facing a relationship that was starting out as poorly as her parents'—although for a different reason.

John Mackenzie had felt trapped, deceived into marriage, and Margie Curran had paid the price for the rest of her miserable life. Over the years she had allowed her husband to destroy her confidence, her ego, and her self-respect until there was nothing left but a defeated, subdued woman.

Staring blindly at the moonlit window, Elle wondered what her own price would be.

Jordan watched the shudders rack her body. From her breathing he could tell that she was no longer awake. She was like a little girl that had been punished and cried herself to sleep. He thought of his own mother and sister, so protected, so cherished by him and his father, and he couldn't imagine what Elizabeth went through as a child. But reality set in. During the War he had seen a great many horrifying things, things that challenged the sheltered way of life he'd known. In a genteel society, children weren't sent out to fight grown men and die for a cause that they weren't even old enough to understand. Women weren't raped by conquering armies . . . not in the world he'd grown up in. But that world no longer existed. He shouldn't have been shocked by Elizabeth's words, but the anger was there nonetheless. A surge of protectiveness welled up inside of him and he curled his arm around her waist, bringing her closer to his chest.

He told himself it wasn't the woman that he was cradling who had deceived him. It was that little girl whose innocence had been so cruelly shattered.

Taking a deep breath, he closed his eyes and tried to relax. Within seconds, his eyes opened and he stared at the silhouette of her head. What was that word she used? *Telephone?* Not telegraph . . . telephone. How odd. And she seemed impatient with him for questioning, as if he were a child and it would take too long to explain.

He must remember to ask her about it tomorrow.

Chapter 22

The three of them just sat in the wagon and stared.
None of them could believe their eyes. Peachtree Point.
It was, quite simply, magnificent.

They had passed out of the grassy plains into a rolling
timberland, thick with forests of cypress and pine where
the air seemed cleaner and cooler. Ahead of the cattle,
Elle had stopped her wagon as they left the woods behind
them. In the distance was the most beautiful place she
had ever seen. Reminiscent of the Greek Revival
mansions of the deep South, the house stood off to one
side of an immense clearing. It was constructed of soft
peach-colored brick with black shutters and four stately
pillars on the front and on each side. The roof of gray
slate sloped down to meet the pillars and shelter the
second story's lacy balcony that wrapped around the
house. On either side were groves of young peach trees,
planted in straight rows. Off in the distance barns stood
next to a long rectangular structure that was white-
washed. And beyond the buildings were grassy fields
where a formidable herd of cattle lazily grazed.

"This is it?" Julie questioned in an awed voice.

Elle blinked and gulped down the moisture in her mouth. "I guess," she said numbly. *This was Jordan's home?* My God. And she had thought him nothing more than a rustic cowboy, keeping his cattle on the back forty. Try four hundred acres; maybe even four thousand. It was intimidating as hell. Suddenly, Elle knew why Jordan had thought she was only after a free ride. The man was wealthy, at least in land and possessions.

"Well, what'da think?"

She and Julie turned to Kyle who had ridden up beside their wagon. Julie started to giggle. "We're going to live here?" she asked incredulously.

Kyle's smile was filled with pride. He nodded. "Yup. In the big house." He turned back to the impressive home. "That's Miss Hester comin' out on the porch now. 'Spect she'll tell you where."

Elle squinted to see better. She could only make out white hair and a long, wide, gray dress. Hester? Where had she heard that name? Had Jordan told her— Just then her memory kicked in. It was his mother-in-law. Charlotte's mother. The breath left Elle's body in a quick, deflating rush.

She was sure they wouldn't be greeted with warmth.

Home. Just thinking the word lightened Jordan's heart. And seeing Peachtree Point brought a smile to his face. It had been one hell of a cattle drive, one hell of a trip. But now he was back, and he swore it would be a long time before he again left. He let his gaze slowly roam over The Triple Cross. The house was called Peachtree Point, but the ranch itself carried the more Texan handle. He noticed Hester on the porch, her hand shielding her eyes as she looked in his direction. Even though the woman was well into her sixth decade, he knew her vision had picked up Elizabeth and the children.

And he wasn't looking forward to the explanation. He wasn't even sure *how* he could explain returning with a wife and two children. Spurring his horse on, he made up his mind to get it over with as soon as possible.

"Hester, this is Elizabeth. Elizabeth . . . Hester Morgan, my," there was a slight hesitation, "my mother-in-law."

Elle smiled with what she hoped was friendliness. "How do you do?" She held out her hand and cringed to see the skin streaked with sweat and dirt. Dear God, she should have cleaned up before this meeting.

The older woman eyed her suspiciously, and shot Jordan a confused look before extending her own soft, white hand. A lady's hand, Elle thought as she shook it. There were no calluses from driving a wagon across three states, nor was dirt embedded into the creases of her palms. The differences between them were dramatic. This woman stood on the brick veranda, with its lacy wicker furniture, coiled and frilled by the finest craftsmen. Her appearance was that of a guarding matriarch protecting what was hers. Elle guessed her to be in her sixties, yet her skin was remarkably smooth, like someone who hadn't been in the sun for most of her life. Her hair was white-gray, without any of the yellow that can detract. Her eyes were an intelligent blue and they were now fixed on Jordan, waiting for an explanation for the strangers who had showed up on her doorstep.

345

Jordan cleared his throat and took off his hat. He seemed uneasy as he brushed dust off its rim. Looking down at the older woman, he forced a smile and said, "Elizabeth and I were married in Decatur yesterday."

"*What?*" Hester looked as if someone had punched her in the chest. Her eyes were wide with horror.

Jordan, knowing she had heard and understood his words, didn't repeat his statement. Instead, he motioned for the children who stood behind Elle to come up the step and join him. "And this is Julie and Cory. Elizabeth and I adopted them. They'll be living here with us."

Hester Hunt Morgan clutched the white lace collar of her dress and stared at the people in front of her. Clearly in shock, she tried to gather her senses about her. "Jordan, what are you talking about?" she demanded. "What happened to Cynthia? Who *is* this woman? And these children? You've *adopted* two children? What have you done?" Her last word sounded as if it had been forced through her throat.

"Hester, I know this is all a shock to you, and I apologize. If there was any way to prepare you, I would have. But I knew I would have arrived before any word could reach you. I thought it best if I explained everything myself." Jordan looked out to the men who had already led the Herefords into the new corral and were now bringing their gear into the bunkhouse. "I think you should sit down. Why don't we continue this conversation inside?"

Thinking the woman looked like she needed a drink to steady herself, Elle smiled sympathetically. It was an awkward moment and she didn't know what to say, so she took Cory's hand and waited.

Hester stared at Elle's hand clasping Cory's for a few

moments before nodding and leading the way into the house. Letting out her breath in relief, Elle realized that for a second or two she thought the woman was going to demand that they leave. And maybe she couldn't blame her if she did. Smiling at Julie with false encouragement, she followed Hester through the massive front doors.

The moment the tall, polished doors were closed behind them, Elle's first impression was of a dark and sheltering enclosure. The foyer wasn't forbidding or unpleasant, but comforting. Almost churchlike. The hallway was designed to make one feel shielded and protected from the harsh Texas sun, to muffle the sounds of a working ranch and create the illusion of a firm barrier separating the outside world from this home. It took a moment or two for Elle's eyes to adjust to the dimness of the light filtering through the small stained glass windows that framed the front door. This warm light was supplemented by a hanging lantern that, at night, would cast a rich glow on the satiny finish of the dark wood wainscoting. It would pick up and reflect the fertile greens, the oxblood red and burgundy in the heavily patterned wallpaper.

Elle watched as Jordan hung his hat on a massive hall tree with its twisted and spiraled branches that encircled a narrow mirror. She noticed a huge grandfather clock that silently announced the moment she walked into this house. Four fifty-three. The sharp odor of homemade furniture polish, of linseed oil and vinegar, emanated from the wide center stairway, with its gleaming dark wood spindles and shiny balusters, its steps paved with runners held in place by brass carpet rods. Elle was so engrossed in her observations that she was startled when Jordan said, "Let's go into the drawing room, all right?"

347

He held out his hand to indicate the way and Hester walked stiffly ahead of her and the children, leading them into a room that could only be described by seeing it.

It was a fantasy of color, pattern and design.

The high walls were covered in a light-cream damask and the woodwork at ceiling and floor painted in tones of ivory, flecked with gold. Gracing the space in between were large paintings that appeared to Elle's untrained eye like works of the Grand Masters of Europe. There was a huge fireplace in the center of one wall with a mantel of soft-pink marble. Sitting at opposite ends were tall Japanese urns that perfectly matched the light green, rose and pearl-gray hues in the medallion and serpentine-back sofas, loveseats and settees. A quick guess was that twenty people could be seated with ease. She had never seen anything like it outside of a movie set, and glanced at the sumptuous drapes that graced the long windows. They were works of art, like any woman's gown, with an abundance of fabric, cords and fringe. No wonder Scarlett O'Hara was able to fashion her famous green velvet dress out of her mother's precious portieres, complete with tassels, braid and trim. It was all there.

Hester nodded to a small loveseat, upholstered in pale green and rose, and indicated with her hand that Elle and the children should sit down. The expression on the woman's face clearly showed that she worried they might stain it. Conscious of the way they looked, Elle took Cory's hat off his head and handed it to him. She sat on the edge of the seat, making room for a child on either side of her. Elle waited, poised, on her best behavior, as though she were a child herself.

Jordan sat opposite his mother-in-law. It didn't seem to concern him that his clothes weren't clean as he leaned back and ran his fingers through his hair. He appeared anxious, uncertain how to begin. Finally he said, "Cynthia turned back in Kansas. She changed her mind. I suppose she saw a few sodhouses and pictured herself living in one. She went back to Atlanta. That's all there is to say about it."

Hester swallowed down several questions. Instead, she glanced at Elle and the children. "And what about this? How could you have married someone you didn't even know? And adopt these children? You want children that badly, then have your own."

He knew it was difficult for her, bringing another woman into the house, especially a completely different woman than the one she was expecting, but he also didn't care for the proprietary tone in her voice. Nor her rude questions. This was, after all, his home. And it was his life. She wasn't his mother. He was never sure that she even cared for him, or just put up with his presence here because he had provided the proper life she'd required for her daughter.

"I've known Elizabeth for over a month. She's my wife, Hester," he said. Not that he actually felt that way, but he wanted to make a point with his mother-in-law. Ex mother-in-law now that he thought about it. "And Cory and Julie are to be treated as my children. Now, if you'd show them to their rooms, you and I can discuss this matter privately at a later time. Right now, I think we'd all like to settle in. We've had a long trip."

Wondering why Jordan didn't tell the complete truth about their unorthodox union, Elle watched as Hester hesitated, studying the man opposite her. Then, as if coming to a mental decision, she rose gracefully from her chair and turned to Elle and the children.

"If you'll come with me, I'll lead the way."

Elle smiled, trying so hard to exude friendliness. She stood, and the children followed. Before they left the room, she turned back to the man who called himself her husband.

"Your home is beautiful, Jordan," she said sincerely.

He seemed preoccupied for a moment before saying, "Thank you."

She waited for him to continue, to say anything that would indicate her place in this household. Yet he added nothing more.

Nodding shyly, Elle turned back to follow Hester out into the foyer and up the grand staircase. Holding each of the children's hands, she squeezed hard to let them feel her support. Children were sometimes smarter than adults in picking up attitudes. And Hester Morgan's attitude was pretty easy to read.

They were not welcomed additions to this house.

"I'll instruct Nina, our housekeeper, to air out the rooms and replace the linens," Hester said primly as she led them into a lovely bedroom decorated in yellow and white. "I had no warning these rooms would be used. This will be for the girl," she announced, her expression clearly showing her annoyance. "The boy can take the smaller room down the hall."

Elle watched Julie's pleasure as the girl stared at the bedroom. This one room was bigger than her entire home in Kansas. The feminine decor of white lace curtains and the daisy quilt must have seemed almost regal to the child who grew up in a sodhouse. Yet when Hester announced that Cory would be put down the hall, Julie spun around to Elle with a startled look on her face. Cory clutched Elle's hand in a death grip and she knew the two of them were terrified of the woman.

Trying to be diplomatic, Elle smiled and said, "Do you think, Mrs. Morgan, that the children could stay together for a little while until they get settled?"

Hester looked at Julie and Cory and then back to the room. "There's only one bed," she stated, as if Elle had lost her senses.

"Yes, I know," Elle answered in an even voice. Not wanting to discuss the situation in front of the children, she added, "Perhaps Cory can wait in here with Julie while you show me where I'll be sleeping?"

Hester didn't say anything, just nodded stiffly and brushed past Elle. Winking at the children, Elle followed. At the opposite end of the hallway, she was shown into a large bedroom decorated in cream and soft muted blues. A lacy crocheted bedcover graced the high canopied bed. Elle noted that the furniture was not as elegant as downstairs, yet just as tasteful. Chintz slipper chairs nuzzled up against a small fireplace, carrying the same floral pattern as on the drapes. There was a marble-topped bureau, a nightstand, a washstand and a huge armoire with oval mirrors on the doors.

"This was my daughter's room," Hester announced in a tight voice.

"Perhaps I could use another then. I don't mind." Truth was she didn't want to alienate the woman any further.

Shaking her head, Hester said, "This room adjoins Jordan's. As his wife he would expect you to occupy it."

351

Elle looked at the connecting door. So he and Charlotte didn't sleep together. Now that was interesting . . .

"I believe your purpose in leaving the children was so that we could discuss their sleeping arrangements. I must say that I find your suggestion of them staying together to be highly unsuitable and, quite frankly, improper. A young boy should not be in the same room as his sister, especially one of . . . what was her name? Julie? Julie's age."

She came right to the point. The businesswoman in Elle liked that. There wouldn't be any beating around the bush with this woman. Hoping Hester would respect that trait in another, Elle said, "I can understand your reluctance, Mrs. Morgan, especially since you didn't know anything about us until our arrival. It might help if I told you that until yesterday, Julie and Cory were orphans. Jordan and I were with the children when they saw their parents killed and we took them with us. They've been together all their lives and to separate them now, when they have to make another new adjustment, might prove detrimental. Cory hasn't spoken since his parents' death," she added. "I just don't think putting him in a room by himself right now would be a wise decision."

Hester Morgan clenched her back teeth in irritation. "I do not know your background, but I will attempt to instruct you in propriety, since it appears your mother failed to do so." She crossed her arms over her ample chest, clearly ill at ease. "During sleep the body exudes emanations, effluvia—if you will, which contaminate the room and everything in it. These nightly vapors are different for the male and female—thus the reason for separate bedrooms. On the best American and British medical advice, it is highly recommended that males and females sleep apart."

"Why?" Elle interrupted, amused and curious. What the hell was *effluvia*? It sounded like an African lung disease.

Hester appeared annoyed and sighed deeply before continuing. "Honestly, you are not exactly a young girl yourself. I shouldn't have to explain such things to someone of your age. I can see that your training in running a household is sadly lacking."

Elle was about to tell her that she'd graduated Rutgers in the top ten percent of her class, but she knew it wouldn't make any sense to the woman, nor any difference. "I am curious, though," Elle said honestly. "What is this effluvia? I've never heard of it."

"Perhaps you should ask your husband to explain," she answered stiffly.

Elle noted that she said the word husband as if it were forced from her lips. Nodding, Elle said, "I'll do that, then. And until I do, I would appreciate if Cory and Julie remained together."

"That's unacceptable. I will not permit brother and sister to share the same room."

She was about to tell her that this particular brother and sister had shared a single room for their entire lives, a room where the whole family ate and slept and washed, and God knows what other night-time activities occurred and were witnessed, but she knew Hester would be shocked. Instead, she realized that this was a confrontation. This issue would determine who the mistress of the house would be . . .

Elle decided to try reasoning once more. "Look,

Hester," and she used the name with more friendliness than she felt, "I have no intention of usurping your place at Peachtree Point. It's obvious to me that you run this house far better than I ever could." She didn't add that in her own time she had trouble keeping her five-room apartment orderly. "I don't want to take your place, or your daughter's place. I only want some peace, for myself and the children. We've all been through enough, especially them. Now, unless you can give me a better reason than this mysterious vapor thing, then I'm going to have to insist that they stay together. At least, for now."

Hester stared at her as if she were no more than an insect that had invaded her home. Seeing how meticulous the woman was about cleanliness, Elle felt like squirming to avoid the inevitable squashing, but she stood her ground.

Finally, Hester said in a tight, barely controlled voice, "I find it highly distasteful that I am forced to instruct you in matters of breeding and gentility." She took a deep, steadying breath and walked further into the room. Wiping her fingers over a wooden bedpost to check for dust, Hester said in a schoolmarmish voice, "For many years it is accepted, and gentlemen have been warned, of the emanations of the sleeping female, emanations that are carried in the air. It is an established belief that the "vital forces" of each, male and female, might be unknowingly exchanged as a result of too frequent nightly . . . intimacies." The last word was whispered, with obvious distaste. "These . . . these things might cause the wife to show masculine appetites and the husband to demonstrate effeminate ones. Thus separate bedrooms, to safeguard each from the other. You will

354

have the key to this room to protect yourself and your privacy, to provide you with the means of avoiding undressing in one another's presence. Because this, too, is believed to inflame excessive emotion."

She turned to look at Elle. "Now can you understand why Julie and her brother cannot share the same room?"

Elle had to bite down on her bottom lip to keep from laughing. *Vital forces!* This woman actually thought males and females might suck the very aura of their sleeping companions? It was ludicrous, and hilarious . . . yet she could tell that Hester Morgan firmly held this belief. "Cory and Julie are brother and sister, not husband and wife. If it would make you feel any better, maybe we could set up a cot for Cory across the room? And it would only be for a few days, just until they become more comfortable here."

The two women stood, staring, measuring each other, for what seemed to Elle like endless, tortuous, minutes. Neither wanted to back down, both knowing the resolution would determine an already rocky relationship. Finally, Elle decided to speak, to strike a deal. It was, after all, the one area she knew about.

"For three days Cory sleeps on a cot in Julie's room. During that time we'll get him used to the separation. We'll put his things into his room, let him play in there and become comfortable. After that, it's your way. Separate bedrooms."

Hester didn't say anything, merely continued to stare—evaluating the situation and the young woman in front of her.

"Please, Hester," Elle appealed. "Don't do it for me, because I'm asking you. Do it for those two scared children down the hall."

Blinking several times, Hester Morgan turned toward the door. Before reaching it, she said, "We dress for dinner. Paulo will bring your things. We always sit down at seven. Exactly."

"We'll be on time," Elle responded.

Grasping the brass door handle, Hester added, "Three days. That's all."

Even though the woman couldn't see her, Elle smiled. "Thank you, Hester," she said in a low voice filled with gratitude.

The door simply closed quietly.

Chapter 23

"She scares me. She's like those women in Caldwell, the church women that look at you like everything you're doing is wrong." Julie nervously checked the buttons on her one good dress, the blue-and-white striped muslin.

Combing Cory's hair, Elle smiled. "Don't be scared. Either of you. Mrs. Morgan just didn't expect us, that's all."

"But what if we do something wrong? This is like living in one of those fairy castles in the storybooks. And she's the evil queen."

Elle looked over to the girl. "Don't frighten Cory. And that isn't true. Let's give her a chance to get used to us before making judgments." God, she even sounded like a mother! Maybe this role was made for her. She was certainly slipping into it easily. "And don't worry about dinner. Just watch me and do everything I do. Do you hear, Cory?"

She looked down to the silent child in front of her. His blond hair was parted and neatly slicked back. He needed a haircut, she thought maternally, and made a mental note to ask Jordan about it. The collar of his white shirt was buttoned to the neck and his black pants had been neatly pressed. Nina, the housekeeper, had fussed over the children and earned Elle's loyalty by making sure that they would walk downstairs to dinner clean and at least pass Hester's scrutiny.

Elle had immediately liked the large woman with her dark Mexican eyes and kind face. Nina seemed delighted with the children and indulged them by bringing up tiny sugar-covered cakes and iced lemonade while she set up Cory's cot. She had even fussed over Elle, helping to put away Cynthia's things in the armoire, setting out the silver-handled brush and mirror and clucking over Elle's lack of wardrobe. When the woman had left to go down and supervise dinner, Elle was sure she and the children had made at least one ally. And that knowledge was comforting.

"Cory? Do you understand?" Elle repeated. "All you have to do is follow what I do, okay?"

The boy nodded solemnly.

She led him over to Julie and the three of them looked into the oval mirrors on the armoire. They stared at their reflection, each filled with their own thoughts. Finally, Elle said, "Okay, people, I think we'll pass. Now let's eat!"

Cory smiled and Julie deeply inhaled, letting out her breath slowly. "I hope Kyle's there," she whispered as they headed for the door.

Elle knew what the girl meant. A friendly face would be welcomed. Leading her troop toward the wide stairway, Elle wondered about Jordan. She hadn't seen him since their discussion in the drawing room. What was he thinking, now that they were finally here? What did he plan to do with her? Would he divorce her? Wait until the children were settled before asking her to leave?

She shook her head to drive out the thoughts. Jordan McCabe was never an easy man to read. But right now there was a dinner to get through. Figuring out Jordan would just have to wait.

"Don't touch anything," Elle whispered to the children as she viewed the elaborate dining room. It looked ready for a banquet. The table was a mass of antique linen, Irish crystal, bone china and silver. A tall centerpiece of gilded sterling stood two feet high so not to block the view of those dining. It was filled with summer flowers and lit candles. Double-tiered ornate silver trays held an array of delicious-looking fruit and added to the assault on the senses of sight, taste and smell. Tiny crystal and silver bowls were filled with pink and white mints at one end of the table and shelled walnuts on the other. There was even a plate of sugar-coated jellies in the shape of flowers, protected by a wire and crocheted lace "safe," to keep away flies. But what really startled Elle was not her surroundings. It was the man rising from his chair at the head of the table.

Gone was the cowboy she had known on the trail. The only trace, the only thing familiar, was his neatly trimmed mustache. Instead of jeans and cowboy boots, Jordan wore a finely tailored black suit, almost modern in style. Even from a distance, Elle could tell his shirt was of snowy white cotton and crisply starched. He wore a black string tie held at his throat by a silver and turquoise clasp that she knew would exactly match his eyes. She noticed that his hair was trimmed and combed back off his forehead and she had the most irrational urge to run her fingers through it. Jordan McCabe was the picture of the perfect gentleman.

Melt my heart, Elle thought giddily, as a warm rush of pleasure raced up her body. The man was drop-dead gorgeous!

Jordan smiled at them and held out the chairs to his right.

"Cory. Julie. Why don't you two sit here?"

Elle nodded to the children and watched as they hesitantly walked up to Jordan. He seated Julie and then pushed Cory's chair in for him, patting the boy's back as he left them to walk around the table to the other side.

"Elizabeth?"

He held out the chair on his left, next to Hester. So, Elle thought happily, she was to have the honored seat next to her husband. She took it as a good sign. Smiling first at Jordan and then Hester, Elle sat down. She looked in front of her. The dishes were rimmed in bands of cobalt blue and gold. The wine glasses and water goblets were of finely cut crystal and she could tell that the silver knives and forks would be weighted and pure. Okay. She could handle this . . . nothing to panic about.

Reaching out, she daintily picked up the starched napkin and placed it on her lap. She looked pointedly at the children and smiled when she saw them follow suit. It was going to be all right. She would show Hester Morgan that these kids had potential.

Hester nodded primly to her as a form of greeting and

then picked up a porcelain bell and rang it. Immediately the dining room door opened and young Mexican women brought out silver platters brimming with food—beef tenderloin wrapped in delicate pastry, roasted chicken with herb sauce, green vegetables decorated with sprigs of mint. Elle was impressed, and knew the children had never seen anything like it in their lives. She saw Jordan serve himself and then, as if he had done it for years, help Cory. Her heart swelled with gratitude as she observed him cutting Cory's meat while keeping up a conversation with Hester about the ranch. He did it casually, without making a point of it, and handed Cory his fork with a smile.

That simple act, done so effortlessly, endeared him to Elle more than she thought possible. Tasting the chicken, she saw Cory fidget, as if uncomfortable, and grinned reassuringly. The boy was trying so hard to please. She turned her attention to Jordan and Hester, trying to listen to their conversation.

"Look what happened to the King-Kenedy ranch. Now it's divided between the two of them. From what I hear Mifflin Kenedy regrets the day that happened," Hester said, cutting off a tiny piece of beef. "It's Richard King that has prospered."

Jordan sipped the dark red wine. "King made a fortune during the war trading in cotton. He used steamboats to carry it to the British ships at Brownsville. That's the money he used to expand."

"How large is his ranch?" Elle asked, wanting to join the conversation.

"Around three hundred thousand acres," Jordan said casually.

Elle blinked. "Three hundred thousand?" It sounded enormous.

Jordan merely nodded and chewed his meat.

"How big is the Triple Cross?" she asked. In truth, she was dying to know.

"Three hundred and twenty thousand," he answered as if it weren't an outrageous statement.

"You're kidding?" Elle was shocked. She couldn't even comprehend such a vast holding.

He paused and looked at her. "No. I'm not. The Goodnight–Adair J&A Ranch is almost a million acres, so we'd be considered pretty small in comparison. But we're not doing too badly. We have almost seventy-five thousand head of cattle, most of them grazing on our land. Some on the government's open range, but very few now that we drove almost a thousand to market."

Elle couldn't help grinning. She was impressed. "And you own all this, Jordan?"

"Two-thirds. I have an investor, a partner, John Magonicle, from Scotland." He was looking at her strangely, as though seeing something in her he hadn't seen before.

Elle turned to Hester and laughed. "And I thought he was some Texan who kept a few head of cattle out on the back forty . . ." She shook her head in amazement.

"It's quite impressive, Jordan," she added with a chuckle and looked around the dining room. "All of it. Congratulations."

Her laughter was contagious and Jordan smiled. "Thank you."

"So you really didn't know that much about Jordan when you married him?" Hester asked, interrupting the moment.

Elle turned to her left. "I didn't know about all this," she answered truthfully. She glanced back at Jordan shyly before turning her attention to her dinner. "I knew enough, though," she added in a quiet voice.

"Where are you from, Elizabeth?" Hester asked. "Jordan never said."

It was an innocent question, certainly one someone would ask under the circumstances, yet Elle quickly looked up to Jordan and saw the slight narrowing of his eyes. She knew he was afraid she would tell Hester the same story she had told him. About the future . . .

Elle sipped her wine and stared across the table at Julie. Even the girl was patiently waiting for the answer.

"I'm from Bucks County, Pennsylvania," Elle began. "My parents are Margarie and John Mackenzie."

Hester took that information and asked, "And what business occupies your father?"

Such a quaint way of rephrasing the real question: What does your family do, and are you good enough to be sitting at this table?

Elle calmly picked up her napkin and wiped the corner of her mouth. "My father is involved in the manufacturing of ale in Philadelphia." It wasn't a complete lie. John Mackenzie had held down a job at Schmidt's Brewery for almost two years—a record for him. Of course, he had probably consumed an equal amount to what he'd manufactured, but she didn't have to tell Hester that.

"How interesting," Hester said in a voice that indicated the exact opposite. "Do you have a large family?"

"I'm an only child," Elle answered and a vivid picture

363

of her mother flashed across her brain. How she would love this place, Elle thought. She had always been so wrapped up in her late-night movies and her magazines that told of the glamorous lives of the stars. Living in a rented two-bedroom apartment outside of Philly, Margie Mackenzie had found an escape in her fantasies. Yet Elle was sure none of the layouts her mother pored over could hold a candle to the real thing—Peachtree Point.

"Are your parents alive?" Hester asked.

She was about to automatically answer yes, when she realized the opposite was true. In this time they didn't even exist yet. "No. No, they're not."

"I'm sorry," Hester said quietly, and busied herself with her meal.

An awkward silence followed, and Elle frantically searched her brain for a subject to fill in the void. Nothing came, and everyone continued the meal quietly. The only noise was of silver forks against china, crystal goblets filled with milk against young teeth—all infractions of proper etiquette. Elle mentally made a note that tomorrow she would have to have a private meal with the children—a real hands-on lesson. She noticed that Cory was still squirming nervously as he clutched his fork in his fist. She'd teach him the proper way to hold it, before Hester pointed it out. Julie was older and had carefully studied the others at the table and followed suit, but Cory was obviously uncomfortable and everyone was beginning to notice his restless movements.

"What is wrong with the boy?" Hester finally asked in an irritated voice. "Must he fidget so?"

Everyone looked at Cory and the child's face reddened with embarrassment.

Immediately, Elle's maternal defenses rose to the surface. If Hester knew the children's true background, she wouldn't be so critical. They were performing. They weren't enjoying this meal. Maybe Cory was uncomfortable because he was scared of making a mistake. Maybe he had to use a bathroom. Or, perhaps he was flat-out terrified of the woman. Elle would bet on the latter.

"Sit still, sweetheart," Elle said softly and smiled with reassurance.

Jordan asked, "Are you all right, Cory?"

The child's eyes were brimming with tears and his hands were under the table, as if adjusting his pants . . . or something. Elle saw Julie's eyes widen with horror when she looked at her brother.

A quick feeling of dread washed over Elle as Hester called out, "What are you playing with under the table? A child's hands should always be in sight. Now please bring them up."

His lower lip trembled, fighting the urge to cry, as he slowly obeyed the woman.

"No, Cory . . ." Julie whispered in fear. "Don't!"

But it was too late. Confused, not knowing what else to do, Cory lifted his hands and revealed what was causing his trouble.

Noah!

Hester Morgan saw those two beady eyes peeking out from that hairy, pointed face and shrieked with horror.

Startled by the woman's scream, Cory jumped in fright and Noah escaped his clutch. The mouse scurried across the table, causing Hester to bolt up and knock her chair to the floor.

Even Elle stood up, trying to head off the thing before

it jumped off the table and was lost behind the furniture or draperies. What ensued next could only be compared to a Keystone Cops serial. Hester remained transfixed in terror, clutching her face and making tiny screeching noises. The rest of them made diving attempts to capture the wily rodent who avoided outstretched hands by scurrying over the table. The mouse dived in and out of the vegetables with lightning speed. Julie made a heroic attempt to snare it but only succeeded in knocking the plate over and scattering peas across the table. Next, Noah ran up toward Jordan.

"I've got him! I've got him!" Jordan yelled, swooping down to trap the mouse. Noah was quicker than any human, including Jordan, whose elbow connected with his wine glass, spilling the contents to the table. Everyone watched the deep red stain spread across the white linen.

"My cloth . . ." Hester whimpered as several Mexican women rushed into the dining room.

Desperate to avoid irreparable damage, Elle reached across the table and picked up the lace and wire tent that was sheltering the sugary confections. "Jordan, get ready to move those flowers," she ordered, spying Noah huddled at the base of the centerpiece.

She looked at Jordan and saw he understood what she was planning to do.

He leaned over the table, holding the center of the gilded piece and glanced at her. "Are you ready?" he asked, knowing timing was everything.

Elle stood poised, the elegant "tent" in hand. She took a deep, steadying breath. "Now!"

Jordan's arm went up; Elle's came down. And Noah

was trapped inside a dainty lace prison.

Everyone stood, for just a few seconds, staring at the mouse, until Jordan said, "All right, I'll handle this. Nina, bring me a box, an old hatbox or something."

"You are not keeping that thing in this house," Hester muttered, her face an alarming color of red.

"Yes, I know," Jordan answered shortly and looked at Cory. "Noah can't stay here. I should have told you that earlier. Don't be upset," he said to the crying child. "This is my fault for not remembering. He'll stay with Kyle out in the bunkhouse and you can see him any time you want."

The housekeeper rushed back into the dining room carrying a large bandbox. Jordan took it and picked up his knife. He punched several holes in the top before taking it off. Almost nonchalantly, he transferred the mouse into it and closed the box. Handing it back to Nina, he said, "Please bring this to Kyle Reavis and tell him he's in charge of Cory's friend."

The woman held the box out in front of her as she hurried out of the room and Elle sank back to her seat in fatigue. Hester glared at them, her table, the servants, and gave a disgusted look. "If you'll excuse me," she said to everyone in general. "I believe I shall retire early."

Like the Queen Mother, she turned and swept from the room, leaving the rest of them to stare after her. Within moments, Elle started to giggle. She couldn't help it. It was a mixture of nervousness and hilarity. They had tried so hard to impress and it had turned into disaster. "Oh, Jordan, I'm sorry," she said, trying to be serious.

She looked at him and saw the corner of his mouth lift in a smile. Nodding, Jordan sat down and it looked like he was biting his bottom lip to keep from laughing. Soon his shoulders started to shake and he was no longer able to control it. Throwing back his head, he started chuckling. It soon became full, deep belly laughs that even Julie found contagious. Cory sniffled, confused by everyone's reaction, but soon he started giggling. Elle leaned over and straightened Hester's chair.

"I don't think we made a great impression," Elle said and laughed regretfully.

"Oh, it was an impression all right," Jordan answered with renewed laughter. "I don't think Hester's had this much excitement since she left Georgia."

Elle looked at him and her heart constricted. He appeared so young, so carefree, as he wiped at the corner of his eye. He was looking at her and the children with what seemed like genuine affection.

"Look," Elle began, anxious to repair the damage with Hester, "I'll clean up everything and—"

"The servants will do it," Jordan said, leaning over and tousling Cory's hair. "It's all right. I told you it was my fault. I forgot about Noah."

"No. I'll do it," Elle countered, leaning over to pick up his wine glass. The wine stain had spread to over twelve inches in width. This cloth was probably in Hester's family for generations. She stood up and looked at one of the young girls who waited by the doorway.

"Perhaps you could make up something for the children to eat in the kitchen?"

The girl nodded. "Si, señora." She turned and left.

That was easy, Elle thought. "Now Julie and I will take care of this. You go have brandy and a cigar someplace else, okay?"

He merely stared at her.

"Isn't that what gentlemen do after dinner?" she asked with a laugh.

He shook his head in defeat as he rose. But Elle also saw that he was smiling. It was a good sign.

When Jordan was gone, Elle said to the children, "Cory, you aren't in trouble, but we do have to make this up to Mrs. Morgan. First go into the kitchen through that door and finish eating. Then you can help me with this tablecloth. The two of us are going to get this wine out."

Looking at the ever-darkening stain, Elle vowed she would scrub it until her knuckles were raw if that's what it took to restore the beautiful white cloth to its former condition.

Somehow, she would make this up to Hester.

Chapter 24

"Momma used to tell us bedtime stories sometimes."

"Really? I don't know, Julie. I don't think I'm very good at that kind of thing." Elle tucked the sheet under Cory's chin and touched the soft skin of his cheek in a gentle caress. "What kind of stories?"

"Mostly from the Bible," Julie answered, sitting up in bed and smoothing the daisy quilt over her lap.

Elle sat on the edge of Cory's cot and took his hand in hers. "I don't know that many stories," she said thoughtfully, "but let me see . . ." She searched her brain for one that the children would like.

And then it hit her. She smiled with anticipation.

"Okay, I've got one. Now listen . . ." She smiled at both children. "Once upon a time, in a time far into the future, there was a girl named Dorothy. Dorothy wanted something better than her own life and she knew it was out there. She just didn't know how to get it. So she decided to leave her home and her family and search for it. She took a huge airplane, a ship with wings that flies high above the clouds, and landed in a strange land—a place much different from her home. She doesn't fit in and she's frightened because there's nothing familiar about this place. She has, in fact, gone back in time—"

"Back in time?" Julie asked. "To when?"

Elle nodded. "To now. To this time. It would be as if you went to sleep and woke up a hundred years ago, during the Revolutionary time, when America was ruled by the King of England. Think how you would feel."

"I wouldn't like it," Julie said emphatically.

"Neither did Dorothy. Anyway," Elle continued, "Dorothy is all alone in this strange place. She regrets leaving everything familiar and thinks 'there's no place like home' and she desperately wants to get back. But then . . ." and Elle paused for emphasis, "she meets a prince."

Julie sighed with appreciation, sure the story was now going to be to her liking.

"The prince offers to help her, to rescue her, and she goes away with him on a grand adventure. They meet up with Indians and cowboys and thieves, but the prince is very strong and very smart—"

"And very handsome," Julie interrupted, as though it were a necessary element to the story.

Elle laughed and said in a sincere voice, "Yes. He was very handsome with dark hair and blue eyes so light they reminded Dorothy of the water in the Caribbean. And a tiny scar over his left eyebrow to show that he was a great warrior and very brave."

"What's the Caribbean?"

Elle blinked, realizing whom she'd been describing. She glanced at Julie and said, "Never mind. It isn't important. Anyway, on one of their adventures they meet up with two children, two little munchkins, who also need rescuing," and she tickled Cory's belly until he laughed. "Dorothy secretly strikes a deal with a Great Wizard that if she helps the children then he will send her back to her time, so she and the prince start looking for somewhere special to place their charges. At first the prince tries to solve all their problems, but everywhere they go just isn't right. There's always something that makes them search even further. Finally, because they are so close to his castle, he decides to take them there until they figure out what to do. But then Dorothy realizes that this is where they all belong. This is the perfect place, exactly what they had been looking for. But she was afraid the prince might not let them stay—"

"Why?" Julie demanded. "Because of the Wicked Witch? There's always a wicked witch."

Elle sighed with resignation. She hadn't intended to introduce that factor. "Okay, because the Wicked Witch didn't want them there. But the children didn't need to worry, because princes aren't the only ones who can fight. Dorothy is also very smart, and remember she has knowledge about the future and secret things no one else in the prince's time knows about."

"What does she do?" Julie asked, leaning forward with interest.

Elle thought for a moment, unsure herself. Finally she said, "She makes up a magic potion of love and weaves her spell around the prince and the witch—who was really just a very lonely and sad woman. Soon the prince begins to see Dorothy and the children for who they really are. He realizes how important they have become to him and knows he doesn't want them to leave."

"What does he do?"

Elle looked at Julie and felt her throat closing with

emotion. "He . . . he tells Dorothy that he loves her. That he wants her to be his princess and live happily ever after. Like in all the good stories."

Julie twisted the long braid that hung over her shoulder. "But what about her family? She never goes back home?"

Elle felt a chill run up her back as she grasped the ending to the story. Her voice was low, thoughtful. "But don't you see? She is home, Julie. There *is* no place like home when somebody loves you."

They sat in silence for a few moments and then Julie said, "I liked it. You made it sound like us."

Elle leaned over and kissed Cory's forehead. She rose and walked over to the teenager. Bending down, she placed a light kiss on Julie's cheek. "I'm glad you liked it. But it was only a story."

Elle walked toward the door. "Now go to sleep. Both of you. Tomorrow's going to be a busy day."

"Why? What are we going to do?"

Elle looked at the two children and a wave of love washed over her. "We're going to start figuring out how to fit in here. That's what."

She blew them a kiss. "Now, turn down the lamp. Good night, munchkins." Smiling when she heard Cory's low giggle, Elle left the room.

If her timing had been different, she would have come face to face with the man who had been standing outside the doorway for the past ten minutes, listening to her fairy tale.

Of course, even princes knew when to beat a hasty retreat.

* * *

She heard a noise beyond the wall and stopped brushing her hair to stare at the connecting door. He was in there. Placing the brush back on the table, Elle glanced at her reflection. The thin white gown of silk must have been what Cynthia planned to wear on her wedding night. Unconsciously, Elle realized she had been preparing for just such a night. She had bathed, rubbed jasmine-scented oil into her skin and brushed her hair until it shone in the soft yellow light from the lamp.

But there would be no wedding night. Not tonight— maybe not ever.

This was not the fairy tale she had told the children. This was reality, or what passed for reality right now. And the simple fact was that although she was a wife, she was not wanted.

Climbing into bed, she lowered the wick on the oil lamp and cast the room into darkness. As she lay back against the plump feather pillow, she stared at the door opposite the bed and wondered what she should do. What if he came in? *What if he didn't?*

Minutes passed in a quiet torture of indecision. Face it, Elle, she told herself, he's not coming. He doesn't consider you his real wife.

But what do you want?

The question repeated itself in her brain, until she pressed at her temples to drive it out. When she was successful, it was only replaced by another, one even more haunting.

Do you love him?

She pictured the morning she had seen him and Cory sleeping in Alexander, the morning she realized that she was the one that would be hurt in this relationship. She had accepted it then, knowing it would never work out for them. But now . . . mental images of Jordan and the children together on the trail, of the magical night in Decatur when they had made love, flashed through her mind. She saw him dancing with Julie at their wedding, carrying Cory up to bed in the hotel. Cory brought out a side to Jordan that even the man hadn't known existed. There was a special bond between them and she loved to see them together. Like tonight at dinner. Already he treated the child like a son.

But do you love him? she demanded of herself.

Yes! The answer was immediate, and in her heart she knew it was the truth.

Then do something about it—before it's too late.

Who was this, filling her mind with questions and demands? Was it her conscience? Or—

Suddenly her eyes opened wider and she stared about the moonlit room.

She knew.

Okay . . . I'm here. Can we re-negotiate? This is the perfect place for the children and I know I said once I found that then you would have to take me back to my own time. That was the deal, but I want to change it. I don't want to go back. Her eyes filled with tears. *I want to stay. I want to make him love me. I don't want to leave him or the children. Can't we think of something else I can do? Can't I give up something else? Not him. Not the children. Please . . .*

Some might think it was arrogant to back out of a deal with God, even to re-negotiate a new one. Some might call it disrespectful or irreverent. For Elle Mackenzie McCabe it was a desperate, fervent prayer. One that she might never know was answered, until it was too late.

*   *   *

It was good to be home, to enjoy the comforts he had worked so hard to provide. There was a great deal of satisfaction and pride when he looked about the large bedroom. Sitting in a striped wing chair, Jordan sipped his brandy and stared at the oak-paneled door. He was clad only in his underwear, the short cotton longjohns that Nina had cut and hemmed above the knees.

She was in there. And that knowledge created an unwelcomed ache in his groin. He shouldn't want her. He should contact his lawyers and get rid of her. Send her away.

But he knew he wouldn't. In truth, he was fighting a battle inside his head, a war of indecision. Should he open the door and go in to her? They could just talk. It wouldn't have to lead to sex. Who the hell was he kidding? He wanted it to lead to sex. That would be his real motivation.

He ran his fingers through his hair in frustration. Now that he had heard her story to the children, he wanted her more than ever. In the quiet of the night, he admitted that he had always wanted her. From the very first. Even when he had seen her with Kyle and Traver as they came up to camp outside of Wichita, even then he had been taken with her. He laughed aloud when he remembered how she spoke to him the first time. Hearing her slurred speech, he'd thought she was deficient, even feeble-minded. Elizabeth Mackenzie had certainly provided him with more food for thought, more frustration and more laughter than he'd had in many years.

But it was the laughter, the good feelings she created, that made him want her even more. He missed being happy, and he didn't know how much until she had come into his life. Sure, she was smart and capable of

377

manipulation. But she wasn't disloyal, or unfaithful. Now that he thought about it, most of her manipulations were done for the children. That's where Elizabeth was her best—with the children. She was a natural mother.

And that bedtime story? Now what did *that* really mean? He had only gone to the children's room to say good night when he'd heard her voice. Stopping in the hallway, he'd listened. At first he had been amused, as entertained as the children with her little fantasy about the girl named Dorothy from the future. But soon it became apparent that she was talking about herself . . . and him.

Did she love him? The question seemed foolish, except he remembered that night in Decatur. It was a torturous memory that no amount of concentration could wipe out. If he had asked that question in Decatur, the answer might have been easy. But now? He wished he could have seen her face while she told her story. He was sure it would have revealed a lot, especially during the part where the prince told the girl of his love. What did she say in the end? That there was no place like home when somebody loves you?

That was so true. Yet he'd never really felt that kind of happiness here at Peachtree Point. Maybe now . . .

He held his breath when he heard the noise coming from her room. It was soft, muffled, like the sound of someone crying.

Why was she crying?

He got up and walked to the door. He barely breathed as he stood before it. Waiting . . . If he heard it again, he was going in.

It would be the perfect opportunity.

*   *   *

The dream was so real. She knew she was sleeping yet, it almost felt as if she could reach out and touch her mother. Frightened, yet compelled, Elle's fingers moved forward . . .

Margie Mackenzie's skin felt cool. It was as if her body temperature was lower than others because she rarely went outside. She was reading her magazine, studying the pictures and the captions that described the glamorous places she would never see in person.

At eighteen, Elle should have been used to her mother's preoccupation but now she needed her. She had spent two hours in her bedroom trying to build up the courage to come out and speak, and she had less than an hour before her father came home.

It was now or never . . . Silently Elle wondered why it couldn't be "never." She couldn't believe that she was about to have this conversation. But then, probably every girl in trouble tells herself it can't happen to her. Only to other people . . . But she had thought—it didn't matter any longer. How could she have been so stupid? So gullible?

"Mom, I have to talk to you."

Her mother looked up and smiled. "What is it?"

Elle could only stare back. Already she felt the tears coming to her eyes. How could there be any tears left? Ever since she had found out five days ago, she'd done nothing but cry. "Mom, I . . . I'm . . ." She couldn't say it. Instead the traitorous tears rolled down her cheeks.

Margie closed her magazine and asked, "What? What's wrong?"

Elle swiped at the moisture blurring her vision and clutched her mother's hand. Her throat closed off and she couldn't force the words past. She just stared at her mother, silently begging her to understand.

Suddenly, Margie's eyes widened in horror. "Oh, my

379

God! No! Please, Elle. Please . . . No!"

Sobbing, Elle nodded. "I'm pregnant."

There was a flash of true sorrow on her mother's face, only to be quickly replaced by fear. "Oh, my God . . . your father! What will he do?"

"Mom, please—forget about him for a minute! What will I do?"

Margie stared at her daughter, so bright, so pretty. She had already been accepted to the State University in the fall. All Elle's plans for a better life were ruined. It was so unfair for the sins of the parents to be visited on the children. Filled with anger, Margie asked in a tight voice, "Who's the father?"

Elle shook her head. "It doesn't matter."

"Of course it matters! He'll have to marry you, that's all."

Elle was desperate. "Mom! I can't marry him. I don't want to marry him! And he feels the same way. The most he'll do is help pay . . ." Her voice trailed off. How could she say this?

"Pay what? Your medical expenses?" Her mother's voice held a distinct note of bitterness.

"Yes," Elle muttered. "Medical expenses."

"And then what?" Margie demanded, clutching her hands together in front of her. "How will you support this child? We're barely getting along as it is. Why, your father will—"

Elle interrupted, "I don't expect either of you to take care of me or . . . or anything else."

"You would put the baby up for adoption?"

"I can't have it," Elle moaned in desperation. "I can't!"

It only took a few moments for Margie to grasp her daughter's meaning. Her eyes widened with shock. "Elle!"

It was finally out, and Elle was crying like a six-year-old.

380

She was so ashamed, so aware of her mother's shock. Her mom had always been so proud of her, bragging to her aunt of Elle's accomplishments. And now this.

Margie ran a hand over her eyes. "Okay . . . there are other ways out."

"No there aren't. Don't you think I've thought over everything? I wanted to run away to save you the embarrassment, but I had nowhere to go." Elle's nose was running and she wiped at it with the back of her hand. "Mom . . . Please! I'm all alone in this." Her hand fumbled with the paper in the back pocket of her jeans. She tore it out and slid it across the table. She was crying so hard that speech was almost impossible, but she had to get it over with. "If . . . if you'll just sign this, I'll take care of everything else."

Unfolding the paper, Margie read it quickly. She looked up to her daughter with a startled expression. "This is a permission slip for a . . . an . . ." She couldn't even say the word. "How can I sign this?"

"What else can I do? Do you think I want to do this?" Elle sobbed. "Don't you understand? There is no future with the father. He doesn't even want to hear any more about it. He gave me two hundred dollars and an address if I can't go through the clinic. I'm the one with the problem, that's what he says. He's going to college in the fall. His life goes on. Mine stops here unless I do something—"

The front door opened and John Mackenzie walked in, making a good show of acting sober, even though his family could tell the second they saw him that he'd been drinking.

"What's goin' on?" he mumbled, dropping his lunch pail on the table.

Margie made a swipe for the white piece of paper, but John grabbed her arm. "What'cha got there?" he demanded. "Another shut-off notice?"

Margie frantically tried to retrieve the paper. "That's it. Just let me file it away with the others, okay?"

"Wait a minute . . . wait . . ." He attempted to focus his vision and read the typed words. "Permission to terminate pregnancy?" He stared at his wife and then back at the paper, as if not believing his eyes. And then he read the name . . . Elizabeth Mackenzie.

He turned on her like a wild animal. "Whore! You whore!" His fist reached out and connected with the side of her head, sending Elle off the chair and onto the floor.

Margie screamed and ran to her daughter. Cradling Elle's head in her arms, she shouted back, "Don't you ever touch her again! I'll kill you if you do!"

"Oh, you will, will ya?" He reached down and grabbed his wife's hair, pulling her away from Elle. "What more should I expect, huh? Like mother, like daughter. The two of you—like bitches in heat!"

Dazed, Elle saw him throw her mother against the wall and she crawled to her feet. It was hate that forced her to rise, to swallow down the nausea, the dizziness, the scream. "Leave her alone! She didn't do anything!"

He turned back to her, an equal amount of hate showing on his face. Slowly he walked in her direction, and Elle backed up. "No, she did her damage eighteen years ago with you and I've been paying for it ever since." His voice was like a dull razor, uneven yet deadly—and it sliced through her.

"All that time spent with your head in those books . . . just pretending, just waiting." He kept coming and Elle kept backing away. "You're nothing more than a slut," he spat out, ripping up the permission slip and throwing the pieces to the floor. "And now you think you can just get rid of it? Didn't those nuns teach you anything in the twelve years I sent you to that school? Answer me!"

Elle could barely think. She had never seen him this crazy. The look in his eyes was terrifying and she felt cornered. "Yes," she cried. "They taught me rules made up by men— men who'll never have to worry about becoming pregnant."

The fury building inside of him caused his face to turn a mottled red. "You've got an answer for everything," he yelled. "Everything but this!"

He backhanded her across the face, so hard that she spun around toward the stairs. She tried to stop her fall, but it was too late. She never remembered actually falling, only staring into her mother's face as she lay in the tiny foyer that led to their apartment. For a few moments there was no pain, only stunned shock and confusion. It wasn't until her mother took her hand that she saw the blood soaked into the sleeve of her yellow sweater. Then she started shaking . . .

"Elle—can you get up? Can you walk?" her mother asked softly, calmly.

Surely her mother wouldn't be that calm if she was really hurt. Confused, Elle nodded and tried to sit up. She felt battered and bruised inside, as if something were out of line. Something was wrong. She stood with her mother's help and sat on the bottom stair.

"I'm going to go upstairs and get my purse and yours, and then we're going to go to the hospital. Okay?"

Now Elle knew what was in her mother's voice. It was controlled panic. Trying not to think, Elle nodded. Maybe she was dying. Maybe this was her punishment . . .

Even though Margie Mackenzie fought like a lioness, they were refused medical attention at two hospitals because they had no insurance. A kindly nurse shoved gauze and foil packets of antiseptic into Margie's hands and told them it was all she could do. Enraged, Margie helped Elle back into the car and bandaged her scalp. While driving to the third hospital, the cramping started. It came on slowly, nothing too different from all the other aches and pains in her body. But then it increased. It was more than cramps and soon Elle was curled up against the door, crying.

"Mommy," she whispered, like the frightened child that she was. "I—I think I'm—I'm bleeding."

"It's all right, honey. I stopped the bleeding. Don't you remember? With the bandages. It's not coming through."

Elle's fingers were shaking as she put them between her legs and felt the dampness. "No," she whimpered and raised her hand.

It was covered in blood.

"Oh, my God!" Margie sounded as frightened as her child. She pulled the car over to the side of the road and clutched Elle's hand. She had to do something! This was her child! Two hundred dollars. That's what Elle said she had. Margie knew it would never pay for the D&C her daughter needed to stop the bleeding. No hospital would touch them. Finally, with more courage than she had ever summoned in her life, she said, "Do you have that address that boy gave you?"

Elle's shoulders were shaking; her body was racked with sobs, and pain, and deep humiliation. How could she do this to her mother? How could she make her mother a part of this?

"Elle. Please! Listen to me. Do you have it in your purse? You're already losing the baby. You're not going to lose your life. We're going to get you some kind of medical care— somewhere! Now, is it in your purse?" She was already looking in the small fake leather bag.

"In . . . in my wallet," Elle gasped as another contraction wrapped itself around her abdomen and doubled her over in intense pain.

Margie switched on the inside light and took out the

wallet. She threw pictures of smiling girls in high school uniforms on the seat until she came upon the small, tightly folded piece of paper. Her hands were shaking as she held it up to the light.

"Kensington and Allegheny. In Philadelphia?" It couldn't be worse. She picked up the wallet and continued her search until she found the money. Stuffing it into her own purse, she said, "I'm going to take care of you, Elle. I promise." She picked up her daughter's hand and squeezed it tightly. "Hold on to me," she said, while throwing the car into drive with her free hand. "Yell, or scream, if it gets too bad. I won't let go of you. I won't let anything else happen to you. I promise."

Within minutes they were on Route 1, heading south toward Philadelphia. Fifty-five minutes later, Margie was arguing with a gray-haired woman with a cigarette hanging from her bottom lip, telling the woman that her daughter had already miscarried in the car and needed help. In less than two hours they were back on Route 1, heading toward Margie's sister's home in Newtown. It would take years before either of them knew the extent of the mental and physical damage rendered that night.

Elizabeth Mackenzie would never be able to have children.

Elle always considered it just punishment for what she had been considering. She hadn't wanted to be pregnant. And now she never would. But it seemed so unfair, so cruel. And there was a part of her that raged against such retribution. It taught her one thing, though, one valuable lesson:

There is no easy way out, and you can't get away with anything.

The room was cast in shadows, yet he followed the

385

sound. It reminded him of the whimperings of an injured child—soft, plaintive, reaching in and grabbing your gut because you knew someone helpless was suffering. He walked over to the bed and looked at her.

She had twisted the bedclothes around her and was moaning. The sound that came from her reminded him of someone mourning, and he whispered her name into the night.

"Elizabeth?"

She didn't respond, so he sat on the bed and touched her shoulder. "Elizabeth, wake up. You're dreaming again."

Awakening with a start, she called out, "Mom?"

"No. It's Jordan. You must have had another nightmare." He reached out and pushed a strand of hair off her forehead. Her skin was damp to the touch.

"Jordan?" She sounded confused, yet relieved.

And then she did the most startling thing. She reached out for him, curling herself against him, and he instinctively wrapped his arms around her.

"Oh, God—it was so real. Like it was happening again." She cried against his shoulder.

"Do you want to talk about it?" he asked gently.

She sniffled and shook her head. She buried her face against his chest and his arms tightened, as if to protect her from whatever torment gripped her at night.

Neither of them said anything, and Jordan waited in silence for her to calm down. But his brain was filled with thoughts—thoughts of Elizabeth at dinner, so pretty and trying so hard to make Hester like her and the children. He thought about the way she had shown an interest in the Triple Cross, wanting him to know that she was impressed with his home. Hester had told him about the deal Elizabeth had worked out for Cory and he admired the way she'd handled that. Instead of screaming at Noah, as the mouse scurried across the dinner table, she had calmly captured the creature and then given in to spontaneous laughter. Laughter . . . he hadn't heard that kind of merriment in this house in many, many years.

And he knew now, now that his arms were around her, that she belonged here all along. That maybe, somehow, Fate had stepped into his life and brought him the right woman after all. She wasn't perfect. She had a shadowy past and delusions of being from the future. It was frightening to hear her speak of it, yet she sounded so convincing at times that he almost believed her. But not quite. They could deal with that later. Right now, he had an important decision to make.

If he wanted her as a wife, a real wife, a real mother to Cory and Julie, then he was going to have to do something about it. This was their first night together under this roof, and if he walked out of this room alone it would set a precedent for the marriage.

It only took a moment for him to decide. This time, this marriage was going to be right. He knew what he must do.

Gathering her up in his arms, Jordan rose from the bed.

"What are you doing? Where . . . where are we going?" she asked sleepily, holding on to his shoulders.

He smiled, thinking of her story to the children. "C'mon, princess. We're going home."

387

Chapter 25

She snuggled against the heat, reluctant to open her eyes. Something tickled her nose, but she tried to ignore it, wanting to enjoy the comfort found moments before complete awakening. Again, she felt the sensation and sleepily raised her eyelids.

Hair. And skin. Not just hair, but soft, curling hair—the kind of hair on a man's chest. Instantly awake, her eyes widened with surprise.

Jordan. It was Jordan. What was she doing against Jordan? Without raising her head, she looked around the bedroom, decorated in burgundy and hunter green. Ralph Lauren would feel right at home with the color scheme and the rich, heavy furniture. She was afraid to move, for fear of waking up the man beneath her. But what if he were already awake? What if he were looking at her, waiting for her to move, to get off him? Frantic questions seized her mind and she froze, afraid to even breathe too heavily. Unable to stand it any longer, Elle slowly turned her head.

He was still asleep. She breathed a sigh of relief and

took a moment to study him. A dark shadow was beginning to show on his face, where his beard had grown overnight. His skin was firm and deeply tanned and his hair was tousled and falling onto his forehead. Dear God, but he was handsome.

And you love him, a voice inside her announced joyfully.

She smiled and rested her head back against his chest. It felt right. She remembered now that Jordan had brought her in here last night. Again, she'd had a nightmare, and this one was worse than before. But she wouldn't think about that now. Now she wanted to concentrate on the moment, for it might not last very long. Any minute now he could wake up and that would certainly prove awkward. Right now she wanted to enjoy him.

His hand was resting on his stomach, inches away from her face, and she studied his fingers—the lines around his knuckles, the tiny hairs below that. They were strong hands, hands that had gently caressed her hair last night as she fell back to sleep, hands that had done astonishing things to her the night before they were married. She felt a tightening deep in her belly when she thought about the one time they had made love. It only made her want him more.

But what should she do? Court him?

Court him? Hmm . . . the idea had merit, Elle thought. What could she lose? After traveling the Chisholm Trail through three states, she had very little pride left. Now how did one go about courting a man—a gentleman of the nineteenth century?

She could play the shy, Southern belle routine, but Jordan already knew her to be the exact opposite. That wouldn't work.

Just be yourself, she thought. And somehow show him how you feel. Deciding to be brave, Elle lifted her hand and touched his fingers. The tips of her own fingers barely grazed his, and she let her nails travel up his wrist. She smiled when she saw how his skin reacted. His arms broke out in gooseflesh. Ahh . . . Jordan McCabe, she thought with satisfaction. Your body betrays you. He brought his arm up and stretched, causing his chest to rise and her along with it. She pretended to awaken with him and lifted her head with what, she hoped, was a very sleepy expression.

"Good morning," she said with a yawn.

He issued a knowing smile and said good morning without a yawn, or any trace of being asleep.

He couldn't have been awake, Elle reasoned. Or, was he?

"Thank you," she said in a hesitant voice. "Thank you for letting me sleep here."

"You're welcome." He still had that grin on his face.

"I—I don't know why I keep having nightmares. I never used to, not since I was a child."

Nodding, Jordan brushed the hair back off his forehead. "You've had a lot of changes in your life. It's understandable."

She accepted his reasoning and added, "Last night— well, I suppose I needed the presence of another human, and I . . . I just wanted you to know I appreciate it."

Why was he still grinning at her like that? It was beginning to get unnerving.

"Elizabeth," he finally spoke. "You don't have to keep thanking me for bringing you in here. This is where you sleep."

Now she was puzzled and she moved away from him. "What? In here? But Hester said—"

Jordan sat up and Elle noticed the sheet didn't move with him. He wore white underwear that came down his thighs. "Forget what Hester said," Jordan interrupted. "This is where you are to sleep. In here. With me."

He stared at her, waiting for her objection. Elle stared right back. In truth, it would have been hard to look away. She knew he was half expecting her refusal. Instead, she nodded. "All right," she said simply.

He nodded back in agreement. Satisfied, he swung his legs over the side of the bed and stood up. "I'll be working in my office most of the day, going over accounts for the house and the ranch. Perhaps if you feel like it, later, I can show you and the children around the Triple Cross."

"We'd love it," she said, happy with his suggestion. She sat back to watch as he opened his wardrobe and picked out a gray pair of trousers and a white shirt. It was just like being married, she thought cheerfully and stopped herself.

I am married, she mentally corrected, and a wide smile appeared at her lips. Isn't Hester going to be shocked to learn she and Jordan might have exchanged "effluvia" last night? She had to bring her knuckle up to her mouth to stop from giggling. Heck, with any luck, they might get to the vital forces and excessive emotions part the older woman found so distasteful.

Hidden by the sheet, the fingers on her left hand were crossed.

Hester Hunt Morgan had left Atlanta, Georgia, as soon as she had found out her daughter was pregnant. On the trip west, her mind had conjured up every story she had heard about Texas. Blistering heat. Marauding Indians. Desolation. Her heart had been heavy, and her only consolation was the fact that a large contingent of Atlanta folk had picked up after the war and settled into northeast Texas—building a new Atlanta with its graceful homes and warm hospitality. She hadn't expected much from Jordan McCabe, for the man was near penniless when he went to seek his fortune. Like so many others, Jordan had lost everything, including family. Hester had been hoping for a small, clean home in the new settlement. What she had found, even now, sometimes took her breath away.

Peachtree Point would have been a showplace in any time, any state, and Hester took it as her God-given duty to keep it that way. Charlotte hadn't had the interest, God bless her soul, in housekeeping or supervision. She was such a child at heart. Yet, who could blame her? Her childhood, and the years following the war, had robbed Charlotte of the carefree times that were her right. She had only been trying to get them back when times were good. That's why she and Jordan had furnished the house with only the best. Jordan had indulged her daughter's every whim, and perhaps, that was why Charlotte's head could so easily be turned by attention.

Hester refused to think about the filthy rumors that had circulated after her daughter's death. That's all they were—rumors, dead and buried along with the only grandchild she would ever have. That grieved her more than she had ever let on. To this day she couldn't understand why God had punished her so cruelly—to take away her only daughter and the babe along with Charlotte.

393

Now she had nothing. Nothing but Peachtree Point.

But now the house had a new mistress. Fear gripped her heart when she realized that her own place in the household was questionable. By all rights, Jordan could ask her to leave.

She had nowhere to go, not anymore. Hester had no desire to go back to Georgia. The war had changed the face of Atlanta, and those who had rebuilt were not the same genteel families that she had known. All the letters from her old friends told of Carpetbaggers sweeping down over the city and taking over. Why, even the VanScivers were living in a three-bedroom house on Jackson Street in a neighborhood Hester had never set foot in. And she refused to live on charity extended to her by those who had rebuilt here in Atlanta, Texas.

Realizing her situation might very well be grave indeed, Hester pulled herself up the stairs—not even noticing that the banister rails had yet to be dusted this morning. Her mind was filled with thoughts other than housekeeping—like the fact that Nina had happily announced she had brought Señora McCabe's coffee into the master bedroom. So they had spent the night together ... It *was* a marriage then, Hester thought grimly. For a short time yesterday, she had entertained the notion that Jordan and Elizabeth were not the picture of a happily married couple. Obviously, she was wrong.

And Elizabeth was surprising, too. She had stood up for the boy yesterday, even though Hester had done her best to make the easterner back down. The fiasco at the dinner table last night had nearly undone her, yet the young woman had been a surprise. Nina had said Elizabeth had washed the wine stain out of the tablecloth herself, and had left instructions that when it was dried this morning, no one but her was to iron it. She didn't have to do that, Hester admitted. But she knew in her heart she would have done the same thing. Hester had been expecting Cynthia Warden, a woman from a family that she knew. The adjustment wouldn't have been easy, yet eventually they would have come to an understanding—being from like backgrounds. But this? Who was this woman, Elizabeth Mackenzie?

She and the boy were accompanying Jordan on a tour of the ranch and, as Hester walked down the hallway, she wondered how she was supposed to go on living here. Still, how could she bear to leave? Elizabeth said she didn't want to take Charlotte's place, yet that was already accomplished. And she also said she didn't want to take over the running of the house. Perhaps, when the time was right, she and Elizabeth should sit down and discuss what was to happen.

In her mind, she had always thought of Peachtree Point as Charlotte's home. But Charlotte had been gone for years now. It was Jordan's—and now his wife's.

She stopped at the doorway to the children's room and watched as the young girl ran a faded cloth over the dresser. She had wondered why Julie didn't go with her brother to see the ranch. She'd thought perhaps the girl was sick and had wanted to rest. But there was something about the child, something about the way her hand lovingly rubbed the oak wood, almost in a caress, that made Hester continue to stare. Soon, the girl noticed her and jumped, standing straight up and twisting the cloth in her hands, as if she had been caught doing something she shouldn't.

"We have servants to dust," Hester said stiffly.

"Oh, no, ma'am," Julie quickly replied. "Nobody has to clean up after me. I don't mind. I—I—"

"Yes?" Hester walked into the room. The bed was neatly made. There were no clothes lying about. If it were not for the cot, Hester wouldn't even know it was occupied. The child was neat, if nothing else. "What were you going to say? You don't have to be afraid to speak, you know."

Julie swallowed nervously and then took a deep breath. "I—ah, I never had anything so fine as this before," she said, glancing about the room. "It's a pleasure to keep clean. The wood shines so pretty when you rub it. And . . . and the quilt. My momma made a patch quilt once, but it wasn't near as beautiful as this daisy one. Somebody sure put in a lot of work on it."

Hester gazed at the bed covering. "Yes," she said thoughtfully. "I did."

Julie looked surprised. "You made it?"

Hester nodded and walked over to the bed. She traced a white petal with her fingertip. "Many years ago. In Atlanta. I was a young woman then. I made it for my daughter." Hester recalled how Charlotte had taken it for granted, spilling tea on it, never remembering to remove her shoes before putting her feet up. It was still lovely, though, but not quite good enough for the main bedrooms. "Do you sew?" she asked the child.

Julie nodded. "My mother taught me." She shrugged. "Not like this, though. We made a dress once. For the O'Learys' barn raising."

Hester stared at the girl. "You're from Kansas?"

Julie nodded.

Hester didn't imagine a farm girl would have an extensive wardrobe. She was wearing the same dress she had on last night at dinner. Making up her mind, Hester said, "Come with me. I want to show you something."

She turned, knowing the child would follow. She led Julie down the hall to the last room on the right. Opening the door, she announced, "This is the sewing room. Nina and the girls use it to repair linens and such. But over here," and she crossed the room to a huge chest and raised the lid. "In here is material that hasn't been touched in years. Perhaps you would like to make yourself a dress."

Julie stared at the muslins and cottons, the satin and silk remnants. She was stunned. "But I don't know how. I only helped with momma's dress. It wasn't for me."

"Well, of course, I'll assist you," Hester said shortly. "We can start right now, if you'd like."

Julie was speechless. She could only nod.

"Fine. Now, which of these materials do you prefer? Personally, I think the sprigged muslin would be suitable for a young lady like yourself." Hester picked up the pale blue cloth with tiny white flowers and ran her hand over it.

Julie continued to stare at the woman's hand. It was lined with age and she wore an odd, braided ring on her finger.

"I made it," Hester said, reading Julie's mind. "It's my daughter's hair."

Julie had heard of such things . . . when a loved one died to make a thin ring out of their hair. She had never seen one before. "I wish I had some of my momma's hair," she whispered. "Her hair was like that."

Hester saw the tears filling the child's eyes and something broke inside of her. The tight band of pain and resentment around her heart lessened. She looked at

Julie's blond hair and said, "Then you must have your mother's hair. My Charlotte's was lighter than yours, but yours is much thicker. She always wanted thick hair. I think she would have envied you for that."

Julie touched her hair. "Really?" To think someone who had lived here could want anything of hers seemed ridiculous. "You must miss her," Julie said impulsively. Somehow Miss Hester didn't seem like a wicked witch right now.

"I miss her very much," Hester answered. "Very much."

Julie felt sorry for the older woman. Maybe Elle was right. Maybe Miss Hester was only sad and lonely. "I miss my momma," Julie muttered.

Hester nodded. "Yes. I imagine you do. It's always hard to accept when someone is taken before their time. All we can do is live out our lives in a way that would make them proud."

Julie blinked, causing the tears to rush down her cheeks. She quickly brushed them away. "I think she would be happy that Jordan and Miss Elle adopted us."

It was unexpected, this sudden affection she felt for the girl. "I'm sure that she would," she said softly. Clearing her throat, she added, "Now, let's look through the pattern books. This will be our project, just the two of us. Come here and we'll take measurements."

As the young girl stood before her, Hester felt a surge of happiness. Julie reminded her of Charlotte, with her blond hair and large inquisitive eyes. Perhaps she could teach this child all the things her daughter had refused to learn. Filled with a sense of purpose, she brought out the heavy book, *The Ladies' Treasury—a Direct System of Ladies' Cutting.*

"Shall we get started?" she asked, and Julie nodded in agreement.

Hester actually smiled.

Elle sat up in bed, her head against the pillows. She arranged her hair over her shoulders and undid another tiny pearl button on the front of her nightgown. Smoothing the sheet over her thighs, she took a deep breath. There, she thought. When Jordan comes into the bedroom, everything will be perfect. She glanced at the clock encased in a glass dome. Ten forty-three. He was working late. Any minute, though, he'll come through the door and see her. His wife. His bride. A chill of anticipation rushed through her and she wet her lips, adding the finishing touch. Maybe she should pinch her cheeks for color? No. She didn't want to look blushing, just sexy. Womanly.

She waited nervously. To pass the time, she thought over the day. All in all, she was very pleased with the way it had turned out. She'd had breakfast with the children, and Emily Post would have been pleased with their table manners. Then she and Cory had taken up Jordan's offer of a tour of the ranch. She was sure Hester was scandalized by her riding attire. Elle had worn a simple white blouse tucked into her twentieth-century slacks. And her ten-gallon cowboy hat. She was proud of that hat—every smudge and crease had been earned—and she wore it with honor. Cory had stopped off at the bunkhouse to play with Noah and she and Jordan had continued on their own. He took her off into the hills and showed her the huge herds of cattle. He said it would take over a day's ride to reach the end of the Triple Cross. She couldn't imagine anything that big, let alone one person owning it. In her time farmers were selling off their property to make way for houses and shopping malls. Seeing so much land, natural and uncluttered, had been breathtaking. Even though she was a novice, she had enjoyed riding with Jordan. He seemed particularly pleased with her interest in the ranch and was happy to answer all her questions. He had even flirted with her, making comments about her slacks. She had told him that if it was good enough for Barbara Stanwyck and Big Valley, then it was good enough for her. To say he was confused was an understatement, but Elle had no intention of trying to explain television to a man that hadn't grasped the concept of the telephone.

They had returned in time to pick up Cory, who was quickly becoming the mascot of the ranch. An old cowboy had been trying to show him how to throw a lariat, and she had glanced at Jordan. He was smiling at the boy, and she was sure it was pride that showed in his expression.

Yes, it had been a pretty good day. Hester was almost nice to her when they returned to the house. She and Julie seemed downright friendly, and Elle was glad the woman was thawing. They really were starting to fit in with the household. Nina had helped with the tablecloth, clucking over *the Señora* doing her work. Even using the old-fashioned iron had proved quaint, rather than burdensome. Of course, she was glad that she wouldn't be required to use it too often . . .

Where *was* he?

Elle crossed her arms over her chest and stared at the door. Enough was enough. And she couldn't hold this position too much longer. Frustrated, she got up and put on her robe and slippers. Oh, well, she did say she was going to court him. But this was pushing it.

If Muhammad won't come to the mountain . . .

She knocked on the paneled door and waited for him to answer. It wasn't until she heard him say, "Yes?" that she thought about what she was going to say. She had no idea. Realizing that she would look like a fool if she walked away, she turned the handle and opened the door.

He was behind a massive desk. Papers were scattered in front of him, and when he looked up at her she could see the strain in his face.

"Elizabeth? Is something wrong?"

Her heart started pounding behind her breast. It was irrational, and even embarrassing, that she would feel like a bashful teenager at this moment. "Well, no," she began, wondering why she couldn't have just waited for him in the bedroom. "It's after eleven o'clock. I—I thought you fell asleep down here." Nervous, she touched the locket that hung from her neck, her birthday present.

"I'm sorry. I should have said something to you earlier." He looked at the papers in front of him and sighed. "I didn't think it would take this long."

"What is it?" she asked.

He ran his hand over his eyes, as if to clear his mind. "Just columns of figures that, no matter how I add them up, tell me the same thing."

She came closer to the desk and sat in the large leather chair opposite him. "And what's that?"

"That after I make this quarter's payment to my Scottish investor, my resources will be strained. The Herefords and the bull set me back more than I had first thought."

401

Elle saw the tension around his eyes. "It must take a great deal of money to keep all of this running. The house and the ranch."

He nodded. "A great deal." Then, suddenly, he looked at her. Really looked. And he smiled. "Does it strike you as odd that you're sitting here in your robe discussing finances?"

She grinned. "No. Not particularly. But, since we are on this subject, can I make a suggestion?"

He sat back, relaxing as he stretched his arms. "Go ahead," he said with a laugh.

She cleared her throat and straightened, as if to impart something of importance. "I think you should invest, Jordan."

"I did. With the Herefords and the Aberdeen Angus. I plan to cross-breed them with the Longhorns."

She was shaking her head. "I don't mean that. Not here. Up north."

"North? Why would I invest in the north, and not in my own ranch?"

"Listen, the Industrial Revolution is coming. I told you about it before. Machinery is going to replace manpower. Factories are going to be built. Hundreds and hundreds of them. You should get in on it. And it's going to start in the north."

"Elizabeth—" He said her name like a reprimand.

"No, wait," she countered, standing up to pace behind the chair. "I'm not going to talk about coming from the future. I just want you to remember what I'm telling you, in case . . . in case something happens and I'm not here to remind you."

"What are you saying? Where would you be?"

"I don't know. But you have to remember everything

402

I'm saying."

"Do you want to leave?" he asked in a strained voice.

"No," she answered impatiently. "I want to stay here. But if something should happen—look, maybe you should write all this down."

"Maybe we should change the subject."

She stared at him, holding his gaze, and then said slowly, "I heard you talk about the barbed wire the farmers are starting to put up in Kansas and Oklahoma. You're beginning to see the change, Jordan. The days of driving your cattle to market up the trails are about to end. You should petition for a railroad spur to come through the nearest town. Invest in transportation and communication."

"I thought you said to invest in factories up north."

"Diversify. Spread out your investment. What is this? 1876? Sometime soon, Alexander Graham Bell is going to invent the telephone—"

"You talked about that before, and I was going to ask you to explain."

She leaned on the back of the chair and held up her hand. "This is going to sound crazy, but it's a device you talk into. It has something to do with converting the sound waves in your voice into electrical currents." She shook her head with frustration. "I can't explain it. Just remember to invest in this sucker, because it's going to make billions."

He was clearly amused.

She ignored his expression. "Laugh if you want, but someday you'll see I was right. And oil! God, we're right here in Texas. Black gold. Texas T. Grampa Clampett's ticket to fame. Listen, Jordan, you might be sitting on a fortune right under the ground." She was about to tell him that they should start drilling, but the thought of derricks sprouting up on the Triple Cross was depressing. "If you ever hear of someone drilling for oil, this black goop deep in the earth, then get in on that, too."

He was looking at her as if she'd come from another planet, which wasn't all that far off the truth. "Anything else?"

She smiled. Poor thing. She had thrown quite a bit at him all at once. "No. That's enough for now. If I think of another great investment later on, I'll let you know."

"I'm sure you will." He reached across his desk and turned down the wick on his lamp until the room was cast in darkness.

"What are you doing?" she whispered in a nervous voice.

"I can't work now. I don't know how I could concentrate after hearing about telephones and Grampa . . ." He tried to remember the name.

She giggled. "Clampett," she filled in.

"Let's go to bed, Elizabeth," he said, coming around the desk and taking her arm.

She was glad it was dark. He couldn't see her smile.

She watched him undress and it was hard not to reach out her hand and run her fingers down his back when he took off his shirt. He was gorgeous. Once, so very long ago, she had thought he looked like Mel Gibson, but he didn't. He wasn't as pretty. He was more rugged, more male. And she wanted him more than she thought possible. She was already excited—waiting for him to come to bed.

He took off his pants and laid them on the chair and

then his hands went to the waistband of his shorts. As if they had shared the same room for years, he pulled them down and threw them over the pants.

He was nude! And he was coming to bed!

Knowing her eyes were wide with shock, Elle quickly looked away as he walked over to the lamp and turned it down. He just completely disrobed, as calm as could be! Never in her life had she possessed that much confidence, and she envied the male species that could be so casual about their bodies.

He got into bed and pulled the sheet up to his waist. In the moonlight she could see him run his fingers through his hair as he sighed with exhaustion.

"Elizabeth?"

"Yes?"

"If I ask you a question, will you tell me the truth?"

She didn't even hesitate. "Yes. Yes, I will."

"Do you think this marriage has a chance in hell?"

Thank you, God. "I do," she said truthfully. "I want it to work." She waited for a few seconds. "Do you?"

He didn't answer immediately and the muscles in her stomach contracted with the suspense of waiting. Maybe this wasn't going to turn out the way she'd hoped.

Finally, he said, "I want to be happy, Elizabeth. I want a partner, someone to share my life. You should have seen yourself tonight. You were so excited, trying so hard to help. And no matter that three-quarters of what you said sounded crazy, you *were* trying. I've never had that before."

"Jordan," she whispered his name. "Someday you'll see that everything I was saying is true. It's all going to happen."

He turned on his side, facing her. "Are you saying you

can foresee the future? Like a fortune teller?'' There was a note of laughter in his voice.

She shook her head. ''No. I've been there. I've lived it. And I know about money and investments. All I did was make money. I had no life. I just wanted to prove I was as good as any man, and better than one in particular.''

''Your father?''

She nodded. ''But that doesn't matter anymore.'' Taking a deep breath, she put it all on the line—everything, and said what was in her heart. ''I want to share my life with you and the children. I want to stay here.''

He didn't say anything for a moment, and then he reached out and raked his fingers through her hair. Pulling her toward him, he whispered, ''Come here, Elizabeth. I want you to stay, too.''

His mouth covered hers in a possessive kiss and Elle rejoiced as his arms wrapped around her, drawing her even closer into his embrace. His hands pulled at her nightgown, and she broke his kiss to reach down and eliminate the barrier between them. When she was nude, his hands cupped her breasts before moving to her back. Applying the slightest pressure, he brought her forward, until they were lying, face to face, their bodies pressed together.

She deeply inhaled with pleasure at the touch of his skin upon hers. He was so warm, almost hot, and she lightly ran her fingers down his back. He kissed her again. This time it was deep and passionate, as if branding her as his. Elle allowed his tongue to explore her and moaned with disappointment when his mouth left hers. His lips were gentle as they placed small kisses along her neck and shoulder, sometimes nipping at the tender flesh. Her skin felt on fire as he continued down her body, lavishing attention on one breast and then the other, until she thought she would go mad from wanting . . .

And then she touched him, running her fingers through the hair on his chest, allowing the tips of her nails to graze over his nipples. She felt them harden with desire and heard his sharp intake of breath.

He grabbed her shoulders and, turning her over, stared into her eyes.

"The past doesn't matter," he whispered, and his voice was thick with emotion. "Not yours, or mine. This marriage begins now."

Overwhelmed with tenderness, her eyes filled with tears. She reached up and caressed his face, running her hands over his eyes, his cheekbones, his mustache. "All right," she whispered, tracing the outline of his bottom lip. "It begins now."

Jordan lowered his head and kissed her softly. He hesitated, then kissed her again with the same gentleness. His skin was hot against hers and she reached around him to run her palms up and down his back. His mouth settled against hers as his tongue slipped between her lips. Slowly, suggestively, he worked it in and out, making love to her mouth until Elle moaned with a hunger for something more. She pressed her palms against his back, pulling him into her, yet still he seemed content to hold her face between his hands and kiss her. But she wanted more. Her body was burning with desire, to feel the friction of his skin as it moved over hers, the hard against soft. She ran her hand down his thigh, placed it beneath his hip, and drew him closer to her—inviting him into her, and into her life.

He entered her with maddening slowness, as if afraid of

hurting her, and Elle grew impatient.

"Jordan," she breathed against his mouth. "I want you."

"I know," he answered, and swiftly buried himself inside her.

Elle's body responded instantly, sending small shudders rippling through her. "Oh, God . . ." It was so perfect. The male against female. Man and woman. Husband and wife. She clung to him, working with him in partnership, meeting each thrust with an answering stroke. Throwing back her head, she closed her eyes and reveled in the sensations that were growing inside. She could hear his breathing, the low moans of passion coming from him, and she delighted in her power, that she was able to return to him the same pleasure he was giving to her.

But soon she was beyond thinking. Her entire being was centered on feeling . . . the brush of his lips over her shoulder, the grazing of his mustache as it tickled her skin and sent waves of excitement racing through her. Each rhythmic stroke of his body propelled her closer to the edge. And she raced with him, harder and faster, until she was over . . . falling . . . bringing him with her, clutching him tightly against her as if their bodies could meld into one.

"*Elizabeth!*" He called out her name in a hoarse cry as he came within her, scalding and fierce, bathing her in the heat of possession. It was an astonishing moment in time, a slice of eternity that they had dared to reach out and grasp—and both of them knew their lives would never again be the same.

They didn't move for a full minute, each too weak and too reluctant to break the spell. Finally, Jordan raised his head and kissed her temple. He eased himself off of her and lay on his side, reaching out and gently brushing the damp tendrils of hair off her forehead. His fingers traced a path over her temple, down her neck, and settled on the chain she wore. He touched the gold heart that lay nestled in the hollow of her throat and held it in the palm of his hand.

"You always wear it, don't you?" he asked, his voice not yet steady.

Nodding, she smiled with happiness and contentment. "It's my birthday present. I never take it off. Every time I thought you were going to send me away, I would reach for it and start playing with it. Maybe I thought if I held it tight enough, you would change your mind. It's silly . . ." Her voice trailed off sleepily.

He picked up her hand and kissed her fingers, one at a time. And then he stopped and just stared.

Elle felt the change in him and turned her head. "What? What's wrong?"

He dropped her hand and slid off the bed.

"What are you doing?" she demanded, rising to her elbows as she watched him cross the room to the large armoire.

He opened the doors and pulled out a drawer, searching through it impatiently. Within seconds, he grunted in satisfaction and came back.

"Sit up, Elizabeth. This is important."

"Jordan—"

"No, listen." He took her hand in his and said in a serious voice. "Our wedding was legal, but Slaughter left out an important detail—one I never thought of, until now. Give me your hand."

He slipped a thin gold band onto the fourth finger of

her left hand. "It was my mother's," he said quietly. "No one else has ever worn it."

She knew what he meant and was touched that he made that point. She raised her hand to look at the ring. It was a simple band of gold. The mark of a wife.

Moved beyond words, she forced them past the tight lump in her throat. "I love you, Jordan."

He took her in his arms and whispered into her ear, "I know. I heard your story to the children. Be my princess, Lizzie? And let's live happily ever after." He kissed away the tears that fell past her ear. "I love you, too."

Chapter 26

Mrs. Jordan McCabe . . .

Elle looked at the gold band on her finger and sighed with happiness. She was truly married—in every sense. And Jordan loved her! How could one woman be this happy, this blessed?

Last night they had given a "small" dinner party for the neighboring ranchers to introduce her and the children. She should have remembered that she was in Texas, and small meant eighteen guests. She was a nervous wreck until Hester, of all people, had sat her down and explained in her no-nonsense voice that as the new mistress of Peachtree Point, these people would be seeking her favor, not the other way around. Hester had told her that her position was to be envied and the ranchers and people from Atlanta would be more nervous trying to impress an Easterner with their own good manners. She had then involved Elle and Julie in the plans for the party, keeping them so busy with every minute detail that before she realized it, Elle was hurrying to get dressed.

Hester. Her turnabout was the biggest surprise. She had even stopped grumbling about Elle's riding attire. Every afternoon, she and Cory went riding across the vast grasslands that made up the Triple Cross. Cory was far better at it than she, but Elle was determined to fit in. And living on a working Texas ranch meant learning to ride was a priority.

Walking past Julie's bedroom, Elle stopped and watched the young girl. Julie was busy working over a small pillow.

"Are you sure you don't want to go riding with us?" Elle asked, walking into the room.

Julie looked up and smiled. Shaking her head, she said, "I can't. Melinda Hartford is coming to spend a few days and Miss Hester said proper Victorian ladies always made a gift to show their guests that they were welcomed."

Elle grinned. Julie was fitting in better than any of them. Since Hester had taken the girl under her wing, Julie had turned into a happy child. She was so eager to please Hester that, at times, Elle had felt a twinge of rivalry. She had to admit, however, that Julie was blossoming under the attention and satisfied herself with the knowledge that she was Julie's legal mother. There was a bond between Julie and Elle that could never be broken. To give Hester her due, she did seem happy to settle for the role of grandmother.

Elle shook the thoughts out of her head. Everything was turning out perfectly, and she should be grateful. They were a family, and now Julie even had a friend. The Hartford girl was from Atlanta and a year younger, but the two of them had hit it off last night and plans for a visit were quickly formulated between the two girls.

"What are you making?" Elle asked, looking down at

412

the lace-edged pillow.

Julie turned it around. "Miss Hester showed me how to make this pillow and spell out Melinda's initials with glass beads. She can take it home with her when she leaves."

Elle reached down and touched the lace edging. "It's beautiful, Julie. I'm sure Melinda will love it."

"I hope so."

Smiling, Elle turned to leave. "Don't worry. She will. Oh, and tell Hester that Cory and I will be back in plenty of time for dinner. Bye, sweetie."

From behind her, Elle heard, "Be careful."

She laughed. Julie sounded as old as Hester.

"C'mon. Let's go back to that creek we found yesterday," Elle called out to Cory. "We'll water the horses and then we can head for home."

Cory kicked the sides of his horse and followed her. Traver had fixed the saddle so the stirrups were just the right size, and he smiled as he pushed the horse up a small hill. He was better at it than Miss Elle, he thought with pride. But then she never grew up with horses, so it was all right. He loved the ranch, every bit of it—especially the bunkhouse and the men. Each morning he went in and fed Noah and all the men talked to him and taught him things, important things for being a cowboy. Miss Elle, and especially Miss Hester, would be mad if they heard all the cuss words he knew. But he wouldn't tell. Kyle and Traver and Andy and Mose and all the others were his best friends, and friends kept secrets. Like the way Kyle and Julie met every night after dinner and before bedtime down at the feed barn. He couldn't figure

413

out why Kyle wanted Julie to be his best friend too—she was a girl—but he guessed it was all right. Julie had stuck up for him when they first came to the big house and let him sleep in her room. He remembered being scared then. But now he slept in his own room. Sometimes he got afraid when the wind made funny noises and blew the curtains on his window. Last night he thought they were ghosts. He knew his momma wouldn't hurt him, but he was still kinda scared that his daddy might come back. He couldn't rightly remember what his parents looked like anymore—

Lost in thought, Cory was startled as Miss Elle's horse suddenly reared back! From the corner of his eye, he saw a small animal scurry into the tall grass, but he didn't have time to tell what it was. All he could see was Miss Elle trying to control her horse as it stood on its hind legs, trying to throw her off.

He wanted to shout out to her, to tell her to jerk back hard on the reins, but his mouth just opened in shock. It happened so quickly that Cory could do no more than stare as the big horse lunged backward again and threw her to the ground. He heard the sound of her body as it hit and his bottom lip started to tremble as he watched her horse run away. Scrambling down off Lightning, he ran to her.

And that's when he started crying.

He thought she might be asleep, 'cause her eyes were closed. Kneeling next to her, he touched her shoulder. When she didn't wake up, Cory wiped his nose on the back of his hand, and tried again. She looked real funny . . . she wasn't dead, 'cause he heard her make a noise, but she wasn't waking up or moving . . . and her face was the same color as the sky just before it rains.

He ran his hand over his eyes to wipe away the tears. He wasn't supposed to cry, but he couldn't stop. He looked around him for some help. There was nothing, except grassy meadows and the tree line. What was he supposed to do?

Picking up her hand, he squeezed it hard, to make her open her eyes. But she wouldn't! She wouldn't even move! *Miss Elle!*, his mind screamed. *Don't die . . . please, wake up!* He was so mad at himself. He was supposed to watch out for her. And now she was . . . she was . . . maybe she really was going to die out here! *Just like his momma and . . .*

Crying harder than before, he raced back to his horse and struggled to get on. It was too high. Traver had always given him a boost. Shit for being so goddamned, piss-ant little! He used all the cuss words he knew as he jerked on the stirrup. Frantic, he looked around until he saw a rock. He pulled Lightning over to it and climbed on top. When he was again in the saddle, Cory looked once more at Miss Elle's twisted body and bit his bottom lip to stop crying—but the tears nearly blinded him anyway. Kicking hard at the horse's belly, Cory headed toward Peachtree Point.

He heard the commotion in the hall and looked up from his papers. Without warning, the door to his office shot open and Hester, Kyle and Traver ran in. Traver was holding Cory. The child was crying, whimpering into Traver's shoulder.

For a second they all stared at him, shocked, until he demanded, "What's wrong? What's wrong with Cory? Is he hurt?"

Traver took a step further and even before he opened his mouth to speak, Jordan was filled with dread.

"Cory and Miss Elizabeth went out riding this afternoon. The boy just came back, holding onto his horse like the devil was after him. I can't get nothin' out of him, 'cept he keeps pointing out to the north."

Jordan was already out of his chair. He took Cory from Traver's arms and turned him around to see his face. It was streaked with dirt and tears, and he had that sound of a child that's been crying long and hard. "Cory," he said with false patience, "where's Miss Elizabeth?"

Whimpering, Cory pointed outside and started shaking his head.

"Cory, listen to me. Is she hurt? Is that why you came back alone?"

Cory vigorously nodded.

"Where is she?" Jordan demanded, fighting down the panic. "What happened?"

The child was gulping down tears, opening his mouth as if struggling to speak. He made little wailing sounds in frustration.

And then the sound came, slow at first. "She, she fell! Her—her horse threw her and she fell down and got hurt."

"My God," Hester whispered. "He spoke!"

Jordan ignored the miracle and asked in a tight voice, "Where is she, Cory?"

The child started to cry again and Jordan held him close. "I'm not mad at you. I need you now. We have to help her. Where is she?" he repeated, fighting for his own control.

"We—we were going to the lake," Cory stammered.

It was all Jordan needed. Carrying the child in his

416

arms, he said, "All right. You show me. Traver, you and Kyle follow in the wagon. Hester, give them bandages and whatever else you've got." He threw open the wide front door. "We don't know what to expect."

For just a moment, Hester stared after Jordan and the muscles around her heart twisted in pain. It was just like before, she thought. All those years ago . . . with Charlotte. And she knew Jordan was thinking the same thing. God wouldn't do this to them again. He wouldn't . . .

"Miss Hester," Traver said impatiently. "The bandages?"

Blinking back her own tears, Hester stared at the ranch hand. "Yes. Yes, of course," she muttered, and hurried to the kitchen. Dear God in heaven, how was she going to tell Julie?

She fought against the darkness, forcing her eyelids open. She could hear a buzzing in her ears and feel the pain ripping at the scar tissue from her old head injury. When she looked up to the sky, Elle felt dizzy, as everything started to spin around her. The clouds whirled in a crazy pattern; the scene above her rapidly changed, replacing the clouds with trees and she shut her eyes to stop the illusion. She felt like she was floating in darkness, in a black, shadowy cocoon that wrapped around her and took her away from the pain . . .

"Can you hear me? Are you all right?"

Elle almost smiled. Jordan . . . He'd come for her. She knew he wouldn't leave her alone—

But it wasn't Jordan's voice.

It was soft and concerned.

And feminine.

In the distance she heard music and a deep, sexy voice announce, "This is your Hyski, Hy Lit, bringing you the number one record in this fifth year of rock 'n roll, 1959's biggest hit—Bobby Darrin's Mack The Knife . . ."

Mack The Knife? 1959!

Stunned, Elle forced her eyes open as the song began. A young woman was bending over her with a worried expression on her face. Elle blinked a few times and brought her hand up to shield her eyes from the sun filtering in through the trees. The woman above her became more focused—the thick blond hair, the bright blue eyes lined with black eyeliner and light blue shadow. The full mouth colored in peach lipstick. Elle caught her breath at the achingly familiar face.

Her heart started pounding and her skin broke out into a sweat. It couldn't be! No . . . it wasn't possible!

The young woman looking down at her and smiling was the picture of . . . of . . .

"Who are you?" Elle breathed in fright, terrified of the answer.

"Margie Curran. Are you okay?"

Oh my God! My God! It's my mother!

Only it wasn't the woman Elle knew. This wasn't the sad picture of a defeated, middle-aged woman, robbed of ever finding happiness. This woman was young and beautiful and . . .

"Maybe I should get the police," she said to Elle and raised her head to search for help. "You don't look real good."

Elle grabbed her hand. "No," she cried, afraid the vision would vanish. "Please . . ."

Margie looked back at her. "Hey, I never saw anyone

418

faint before. I don't know what to do. Can you sit up?"

Elle nodded and forced her body to move. She was on the grass. In a park. She turned her head and saw familiar buildings. In Philadelphia . . .

How did this happen? 1959? How could she be in 1959? Where was Jordan—and the children? Her head hurt from thinking and she held her hands over her eyes, as if it would shut the insanity out.

"What's your name?" Margie asked, and Elle slowly brought her hands down.

It was her mother! She'd seen pictures of her mother when she was young . . .

"Your name? Do you remember? It looks like you hit your head when you fell. Geez, I don't know what to do. I think I'd better get help."

"My name is Elizabeth," Elle said quickly. "Elizabeth Mackenzie."

She watched for a sign of recognition. There was none. Her mother didn't know her!

Margie Curran gave her a friendly smile. "I don't know what happened. I was eating my lunch and I looked up and there you were, lying over here." She shook her head, as if amazed. "I'm glad you're okay. Do you want some Coke? Something to drink?"

Dumbfounded, Elle could only nod. She watched her mother get up and walk to a nearby park bench to retrieve her lunch. She was dressed in a light cotton shirtwaist dress that almost matched her hair. A black barrette held the blond curls off her forehead. Her heels were high and patent leather, and sank into the soft ground as she walked. Coming back, Margie knelt next to her and held out her hand.

Coca-Cola in a pale green bottle. Elle hadn't seen that

since she was a child. She watched as Margie took out a lacy handkerchief from her skirt pocket and wiped the neck of the bottle and then offered it again.

"Sorry, but I don't have a paper cup."

Elle wanted to tell her what they had shared over the years and that she shouldn't be worried, but she knew it would only frighten her. She continued to stare at the young, pretty woman as she sipped the Coke.

Why did this happen? her brain demanded. Why was she taken to this time? Hadn't she made a deal with God? *Hadn't she? What are you doing to me? We had a deal!* she raged inwardly, fighting the panic. What was it again? Something about—

"Do you want to sit with me for a while?" Margie interrupted her thoughts. "Just till you get your bearings?"

Elle stared at the vision next to her. She was so pretty—her face not yet lined from years of worry; her eyes bright, intelligent, not showing the unhappiness that was to be her fate. Elle handed her back the bottle and tried to rise. Her body felt sore and her head ached. As she stood with Margie's help, a wave of dizziness washed over her and Margie put an arm around her waist to steady her.

"Whoa . . . be careful. Here. It's only a few more steps."

Elle collapsed onto the wooden bench and Margie sat on the other side, a lunch bag, a sandwich wrapped in waxed paper, a large black purse and a radio, separating them.

Picking up the sandwich, she held out half. "Would you like some? It's tuna fish. I made it myself."

Elle shook her head. "No thanks. You go ahead." Was

it really possible that she was sitting in a park in Philadelphia, listening to Ray Charles belt out "What'd I Say" and talking to her mother at age—what age was she?

Elle glanced at her, trying to guess. Nineteen? Twenty? And why was she here in Philadelphia? She'd said she had always lived with her parents until she was married. Elle searched her fingers for a wedding band. There was none.

"Do you live here in the city?" she asked.

Chewing her sandwich, Margie shook her head. She swallowed quickly and said, "No. I just work in Philly. I'm a legal secretary."

Her mother was a legal secretary? Why didn't she ever know that? She knew her mother worked in an office, but that was it. Elle suddenly realized her mother never really told her about her life before she was married. Why was that?

"What do you do?" Margie asked. "Are you sure you don't want something to eat?"

Again, Elle shook her head. "I . . . ahh . . . I'm a secretary, too," she finally said, knowing her mother wouldn't have heard of computers yet.

Margie glanced down to Elle's slacks and grinned. "Boy, are you lucky. We have a strict dress code at the law office. When winter comes I'd love to be able to wear slacks, but our clientele is mostly Main Line and we have to dress like we're living in the Middle Ages. It really bugs me how strict they are."

Elle brushed grass of her leg. Her mother was bugged? *Bugged?* "Yes, well, my office is real . . . informal," she muttered.

"Where do you work?"

Elle looked at her. "Mictronix," she answered truthfully. Dear God, she was older than her mother! By a good ten years!

Margie scowled, concentrating. "Nope. I've never heard of it. Is it in the city? Do you live here?"

Elle shook her head. "I live in Texas." It was the truth. That's where she wanted to be—

"No kidding? You don't sound like you have an accent."

Elle tried to gather her thoughts. Lying to her mother. Even now, in this incredible circumstance, it could still make her feel guilty. "I'm just visiting."

"Hey that's a great . . . oh, listen!" She held out the small transistor radio so Elle could hear. The sexy voice was telling his listeners to come to a canteen, an under twenty-one club, tonight to hear Frankie Avalon sing his latest hit—"Venus."

"I'm going," Margie said in an excited voice.

Remembering her mother's love of celebrities, Elle asked, "For Frankie Avalon?" Her mother . . . a groupie?

Margie shrugged. "Not just for that. This club's down by the Naval Base. My girl friend, Natalie, called at the office this morning and said the guys will be shipping out tomorrow for two months, so the place will be packed."

And then it hit her. It all became clear. Her father was in the Navy when he'd met her mother. Was it tonight? Did her parents meet tonight? Without thought, Elle said quickly, "Can I come? Or, are you meeting someone special?"

Margie smiled. "I don't have a boyfriend. Sure. Come. It'll be a gas."

A gas? This was her mother speaking?

Margie looked at the thin watch on her wrist. "I have

to get back to work, or I'll be late. Are you sure you're okay? You look better. You have some color in your face. Geez, you should have seen it before. All gray and pasty." She shuddered and stood up. Crumpling up the waxed paper, Margie threw it in the brown bag. She turned off the radio, put it in her purse, and then hung the purse in the crook of her arm.

Elle thought she looked like a very proper young woman, full of life and purpose, so different from the one she remembered.

Almost absently, Margie smoothed down the full skirt of her dress. "Where will I meet you? Down at the club?"

Elle shrugged. "I don't know." In truth, she was more confused than ever.

"Listen. I'm going to work late tonight and go right from there. Why don't you walk me back to the office and then we'll meet—say, seven?"

Nodding, Elle rose. "That sounds good." She was unsteady for the first few steps but it didn't last. She noticed that Margie slowed her pace and she wanted to reach out and hug her, to thank her for showing her mother as she really was, before Fate had turned her life around. She wanted to beg this young, vivacious girl not to go tonight, to stay away from all sailors, and one in particular. But she knew she couldn't. Margie would think she was crazy. And the cardinal rule applied . . . you couldn't change the future. You can't tamper with Fate.

So tonight she would go, and watch helplessly as her mother made the biggest mistake of her life.

"Did you see it?" Margie asked, while pointing to a movie marquee. "Didn't you just love it?"

Elle looked up and saw a billboard showing Audrey

Hepburn in a white habit. *Nun's Story*. She remembered watching it on television late one night when she was at college. "Yes. It was very good." She tried to remember the plot.

Margie sighed. "I was glad she left the convent. I wish she would have found the doctor, though. He really loved her."

Elle grinned at the woman next to her. She was always a romantic. Looking down the street, Elle saw a row of movie theaters with multicolored neon lights advertising *Ben Hur, Rio Bravo, Room at the Top, Gidget*. God, no wonder her mother had obsessed on movies!

"Here we are," Margie said, stopping in front of a large office building. "Seven o'clock. Right?"

Elle nodded. "Seven o'clock. I'll be here."

"Great," Margie answered and gave her a quick smile. "See you then."

Elle watched as her mother opened the heavy glass door and she was filled with a sense of urgency. What if she never saw her again? "Margie, wait!"

Her mother turned around.

Elle just stared for a few moments, memorizing her face, her expression of vitality and innocence. "Thanks," she said slowly. "Thank you for everything."

Margie laughed and waved, as if to say it was nothing.

Elle's eyes filled with tears as the door closed and blocked her view.

But it was everything. Margie Curran had given her more than she knew.

It dawned on her as she walked the city that she had no money. She looked in the window of Wanamakers at the proper Chanel and Christian Dior suits saluting the approach of fall. A block further on Chestnut Street another store tried to cash in on the warm September weather by offering an Indian Summer sale on the new daring bikini, and more sedate bathing suits with little flared skirts. She walked into Woolworths and stood before the magazine rack, soaking in the culture of an innocent era. The more newsworthy told of Alaska and Hawaii becoming the 49th and 50th states, that Khrushchev is expected to tour the U.S. in response to Vice President Richard Nixon's heated kitchen debate in Moscow. She read with fascination that "Lady Day," Billie Holliday, died in New York City and that before her death, she was arrested in her bed on a drug charge. The police even confiscated her magazines, radio and a box of Whitman's chocolates. "Lady Chatterly" was still too hot for America, and D.H. Lawrence's classic was banned as being too filthy for postal workers to handle.

Shaking her head in amazement, Elle saw that the innocence of this era was about to be shattered as she read a story of mob violence and tension in Little Rock, as Negro students registered for the coming school year. She picked up a small item at the bottom of the page, quietly stating that Communist guerrillas had killed two American soldiers at Bienhoa, South Vietnam. Filled with sadness, she turned the page and saw a picture of a healthy, smiling man in his prime—a young senator from Massachusetts who had just been nominated as the Democratic Presidental candidate. Elle closed the magazine and slowly placed it back in the rack, wishing with all her heart that she didn't know this country was going to be torn apart with race riots, that tens of thousands of young men not old enough to vote would die in that little

Asian country. And Jack Kennedy would be dead in a few years. . . .

She looked around her, wondering if she told someone would it make a difference? Would anyone believe her? She knew it was useless. No matter what, you can't change the future. You can't alter the course of history. She glanced back to the rack of colorful magazines and saw that this time, this America, was basking in tranquility and prosperity—the Yankees were baseball's dynasty. Hoola hoops and stuffing phone booths were the craze. *Leave It to Beaver* actually seemed to mirror real life, when, gee whiz, the worst that could happen was that the Beav might get caught smoking. No one would listen to her. And could she blame them? It would be the young people, her mother's age, that would get involved. But right now they were still grieving over the deaths of Buddy Holly and Richie Valens, waiting for Elvis to get out of the army, standing in line to see Rock Hudson and Doris Day in *Pillow Talk*, or trying out Metrical to lose weight or Breck Shampoo because the ads had the most artistically beautiful women in the world. No one would want to hear about civil rights, Southeast Asia, or a sniper's bullets.

She was distracted by the cries of a little girl down the aisle, pleading with her mother for one of the new Barbie dolls, and Elle shook her head as she walked away. Through the years that doll, with its absurd proportions, had done more damage to the female anatomy than whalebone corsets. Shrugging, Elle wondered what ever became of her own Barbie. How she had loved that feminine rite of passage in the sixties—all the outfits, dating Ken, dreaming of the time when plastic would be transformed into living and breathing boyfriends. It was so long ago . . .

Passing a small mirror, she stopped at the counter and looked at her reflection. She was a mess! Her hair was tangled. There was a smudge of dirt on her cheek, and in a time of eyeliner and bright lipstick she wore none.

She looked up and down the aisle. Everyone seemed busy, even the young girl behind the counter. It wouldn't be stealing, not really. And she did have a dance to go to later on . . . Making up her mind, Elle picked up the comb and walked away to find a sales clerk. She was directed to the bathroom and, after washing her face, she pulled the wide-toothed comb through her hair. Looking in the mirror, she thought of Jordan—what he was doing, what he was thinking. Would he believe that she left the Triple Cross, that she ran away? He couldn't. What about Julie and Cory? She even thought about Hester. She would give anything just to see the old woman's face again. To be back where she belonged.

Don't think about it, she told herself, washing out the comb and drying it on the roll of white linen. Just get through tonight. Catching the eye of a teenager who was applying even more blue eyeshadow to her lids, Elle smiled. My God, tonight she was going to a dance with her mother! She truly had landed in Oz.

Replacing the comb in its bin, Elle moved further down the aisle. It was all here. Lipstick in exotic shades. Eyeliner. Shadows. Rouge. Checking first to make sure no one was paying attention, Elle reached out for a tube of lipstick. She turned it over and read the name. Angel Fire. A smile appeared at her lips. It was appropriate. She took the top off and applied the bright red color. Next, she moved to the rouge and then the eyeliner and shadow. It was while she was applying mascara with a

427

tiny brush that she smelled food and her stomach muscles tightened in response. God, she was hungry!

Turning around she spied a lunch counter against the wall and made her way over to it. She was salivating as she watched people chewing hamburgers, sipping Cokes and milkshakes in tall fluted glasses. She didn't have any money, but maybe she could get some water. They didn't charge for water, did they?

There was one woman behind the counter, looking frazzled as she tried to serve everyone herself. Hoping to be friendly, Elle smiled as she rushed past. The woman ignored her as she dropped a plate of spaghetti in front of the man seated next to her. Elle looked longingly at the dish.

"What can I get'cha?" The voice was impatient, not at all friendly.

Swallowing down her hunger, Elle again tried smiling. "Could I have some water, please?"

The woman rolled her eyes and walked away. She had bleached blond hair, too much makeup, and a pink-laced handkerchief fashioned into a corsage at her breast. The name Trudi was stamped on her name tag. She carried the glass of water in one hand and a plate of french fries in the other. Dropping off the fries for a young boy, she slid the water in front of Elle.

"Now, do you want to order?" she demanded. "I got twenty people here waiting."

Elle was embarrassed, and shook her head. "No. I can't. But thanks for the water."

Trudi muttered something before rushing back for her pickup. Elle watched her, fascinated by the efficient, if brusque, manner of the woman. Pickup from the cook. Delivery to the customer. Ring up receipts at the cash

428

register. Elle knew she could do it. All she needed was courage.

The next time Trudi raced in front of her, Elle called out her name.

"Yeah? You gonna order now?"

"Can you use some help?" she asked hopefully.

Trudi issued a sarcastic laugh. "Can a train use tracks?"

Laughing, Elle nodded. "I can help you for a couple of hours. I waited tables in college."

"Hey, Trudi! What about my chicken salad?" a large man yelled down the counter.

"Hold your horses," she yelled back, and looked at Elle. "You're not kidding me?"

Elle shook her head.

"Mary Ellen went home sick and they left me alone. They don't care if I'm dyin' back here," Trudi said, looking out to the body of the store. "I guess I can give you a couple of dollars if you work until the dinner crowd is over. And you can eat whatever you want before you leave."

"*Trudi!*" The man was obviously in a hurry.

"I'll be there when I get there. If you can't wait, go across the street to Sun Ray Drugs, why don't ya?"

She looked back at Elle, waiting for an answer to her proposal.

"I'll do it. Got an apron?"

She pointed to the end of the lunch counter. "C'mon back, kiddo. You're hired."

Chapter 27

They stood in line at the entrance to the canteen. "It's a dollar," Margie said, smoothing down her hair while checking it in a compact mirror. "Keeps the younger kids out."

Elle nodded, queuing up. She was nervous. It seemed silly. She was older than all of them, from the girls who looked too young to be in heels to the boys with their crewcuts and baggy sweaters. Her mother's friend, Natalie, was right about one thing, though. There were a lot of sailors. They stood in their white uniforms, smoking cigarettes and eying every girl that passed.

"Elle?"

She looked down at her mother—who was shorter, younger and prettier than she. God . . .

"I don't mean to pry, or anything. And you don't have to tell, if you don't want . . . but, isn't that a wedding ring you're wearing?"

Elle looked down at the thin gold band. "Yes," she said quietly. "It is."

Margie stared at her. "You're married?"

Smiling, Elle nodded.

"Is he . . . like dead, or something?" Margie looked upset.

"No, he's—" *But in this time he was* . . . Elle refused to think about it. "He's away," she finally answered.

"And he doesn't mind if you go to a dance?"

Shaking her head, Elle said, "I love him, but I don't think he'd mind tonight."

Margie's expression showed her surprise. "Wow. Married! I don't think I'll get married until I'm at least twenty-five."

"No?" How Elle wished that were true.

"There's too much I want to do."

"Like what?" Elle was really interested, and she realized what a miracle this was—to meet her mother as a young, vibrant woman, full of life and promise. Every daughter who ever fought with her mother, who thought they were too old and would never understand them, should be granted this moment and see the truth.

Margie smiled dreamily. "I want to go to Paris. I have about six hundred dollars saved. Hopefully, by this time next year, I'll be having dinner at the top of the Eiffel Tower."

Elle didn't know what to say. Margie Curran would never make the trip.

"Here we go," Margie pointed out, handing a man her dollar. The man took the money and stamped her hand with a red star.

She turned as Elle held out her money. "Hey. Not a silver dollar! Don't you have anything else?"

Elle wanted to get rid of it and keep the lighter bill, but she shrugged and made the exchange.

As they walked into the dance, Margie yelled over the

music, "My boss says they're going to be worth something one day. Keep the silver dollar." She pressed it into Elle's palm and smiled.

Nodding, Elle looked out to the crowd. Kids were jitterbugging all over the place. It was hot and smoke hung in the air like a vaporous cloud. Obviously, the Surgeon General's warning had yet to take effect.

"C'mon," Margie said, and pointed to one side of the room. "I see Natalie."

She followed her mother, watching as Margie walked in front of the young men and sailors who leaned up against the wall, passing judgments on the females who crossed their line of vision. Elle heard a few comments addressed to her mother and she had the irrational urge to walk up to the jerks and slap them silly. This was her mother! But Margie ignored them, happy to be with her friend.

"Elle, this is Natalie," she said, smiling at the small dark-haired girl.

"Hi." Elle thought Natalie was pretty in an exotic way. Her brown eyes were ringed with thick lashes and her smile was warm and friendly. She made the perfect foil to her mother's light beauty. No wonder the two were attracting attention.

A guy, about twenty, came up to her mother and pulled her onto the dance floor. Elle turned to watch, fascinated . . . she was so full of spirit and energy. No wonder she loved to look at old movies and listen to the oldies on the radio. This must have been the happiest time of her life. Tears came into Elle's eyes as she stared at her mother. The fast song ended and her dance partner took her in his arms and slow-danced to Phil Phillips's "Sea of Love."

"Wanna dance?"

Elle blinked, not sure she'd heard correctly. She looked to her side and saw a young man, a good ten years younger than she. He was waiting expectantly for an answer. Smiling nervously, she shook her head. "No thanks."

"Oh, go on," Natalie urged, cradling the arm of her own partner.

The boy waited. He was tall, with red hair and freckles. Not quite a nerd, but close. And looked about as nervous as she felt. Sighing in defeat, she nodded. "Okay. Sure. Let's dance."

She spent the next hour and a half trying to keep tabs on her mother. Why didn't she ever realize her mom was such a good dancer? It was ironic to be in her own prime and stand on the side while her mother was more popular. But she wanted Margie Curran to enjoy every dance, every moment—

And then she saw him.

He was hard to miss. Dressed in Navy white, he walked with a swagger. He had the look of a man that knows he's attractive. He was alone. A man like him doesn't need friends, Elle thought. He wants to stand out, to be noticed. John Mackenzie stood, one hip thrust out, and put a cigarette to his mouth. Striking a match, he deeply inhaled and then looked out to the dance floor, as if assessing anyone worthy of his attention.

He doesn't know her yet, Elle thought quickly. He hasn't even seen her. I can stop this. *No. No you can't. You can't change the future. He's going to ship out tomorrow, so it has to be tonight that they meet. Something will happen between them, some spark of white-hot passion, and you'll be conceived.* Elle searched the dance floor for her mother.

She was laughing in the arms of another man. *And she'll pay for the rest of her life.*

Starting to cry, Elle took a deep breath and struggled to control her emotions. She tried to think logically. Maybe he wasn't her father. He had always denied it, had always thought he'd been tricked into marriage. But she looked at him, young and handsome. Her hair was the same color as his. Her eyes were the same amber brown. He could be her brother. Though in her heart she knew the truth. He was her father.

What would happen if she got her mother out of here?

You won't be born—you'll no longer exist. And if you do this, then nothing else in your life will exist either. But what had she ever done that was so important? What will she really leave behind? Nothing, except a lot of mistakes.

Jordan. He wasn't a mistake. He was everything to her now.

What will happen to Jordan? And the life she desperately wanted to return to? Maybe this was why she was brought to this time. What was the deal again? She frantically searched her brain for the answer. Give up something else besides Jordan and the children? What? *Her life?* Isn't that asking for the ultimate sacrifice? And what if it doesn't work?

She had little time to reason out the answers to her questions as she watched her father's face. He showed interest in someone on the dance floor. Following his line of vision, she saw he was looking at her mother.

Fear clutched her heart. She had seen the same look in too many men, in too many singles bars, in her own time. John Mackenzie didn't want to really know Margie Curran. He wanted something fast and carnal, something

435

he wouldn't have to think about after tomorrow.

And she couldn't let it happen.

Driven by love, Elle rushed out onto the dance floor. She pushed couples out of her way in her haste to reach her mother.

"Mom . . . Margie! Come with me. Quick!" She reached for her mother's hand.

Margie pulled back, confused. "What? What's wrong? Are you sick again?"

Elle nodded. "That's it! I'm sick. I need you."

Margie looked to her partner and shrugged. "I'm sorry. Maybe we can dance later."

The young man nodded and watched as they walked away.

"Do you want to go into the bathroom?" Margie asked.

Elle shook her head. "I . . . I need fresh air. All this smoke."

When they stood on the sidewalk, Elle's heart was still pounding with fear. She had to get her mother away from here.

"Are you okay now?"

Elle shook her head. "Maybe we can go and get coffee, or something. I have some money," she added quickly.

"I can't leave," Margie protested. "What about Natalie?"

"She'll be fine. She was dancing with the same guy all night. He'll bring her home."

"But I haven't even seen Frankie Avalon yet. He's supposed to be here tonight."

Desperate, Elle blurted out, "What's the big deal? He gets married and has like a dozen kids, or something."

Margie stared at her. "What?"

Shaking her head, Elle said, "Look, I'm sorry."

They both stopped speaking as a large black Cadillac, with fins Jaws would have envied, pulled up to the sidewalk. The door opened, and Elle watched as her mother nearly swooned at the sight of a skinny man emerging from the dark interior.

"Oh my God—it's *him!*"

Elle wasn't all that impressed. It wasn't like he was Elvis Presley, or one of the Beatles. Even she would have been excited. But he was sort of cute, and he had a great smile, even if his hair was styled in a pompadour.

"C'mon," she urged. "Let's go meet him."

"I can't!" Margie protested.

Elle turned to look at her in astonishment. "Didn't you just say you couldn't leave because you wanted to see him? Well, there he is, and he's going to be gone in a couple of seconds if we don't move."

She took her mother's wrist and nearly pulled her up to the man. "Hi, Frankie," Elle said, as if she did this sort of thing all the time. "This is Margie Curran. Can you give her an autograph?"

The young singer flashed them a brilliant smile. "Sure." He reached inside the jacket of his black sports coat and brought out a pen. People were starting to gather around them when he said, "Got any paper?"

Elle looked at Margie, who was staring at Frankie as if she'd just died, gone to heaven, and was gazing on the face of a deity. Realizing her mother wasn't going to be of any help, Elle again reached down and took Margie's wrist. "Just sign her hand. She'll be thrilled."

"Hey, cool." The singer laughed and wrote his name. He looked up at Elle. "You want one, too?"

Elle grinned. "Sure. Why not?" She let her mother admire her hand as she held out her own.

"I got to go," he said after signing his autograph to her skin.

He was led away by several men who pushed back those who'd gathered on the street. Impulsively, Elle called out, "Hey, Frankie!"

He glanced back.

"Give my regards to Annette," she shouted, laughing at his confused expression. He shook his head, as if he didn't hear and was swallowed up in the crowd of admirers.

"Nice guy," Elle muttered, looking heavenward. It was no accident that he had appeared just at the right time.

"He's wonderful!" Margie gushed, holding her hand out in front of her, as though it were something sacred. "Oh, Elle, how can I thank you? Frankie Avalon wrote on my hand! And you told him my name!"

Elle was pleased for her, but she still wanted to get Margie away from this place. "Do you want to know what you can do for me?"

"Yes. Anything. Just tell me."

Elle took a deep breath. "Go home."

Confused, Margie stared at her. "Go home?"

"Get on a bus, or train, or however you get back from the city. Just do it now. Okay?"

"Okay," Margie said, still looking confused. "I only came tonight to see him, so I might as well go. I take the E bus. Oh, Elle, nobody's going to believe this! I wish Natalie could see it."

"I'll walk you to the bus," Elle said firmly, and took her mother's elbow. "Let's go."

They stood on the street corner, waiting for the bus.

There was so much Elle wanted to say to her. She wanted to tell her that she loved her with all her heart, to thank her for the love she had always shown, but she knew she couldn't. Instead, she listened as her mother went on about Frankie Avalon. Elle couldn't stop staring at her and, when the bus came, she pulled her mother into her arms. Hugging her tight, Elle caught the scent of Evening in Paris and her eyes filled with tears.

"I'll never wash my hand," Margie whispered into her ear and giggled.

Elle sniffled and laughed, as Margie pulled away from her.

"Are you going to be here tomorrow?" she asked when the doors to the bus opened.

Elle shrugged. "I don't know."

"Well, if you are, maybe I'll see you in the park tomorrow. You can give me your address and we can write each other. Okay?"

Nodding, Elle bit her bottom lip to keep from crying as her mother walked up the steps.

She turned before paying her fare. "Thanks for everything, Elle. I'm so glad we met."

The tears fell down her cheeks freely. She couldn't stop them. "Me, too, Margie. Me, too . . ."

The doors closed and Elle followed her mother's image as she found a seat. Margie held up her hand to show off the autograph and laughed as she waved goodbye.

Brushing away tears, Elle waved back. "Go to Paris," she shouted as the bus pulled out. "Promise me, you'll go!"

She didn't know if her mother ever heard her, but she stared after the bus, wishing with all her heart that she did.

Bringing her hand up to her mouth, she tried to stop her lips from trembling.

Goodbye, Mom . . .

She had nowhere to go. It was dark and late, and she didn't want to roam the city at night. What's going to happen to me? She looked down at her hands. One had the scrawled signature of a teen idol, the other a stamped star. She could go back to the dance and then decide. At least there were people, and she wouldn't be alone.

She walked back into the canteen to the pounding rhythm of Little Richard's "Good Golly Miss Molly." Everyone was dancing and the wooden floor vibrated with the pounding of their feet. Her head ached from the loud music, and her body was trembling with emotion. Her mother . . . there was so much she had wanted to tell her. Reaching into her pocket, she felt the silver dollar and pressed it into her palm. It was warm and comforting.

She saw him. Through the couples swinging each other, he caught her eye. They stared across the room for endless seconds and Elle's heart beat wildly inside her chest. The pores on her skin seemed to open and sweat broke out over her body. He was coming to her, weaving his way across the dance floor. Her father. He was walking straight up to her! Fear took hold and she tried to move, but her legs refused to help. Tremors started in her hands and worked their way up her arms, until her entire body was shaking. She felt dizzy with panic. The music was drowned out with a loud buzzing in her ears, and her vision started to darken, as if she were seeing him through a shadowy tunnel. How could he have denied her all those years? How—

440

Elle's eyes opened wide with fear as she realized she was going to fall. She reached out, desperate to connect with someone, something, anything, to keep her anchored.

But the darkness enveloped her, and the pain in her head was unbearable as she fell. She opened her mouth to cry out, yet no sound emerged. There was only darkness and pain and the eerie sensation of someone calling out to her . . .

"Elizabeth! Can you hear me?"

Was she dying? Was this it? She was paying the price for preventing her own conception. She desperately tried to hold the image of Jordan in her brain, to see him and the children, but it was impossible. Was she supposed to follow the swirling lights in her mind's eye? But the pain— Dear God, the pain!

"Open your eyes, Elizabeth. I know you can hear me."

She fought the heaviness at her lids, desperate to see him.

It was Jordan's voice!

Jordan!

She forced her eyes open and stared at the beautiful face in front of her.

"Jordan?" Her voice was raw with emotion and disbelief.

"I'm here," he said gently, cradling her head against his chest. "Are you all right?"

She looked up to the sky. "Where am I? What . . . what happened?" Dear God, her head was pounding, and she felt nausea rise in her throat.

Closing her eyes, she heard him say, "You were riding with Cory and your horse threw you. We brought the

441

wagon to take you home, darling. You're going to be fine."

He kissed her temple and Elle started to cry. Was it all a dream? Her mother . . . did any of it happen?

"Don't cry, Miss Elle."

She opened her eyes and saw Cory kneeling beside her.

"You talked!" she muttered in astonishment.

The young boy grinned sheepishly.

"He came back and got us. We're all real proud of him." Jordan reached out and tousled Cory's blond hair. "C'mon, let's get you in the wagon. There's nothing broken, is there?"

She tested her limbs. Her entire body felt beaten and bruised, but she shook her head. "I don't think so."

"Okay. Hold on to me." He lifted her up and she clung to him, never wanting to let go. She inhaled the scent of him, felt the texture of his shirt, and pressed her head closer to his chest. She was with him. That's all that mattered.

She saw Kyle and Traver standing by the wagon and almost laughed at their forlorn expressions. Dear God . . . wasn't this how it had all started? If it wasn't for their mistake, she never would have met Jordan, or the children.

"Thanks, guys . . . for everything," she murmured, meaning every word.

The two men stared at her, clearly embarrassed, until Traver elbowed Kyle in the ribs. "Don't just stand there, catchin' flies with your mouth. Go get the Cap'n's horse. I'll be takin' Miss Elizabeth home."

Home. The word never sounded so sweet.

Jordan deposited her in the back of the wagon and got

442

in beside her. He took her in his arms and held her tightly. As the wagon began to move, he lowered his head and whispered in her ear, "I was so worried. I don't know what I would have done if anything happened to you. I love you, Lizzie."

She closed her eyes and snuggled against him. "Oh, Jordan, you'll never know how much I love you. And I promise I'll be a good wife. I'll even do the obey part and never talk about being from the future. It's all over. I want to stay here with you forever."

"Ahh, Elizabeth?"

She heard the tone in his voice and looked up at him. He had a funny expression on his face, kind of scared and yet awed.

"What is it? What's wrong?"

Reaching into his shirt pocket, he held out his hand. "I found it on the ground, next to you."

Cradled in his palm was a shiny silver dollar that caught the last rays of the fading sun.

Her hand shook as she ran her fingertip over the raised image of Lady Liberty, the year 1921, and the words, "In God We Trust." The scrawled ink signature on her hand was smudged and stained the skin.

Oh, Mom... She knew Margie Curran would go to Paris after all. Somehow, Elle had broken the circle of unhappiness.

"Elizabeth? It was minted in 1921. How can that be?" he asked in amazement. "I mean—look at it!" His voice was almost reverent.

Filled with joy, she threw back her head and laughed. "Maybe now you'll believe me. Oh, Jordan, wait until you hear where I've been!"

Looking out across the vast meadow, Elle saw Peachtree Point in the distance, so beautiful, so welcoming, and her throat tightened with raw emotion. It all became clear to her. The only reason she was alive anywhere, in any time, was because of the love she had found here in the past. Letting the tears fall freely, she pressed her face against Jordan's chest and smiled as she listened to the steady, sure beat of his heart. It wasn't the past, she corrected herself.

It was now her future.

"We're almost home," he said gently, interrupting her thoughts.

Looking up at him, she breathed a sigh of contentment and shook her head. "No, Jordan," she said slowly, sincerely. "I'm already there."

She was finally alone. She had waited patiently for everyone to leave, and if truth be told, she couldn't seem to stop touching the children, nor staring into Hester's wonderfully maternal face. She let them fuss over her— feed her, read to her, prop mountains of pillows behind her back. Anything they wanted to do was fine. She had all the time in the world.

But now . . . now she was alone. Jordan had told them she must rest and regain her strength. And she intended to do just that. But first, first there was something far more important.

Ignoring her aching muscles, Elle pulled herself up from the bed and walked over to her dresser. Lying flat against the crocheted doily was the silver hand mirror.

Even though her heart told her one thing, she needed

this reassurance that Margie Curran hadn't been defeated by life. Elle's hand was shaking as she picked up the mirror and turned it over. She stared into the broken glass, seeing nothing but her own reflection. She concentrated, willing an image to take the place of her own, yet the effort only produced a dull headache. Disappointed, Elle turned back to the bed. She just wished she could have seen *something,* some sign.

The pillow behind her head was soft and comforting and she closed her eyes. Jordan was right. She should sleep. There was so much to be done. Now that she knew she was staying, she intended to really get involved, to use her knowledge of the future. She would study the newspapers, try to remember her history—

Suddenly the dancing lights behind her lids took shape and form. It took only a few moments to see a face. The face of an older woman. In her fifties. Graying hair, stylishly cut. Impeccable makeup, light, yet enhancing the natural beauty. And she was smiling. Happiness radiated from her eyes and the soft line of her mouth.

Elle caught her breath when she recognized the likeness. It was her mother! *And she was happy!* Grateful, so very grateful, Elle started to cry, yet the tears gently washed away the vision. Moaning in disappointment, she tried to recapture the image but it was gone.

It had been enough, though. She had seen enough to know that Margie Curran had been given another chance at happiness.

And so had she. This time it wouldn't be wasted. Closing her eyes against the tears, Elle whispered a sincere, fervent prayer.

"Thank you . . ."

She knew it was heard.

Nine months later, almost to the day, another miracle occurred. Jared Mackenzie McCabe came into this world, bringing with him the promise of the future. His father's gift to his mother was five hundred shares of stock in the newly formed Bell Telephone Company of Boston, Massachusetts.

Afterword

Every child comes into this world, into this time, with the message that God is not yet discouraged by man.

Anon.

ROMANCE FROM FERN MICHAELS

DEAR EMILY   (0-8217-4952-8, $5.99)

WISH LIST   (0-8217-5228-6, $6.99)

AND IN HARDCOVER:

VEGAS RICH   (1-57566-057-1, $25.00)